I0653994

LAST
ONE ALIVE

An absolutely gripping crime thriller with a massive twist

CHARLIE GALLAGHER

Detective Maddie Ives Book 7

JOFFE
BOOKS

Joffe Books, London
www.joffebooks.com

First published in Great Britain in 2022

Cover art by Nebojša Zorić

ISBN: 978-1-80405-518-2

PART ONE

The brightest sun casts the darkest shadow.

CHAPTER 1. PAUL MORGAN

Monday, 7 November 2022

I am not the sort of person to write a journal and this isn't one, so don't be fooled by me writing out the date at the top of the page there. It just felt right and maybe that's a generational thing. We all do it, right? Sit down and write something important and we feel compelled to put the date at the top, conditioning from right back when we were kids given that very first schoolbook.

So, this isn't a journal entry about Monday 7 November and trust me, you wouldn't want to read that anyway. Monday 7 November will be uneventful, hell, I reckon I could write a journal entry for tomorrow already with pretty good accuracy, just as long as I was careful to ensure nothing happened but the weather.

People get depressed in the winter and I know I'm one of them. I know why, too; the cold and rain might be never-ending but it's the darkness that does it for me. Even on a bright day (and it actually has been sunny for the last few, today included) the sun is never high enough to really chase off the shadow for good. There is a row of conifers in my garden that I can see from here, from this kitchen table, and at just past the middle of the day here those shadows are already starting to reach back towards me like a clawed hand in those old Hitchcock horror movies, ready to grab this old house whole.

The wood burner might be roaring but, come the night especially, it doesn't seem to add the light and warmth that it used to. Strange how a family home stripped of a family can make it feel that way. Sometimes I think this is a home that has gone cold to its bones.

That'll be enough of that. I told myself that this was not to become *the memoir of the sad old man* and how he lost everything he cared about. I told myself I would stay on track and only write what I need to write — what you will need to know — but I'm no storyteller, no writer. I do remember the most basic rule for telling a story, though: start at the beginning.

So, I should start again.

New Year's Eve 1999, the Millennium.

I remember the papers in the weeks and months leading up to that night (people actually used to read newspapers then) talking about the "Y2K" computer bug that would have everything with an electric brain crashing. Planes and satellites were gonna fall out of the sky — the whole world was going to come to a complete stop. That night the world did stop, but not as predicted, just for two young women who had otherwise been minding their own business. Talking of business, I was minding mine: *The biggest night for a thousand years*! was the promise I had put out on flyers all over town so people would know where to head for a good time. I say *mine*; I owned forty percent of that nightclub — a good chunk, just not quite enough to be able to pick the name. The Ugly Sisters was ticket-only for Millennium night and it was sold out as far as any fire inspector was aware, oversold in truth, once you factored in the punters we let pay at the door. Everyone did it, I guess we all had the same idea that the fire inspector was going to be having a busy night.

It was hot in the club. All three floors were searing hot, enough to have me checking the thermostat. There was nothing wrong, it was a combination of a lot of body heat and the sort of ventilation that would have that same fire inspector in a bit of a tizz if he had looked too closely. It was always hot when it was busy, I was never good working in the heat so I used to spend a lot of time standing at the door, watching out over people waiting. The people that worked for me then all said that they knew to judge my mood on how big the queue was. I always wanted it good and long, it's an old club trick that you learn pretty early: to run a nightclub that people want to go to you have to make it look like a place that people want to go to — and that means a stack of punters right out front. Once people have that in their mind, you can turn the lights down on filthy floors, water down the spirits and think up a ticket price to double it and they will still keep coming. These are not my words by the way, that other sixty percent was Eric Uggla, a Swedish man who lent his name to the club and some rather brutal ideas to the running of it. We didn't have filthy floors either, not at the start of a night at least.

The Millennium, then — that was one hell of a Friday night! It was three a.m. when the last of the punters were pushed out of the door into the freezing beginnings of the next two thousand years and we only shut then because the booze was starting to run dry. It was easily four a.m. before any of my staff made it out. Most had talked about keeping something bubbly on ice to toast when they got home but I watched them leave, all with that walk you get when you're proper exhausted — like one leg is dragging the other — and I reckon just about every one of them ditched those plans in favour of a hot shower and cool sheets.

I was sure to talk to every member of staff as they left; that was my style, unlike Eric who was never really seen, leaving the hands-on running of the place to me. Hands-on I was, too, I shook hands with the blokes and kissed the women on the cheek (you could do that then) and that meant Denise Tutthill and Christine Matheson got one of my smackers. You should know right from the start that

4

Christine was a little different to the rest, to anyone really. She always had such good energy about her and I remember that she wrapped me up tight in that energy for a hug on her way out: *We did it, Morgs!* That was what she called me, actually it was what they all called me and it didn't matter that I was the boss and that I didn't like it at all. They took my real name: Paul Morgan — respectable and decent sounding — and reduced it to something that sounded like what you might call the alien character in some naff sitcom about an alien living with a normal family: *Morgs*. I might have hated that name but it was different when Christine said it, better somehow. How I wish it wasn't the last thing I would ever hear her say.

I watched her leave too, giggling and bumping shoulders with Denise, her walk exhausted like the rest but there was always something about her, a good feeling: hope maybe, innocence for sure. I already said I'm no writer and I'm cursing that now; Christine was special in a way that I can't think how to describe. *Something about her* doesn't seem enough but I'll have to leave it at that and hope that you get an idea of what I mean. You also need to understand that I wasn't the only one who watched her leave. For a long time after, I beat myself up for what happened, like I should have gone with her, made sure she made it home and if I had done that, well, she would still be here today. I'm a little more at peace now, it's like my Helen said, you can't walk the whole world home. There was nothing about that night that had my hackles up, nothing out of the ordinary and nothing but a good feeling in the air. Thinking back, I reckon that was why it had such an impact on us all, we all learned the lesson that some things in this world really can come from nowhere — and nothing does it like death. That night, death was hiding its face in the shadows of those freezing streets and when Denise and Christine stepped out, it followed them all quiet.

Denise Tutthill and Christine Matheson would barely know the year 2000 and yet it was destined to linger over their memory forever, chiselled out in grey marble above a whimsical summation of lives lost before they had even begun.

That night was an ending for those two young women, but, like I said, it is the beginning of what I have to tell. I knew I would have to one day, I even went out and bought this lined book special, part of making sure this is one story I get right. I owe that to myself, to Denise and to Christine — the young woman with *something special about her*. And don't worry about the time that has passed, I can still remember that night and all that has happened since and I guess that's how it happens when you go over something every day in your head, rain or shine — those memories can never get any older than just yesterday.

Maybe this can help. I reckon if I tell the story once and for all, getting it right and written down, then I might be able to put it to bed and let those memories get old enough to fade. Then, who knows, maybe I can even get some of the warmth back into the bones of this old house.

CHAPTER 2

Consciousness, Daisy-Mae Adams was sure of it. The dreams had been surreal: colour and sound, swirls of movement, blurs of running as hard as she could. Now she was awake. It wasn't the cutting breeze or the musty smell that had her convinced, it was the pain. You can't dream pain.

She felt it in her wrists first, then her head the moment she tried to look for the source. She was being held down, something tight over her arms, her chest too. The movement of her eyes felt mechanical, she could feel the individual sinews working to move her eyeballs in their sockets and it sparked a pain in her head that was liquid, starting behind her eyes to flood outwards.

The pain in her neck was worse still; sudden, lying in wait for when she rushed a breath and attempted a swallow. It felt like her throat had been stuffed with wooden splinters that gripped and nipped at the lining. Her gasp came back at her as an echo, the acoustics of an empty room where she could see the ceiling.

Calm, Daisy-Mae, stay calm.

She was breathing, she could breathe. It was hard and it was painful, but she was breathing and she was starting to remember when she couldn't. The lurid visions from her dreams were unmerging from the reality of what had happened to her. She remembered a sound first; knocking, not rhythmic but irregular, some knocks louder than others, but constant. She remembered focusing on that noise, she couldn't remember why. She had been grabbed, *by her wrists*. She tried to lift them now, forgetting they were restrained, but there was some movement. She wriggled her arms more, her face a grimace, the pain got too much when combined with a swallow and she had to stop everything for a moment to recover. She wanted a deep breath but her chest had a burn that matched her throat, her whole diaphragm was like the embers of a firepit; red-hot when disturbed.

The punch!

Another image became clear in her mind: there had been a man, and he had hit her — hard and in the stomach. It had forced her to lean into him, his face hot and prickly, his breath sour, emitted with a subtle purr. He'd purred right in her ear.

She retched, the memory and the pain conspiring and she jerked onto her side, pushing her mouth out to try and vomit away from her own shoulder. She heard it splash onto a solid floor below and the smell was instant, acidic and cloying, flooding her senses. Then came the pain. Now it was everywhere, her punched stomach, her splintered throat, the mechanics behind her eyes and she had to return to lying on her back, her eyes tightly closed while she rested, waiting for it all to fade.

She wasn't sure how long passed, it seemed like barely a minute but when she opened her eyes again it seemed darker. The pain had abated; enough to try and move again where every instinct was roaring at her that she had to. Her left hand was no longer bound, it must have come free when she rolled to her right. The ceiling was white tiles, the style she'd seen in office blocks, only some were peeling for chunks to hang off in grey strips, the rest mottled and water-stained. She pushed her head back to see more; the ceiling had a black eye where a tile was missing completely. Beyond that was a door framed in nicotine yellow. A light too, the size of a tile but plastic and frosted that flickered and died as she watched, leaving the only light source as a pinch of weak daylight from the other end of the room.

She positioned her free hand in preparation to sit up. She was laid out on something that had some give, blankets perhaps or bedding and she dug past it until she could get a firm base. Then she pushed, trying to sit up from her stomach. She couldn't, the pain was too much and the strength wasn't there.

She flopped back, her throat searing as a groan was torn from her, her head beating in a strong and painful rhythm. She would need to free her other hand. The only restraint she could see was a sheet tucked in tight, and already it felt looser. She just needed another moment to rest.

She turned her head for a different view: a whitewashed wall, faded by time, scuffed to add to the impression of a building deserted in a hurry. But there was something in the room that looked fresh: graffiti; large letters on the wall, tall and black, the runs in the paint like fresh tears dragging mascara down a pale face. The letters spelled out three words that were enough to have her retching again: *DON'T WAKE UP.*

CHAPTER 3

Detective Inspector Maddie Ives was a tea drinker in a room full of coffee people. Together they formed a ring of nine and every one of them held a *Kent Police* liveried mug, the scent visible as droplets that caught in the thick slice of sunlight piling through the large windows of the conference suite of Headquarters. They weren't supposed to be in such grand surroundings, the venue on the email had been a far smaller, dingier (and far more apt) room just off the canteen of the newly named Kent Police Headquarters. But that room had been occupied, a stern-looking meeting in full swing with papers and reading glasses strewn over the table. The man leading Maddie's group was not the sort to tap on a door like that and he didn't have it in him to glare and tap his watch to state that they were overrunning like she would. Instead, he had scurried away like a discovered rat to the next empty room; a room so grand it was named after a former chief constable. But still, their group leader couldn't settle, he was a bag of nerves, his attention only half on the ring of coffee-soaked misery in front of him, the other half on the door they had come through, waiting for the Senior Leadership Team to bang on the glass and demand to know who the hell he thought he was using their empty room.

Group Support: Maddie fucking despised it.

That wasn't what it was called, either: *MIND Support Group* was the official title where *MIND* was an acronym for something shit and back-slappy and Maddie only knew the first word was *Mental*, which just about summed up the eight other coffee-drinking sad sacks all sat avoiding eye contact. It was an hour long too, an hour of her life lost every week, her attendance required as part of her step up to the rank of detective inspector and *the conditions that had led to it*. That was how the instruction to attend had been worded, but they could have worded it more simply: *after your last case*. It had been harrowing, a sprint of an investigation and there had been no time to breathe between bringing that case to some sort of conclusion and stepping up to lead a team of people just as shell-shocked as she was. The Senior Leadership Team had endorsed her promotion, then hastily moved her sideways, away from what they deemed *serious* investigations, and made MIND Group Support part of the conditions. Maddie saw it for what it was: a tick-box exercise where they could insist they had done all they could for her welfare: *Maddie Ives' mental health well-being — job done*.

'Maddie?' Someone was talking to her. The bald-headed, glasses-wearing streak of piss scared of his own reflection in the window of a full meeting room was talking to her, more specifically.

'Sorry . . .' Maddie said, then, with annoyance clear in her voice she said it again, but softer. 'Sorry. I was a mile away.'

'I could tell!' Their group leader grinned, pushing his glasses back was a sign of his nerves, they were already fixed on his nose, nervous perhaps that he should be addressing Maddie's attitude, but of course he wouldn't. 'We were just talking about sharing our experiences. We're all police officers in here, we're all exposed to the same things and Harriet, well, she was just saying that she thinks we should all talk about what brought us here, the reason we felt the need to seek comfort in our colleagues. Cards on the table, as she said.' He gestured at Harriet who was too slim and sitting in a permanent hunch, her hands in her lap, her expression that of a child expecting to be scolded. Harriet seemed to be taking this more seriously than most, like it was the meeting that might save her, even, and Maddie felt a pang of guilt that she wasn't as invested.

'I just said . . .' Harriet started but faded out fast, there was an awkward pause before she started up again. 'Well, we all know The Job and what it brings, but under this uniform we are people. We all break the same and I think we all repair the same way too. If we can talk about what broke us, then there's nothing more to hide, nothing more to worry about. This is a safe place and I think it should also be an honest place.'

The streak of piss nodded enthusiastically, delighted perhaps that someone else was helping fill the time with meaningless bullshit.

'OK.' Maddie sighed. 'And what, is it my turn or something?'

'Not necessarily, Maddie . . .' She hated the streak of piss using her first name. She had never been the sort to care about rank and, after eight months as an inspector she already knew she was never going to like being called *ma'am*, but it rankled with her that the PC leading this group had taken it upon himself to refer to her like they were mates now. 'But you've been coming to these sessions for a little while now and you haven't shared anything yet. I think we know a lot about most of the people in here. Do you not feel that you might feel a little . . . *lighter* if you shared?'

'What would you have me share?' Maddie was conscious of her tone again.

'Like we just mentioned, the reason you're here.'

'I'm here because of an investigation that got away from me, from us all, that still has me wondering if I could have done it different, taken time to think and maybe the outcome would have been different. Better. But sometimes policing is about moments, isn't it?' Maddie heard agreement from the streak of piss, he started to talk too; more bullshit and she was quick to cut him off. 'Well, in that moment I killed a man, I crushed his head with a pair of steel bolt croppers, and in the next moment I watched a child drown because I hadn't got there in time. And in the moments that have followed since I am glad that I killed that man and I have fought myself over that. But you know what? Eight months later and I would kill him all over again, so it was the right decision, it has to be.' Maddie's eyes had glazed, the ring of sorrow was a blur that came back into focus as a shocked silence and she realised that she might have shared too much.

'And what impact did that have on you, Maddie?' Their group leader finally found something to say, the use of her name — now as part of a stock response — narked her the most yet and she found herself fantasising that he was attacking her so she could swing another pair of bolt croppers.

'Well, I'm not really sure, to be honest. I'm tired, I know that much, there's this internal dialogue . . . not dialogue; *battle* that goes on. I still don't know how to feel about what I did, or about what I wasn't able to do and I'm angry too, angry that the person I leaned on more than anyone decided that he couldn't cope, that he wasn't going to *try* and cope and he just walked away when I needed him most. And you know what? He dressed it up like he was doing me a favour because *now I get to be the inspector*. Whoopee shit. I get to be called *ma'am*, have my workload doubled, my attendance required at pointless meeting after pointless meeting and I have to come to shit like this and waste an hour of my life and I can't even get a cup of fucking tea!' The shocked silence continued; thickened even. At least now there was eye contact: all eyes on her. She was aware her chest was heaving; she could feel her pulse in her temples. It would die away to be replaced by a thick feeling in her head that had once only come after a few glasses of red wine but was now a common part of any given day. She was more aware of her anger than she had been a few months ago; aware enough that she knew she needed to stop talking, that she had said enough. Maybe she should apologise. 'Sorry . . . I didn't mean that last bit.' She spoke directly at Harriet, who needed this. 'I do feel better, though, so I guess that's job done!' Maddie forced a sort of smile out of a deep sigh.

The streak of piss was still staring over at her where everyone else had gone back to inspecting the floor. He looked a little lost, desperate for something to say, finally tearing himself away to flit from mug to mug, breaking out into a smile as wide as he could manage.

'I didn't realise we had a tea drinker in our midst!' The smile was fragile, the one he used when confrontation would be the other option. Maddie fell back silent, her attention drifted longingly out of the window and into the crisp sunlight of early winter, certain that at least she wouldn't be bothered again.

CHAPTER 4. CHARLES SNOW

I'm writing titles up top. You don't need to worry about that, it's for me, it helps me be sure I've covered everything, every-*one* even, that I need to. I have a mind that jumps about, I've always been a bit like that but it's definitely something that's gotten worse with age. I figure that writing out a big, bold title at the top of these pages might just keep me on track. We shall see.

Christine Matheson and Denise Tutthill's case was referred to by the associated press as "The Ugly Sisters Murders", which was something the girls didn't deserve, but then, of all the things that happened to them that they did not deserve, this might be the one to worry about the least. Still, I might have complained myself if I knew who to complain to. No one cared about them, they pretended to, but what sells newspapers are gory details of abductions and murders and, without intending a pun, they bled this one as dry as they could for as long as they could. Of course you can find out all that was written just by searching on your phone these days, I guess I should be relieved at least that they were spared social media, or what it has turned into since then. Back then they called it the Gutter Press, suggesting that some news outlets couldn't go any lower for their material or their opinions, but twenty years later and social media allows anyone at all to shout an opinion up from the sewer.

I know the truth of what happened, all the gory details with nothing left out; a lot more than what was reported. I'm talking the sort of stuff that newspaper reporters would have fallen over themselves to hear. I know it because I heard it over the garden fence, with Detective Inspector Charles Snow standing the other side. He was a tall man, tall and lithe, although *lithe* was to turn to *gaunt* the more this case went on. He joined the police at a time when everyone was tall, they had to be, due to a minimum height requirement that has gone now, but his height meant I always had a good look at his face when he told me his tales. He was a stoic man with strong morals, he had a hard edge to him that I guess a police officer needs but I was never in any doubt that he wanted good things for good people. He was a good man himself was Charles, and aren't those the type of men that struggle the most?

We have one fence panel lower than the rest, the last one before the end of the garden, one I suppose had been replaced after a storm as a patch-up job that Charles never got round to making right. Whatever the story, it was low enough that two men complaining about nothing could be face to face to do it, even with arms resting on top for comfort. I never replaced it either, I think we realised that life can pass better with a conversation panel at the bottom of the garden. It was a place for small talk about small topics: the weather, the price of petrol at the pumps, a football score or how my baby daughter was sleeping (or not).

Until it wasn't.

The first time it was different is one of those memories I talked about that plays out every day, one of the things my mind won't let me forget. I was mowing my lawn. I had a loud old mower then, ran on two-stroke but spat fumes like it ran by shovelling coal into its belly and with a noise to match. I saw that Charles had appeared at the fence with two mugs rested on the top and him having to keep a hold of them where that panel has a rounded edge. That was the first time he ever made me a coffee, the first thing I thought was odd about that day. I didn't know how long he had been stood there waiting for me but that coffee was tepid at best. It was sweet too, far too sweet for me and I shook out the last half in secret. That lawn only needed another couple of runs but there was something that made me turn that mower off and say hello the moment I saw him and Charles seized his opportunity before the engine had fully clattered to a halt.

'What's wrong with the world, Paul?' That was what he said and I knew in a moment that the lawn was going to stay almost-done for a while longer. He was leaking melancholy, see, that was a saying my Helen had and I don't know a better one. It was leaking right over that fence.

'I don't know, Charles, just as long as we don't let it get us down,' I said, feeling the weight of grass cuttings, made heavier from damp, in the bucket in my hand. That's when I noticed that his coffee had a little something with a kick in it. You don't have to run a nightclub to know that a man reacts to strong liquor different to a cup of coffee. He might have been holding a mug that matched mine but he wasn't fooling anyone.

'It does get me down sometimes, it really does,' Charles said in reply and I could tell that he meant it — *as serious as cancer* — another of Helen's sayings.

'What's eating you, Charles?' I said, putting that bucket of grass down for the scent to mix with that sweet coffee and suddenly hoping it *wasn't* cancer and that I shouldn't be choosing my words more carefully.

'Do you know what he did to them?' That was what he said next, no lead-up or any more of a clue what he was talking about, but I knew straight away that it was going to get darker. What I didn't know then was that he had been running a missing persons case that had just become a murder enquiry, that he had just discovered the first body he could match with one of the missing. And it was not to be the last. That was May 1999, before Christine and Denise were anything other than two women feeling good for no real reason, like we all do when we are young and summer is just starting out.

Even then, right at the start, Charles was stood in the shadow of something, a shadow he never really made it out of again and, as he talked out his last few days, that bright spring day got darker for me too.

I let Charles Snow talk. We were neighbours to that point, but I guess you could say we were friends by the time he stumbled to a stop and locked eyes on me like I might have something to say that could make it better. That's what happens when you're vulnerable, you take down a shield so a person can step closer, whether they want to or not. It wasn't a reflection on me, I'm no great listener, but if someone is opening floodgates you're getting soaked no matter what. I don't mean tears either, not Charles — not ever — he was born of a generation without tears, it was horrors those flood-gates had been holding back, the type you need to exorcise. If you get a rotten piece of fruit in a bowl, sure as sure, that one piece will rot the rest and bad thoughts are just the same. He got them right out over that fence, the most evil I had ever heard, evil that had no right to exist on a bright Sunday after-noon just fifty metres or less from where my baby daughter was napping in the shade.

I remember I was glad when he was done. I watched him walk away, glad that he was taking that darkness with him so my day could brighten again.

But now I know better. I wasn't watching evil leave, I had just let it take root.

CHAPTER 5

Daisy-Mae closed her eyes for the impact with the floor, her hands lifted to wrap her head for protection. She took the impact through her elbows and knees mainly, the side of one of her feet too, but that pain didn't register until the ache in her elbow died down. For a terrible moment she thought she might have injured it badly but the pain subsided and the movement remained in all of her limbs. It ebbed away enough that she was able to open her eyes. She was still on her side, her back to the gurney, the leg of which now dug her in the back. Her view out was at the same wall, the same graffiti: *DON'T WAKE UP!*

These were the words that had forced her to move, convinced her that she needed to do something. Help wasn't coming for her, she couldn't just lie there and wait.

She was breathing heavily, the pain in her neck numbed a little, enough that she could gasp for air. The muscles at her core still complained as she tried to pull her legs up, feeling the cold for the first time. She was dressed for hospital in a flimsy nightshirt covering little. She was wearing under-wear at least. The bobbled blanket that had been holding her down had also trapped her in a bubble of her own body heat that was now well and truly burst. The nightshirt was short-sleeved, her arms and legs covered in gooseflesh. There was a draught that hugged the floor. In front of her was a tall, slim stand, the sort that she had seen used to hold bags of fluid for drips. It had a base of four wheels, each with a grey switch to lock them. She reached out for it, her core complained, her throat joined in when she grunted with the exertion. Her left hand got a firm grim of the stand near to the bottom and she pulled with all her might, her legs scrabbling where she was trying to drag herself to her feet. Her stomach flared hot, the pain spreading out to every corner but she gritted her teeth, refusing to give in to it. The wheels moved away, it was sudden, enough to catch her out and she lost her tentative balance to crash back down onto her side. The drop wasn't far, the blow nowhere near as dramatic as the sound of the toppling stand suggested, but it was excruciating and her eyes slammed shut again, her reaction to the pain this time just a hiss.

A minute or two passed before the pain of simply breathing was bearable and she could open her eyes. That same wall, that same graffiti, but a new impact now:

DON'T WAKE UP!

She almost wished she hadn't.

CHAPTER 6

Maddie walked through a door marked "Domestic Violence Investigation Unit" and strode across to a desk out on its own as the only one not part of a bank and that she had positioned against a window. It wasn't quite the glitz and glamour of being based in her own office that would have come with remaining as the DI in Major Crime but you can't miss what you never had. Maddie had been working in that area as a detective sergeant, her move up to DI coming from a concoction of ingredients, the most significant being the previous DI's retirement wishes. She was all set to take up his role but the timing was rotten. Maddie's force was to rebrand itself as "Kent Police" and, it seemed, a new name has to mean new ideas. One of them was for Major Crime to be centralised and run from Kent Police Headquarters. By someone else. Maddie wasn't upset at being overlooked, at least they had been honest with her over the reasons why. She had been told how she was seen as *fragile* after her last case and that she might not be in the right *headspace* to continue in the Major Crime arena. She didn't agree but she didn't argue either, there was no way to do that without making them right.

She wasn't even disappointed, in truth, especially when she had been offered a team investigating domestic violence

— something she had always had a passion for. Domestic violence appalled her, its perpetrators the scum of the earth and if she was asked for her opinion (they never would) she could make a very strong argument that domestic violence should fall into the Major Crime remit anyway.

'Ma'am.' Maddie had made it to her desk to be consumed with rifling through her top drawer, having lost her third pen of the day, when the hulking uniform officer standing on the other side of the desk stopped her in her tracks. Vince Arnold. He was smiling, it was large, lopsided and with eyes that sparkled their mischief. Vince was her go-to officer in work when she needed anything doing and her lover out of it. It was something she tried to keep entirely separate, entirely possible with a little subtlety, but Vince and subtle were not something that went together well. As he was about to demonstrate.

'Weren't you finishing at three?' Maddie said. It was nearly half past.

'Justice doesn't always clock off on time, Mads, you know how committed I am to this place.' His grin held, Maddie couldn't help but mirror it.

'I know exactly how committed you are,' she replied. 'But don't worry, I'll keep it to myself.'

'Why are you being like that? I only came in here to see if you wanted me to stop on the way home. I thought maybe you might want something nice and hot tonight . . .' He faded out to fix on her intently, his smile dropping away just slightly.

'This is the bit where you make some joke where you're the hot thing, isn't it?' Maddie said, her eye now caught by a Post-it note stuck in the middle of her screen telling her to read her email.

'Dammit!' Vince exclaimed. 'Am I really so predictable already?' They hadn't been together long, less than a year but barely a full day apart. It was nothing like Maddie had experienced before as far as relationships went. All of her career before an unceremonious shift to the detective world had been in undercover policing, hardly an environment conducive to letting someone close. But now she could, it almost felt . . . comfortable. Right, even. Much to the amusement of DC Rhiannon Davies, another member of her team who unmerged herself from the throng to arrive at Maddie's desk wearing her own grin.

'Jesus, what do you want?' Maddie spoke to her young DC now, while tripping over typing the password to get to her email.

'You two, you're just so cute!' Rhiannon was barely twenty-one years old but she had already proven herself a vicious talent with a big future. She and Maddie were also close, in the few years since they had first met they had already crammed in enough experiences to make the sort of bond that lasts a lifetime.

'Say that again and you're fired,' Maddie snapped, but again she couldn't stop her humour bleeding through.

'We were just talking about how Mads has got something nice and hot to look forward to, tonight,' Vince said.

'Couldn't resist it, could you?' Maddie said, but her attention was now sucked into her computer monitor, her eyes moving across the text of the email that the lopsided note had made sure she didn't miss before her own shift ended at four. 'And you might have to put your hot idea on ice, I'm afraid.' Maddie straightened up, Rhiannon picked up on her inspector's change of mood and looked expectant.

'What you got?' Vince said, also interested.

'One of our recent DV victims has been reported missing.'

'Missing?' Rhiannon prompted.

'No sus circs as such, but it's out of character. Uniform went out and did a Misper One, but it looks sketchy.'

'Not enough of us to go round. You have to take short-cuts to survive out there.' Said Vince, always defensive of his uniform colleagues. *Misper One* was the name of a form filled out for every missing person report, it was designed to be a coverall for any type of missing eventuality, meaning there could be a lot of information judged irrelevant. Nine times out of ten the officer would be right to miss out large chunks, Maddie hoped this wasn't the one time they were not. The Misper One form also allowed the initial officer to apply a risk assessment based on what they had in front of them: *Low*, *Medium* or *High Risk*, with the latter being fast-tracked through to a Major Crime team. It was Maddie herself who had pushed for a scheme where if anyone was reported missing — at any level — who was tagged as a victim of domestic violence, her team would be made aware. This was the reason the form had turned up in her inbox but the accompanying Post-it suggested someone was a little more concerned than usual. She scrolled to the bottom where the risk assessment was in bold: **Low**. There was a large box to fill out with justification for the rating and in this case there were just three words: *No sus circs.* Maddie wasn't sure she agreed. The CAD — Computer Aided Dispatch — was also attached, effectively the notes the call handler had made and this clearly stated *disappearance deemed to be out of character.* This was all the *sus circs* she needed.

'We're going to need more.' She looked up and out into the white noise around her in general.

'Want me to turn out?' Vince's offer was instant.

'No, go home. You're already late off and I can't authorise your overtime when there's a late turn on.'

'The late turn are just as short as we were, they came in to calls queuing. If you stick it on the box for re-attendance I can tell you now that it will still be there in the morning. The response skipper will take one look at the words *low risk* and move on.' Vince stood taller. He was stripped down to just his black, half-zip top and black patrol trousers. He was well-built, his shape classic of someone keen on the gym — or *meathead* as Maddie liked to playfully tease him — and his chest seemed to grow considerably with a simple change of posture.

'Then I'll go. I'll do it on the way home, I don't need much more,' Maddie said.

'Why does that sound like the start of a sixteen-hour shift to me?' Vince's grin now had a little melancholy to it.

'I'm sure it's nothing, some nineteen-year-old kid who didn't show up for work this morning and isn't answering her phone.' Maddie brought the missing person's file up on the police system to get the name of the officer who had dealt with the DV case. She looked at Rhiannon. 'She was one of yours. Didn't support, minor assault reported by a third party back in January? Some argument in Starbucks that got heated enough for the police to be called.'

'Starbucks . . .' Rhiannon mused, 'rings a bell. She was breaking it off and it got out of hand. The victim played it down, said there was nothing more to it than that. I know we hear that a lot but I remember believing her.'

Maddie shrugged. 'It's already sounding like we're going to find a simple explanation but I still want to talk to the person who reported her missing.'

'What was her name again? About my age, if I remember right?' Rhiannon leaned forward as she spoke to try and see Maddie's screen.

'Just nineteen,' Maddie said. 'And her name's Daisy-Mae, Daisy-Mae Adams.'

CHAPTER 7. BETTY SNOW

Charles' wife, Betty Snow, is all that is left of next door now. Although a woman in her state can hardly be described as being there at all. It's sad for me to write these words at the same kitchen table where we shared meals, Charles and Betty, large as life, sitting here with me and Helen and our Jessica too. Jessica is my daughter; she's grown and gone but all of her childhood was spent living the other side of a thin wall to the Snows. Charles and Betty have two kids of their own but they were adults already when we moved in and they were gone soon after. Betty said herself that it seemed to happen in the blink of an eye; one moment you're young with a young family, then you're old, redundant and starting to fall apart. It was a joke then, we both laughed. Betty wouldn't laugh now.

I guess the cycle of the family has it right: young and strong when you need to protect your babies, then older and weaker when they've gone on to protect their own. Though sometimes right doesn't mean fair.

I reckon the Snows saw us and the buzz, chaos and cheer of our family table as a way of replacing what they had lost at their own. I can understand that — now more than ever — and I was glad to help in that way, in any way, truth be known, as I've been in their debt from the moment we turned up at this place on moving-in day.

I remember how me and Helen had been all day waiting for the keys — who knew how exhausting sitting around nervously waiting for something to go wrong could be — our whole life packed in the boot of a borrowed Vauxhall Cavalier. I remember that the house . . . *this* house looked odd when we finally pulled up outside in the thick darkness that winter brings, even at five p.m. You could say it was foreboding: cold and frothing with rainwater that gushed out of a blocked gutter. Suddenly it seemed nothing like the house we had walked past with longing in our hearts in the months it had taken for the sale to go through. I remember the contrast to the family home it leaned against — the Snows', of course — with all of its windows lit in warm yellow where all the rooms were in use. Betty had colourful flowerbeds too, ones that didn't mind the rain, brutal as it was with sleet mixed in, like walking through frozen nails the Lord himself was tipping out of a bucket. It was the sort of weather you might take as a sign if you were that way inclined, or if you had the time to stop and think about anything other than getting your wife — six months pregnant — through the door of the new family home. I remember stepping out of the car, Helen did too, despite me protesting that she should stay in the warm until it was all opened up. The estate agent jogged to us, his hand over his head doing nothing to save him from the onslaught: a young lad he was, short and overweight for his age who struggled over the lock and, when the front door was finally opened, stepped back like we should enter first while rain rolled down full cheeks flushed red.

And we stepped in.

The floors were cheap laminate, the walls dark grey and bare, the grey darker in patches the shape of picture frames. Mine and Helen's steps seemed so loud as we bunched together for warmth. The estate agent found the light switch and a bare bulb made a *tink* sound as it blew.

'Faulty bulb!' The lad chuckled, then explained it like only an estate agent can: 'It can happen when the heating gets turned off and a place gets a little cold. At least you know the fuse box works!' He then dropped to his knees to ferret around under the stairs that were directly in front of us to look for that fuse box. The sound of his muttering and the view we had of that fat arse all shiny in his cheap suit to stand out from the darkness, well, we soon found ourselves laughing. Helen first, starting out as a giggle, a sound like water gurgling as a natural spring that she tried to conceal behind a fist. But, like a natural spring, a giggle won't be contained and it quickly became full-on belly laughter. Helen was beautiful when she laughed, she was beautiful when she did anything but laughter always suited her best.

That was the moment we first met the Snows. Betty called out through the open front door: *Knock knock!* And we turned to her big smile. Charles was next to her, he'd made the mistake of wearing slippers that left a puddle like he had stepped on a sponge in our porch but he also held the torch and bulb he had gone back for. The fat estate agent was officially useless and made his excuses, leaving just us and the Snows, and the crockpot that Betty held tight in oven gloves. The smell from that pot flooded the cold, dark interior with delicious smells quicker than if that malfunctioning gutter was pointed inwards and, just like that, it felt like home.

'I hope you like lamb,' Betty said and she waited until the bulb was installed to carry it through to the kitchen. Everything was so bare, the floor had a muted thud for every step as we all gathered in the kitchen, the room I sit in now, drawn to what was an open fire back then. Charles bolted back out into the rain, his return took a little longer this time and he came with an armful of kindling and some heavier logs in a bag that hung off his arm. He also came back wearing a more sensible pair of shoes and set about lighting the fire while Betty served up the best lamb stew I've ever tasted — circumstances have a way of doing that to food.

'When does the removal lorry get here?' This was the first thing Charles ever said to me and I remember it so clearly it could be right now, with him still bent over my fireplace, his damp neck reflecting the beginnings of a flame. Me and Helen looked at each other, both mid-chew and both about to struggle to keep hold of the contents of our mouths as we laughed loud and hard for the second time.

'You mean your whole life is in the boot of that car?' Betty had said when we were finally able to apologise and explain. 'Oh no, that won't do, that won't do at all.' I could tell straight away she meant it. And she really did. Betty used connections with local charities that she had from her work with the church and by the end of that first week we had a sofa to sit on, a television to point it at and even a bed frame to put our new mattress on (which was where all our money went, this is the one thing Helen insisted had to be new).

That was 1998; two years before the Millennium but my goodness it seemed like a lifetime. In those two years I was to become 40% owner of the biggest nightclub in the town and a father of a baby girl called Jessica who shamelessly stole her mother's beauty — and my tendency for mischief. We also bought a new sofa, painted over the grey with a more cheerful yellow and fitted the wood burner. But our first big purchase, even bigger than the mattress, was a kitchen table. It was Helen who had all the visions of the family house and what that meant and, as she said a number of times, the true beating heart of any family home is the kitchen table. That wasn't the first or the last time she was to prove to be right. The table that I lean on right now has been the place for meals and laughter, it was where I changed Jessica's very first nappy, where I first read her a story about a greedy caterpillar and it has been a place to dump the trappings of a million stressful days, for making plans, for booking holidays, talking with friends and for living life as a family.

It has also been a place to sit and get older.

That last one has snuck up on me a little bit. For Betty Snow these last few years have seen her break into a sprint, suddenly in a hurry to waste away. Her days are now spent bedbound as far as I know, sporadically hacking layers of her throat up, the sound through the wall like someone trying to start an old car layered in frost. Betty has rolling carers in and all of them react the same way when asked how the old woman is doing: *Oh, she's hanging on* their lips say, but their rolling eyes and sigh say something different entirely: *it's a bit of an inconvenience, to be honest.*

Betty Snow's mind rots like the conversation panel that still separates us and it's a race for which will fall first. The vicar is a weekly visitor next door, reward for Betty's lifetime of service but preparation, too, for an imminent epitaph. I imagine he uses his time to assure her that despite a mind unable to remember a lifetime of love and devotion to her faith, when it comes to her Lord and Saviour, He has not forgotten her. Her place will be waiting.

I only wish I had something I could take such comfort from.

CHAPTER 8

Daisy-Mae leaned on the bed, waiting for the pain beating a pattern behind her eyes to diminish. Her legs tingled with pins and needles, her hip hurt and her core ached but she had made it to standing and it was getting better. She was going to be able to walk out of here.

The room suddenly seemed smaller. She considered it was made for an individual bed, maybe even an operating theatre or some sort of observation room with the specialist equipment and lighting long since removed. The double doors that blocked her exit looked heavy, painted white but fading to yellow, both fitted with plastic skirts that rucked up against the floor to leave a pattern, an arc in the dust, a sign that they had been opened recently. She scanned the floor for footprints and couldn't see any. The paint on the walls had different tones, darker squares like shadows but in the shape of cupboards or peculiar pieces of equipment. The fading was most prominent opposite a window that was now part boarded up, the bottom third ripped away to provide the only light source. The broken planks that had been removed were still lying beneath it.

She pushed away from the bed, lifted her arms for balance but dropped them quickly to her side where the movement tugged at her core. The feeling was back in her legs, her arms still bubbled with gooseflesh. She was wearing a solid cross on a chain around her neck that had thumped against her chest when she straightened and she reached for it instinctively, rubbing it for luck. It might have worked, her first few steps were heavy and lacked coordination, but they worked. She was moving.

To her relief the doors pushed open and took her into a corridor that was instantly cooler where a brittle wind whistled through internal windows littered with small breaks. It was enough to ruffle her hospital gown and chill her to the bone. Her bare feet kicked through tiny shards of glass and the small rocks that might have caused them. Everything was covered in dust layered thick enough to make it look furry. Daisy-Mae turned back to where she was leaving prints, noting they were still the only ones.

The building was smaller than she had imagined. The room she had come out of was at the end of a corridor that cut through the middle, the style in general was distinctive of buildings ran by the NHS, with exposed brick walls polished until they were shiny, beige flooring with anti-slip surface that had a subtle crunch and a uniformity to the doors where each had a metal plate covering the bottom half to protect against the movement of beds bumping their way through. She counted fourteen rooms, equal amounts on either side, none of them big enough to act as wards. It must have been a specialist hospital, a birthing suite perhaps, she knew of buildings dedicated to childbirth that were about this size.

She made it to the main entrance door and it was the first that had no give to catch her out, to the point where she bumped her face against it. She didn't know why she had been expecting it to just swing open like the others had. She took a step back to take it in. It was actually two solid doors locked together, a thick, stone lintel stretched over their top, its grey surface opened up by fresh-looking white slashes. She pushed at the door again, then took hold of the metal handle to rattle it in its housing, prompting a yelp that was a combination of pain from her core and the panic of realising she was still locked in.

'Think, Daisy-Mae.' The words tugged at her throat. When she took hold of the handle this time she focused on the parts that didn't rattle, identifying that the door was secured at the top and bottom by thick bolts. She bent for the bottom one first. It needed some jiggling, the bending and twisting movement giving the pain in her core reason to spread out so it felt like her whole body hurt, but she didn't stop. The bolt came suddenly, jerking her straight, the silver cross again thumping her in the chest. Reaching up for the top bolt was almost a relief, like stretching out was what she had needed all along. The bolt came easier too where she was able to hang her body weight on it.

A freezing wind burst through the open door and she welcomed it. The daylight was weak, ebbing away as she watched to give her the idea of late afternoon. A slate-grey sky met with the concrete of a large car park, the separation marked out by the white lines of parking bays and the large, twisted weeds that were the only thing to be making any use of them.

The instinct that had been pushing Daisy-Mac away from that place was stronger than ever and she fixed on the horizon, focusing on putting one leg in front of the other and trying to ignore the pain that came with every step.

CHAPTER 9

The Ugly Jug: the name of a coffee shop that was unfortunate in its placement near to the top of the Old High Street in the seaside town of Folkestone; unfortunate as the aggressive incline made it the steepest of streets and Maddie had to gulp a breath of air to be able to speak to the young woman fronting her up from behind the counter. She had mousey brown hair tied out of the way of a tight smile, extended eyelashes and a pen ready. Maddie put her considerably younger than the Phil Collins song that was being piped out into the shop from concealed speakers. It wasn't like they were short of places to conceal them either, there was a bookshop theme that they had really gone for and every inch of wall was covered in battered-looking novels.

Maddie's order of a tea and nothing else seemed to cause a moment of confusion with the young woman. The pen hovered for a beat and then she abandoned it altogether. In a coffee shop, it seems, the order of a tea doesn't even get the honour of being written down.

'Did anyone come in and talk to you about Daisy-Mae Adams?' The question was casual by design, not casual enough perhaps, as the young woman suddenly stiffened and gave her a look like Maddie had just demanded all the money out of the till. Maddie continued in the casual vein with the showing of her warrant card and the woman relaxed enough to be able to drop a teabag into a cup.

'Yes, someone was here earlier but I didn't, it wasn't me . . . There's a manager, I'll go see . . .'

Maddie thanked her and swept up her drink. The interior was on two levels and she went carefully up the three steps to take a seat at a huge window that looked back out on people huffing and puffing past on that hill. It was 5.30 p.m., the opening hours had been prominent on the way in so she knew the café shut in half an hour, which might explain why she was the only one in the back section. The street she looked out on was cobbled, given a quaint pattern of orange-and-black shadow by street lights doing their best.

'You were asking about Daisy-Mae?' Maddie turned to a voice. A dark-haired woman, studious-looking with neat glasses that she reached up to take off, leaving them hanging from her fingers. Maddie reckoned she was late twenties, her air far more confident and in fitting with the manager who had been mentioned.

'I was just making sure someone came in. I'm Detective Serg . . . Inspector Ives. Maddie!' Maddie felt her face flush. 'Sorry, even I get confused with all the ranks!' She took her warrant card out again to show, suddenly aware that she might need to authenticate her claim. The woman's stance changed, one hand lifting to her hip and her head angling slightly.

'Someone came in already. In a uniform, they talked to me and wrote it all down. They said they would be back in touch. Said there was nothing to worry about, but . . .'

'But?' Maddie prompted. The window had a length of bench for a table and she was sitting on one of the high stools propped against it. She pulled out the one next to her and the woman stared at it for a moment before accepting the invitation.

'I don't know, it's just so out of character and I guess I thought the police would . . . they would take it more seriously.'

'You don't think we're taking it seriously?'

'I'm sure you are. The lad that came out, I mean he was just that, he looked like he was fifteen to me! Half my age. He asked a lot of questions and wrote down all the answers so I'm sure he's doing what he can . . .'

'But he didn't exactly inspire confidence?' Maddie smiled and got one back.

'I'm not trying to get anyone in trouble with their inspector or whatever . . .'

Maddie waved her away. 'He's not one of mine, and besides, no one listens to me anyway. What happened, with Daisy-Mae I mean? If you don't mind going through it again.'

'I don't, but I don't know what to tell you really.'

'Start with how you met, how she came to be working here.'

'Well, we certainly didn't talk about that before, he just wanted last movements, what her mood was like, if she had talked about future plans, whatever the hell that means.'

'Standard questions for a form,' Maddie explained. 'We all start by sticking to the standard questions but a bit of experience teaches you what else can be important. How did you meet Daisy-Mae?'

'Daisy-Mae . . . So, she left school last year, did well but didn't know what she wanted to do with her life and needed to be earning while she figured it out. We met when she walked in here with my advert on her phone and I took her on pretty quick. She's been brilliant. Good with the customers, learned the drinks easy, hardworking and reliable. You don't get that, not with nineteen-year-olds. And then . . .'

'Then she wasn't reliable,' Maddie chanced.

'She just didn't show. It's never happened before. I wouldn't call the police lightly but . . . this isn't right.'

'Are you and Daisy-Mae close?'

'Close? She's a lovely girl, I adore her. Is that what you mean?'

'Did you socialise, meet up outside of here, do you know anything about her life?' Maddie said.

'Oh, I see. I mean we have a social get-together every now and then, works out about once a quarter but sometimes it can be just a glass of wine in here after hours. We all went out at Christmas last year but she was almost brand new for that. We do get on well, we've sat in here out of hours talking but if you're asking if we've been out on the town, just me and her, then it's a no. I really like her but the difference between nineteen and thirty is . . . well, it's massive.'

'Tell me about it!' They shared a chuckle, the woman suddenly looking past Maddie, her attention waning where she fixed on someone walking past outside.

'I didn't get your name?' Maddie said.

'Megan, Megan Laurence.'

'So, Megan, who would she go out with on the town? Did she ever talk about a boyfriend or a group of friends, parents maybe? Did anyone ever come in to see her?'

'No . . .' The word seemed to die on her lips, like it was supposed to be followed by others.

'What?' Maddie pushed.

'She never talked about it directly, her home life I mean, but sometimes she would say something that made me think maybe it wasn't entirely happy. I can't remember the specifics, just a few mentions of moving out as soon as she could. I don't think she has much to do with her parents. That's something I can relate to, shall we say, I guess we bonded over that.'

'And a boyfriend, did she ever talk about one?'

'Not really. There was someone earlier in the year but she didn't talk about him much and hasn't at all for a while now.'

'And you never met him?' Maddie said.

'No. And normally we do, especially the younger ones. They tend to bring a boyfriend or girlfriend in here pretty soon for us all to get a look at. Even if it's just for a free coffee.' Megan stopped like she was taking a moment, her head gave a subtle shake. 'I was thinking earlier about how she's been here over a year now and I don't feel like I know much about her at all.'

'I wouldn't worry, it takes two. Some people just don't share. Are you friends on social media?'

'Yeah, that's another reason why I think she might have split up with her boyfriend. There was a period when she didn't post anything at all, she made some comment about how it wasn't worth it and wouldn't accept friend requests from any of the men that work here; not even the owner.' Maddie tried to hide a grimace at Megan revealing a classic sign of a controlling partner. 'Daisy-Mae was back to posting but it's all pretty tame, nothing that might tell you anything. She hasn't posted since I saw her last in here either, I did check.'

'Have you ever noticed anyone in here checking her out? Maybe trying to chat her up or getting a little too friendly?' Maddie said and Megan's face suddenly changed, her eyes grew a little larger, her mouth fell open and she lifted one hand to cover it.

'You think someone from in here . . .' and suddenly she was turning away to look around.

'Not necessarily, but I like to ask that sort of question early just in case anything were to take a turn.'

'A turn,' Megan repeated back, then caught her bottom lip between her teeth. 'It's rare but we can get people in here, men I mean, who can be a bit letchy. It's part of the job I suppose and Daisy-Mae always handled herself well, I certainly wasn't as good at it when I was her age. But it's not that sort of place, you know? The people that come in here are decent. Some of the blokes are better at checking out the staff than others, the worst ones are usually those sitting next to their wife!' She snorted a laugh that ran out quickly, then trapped her bottom lip again like it was something she did when she was thinking. 'Do you think something bad might have happened to her, then? Only the police officer who was here earlier, he said that he was sure she would just turn up, even made me feel a bit silly for phoning. I didn't do it lightly. I called her phone first, checked her social media and even knocked on the door to her flat.'

'Sounds like you did a lot more than most people, thank you for that and I wouldn't worry too much. I'm sure there's a perfectly reasonable explanation. My colleague was right to put your mind at rest, experience tells us it's highly likely she'll turn up with a big apology and a well-prepared excuse.' Maddie downed the last mouthful of her tea and stood up. 'I'll pop in tomorrow, grab another tea on the way in as a way of keeping in touch.'

'I'll be here. It's on me, too. I'm sure we can lose a cup of tea.'

'Very kind. We'll be working on finding your friend in the meantime, but if she turns up or makes contact with you, or if you think of something else . . .' Maddie pulled a card out of her wallet and handed it over for Megan to read the front.

'Detective *Sergeant* Maddie Ives?' Megan read. 'You said inspector?' She was clearly thinking out loud and she suddenly looked up from the card to make eye contact with Maddie. 'Sorry, it doesn't matter—'

Maddie waved her away. 'Possibly only a temporary promotion so I didn't bother getting new cards printed up. I can't say I'm bothered either way, I'm still not sure management is for me.'

'I wouldn't recommend it,' Megan said and finally a genuine-looking smile broke out.

CHAPTER 10. CHRISTINE MATHESON

I love my wife. You should know that, maybe even hold it in your mind when I talk about Christine. I know that people at the time thought that I had a thing for her, that I was in love with her even and let me tell you this: I did love that girl, only I am old and wise enough to know that there are different types of love. There is love that is so mixed up with lust that you can't see one from the other, when you can want someone so bad it hurts but it is a physical want that wanes and fades. Then there is another type altogether: a fatherly love, where the only physical desire is akin to cupping hands around a dandelion to protect it from the wind. That was what I had for Christine. I knew I couldn't, I knew I shouldn't, a dandelion is supposed to scatter in the winds and Christine was young and enchanted and bigger than this small town. It *should* have been a wonderful world for her so when it struck her down the anger I felt was like nothing else. I couldn't explain it, I didn't know why it was so intense and it was made worse that I couldn't talk about it either, it was like I had no right to be so mad. Christine wasn't my daughter, she was nothing more than a young woman who worked at my club according to anyone else in the world but she was so much more. And it was mutual.

Christine talked to me like a father. She never had one of her own. Her upbringing had still been happy, she was adamant about that, wouldn't let a bad word be said about a mother who she loved a whole lot. But she was a pretty young thing working in a nightclub where men turned up with their inhibitions and self-restraint long dead from drowning. I watched a million men fall in love with her in an instant but that lust-love type that comes on fast and strong. Most were accepting when she broke their hearts, their want gone just as quick, but we escorted more hapless fools than I can remember out of the back exit and onto a bed of very uncomfortable cobbles in the name of Christine Matheson. I think maybe that summed her up best: everyone fell in love with her; some in one way, some in another.

Despite having her pick of the men, Christine proved adept at picking the wrong ones. The fact that she talked to me like a father meant that I knew about the bad relationships, one in particular was a man I only knew as 'Twitch', a nickname he earned from his big use of recreational drugs. This Twitch could go missing for days and Christine would get concerned like any good lover does, concerned enough to report him missing at least once. Following her report, the police found him at a friend's house. They also found enough drugs on his person for him to be arrested for drug dealing. The charge was later dropped to possession only, due to his reputation as a big user, and Christine was then dropped by a sucker punch from Twitch for getting him arrested in the first place.

Twitch was a regular in the club at one point, that might even have been where they met but he only came in once more after he beat on her and I was waiting for him. That night he got a message loud and clear, from me first and then from those same cobbles I mentioned. Both of us were particularly unforgiving that night.

When Christine herself went missing the police came to the club to ask their questions and I told them about Twitch. I told Charles personally too, how he beat on her and how he might have hit too hard this time. That was maybe the only time that Charles leaked something to me he hadn't wanted to. He knew how I felt, he knew the relationship Christine and I had by this time and maybe that was why he lost control of his reaction. It was subtle, a slight movement of the mouth and a beat too long in his pause that told me that the worst was true. The evil that he had been spilling over that garden fence, that had darkened the summer of 1999, it had taken my Christine.

CHAPTER 11

She was at high altitude. It was a feeling Daisy-Mae had experienced from the moment that door had opened, but now, having walked through the car park and beyond the treeline, a view was in front of her that in any other circumstance would have been beautiful. She was looking down into a valley from the top of one side with grassy-covered hills rolling away from her into a basin of swaying trees. The slope that lifted out of the other side looked steeper still. Most of what she could see was fields divided up by wire fencing. The distant sky seemed to be a deeper grey, verging on purple, like the hill opposite was a volcano and the sky had erupted from its peak.

Daisy-Mae Adams looked out on a huge area of land and fought back her sense of panic.

'Where the fuck am I!' she whimpered, certain that she didn't recognise anything from the view that confronted her. She looked down at her bare feet. They were filthy. One was bleeding where she had nicked it on a shard of glass. The only road she could see was gritty, the edges broken up and falling away. She followed it with her eyes until it dipped out of sight, maybe even stopping entirely. Without it, the going would be either through fields or forest and she didn't fancy that either would be easy. The purple sky in the distance had grey tassels hanging from it, too: rain. She should stay, go back into that building and look for something she could use. A phone at best, a blanket, a pair of shoes or just a place to shelter at worst. But when she turned to take it in, even from a distance, she knew that she couldn't go back in there. A gut instinct or an invisible force was not only preventing her going back, but was actively pushing her away. She moved into the road that ran right to left. It was stained with mud but looked barely used overall. Left would have taken her uphill, so she turned right.

It was at least ten minutes of carefully picking out places to step before she heard a noise that wasn't wind through trees. The drone of an engine. It was getting closer, coming down the hill from behind her. Either side were stone walls, not high, but high enough that it would be a struggle to make it over if hiding had been her first thought. It wasn't. Her first thought was rescue, to the point where she moved out into the middle of the road to make sure she was seen. It was a truck, long and wide so as to just about fill the road. The paintwork was silver and clean enough for the bonnet to reflect the colour of the sky and it was coming fast. She was waiting for the engine tone to change, a signal that it was slowing, but it didn't. Maybe the driver hadn't seen her? She didn't see how that could be but she moved over quickly, her feet coming down on something solid and jagged to make her stumble and grab at the wall to keep her up. The truck bowled past and Daisy-Mae spun to watch it continue down the road ten metres before the brake lights flared a bright red, their colour brighter even than the hi-visibility chevrons that made up the flat back of the truck. There was an orange light on top too, the sort she had seen on recovery vehicles, although this one wasn't lit.

She stayed still while the truck ticked over, its back sodden with rivulets of water running off its side. Wherever it had come from, it had been raining there. When she didn't move, the back suddenly was lit a bright white: reverse lights.

It still didn't move. A face appeared out of the window to stare back at her.

'You OK?' A man's voice, gruff, starting out with a cough. Daisy-Mae was frozen to the spot, staring, she didn't know the answer to that question and her mind was suddenly clogged with confusion. She delayed long enough that the face disappeared, the engine hummed a little louder and the truck rolled backwards. It had a flatbed, and as it came closer she could see *Highway Maintenance* written down its side and into the back where white bags were labelled as animal feed, their tops folded over to keep the rain out. There was a shovel too, laid down with some of the feed congealed on the scoop end. The driver's window came level, still she couldn't speak. The man's unkempt hair and matching beard was the first impression, his hair was dark but infested with grey patches everywhere. The skin that was visible looked creased and dirty, like an old pair of sandals and directly below his brown eyes looser skin was bunched into bags that were deep-filled. He wore glasses with lenses thick enough to pull his eyes out on stalks. One of his arms was lifted to rest on the door sill where he had dropped the window.

'You can't stand in the road like that out here. One fiddle with me radio and I near knocked you down!' He was disapproving as his eyes hunted all over her for a second time. 'You'll catch your death!' He looked suspicious, breaking away to study the road ahead like he might be on candid camera, a team hiding in the bushes to capture his reaction where the ghost from the hospital was stopping drivers to then disappear.

'I woke up in the hospital.' It was all she could manage; it was just about all that she knew.

'Hospital?' The man scowled. 'You mean the old mental place back up the road? Been shut a decade or more.'

'I don't know. I just woke up and I was dressed like this. It's cold. I just want to get home. Can I use your phone?'

'Yeah, if you wanna play a snake game I got, or take a picture mebbe, not much good for nothing else out here I'm afraid. There ain't no signal 'til you get clear of the hills, a good ten miles.'

'Where am I?' she said, already fearful of the answer.

'Where should you be?' he countered and a smile broke out from his dirty exterior.

'I live in Folkestone, near the train station, I—'

'Folkestone? I ain't ever heard of that.'

'Kent?'

'Kent!' His smile grew to laughter quickly and then it was gone just as fast, like he was waiting for her to admit she wasn't serious. 'I would say you're a little way from home.' He tutted, shaking his head. 'I suggest you get in, love, I'm heading somewhere a bit more civilised, some place with a phone signal at least. You're lucky I came past, can't say for sure you'll see another soul out here anytime soon.'

'I don't know where my phone is!' Daisy-Mae's voice came as a whine.

'You can use my phone, sure you can. Call your family or . . .' He hesitated, his eyes again dropping to her feet then lifting back up to take her all in. 'Or there's a police station there. I don't know if there'll be anyone in, but I'm sure we can get someone out to talk to you.'

Daisy-Mae suddenly felt like breaking down, relief flooded through her, weakening her knees where she stood. She held it together, enough to walk around to a passenger door that was heavy to pull. The smell inside was overwhelming: straw and animal feed, the straw dense enough to hang in the air and coat the back of her throat. But it was warm. A pair of muddy boots took up the footwell so she lifted her legs to curl up on the bench seat.

'Thank you,' she managed before she had to clamp her jaw shut, scared that any more words would release the flood.

'Don't mention it. It's a bit of a drive, so you know, an hour from here at least. Phone reception comes back before that, though. You hungry?' He was eyeing her closely again, his eyes running up and down her small frame. 'You look like you need to eat.'

'Thirsty, do you have any water?'

'I got some bottles.' He suddenly seemed pleased, reaching behind where the lid came off a cool box to reveal a six-pack of water wrapped together in plastic. 'I got a Mars bar too, some nuts. Staple foods, keep you going?'

Daisy-Mae took all that was offered, even reaching back for a second bottle of water, hastily tearing at lids and wrappers. Her thirst had been ever-present from the moment she had woken up, but she was suddenly aware just how hungry she was too.

'Thank you,' she said again, this time with her mouth full. He waited for her to finish what she was eating before moving off. The warmth inside the cab quickly formed a layer over her, heavy like a blanket and, with a full belly, she was suddenly overcome with exhaustion. Her eyes fell closed, opening again when the noise of the suspension squeaking was beaten into submission by the sound of something knocking against the roof. When she looked up, her driver noticed.

'It's the light,' he offered. 'It comes loose sometimes. I could get out and fix it back but it'll happen again in a few miles. You ain't got any fillings, have ya? Cause these roads out here can shake them loose! I keep meaning to fix it proper but you get used to it.' Another smile, he seemed to be warming to her, his front of suspicion long gone.

'It's fine,' Daisy-Mae said. It didn't matter to her, sleep was coming and there was nothing she could do but give in. The warmth, the comfort, the feeling of relief and the tension leaving her body were all conspiring against her. An hour from now she would be able to start piecing together what the hell had happened.

And then she could go home.

CHAPTER 12

The "refs rooms" were communal kitchens found in every police station and, unofficially, they were for the exclusive use of the response teams. They were unique places, playing a central role in the immediate aftermath of the unexpected, the horrific, the downright terrifying or the hilariously funny. The tales and quips exchanged over the chipped Formica table dominating the middle of that room would be appalling and abhorrent in any other context but were often utterly essential for the sanity of the officers on duty and for their ability to ever step out of that room and answer a call again. The room also provided a backdrop for every stage of the career of a uniform cop. Maddie noted the *officer-closest-to-retirement* stage was well represented, the officer in question dozing on the too-firm sofa opposite a cheap TV playing a shopping channel, various items of his kit stripped down for comfort. These rooms always had bits of uniform lying about: stab vest, belts and sometimes boots next to a radiator when their owner had been forced to stand out in the rain. The atmosphere overall was forged from a sense of expectation and a fear of the unknown and, on this occasion, it was mixed with the funk of the Pot Noodle steaming in front of just the person she was looking for: PC Gibbons.

Maddie could instantly see where the reference of *half my age* from the thirty-year-old Megan Laurence had come from.

'PC Gibbons?' Maddie said.

The response was like Maddie had poked him with a long and solid stick. 'Yeah!' he said in a rush.

'Inspector Ives.' Another reaction, like she had poked him again. 'I was in a coffee shop in the town and I got talking to Megan in there. She said something about reporting one of the staff missing?'

There was a snort from behind her where a man with twenty years' experience of waking-up-and-looking-busy-in-an-instant kicked in when he heard the word *inspector*. A few seconds later and he drifted past them, his bits of uniform gathered up and clipped back on, his pocketbook open and pen readied, a few words muttered like he was mulling over his entry while he made for the exit.

'Daisy-Mae Adams?' PC Gibbons said, taking his own pocketbook out after a fight with stiff Velcro on a new-looking stab vest. 'My first job. It had been on the box all day, early turn couldn't make it.' There was a touch of annoyance in his voice, like doing something as potentially important as taking details for a missing person was a major inconvenience.

'Daisy-Mae, that's right. I saw it was you who took the Misper One and I just wanted to get your opinion on it.'

'Opinion?' This was another rushed word as he swung back to fearful, like no one had ever asked him for his opinion before.

'Yeah. My spidey senses are tingling a little for this one,' Maddie smiled, trying to get the mix right. She didn't need him defensive. 'Did you get the same thing?'

'Spidey senses?'

'Something doesn't feel right about Daisy-Mae. Her disappearance seems a little out of character to me. I know you did a little more than just talk to the informant. Was there anything you missed off the form that might help?'

PC Gibbons shrugged. 'Yeah, I went out to her address, spoke to her flatmate who doesn't spend much time there anymore as she's basically moved in with her fella. She did say that Daisy-Mae had become a little demotivated about her job recently, about life as a whole even. She wasn't surprised that she might have skipped out on work and switched her phone off for the day. She seemed pretty chill about it.'

'Chill . . .' Maddie repeated thoughtfully. 'Well, she has every right to be chill, seeing as it's not her job to investigate a potential disappearance, is it?'

'No, but—'

'Daisy-Mae was active on social media and that just stopped. People of her age don't tend to break a habit like that, don't you agree?'

'Yeah, but then there was something.' PC Gibbons was now two-handed, one fiddled with his phone while the other lifted a mouthful of the Pot Noodle that he sucked off the spoon. He spun the phone around to show Daisy-Mae's open Facebook profile. There was a comment, posted earlier in the day:

When you're so ill that even breathing hurts!

'Is that the only one?'

'That's it, just over an hour ago now. Illness would explain it.' He sounded pleased with himself.

'So you've called her now that this has appeared?'

'I called the number I have for her, yeah, it went straight to voicemail. My guess is she turned her phone back off so she can sleep it off. I've sent a direct message from the police account too, just asking her to check in.'

'Check in . . . And you *guess*?' PC Gibbons slurped another mouthful of sloppy noodles from his spoon and she had to fight a sudden desire to sweep it off the table.

'We did some phone work. It hasn't pinged anywhere other than the mast that covers her home address. I've put the request back in and I bet it says that it's still covered by the same mast.'

'What's the accuracy? When we're tracing a phone that is switched off using the last mast it pinged?' Maddie's tone should have carried sufficient warning but PC Gibbons seemed immune.

'I dunno, it's a pretty good way of showing she's still in the area.'

'A ten-kilometre square is a good rule of thumb. And it tells us nothing about Daisy-Mae's location, does it? It tell us her phone's location.'

'You're never far from your phone, though, are you?' he replied. Maddie didn't have time to argue, or to make sure he knew never to apply to be a detective. She needed to move this on.

'So she's been at home all this time while police officers and work friends have been knocking on the door? She's just chosen to ignore us?' Maddie was still waiting for some sort of realisation.

PC Gibbons' chewing became thoughtful, then he shrugged. 'Wiped out, by the sound of it.'

'And have you been back to knock again? Now that she might not be quite so oblivious?'

'I had to update the system . . .' PC Gibbons sat straighter, like maybe he was finally catching up.

'Tell you what,' Maddie said with heavy sarcasm, 'I'll go out and knock on the door. Then maybe I can update the system that she's been found safe and sound and you won't even have to do that. Does that sound OK?'

There was a reply, mumbled through the remnants of microwave noodles. Whatever it was, Maddie was glad she didn't hear it.

CHAPTER 13. RACHEL COOPER

He took five in total.

This is where it gets darker, the story I mean, while the garden outside my window does the same. The shadows are stretching out, night is coming and I would rather not be writing when it does, I don't work at night — not anymore. Get older and you realise that the night is for resting.

I was going to stop for the day, pick this back up in the morning under a new sun, maybe go somewhere public with people around me going about their business. Talking about all this, about what happened to those people, can make me feel less human, other-worldly even, forgetting that normal people are out there having normal lives. Charles felt it too, I know he did. He never said it but I could tell a man considering he might have made the wrong choice in chasing down the worst of humanity. Any decent person would be affected, even just reading about what happened, so I guess this is a warning: carry on and read what I have to write, or stop and save yourself . . .

* * *

Brave choice.

Charles told me everything. He never held back on the details, his idea of a purge, of getting as much of the horror out of him as he could and that would have left a mark all on its own. But he wasn't what left the biggest impact, not by a long way.

There were two survivors.

I don't think I can write this down here after all, not in this place, in the quiet of what was once my family home. There are already too many ghosts here. This house is not something I can explain easily other than to say that behind every door is a warm memory that dissolves into a cold truth in a moment. I've stopped opening some doors at all.

Let me make a start at least, see how far I get, seeing as I've written the title out now.

I want to talk about Rachel Cooper.

Rachel is someone that you can read about in the press. She'll be in the same news reports that talk about Christine and Denise and that claim to have the "detail" of the case. The police spoke to Rachel a lot after what happened, seeing as she was someone who lived to tell the tale. She talked to the press too, at first, but she soon realised that was a mistake and the police helped her move when it all got too much, somewhere they couldn't find her.

But I could.

It took a little time, a lot of begging Charles and then, when he finally broke and then changed his mind, a lot of promising that I wouldn't go anywhere near her.

But I did. I had to. Rachel Cooper was among the last people on earth to see Christine alive and she also knew better than anyone else exactly what she had gone through. And I thought I wanted to know too. I thought I might even owe it to Christine to find out.

But I remember changing my mind when I was still stood at her front door.

Rachel opened it herself. I don't know why I wasn't expecting that, I was ready to find barriers between us, I even had a whole pitch planned for whoever did answer, one that I hoped might be enough to get a message through, something that might count as a start. I didn't end up needing a word of it. Instead, Rachel thought I was a reporter, told me to *fuck off* and it was all I could do to blurt something back: '*I was a friend of one of the others!*'

The door was already shut by this time; slammed shut too, probably still vibrating if I had raised my hand to it, but I didn't, I just stepped up real close and I said those same words all over again a little calmer. That was when I knew I should leave and that just being there seemed cruel. But the door unlocked and opened back up for Rachel Cooper to appear. I remember her looking angry and caring at the same time, like when your kid spills a drink all over the carpet but it was a drink they were bringing you. All I was bringing was a kind of shovel with which to churn up a past that Rachel would surely rather leave behind.

She was a good woman, tall, slim and strong in build with a face built for smiling. I might have described her as plain-looking at first but I got a smile out of her, it took me a while, and she was a whole different woman with a smile on her lips. Not plain at all. I didn't make her smile much and not once the first time we met. Eventually we became close enough to call each other friends, for smiling to become a feature of our time together, which made what happened later so much more difficult.

I thought Rachel was getting better, the last time I saw her seemed to be the best of all my visits. She was starting to seem brighter, she was so different from that first version I'd barged in on. What is it they say about the most beautiful flowers? They grow best from shit? I haven't used the right words there at all but you get the meaning. I saw beauty return from a place it had no business coming back from; that woman gave me hope for the whole world.

And then she dashed it again.

I'm jumping ahead. That first visit to Rachel: she showed me in and pointed over at a seat, looked at me stern and said she needed to make something real clear right from the off: *I didn't know those other people. I wasn't allowed to.*

Then she told me a little more, enough that I could start to understand how she could be in a room with four other people for a good period of time and not know a damned thing about any of them. I will make you understand too but not here and now. I will wait for a new sun, I will go somewhere comfortable and warm, a public place with smiles and laughter: *normality*. I know those people won't be smiling and laughing with me but the warmth of strangers trumps the coldness of a family gone, I can tell you that much.

What I will tell you now is that Rachel Cooper was brave and she was strong. That first time she sat me down she stared at me long enough that it got awkward. I assumed she was considering if I was going to get to stay or not. Then she stepped away and I thought she had made up her mind, that she was going to hold open her front door and ask me to leave. She didn't. She got herself a cigarette, holding it in a delicate hand with the slightest of shakes and then she started. She took her time, talked it out at her pace and I never felt like I should interrupt, never needed to. I reckon she had been over it so many times by then that it fell out of her like something she had learned to recite. Her eyes glazed, her voice never moved up nor down so I made the mistake of thinking there was no emotion in them words. I was wrong about that.

I remember how it ended, that first visit, with me feeling foolish and guilty at the same time. Because, when she finally came out of that trance to take a look at me, she couldn't have missed the thick tears running down my face.

CHAPTER 14

Megan Laurence always found the sound of the locks finding their place on the main door to the Ugly Jug Coffee Shop somewhat satisfactory. It was a firm *clunk*; a noise that meant she was done for another day. Staff shortages had her working longer hours but she could hardly complain, knowing the reason behind that shortage.

The day had been clear but cold, though some clouds had now moved in under the cover of darkness. They must have leaked at some point too as the cobbles of the steep hill had a slick layer of moisture, enough for them to pick out the orange from the street lights above. The lighting was supposed to have been upgraded by now to the brighter, whiter LED versions that seemed to be everywhere else, though Megan didn't mind the delay — cobbles washed in warm orange seemed to be more fitting with the ancient and higgledy-piggledy shops tightly formed up in two drunken lines either side.

She paused for a moment to take out her phone, praying for a message or a missed call from Daisy-Mae. When there was nothing, a huff erupted from her as a tight ball of breath that dissipated into the darkness.

Home was a left, down the hill, through the ancient arches of a dormant train track and onto an area called the

East Cliff. Tonight, however, she was going to make the worst decision of her life — she was going to turn right.

Megan had committed to a night out more than a month ago. She had studied history of art in London, met some amazing people doing it and returned to the city as often as possible after graduating with a very respectable 2:1, to meet up. But the split in their paths when they left their student accommodation was to get wider still as each of them launched themselves into new careers. Take Jennifer, her best friend at uni, she had gone back to work for her father's property company and was quickly installed at director level, responsible for some rather impressive-looking marketing campaigns (of course shared on social media). There was Jason, who had been a short-term fling but was far better suited as a long-term friend, he had stayed in the city and somehow blagged a dream posting, working with a company responsible for the movement of high-end art pieces all over the world. Ever wonder how a famous painting or sculpture goes on tour, to be enjoyed in museums all over the world for short periods? Jason could tell you. It was stressful, a good understanding needed of logistics and security more than the art itself but he got to travel to the greatest cities in the world and get up close and personal with the greatest examples of human creation: something which, of course, he also plastered all over social media. There were other examples of other members of that class, or of her housemates studying something different entirely who had leaped out of full-time education to land securely on their feet. And Megan Laurence, 2:1 in Art History with her own dreams of career, travel and exploration? She was a coffee shop manager in the seaside town of Folkestone, trusted enough to lock up on behalf of the owner.

Travelling back to the city meant facing up to that. The others didn't make anything of it, her career was generally skimmed over, but she was tired of being the one dragging the elephant into the room. They were due to eat, at least five others in total and conversation would inevitably include all of the interesting things happening to the group. And what did she have to add into the mix? The police visited her today. That was it.

She huffed again. Turning right for the steep incline to hamper her movement towards the train station, already trying to dream up something interesting to share, totally oblivious to the fact that she was never going to make it.

CHAPTER 15

Maddie still hadn't made it home, finding herself the victim of *just one more thing*, a common concern in the life of a detective. No matter the investigation there was always *just one more thing* that could be done before ending a shift and, in this case, it was to check if Daisy-Mae Adams was indeed at home.

As Maddie approached, the door was opened by a young woman who wasn't Daisy-Mae, with white headphones jutting out of her ears at different angles. She was seemingly talking to herself but reacted to Maddie by apologising out loud, then announcing that she would call right back. She produced a phone from somewhere to portray her annoyance with a firm jab on its screen, then stared at Maddie expectantly.

'Detective Inspector Maddie Ives, Kent Police.' Maddie resisted the urge to congratulate herself on getting her title right.

'Oh, right, the police. About Daisy-Mae?'

'That's right, is she here?'

'Here?' The woman frowned. She looked Maddie up and down then spoke slowly in reply, like how someone might speak to an idiot. 'No, she's missing. The nice policeman told me that.'

'She posted online that she was just sleeping off a bout of sickness,' Maddie said, resisting the urge to bite back.

'Well, she isn't doing it here.'

'Any chance she could be doing it somewhere else?'

'Like I said, I spoke to the police already and I told them I don't know the girl too well. She's a flatmate, I needed a room and she was advertising. We both work most of the day and I spend a lot of my evenings at my fella's now. I was going to talk to her about giving it up to be honest, just as soon as he lets me leave my toothbrush there.' Her expression changed to show a hint of confusion. 'Inspector, you said? And you ain't dressed like a copper, are you CID?'

'Yeah.' Maddie didn't have time to explain the intricacies of who she worked for and why. Members of the public generally understand that you're either a uniform cop answering calls or CID detectives. The structure was a lot more complicated but in that draughty hallway, it really didn't matter.

'Is she OK?' A little bit of her attitude seemed to fall away. 'I thought this was all just a waste of everyone's time, it wasn't even me that called her in missing. She's not local, I just figured she'd gone home.'

'Where's home?' Maddie said.

'Kent, like, still Kent. Tonbridge or somewhere I think she said.' Maddie already knew her parents' address from the earlier Domestic Violence report and a revisit of this address had been tasked to West Kent patrols. It was feasible that someone of their misper's age might sleep off an illness where she could be mothered as part of it, but talking to Megan earlier in the day had given Maddie the impression that Daisy-Mae might not look to home for a warm welcome.

'Does she go there a lot?'

The girl shrugged. 'Like I said, I don't know her so well. I can't say I've known her to go anywhere in the four months I've been here. She's been a bit more distant recently, not like there's been anything wrong or anything. She talked about looking to see what else might be out there other than just working at some coffee shop. I thought she was job hunting and that might be what was getting her down. There ain't much around here.'

'Did she go to any interviews? Is there anywhere specific she wants to work or something she wants to do?'

The woman actually laughed. 'You mean like hopes and dreams? Can't say I know anything about that. We're just flatmates, flatmates that pass in the night really.'

'Do you mind if I have a look?' Maddie gestured at the door.

'Have a look?'

'At the flat, Daisy-Mae's room if you don't mind pointing it out.'

'I did that already. When they came round and they said they needed to search her room. They took her passport, some letter she got from the bank and a few other bits. Didn't get nothing of interest, said it was just routine. Did you talk to that guy?'

'I did, yeah, of course,' Maddie said, her mind filling with the image of a boyish uniform, sucking noodles off a spoon.

'You don't sound like you did and I feel like I'm just going over the same stuff as I did before.'

'I get that and I'm sorry. I guess two people checking is better than no one checking at all. I just want to find her safe and well,' Maddie said gently.

The young woman shrugged. 'I've already given my phone number and my boyfriend's address, which is where I'll be if I'm not here. You can call me if something's changed and there's a reason you need to search my flat again. Until then, I've really got to be going.'

'Can I just see she's not on the sofa?' Maddie said, holding her ground. Maddie didn't expect her to be but she'd also heard a million reasons from people who didn't want to be found when the police show up. The huff from the young woman was timed like it powered her first step back towards her front door. She stomped through her flat, pushing internal doors open firmly enough for each of them to bang and

61

every one was accompanied with: *No Daisy-Mae*! The final one came with the most force.

'Is your boyfriend's flat close by?' Maddie said, almost enjoying the young woman's impatience.

She huffed again. 'Just the other side of town. Sometimes we go out though, you know, we have a life an' that. Do I need to seek permission first now?'

'That's not necessary but thanks for asking.' Maddie put effort into her smile and didn't get one back. The young woman took her phone back out for another firm jab of the screen. A few seconds later and she was complaining loudly to herself about *some policewoman*.

Maddie watched her go. She had another *just one more thing* that had her knocking at a few of the neighbours' doors, extra care taken at those directly above and below Daisy-Mae's flat. Maddie regretted knocking at the one below and asking if they could hear when the tenants were in above as apparently the insulation was *hopeless* and the noise level a *complete joke*. Maddie let the man rant for a good minute before funnelling him down to the answer she needed: he hadn't heard anyone above him for at least three days and he was keen to emphasise his point: *Not only would I hear a mouse if it walked to the bathroom, I would hear it taking a shit too.* Maddie thanked him for his time, if not for the image.

When she stepped back out into a night that had quickly turned wintry, it was with a feeling that she hadn't made any progress at all.

CHAPTER 16. TRAPPED

That seems like the perfect place to end for the night. You have me in tears, in a room with Rachel Cooper and all that she went through and I am the one blubbing while she scurried off to get a box of man-sized tissues (a joke she made at the time) so I could blow my nose like a toddler who'd just tripped over his own shoelace. I feel compelled to continue, to talk more about Rachel and what she told me, but the darkness is now solid and this house is a very different place at night. Those memories I talked about, those that are shut up in rooms during the day and held in place by the sunlight, they can push their way out under the doors at night.

It's time to stop. The time is close for when the last of the carers will leave next door and I will wait with a handful of rubbish to take out, timing it to make sure I am seen, maybe even exchange a wave. I can't even be sure how many times I've started the process of selling up to move, believing that Betty's mind is far enough gone that she wouldn't even know, that I wouldn't have to keep up this ridiculous facade. It's been so long since I've seen her in the flesh that I can almost convince myself that she doesn't remember who I am. But then, on an occasion when I am making sure to be seen and remembered by her carers, when I am making small talk, asking them how Betty is and they are rolling their eyes because *she just won't die*, they will say something like: *Oh, she still asks about you too! Just the other day and from out of nowhere she said is Paul still next door? And of course I told her you were, that you ask about her and do you know what? She even had a little smile for you!*

A smile . . . of course she does. The smile of a woman who, somewhere in the fug and confusion of her rotting mind, still has recall of a moment that changed everything for us all.

Betty Snow knows that I cannot leave this place, not ever, and she sure as hell remembers why.

CHAPTER 17

The return to consciousness was just about the same as before for Daisy-Mae: sudden awareness cutting through dancing, swirling patterns of colour. Only this time it wasn't pain that had her aware, it was cold. Cold and dark. She shifted her eyes but it changed nothing about what she could see — still darkness — only now with a tugging sensation against the skin on her face and a tickle against her eyelashes. Instinctively she sat up, moving her hands to reach for her eyes.

Cold and dark were suddenly invaded by the sound of a tinkling bell.

Her hands weren't moving right either, they were forced together somehow with all her fingers splayed wide against something firm. Something else bumped her in the face when it should have been her fingertips and the tinkling noise of a bell came again and from closer.

Cold and dark were quickly overwhelmed by stinging pain.

The pain was from a blow that knocked her back to the floor with enough force for her to skid on her side, her face was turned down in the blackness and when she tried to gulp a breath something sucked in against her lips to restrict the air. She moved her hands back to her face, confused why she couldn't touch her own mouth and why her movements had a tinkling sound that she could also feel moving as a vibration against her palms.

When the next blow came it rolled her eyes back in her head and marked a return to dancing, swirling patterns of colour.

CHAPTER 18

The light in the room had a dance led by the flames that crackled and popped in the grate of the open fire in Vince's living room. The fire had never been used (by Vince at least) before Maddie had started spending most of her evenings at his place. She had been quick to point out the benefits of an open fire in a room, her nagging soon overpowering Vince's insistence that he would spend time and money on its restoration for it only to be used twice — *three times, tops*. Of course he had been wrong. It had only been up and running a few moments when Maddie had been joined in her worship at their crackling shrine by Vince's collie dog, Alfie. Just like that, a new favourite place for them both was born.

The sleeping dog added to the cosy feeling. Alfie's breathing was rhythmic until dreams came to twitch his legs and make him snort, though no matter how deep his sleep he would still jump to attention the moment his master returned, which on that night, should be soon. Any moment in fact. Vince was out picking up his ten-year-old nephew, Sammy, who was due for a sleepover. Sammy was his sister's kid, they lived just round the corner and the sleepovers were becoming more and more frequent and were not always ideal in their timing. Maddie had no complaints, however; Vince's sister wasn't well, her treatment had recently needed to step up a notch, enough to take its toll on her ability to look after herself, let alone a ten-year-old boy.

Vince had planned out a takeaway and a movie for them all and then, when Sammy was tucked up in bed, the rest of the evening was already allotted to start their search for a place to live together. It was something that Maddie could put off no longer. It wasn't that she didn't want to move in with Vince, she had pretty much done that already, but he was dreaming about a place away from the town, any town, with a big back garden and a third bedroom. The sort of place that came with conversations about *the next phase* in a relationship — and that was what she was really putting off.

The boys were right on cue to bundle in through the door and interrupt her musing. Vince's first action was to turn on the big light, prompting Maddie to sit up and blink at him.

'Wake you?' He beamed, then lifted two large pizza boxes that belched delicious smells. Alfie was already sitting down in front of him like a good boy, the sort of good boy who deserved pizza crusts. 'We couldn't wait so we got it on the way home, it was Sammy's idea!' Sammy appeared, his hair longer than most boys his age (at his mother's insistence) and looking like it had been styled by the wind where his uncle would constantly run his hand over it. Maddie smiled, her gaze lingering on Vince.

'What?' he said and she shook her head.

'Nothing.' She couldn't deny that she loved Vince all the more when he was looking out for his nephew. He really was perfect father material.

But the father wasn't ever going to be the problem.

CHAPTER 19. REGRETS

It is dark and cold and rain is now falling to make a pleasant pattern on my car's metal body. That sound, combined with a view out of the front of my house, is why I came out here in the first place, it's enough to take me back to that very first night when that old Vauxhall Cavalier was taking the worst that Mother Nature had to offer. The rain was icier then, hail mostly and rather than excitement and wonder turning my stomach like a tombola, there is only anxiety left these days. I remember thinking, as I took in the warm and cosy family home that was pushed up against our cold, dark house that first day, how that would all change the moment we got in. You're naïve when you're young, I reckon I'd seen too many Disney movies, but I didn't think for a moment that it would *feel* cold — heating or not — when we stepped in. Or bare.

The feel of a family home is something you have to make, something you have to work on. We did, too. It wasn't long, it wasn't many changes, but the *feeling* did change and it sure was for the better. For a long time I liked the rain, I even found myself liking the winter more. There's not much better than foul weather outside when you're stood in a warm living room, soft carpet under your feet, your baby girl gurgling and giggling, cooking smells mingling with sweet chestnut on the wood burner. And a wife there to share it all.

I had that. I had everything.

It is difficult not to think about regrets, I have long since accepted that I am not someone who has none. That's what they say, right? No regrets, never look back? Here I am doing both, even writing them all down in a journal pushed up against a steering wheel while rain plays staccato above me.

I wonder what regrets linger next door. From every window bursting with life, just two lights remain, both on the ground floor and both a frigid white. The top floor long since abandoned, left to languish in darkness where the children have grown up and gone and where Betty can no longer manage the stairs. She is now confined to the living room. Once filled with Saturday night TV, family movies and Christmas morning, it is now filled with her bed and the harshest of lights directly above her, where her sight is failing. The other light is weaker, hanging from the underside of the porch, a light that the carers leave on overnight so that the first to arrive in the morning — when it is still dark — can see their way in.

Until then Betty Snow will be alone. The rest of the house cold and dark with closed doors holding back the ghosts of family past.

We're not so different, me and Betty Snow.

No matter what she thinks.

CHAPTER 20

The train wasn't busy, Megan Laurence was going the wrong way at the wrong time for crowds; good for guaranteeing a seat, not so good for peace of mind — or just peace. As a lone woman travelling in the quiet belly of the high-speed train from Folkestone to St Pancras, Megan Laurence would have preferred a bit of a buzz, a few more pairs of eyes in the carriage. Creeps don't like an audience and, it would appear, she had a creep for company. There was someone else, besides the creep, at least. A much older man sitting at her seven o'clock who appeared to be mumbling into his own lap; his pair of eyes were down.

Megan had sat at a table, something she wouldn't normally do, but she had been absent-minded as she wandered on, putting her coffee cup down — a nice accompaniment to the Kindle in her bag with the new Mhairi McFarlane novel ready to go — but a table was not a place where you could hide easily and of course it was too much to ask for to be left alone to her book.

The creep had come on later, then hung by the table like he was considering sitting across it before opting to slink into the outside of two seats directly across the aisle. He had instantly adjusted his laces, and it was only when he did it again that she realised what he was doing. She was wearing a skirt, shorter than she might usually, but with one leg crossed over the other to pull it up even more. And the creep was enjoying the view. This was where a busier train would help, with a few more *normal*-seeming people around her she could call him out, ask him what he was looking at under her table and watch him wilt under the disapproving stares of her fellow passengers. But in a quiet carriage any sort of engagement was just asking for trouble, including eye contact. She had seen enough when he had walked in, enough to put him in his mid-twenties, despite dressing like he was still a teenager. He wore jeans low down — enough to show most of his underwear — a baggy hoody and baggier hair pushed out at a jaunty angle from under a baseball cap. He also wore a bag across his chest, a chest that he had turned towards her, opting to sit side-saddle, his legs wide open and slumped forward so his elbows took his weight through his knees.

She would try the book.

The Kindle hadn't even woken when he reverted to noises. She'd seen this play out before, every woman must have. The noises are supposed to force the eye contact, which, to a creep, is basically the same as handing over a letter of consent. He wants a conversation and subtle attempts to shut it down will do nothing, she'll need to get more and more blunt, finally explaining how she would just like to be left to her book. A reasonable request for most people, but Megan knows men like him — only too well — and at that point he either abuses her and moves on or he has already reached his own point where he cannot take no for an answer.

She shook her head, giving herself a ticking-off internally for being judgemental, paranoid even. The whole evening felt like a mistake and she was letting that set her mood. But coming all this way just to sit in the background of a conversation about other people and their successful careers with a well-practised look of faux delight, when she could have gone home and warmed up her tired bones in a bath, was seeming less and less appealing.

The creep giggled, his loudest noise yet, ending with a dramatic snort down his nose. Megan was supposed to look over. She didn't.

'What the hell!' A different voice, this one came from the other man in the carriage, the older man sat at Megan's seven. She didn't turn to that either. She could see enough in her periphery to know that the creep looked over at him, but he didn't linger and was soon trained back on her. He couldn't resist another lean forward, another fiddle with his laces and she actually shuddered, a spasm brought on by the sensation of her skin crawling. She tightened her legs to the point where it was almost painful.

'You're young! Can you work these infernal things?' The older man's voice cut through again, directed at the creep who was quick to reply.

'Nah mate. Not my thing,' he said, doing little to hide the fact he was laughing at the old man. Megan felt angry all of a sudden, angry at the impact one person could have, on her, on the old man asking for help; on anyone else who might dare to sit in the same area.

'Not your thing? I thought all you young'uns spend all your time buried in your mobile phones. That's all I see. I just need to send a simple message,' the older man came back, his frustration and vulnerability laid bare.

'Nah Grandad, can't say I'm an expert.'

But Megan saw an opportunity, snapping the case shut over her Kindle and plunging it into her bag. She turned to the man at her seven.

'Can I help?' she said.

The older man looked up, he had watery eyes that were peering out through thick reading glasses and a mask of frustration that softened, his brow that had been creased into deep rivulets suddenly straightening as he beamed at her. 'Would you mind, love? It'll just be me being a silly old fool, but I can't make head nor tail!'

Megan moved, coffee and all. She ignored the creep who started to protest like suddenly he might be able to help and who stared at her bottom as she moved out into the aisle, holding her skirt down with both hands, and quickly into a two-seat row behind the man. She was the same side of the train as the creep and with at least four seatbacks between them; perfect. She felt herself relax as the man pushed his phone through the gap in the seats, squinting as she took it off him, sure to hold it in such a way that he could still see the screen and see what she was doing. He was trying to reply to a message, a simple task and she took her time showing him. When she handed the phone back she stayed where she was, her bag on the seat beside her, feeling an upward swirl of warm air from a heater and suddenly the whole night seemed like a better idea. She could get through it, but more than that, it might even be nice to see her old group of friends. She still missed them, that was for sure.

Megan should have gone home to warm her bones. It had been a mistake to turn right for the station and not left for home, it had been a mistake to get on a quiet train and to travel alone. But her biggest mistake of all had been earlier, much earlier, when she had talked about her plans, out loud in a busy coffee shop: where she was going, how she was travelling, that she was going alone. A coffee shop is a place where patrons come and go, where they all blur into one and where you never know what sort of a creep could be listening.

The sort of creep who might refuse to take *no* for an answer.

CHAPTER 21

A new day brought with it a change of staff at the counter of the Ugly Jug and Maddie was faced with an expectant-looking man forcing a smile, rather than the nervous young woman with the eyelashes or the quiet confidence of Megan Laurence. Maddie spoke a little louder when she ordered a black coffee, lingering at the counter after payment with the expectation that Megan would appear from the back area. Instead, the man told her in no uncertain terms that she needn't wait, that he would bring it over when he could. His response was abrupt enough for him to stop and take a deep breath like a man steadying himself. 'Sorry,' he continued. 'Stressful morning. I'll bring it over to you is what I should have said.' His smile came back a little more genuine and Maddie was sure to mirror it.

'Don't mention it, I can relate. I don't even like coffee. Rough night for sleep.'

'No staff,' the man said in counter. 'Which means a rough morning.'

'Ah, does that mean no Megan?' Maddie said, turning the man's genuine smile back to the forced version. 'Sorry, I should say I'm a detective. I was in here yesterday and she helped me . . . about Daisy-Mae?' Maddie opened her warrant card for inspection.

'Daisy-Mae, of course. No, Megan's part of my problem this morning, didn't even let me know. I got a call from the shopkeeper over the road to tell me that my business hadn't been opened up.'

'Have you spoken to her?' Maddie asked.

'Phone's switched off.'

'Like when Daisy-Mae just didn't turn up?'

The man seemed to consider this for a moment. 'Never even crossed my mind. But Megan . . . Megan's different.'

'Different?' Maddie said.

The shop door clattered open, it was enough to attract the attention of them both. A woman with a round face and red cheeks was the source of the clumsy entrance; she huffed towards the man serving, then said, 'I came as soon as I could.' She walked around the back of the counter, stripping a handbag and layers of clothing as she went. Her final movement was to slip an apron on, over her head, completed as part of a seamless routine.

'Perfect timing. I just need a moment with this police officer . . . two black coffees if you would,' the man said and the late entry huffed again. The man moved out and Maddie followed him to a table. 'Different,' he said again, falling into a chair and gesturing for Maddie to do the same. 'We've had words in the past, Megan and I. Don't get me wrong, she's become far more reliable but there was a time when she was a little . . . patchy.'

'And you think she might be being *patchy* now?' Maddie said. That wasn't the impression she had got of Megan at all.

'She was going out last night, described it as a big night up in London. She used to do that a lot, that was when the problems would come.'

'So this isn't the first time she's not turned up for work?'

'This isn't the first time she's disappeared. My wife usually deals with her, she's away right now. They had a right old heart to heart, a few actually, she would sit her down and talk to her in here and they would scrap it all out. The wife's got a soft spot for Megan, sees a bit of herself in her, I reckon.

76

Anyway, I thought they had it all sorted. Do you know what my wife's solution was, by the way? She promoted her, made Megan manager.' He was the one who had a huff now. 'I can see the logic, I suppose: up her responsibility level, get her to see the impact of staff letting her down and force her to step up and lead by example. I really thought she was.'

'But you think she's just slipped back into her old ways? You don't think it's a little odd when you take into account that Daisy-Mae was reported missing a few days ago?'

'I suppose so, I really didn't . . . It's been so busy, I was turned out of bed this morning and I've been chasing my tail ever since. Do you think something might have happened to her then?'

'I'm a detective, we always start at the worst-case scenario. Have you checked her social media or knocked at her home address?'

'No . . . my wife will have her home address somewhere.' He took his phone out and swore like it wasn't playing ball, his fingers tripping over the operation and Maddie looked away to take the pressure off. The shop was filling, a low hum already caught between the rows of books from groups of punters chatting and giggling, stirring their coffees and taking pictures of their breakfast: Instagram always gets fed first. A couple of tables were occupied by a lone person with an open laptop and, at the big window, in the seat Maddie herself had occupied the day before, a man was engrossed in an open notebook, his pen a constant fidget.

'Ah, here we go.' Maddie turned back to where she was being shown a phone screen that she recognised as Facebook. She could see the name *Megan Laurence* and a profile picture that matched with the woman she had met the day before. 'Nothing,' the man said, 'not for a few days. She doesn't go on here much though, she updates the page for this place far more.'

'Can I see?' He let Maddie take the phone, she took a picture of Megan Laurence's profile — so she could find it again easily — and scrolled through. There were no posts of interest, none at all for at least a week. Maddie must have been grimacing.

'Is that bad?' She looked at the man who was gesturing back at the phone she still held. 'No news is good news, right?' he offered.

'Good news is good news,' Maddie replied. 'Bad news is coming in here for a morning coffee and leaving with even more questions.'

CHAPTER 22. RYAN SAUNDERS

Tuesday, 8 November 2022

I spent the first ten minutes or so this morning reading back over what I did yesterday. There was more there than I thought I would be doing, more words at least, but I got to thinking that I didn't tell much of the story at all. It can get like that when you're sharing something that you really want to make other people understand. I could say this a lot simpler: what happened, when it happened and by whose hand and it might only take a few lines but this needs to be done right; the best I can at least. I can't promise there isn't waffle, that you won't need to be picking the bits you need out from a lot of what you don't and I don't feel bad about that either. I don't feel bad telling you that it was raining the day that I moved in, that it was cold and that the lights didn't work because, actually, this isn't for you, this is a story that I am telling myself and it just so happened that other people will want to know it too.

This only occurred to me last night, lying awake with the light on (and when a full-grown man like me admits to being scared of the dark, you better know the rest is the truth). This whole thing is for me and my understanding, this is me working out what happened and I guess I think that those answers may well be found among the smallest of details. The fact that I remember it was raining must make it important, otherwise, why do I remember it so strong?

I also thought more about being somewhere warm and buzzy, to be surrounded by people — even strangers — to write this next bit down and you might want to know that that's exactly what I did. I'm in a coffee shop called the Ugly Jug on the Old High Street, Folkestone. The street outside is cobbled and washed in freezing rain and runs right through the heart of the old town. There's a good mix of what I call knick-knack shops, restaurants and some arty places that I couldn't even tell you what they sell, but I can tell you there used to be a top nightclub around here somewhere!

I was here for when they opened up, first customer gets first dibs on a table and I chose one right in front of a tall window where I could watch the world walking past. I sometimes like to get a bit lost in my own mind watching people, imagining their backstory, who they are and what they want from their day. I sometimes wonder if they might have been to my nightclub all those years ago. The entrance doors might have been around the corner but the Ugly Jug coffee shop was carved out of my old building. It can't be a coincidence either, that this coffee place is called *The Ugly Jug*, that has to be a nod to The Ugly Sisters that came before it. I could ask of course, but I came out to surround myself in conversation, not to be a part of one.

The Old High Street — the cobbled slither the other side of the large window — is just about the only thing that hasn't changed a bit; not for centuries, I would guess. Twenty years ago, it was just a steep hill that you could get out to via a fire door at the back of the club and was the area where unwelcome guests were deposited face-first into those cobbles. That fire door also served as an unofficial area for staff on a break or as a door that some would leave through when it was their time to go home. Denise and Christine did just that after their new year shift, right after I gave them both a smacker on the cheek and Christine purred right into my ear: *We did it, Morgs!*

Ryan Saunders was waiting out on these cobbles. He might even have seen that final exchange. Ryan Saunders is a name that you will come to know well, a name that everyone should know well, just like everyone should know what he did. You have to understand that we didn't know it at first, it was some time after Christine and Denise that I first heard that name.

But I know it now. Goodness me do I know it now.

On the night of the Millennium, Ryan Saunders followed Christine and Denise up this cobbled street, his intentions so black it could have been what helped him merge with the shadows. I don't know how long he followed them for, but I do know he had been in my club a lot. After the horse had bolted I sat down and reviewed the CCTV we had and there he was, bold as brass, the camera that showed him up best was the one pointed towards the bar where Christine worked.

It was Charles who told me about Saunders and what he did, but talking to Charles wasn't like talking to Rachel. Charles spoke like a police officer, he used formal words that softened the impact somehow. The newspapers might not have had the detail of the Senior Investigating Officer living next door but I much preferred the language they used when they told their story: Ryan Saunders *snatched* those girls off the street, he *beat* them hard with a steel bar and then he *choked* every last breath out of them. He was clever about forensics, he wore gloves and Charles fancied them to be those rubber types that vets use, the ones that go right up to the shoulder just in case the part of the animal that you're pushing your hand into does the same. He said they found a pair of brand new and unused gloves just like it, near to where they found one of his victims.

But those people. He *tortured* them. How's that for a word? Better than *prolonged assault*, which is what Charles tried to tell me. Here's another good one: *killed*. Ryan Saunders killed more than he tortured and I know how that reads. You see, Saunders had a sort of test, he didn't want to waste his time on the weak so there was like a qualifying heat where he would throttle his chosen victim until their lights went out. This was the point where you passed or failed, where, for some people, they became just a murder victim. Saunders didn't care, he just moved on, leaving them to rot where they had died. Charles used his police language to explain how *victims of asphyxiation* were suddenly being found, at least three that Charles told me about. There were others too, in other parts of the country; other forces calling to say they had bodies turning up in circumstances that matched.

Charles couldn't link them for sure but that didn't mean he wasn't convinced that Ryan Saunders was responsible. At one point he seemed to be convinced that Saunders was responsible for just about all the evil in the world at that time. That man was throttling people until they were unconscious, then leaving it up to fate to decide who came back. Those that did, those that survived came round to find their ordeal was a long way from over.

And still, that isn't even the half of it.

The survivors woke up somewhere else, somewhere already prepared. Charles said they were probably drugged for the transfer, then left to come round. These victims would wake up cold, alone and in pain and with no real memory of how they had got there. They would be terrified, something I probably don't have to say, but he made damned sure they were as scared as a person can ever be when he wrote them out a message to find up on the wall or ceiling: DON'T WAKE UP.

The press never knew that bit. The police gave out what they could that might help find the man responsible but they held back a fair amount too. Charles told me why, and remember, this was before he knew the name Ryan Saunders. At that point his job was to get a suspect arrested and then to get them talking. When that happened, he wanted that person to talk about details that he shouldn't know, details that he couldn't know unless he was the one daubing them words up on that wall. That way, Charles could be certain he had the right person sat in front of him — and a judge and jury would know it too.

He swore me to secrecy, Charles did, but he didn't have to. I wanted the right man to be caught just as much as anyone did, and besides, I don't think I could talk about it anyway. Not like Rachel Cooper did, not like Charles did. That's why I'm sat here having to write it down and I don't mind telling you that I'm doing that with a little shake to my hands.

Christine was one of them that woke up. After she had been throttled. I still think about what that must have been like, waking up hurting all over and seeing that writing on the wall, how confused and scared she must have been. Twenty years isn't long enough to make me any less angry; if anything, it's gotten worse.

People at their most vulnerable are easy to predict.

This was something that Charles said to me in another session over the top of that conversation panel. His head shaking in disbelief, a sign I had come to know to mean that it was about to get real dark. He said this to make me understand the next part, because I might not have otherwise, so now I am doing the same thing for you. You see, Saunders got his victims by the throat and he put their lights out, those that woke up got mocked by the walls and they were hurting like I said, freezing cold, laid out somewhere falling down and thirsty from the drugs. They had never been more vulnerable and Charles was right in what he said: they'd never been more predictable either.

Saunders knew what his victims would do next: they would get the hell out of there; they would go look for help and they would go look for answers.

Saunders made sure he was both.

This bit I know best from Rachel Cooper. Rachel told me how she was left in an old horse-riding school, a building long since left derelict that was being slowly reclaimed by the forest that had it surrounded. She was beaten all over, her broken toes testament to the violence required to get her there, and she woke up to see that message bearing down on her from the walls: DON'T WAKE UP. Broken toes or not, all Rachel could think about was getting out of there and she did, walking too, on bare feet, and if that don't tell you something about her desperation then nothing will. Rachel made it across the barn to a door that wasn't locked. She walked down a private driveway until she came out on the first public road for miles. She turned right, for no other reason than it was directly towards a sun that felt comforting on her face. She didn't know where she was, how she had got there or why she was only dressed in some nightdress that weren't hers. She walked slowly, the pain still bad, bad enough that it should have stopped her but she knew she had to keep moving away. She talked about the relief she felt when a truck came towards her, when it slowed and a young-ish, kinda dirty-looking white fella leaned out of the window and looked her up and down like she was crazy. His truck had writing down the side, she said he was something to do with Highway Maintenance — a working man to anyone looking in and she trusted him. Partly it was due to the way he had looked at her; suspicious almost, but also like he had never seen anything like her before and he certainly weren't expecting to. But it didn't matter that he played a role well; she was desperate, she was in pain and she was too weak to go much further on those broken toes. You hear about wounded animals that would normally run a mile from humans, letting themselves get picked up and taken to help, knowing that it's the only choice they have. I think Rachel was that wounded animal, I think every single one of those people was the same.

Ryan Saunders made sure it was he who came along, who stopped to look her up and down while acting all con-cerned, who had a bottle of water and a chewy bar for her to eat, just like someone she could trust. And it was he who had throttled her and left her for dead in the first place, who had dragged her to that place so rough that she had broken toes and handfuls of hair missing off her scalp. Another thing Charles had convinced himself of, convinced me of too, for sure, was how it must have been a real big thrill for Saunders to play the *rescuer*. Yeah, he mighta been testing to see who was strong and who was weak, yeah he mighta been keeping himself distant so he didn't leave too much of his traces on her until he had to and yeah, he mighta been letting fate play its part in what happened next, but that was set up for his *enjoyment*. He looked them people in the eye when they were at their most desperate, he gave them hope and his thrill was in taking it away again.

Saunders had Rachel thinking she was safe. You should know that when he took them, he did so like a coward, sneaking up from behind to push something over their head, taking them down blind, so there was no chance they might recognise him later through the window of a truck. Instead, his was the face that had them all believing that their ordeal was over.

It's a strange thing to say but Rachel felt bad that she survived when so many didn't. She beat herself up about it, beat herself up real hard and when you do that enough, something has to give. I was sat in front of Rachel Cooper when she had her head shaking, when her eyes were glazed over and she was demanding answers from the world about how she was sitting there at all rather than being laid out in a box. I knew why; Charles had told me, see, but I couldn't bring myself to tell her and at the time I told myself it was because I was protecting her.

But I know now that I was protecting myself.

CHAPTER 23

Consciousness, Megan Laurence was sure of it. The dreams had been surreal: coloured patterns of movement, blurred faces with wisps of hair, nothing that stayed long enough for her to make out. Or maybe there had been nothing to make out in the first place, just an oval face with all features rubbed out. But she was awake now. It wasn't the stillness or the musty smell that had her convinced, it was the pain. You can't dream pain.

The worst of it came from her neck, it caught her out, shooting through her as she tried to move from a prone position, laid out on something that had some give. She groaned — that hurt too — and her head which she had tried to lift fell back onto something firm. She would take a minute, wait for the grey blur above her to grow some features. They came slowly; black patches first, where clumps of painted ceiling were falling away, a ceiling that was a long way above. The sensation of cold came too, rushing her all at once to make her shiver. She tried to lift her legs but only one came, the other complained from the knee and she reached out to find a swollen kneecap that hurt to the touch.

The urgency to get up suddenly increased, panic sweeping over her, faster even than the draught. Her neck complained again, the pain just as bad but this time she pushed through it, planting her hands either side, falling back as the surface seemed to slip beneath her. She looked down to where she was laid out on a series of solid wheels, their shape like empty spools of wire, laid out side by side to make a platform; *some sort of conveyor belt?* Her whole body was rigid with tension, it felt like someone had reached into her gut to grab hold of a fistful that was tightening all the time. Her eyes flicked around, trying to make something of her surroundings, to see if she was alone.

She was in a big building, a small warehouse even; tall and bare, with brick walls that pushed up into a point at the far side. Beneath this were wooden double doors pushed closed that were easily three times her height. Near to the tip of the point was a small, round window that was painful to look at where it bled white light, bunching it up together like a laser to burn straight into her eyes. She was sure she was alone; the place felt desolate for sure, but it was also too open, too bare to provide any hiding place. The long, slim conveyor belt she was laid on, however, also continued through grey flaps of thick plastic hanging down like a baggage reclaim at the airport and she couldn't see where it went.

There was graffiti too, on the wall above the plastic flaps, tall black letters in block capitals, the words tightened the fist in her gut:

DON'T WAKE UP.

She looked away, told herself it was something that had been there a long time, that it was unrelated; it wasn't the only graffiti after all. She focused instead on the fact that the conveyor belt told of areas where someone could be hiding. She needed to move.

Her neck complained again as she swung her legs round. She pointed her toes to feel for the floor and got an immediate complaint from her knee and was conscious to drop the short distance left foot first. It didn't make much difference, the pain still roared outwards from the kneecap, causing the muscle in her thigh to tighten like it might cramp. She lost her balance, stumbling forward, her pain found a voice, a squeal that bounced around the exposed rafters as she fell to a dusty heap. Her palms took the brunt and she made a sort of plank shape to prevent her injured knee from touching the floor. Something clicked right in her kneecap, the pain came all at once and was then gone just as quick. Instinct told her that something had gone back in, fixed itself even, but still she moved gingerly as she went back to standing straight. It was a little better.

She took a moment to assess herself again. Her neck had a sharp pain as she tried to clear it of dust, her stomach, while knotted, was also tender to the touch and her chest hurt on both sides where it met with her shoulders, a pain she had experienced before after a heavy gym session with the focus on pushing weight away.

Pushing away . . . there had been someone!

There were memories, they came and went, mostly they went. It was all such a blur. *She had been on the train with a creep!* She remembered that much. She had moved away but he had been insistent and had moved too, not taking no for an answer. She'd been uncomfortable, she knew that but her head hurt trying to recall any detail. She had got off, she remembered that to; why had she got off? It wasn't London, it wasn't where she had wanted to be. She remembered saying so, arguing . . . *this isn't my stop, this isn't my stop!* No one had listened. Someone had been leading her, the creep? It must have been. She could remember feeling sick, sick and like she was drunk, spilling her coffee, leaving it tipped over on a table. She'd been led off the train, past other people, hearing someone tell them all it was OK, that he was looking after her.

Laughter?

She'd laughed. She remembered, that wasn't part of a dream. She'd been laughing, at that voice, at the idea that he was looking after her, like it was ridiculous.

Her thigh!

She dropped her eyes, she was standing straight now, and still, out in the circular beam of light that flooded her from head to foot with room to spare. She was still wearing her skirt, it was short, shorter than she would normally wear, short enough that she could see a small, round bruise in the centre of her thigh. She remembered it, how it had happened, it had stung at the time, made her jump then evolved to a dead leg.

The creep had injected her? He must have. Just like on the news: *needle-stick assaults*.

She had to go.

She made for the doors, her pace a quick limp, too quick for her innards that were still wrapped up in a tight grip and she had to stop to vomit. It came up hot enough to burn, leaving her gagging at the floor, the scent sweeping back up to make her vomit all over again. The pain was everywhere, she was bent forward, her knee complaining but her stomach suddenly so tight that she couldn't straighten back up again. She was using one of the huge doors to hold herself up and she could feel it start to move, dragging open where she was pulling on it.

Now the light was everywhere. She was barefoot. She had gone out in boots with a low heel but now they were missing and the heavy door scraped over her exposed feet to skim a layer of skin off. She hissed at the pain, then gathered herself, using her hand to wipe away thick clumps of spittle from her lips. The light also came with white noise drifting in from a distance. There was hammering too, a solid noise, like nothing she had heard before, something so huge being driven into the ground that she could feel it through her feet; feel but not yet see. There were buildings all around her, all in the same style as the one she had stepped out of. They were all in a row, end to end, longer than they were wide by quite some way and the ground in front was intersected by rust-coloured train tracks that split to push into the larger buildings. A squeal unmerged itself from the white noise, distinctive as the sound of a train passing. She walked a little further out, enough to see further down the road between the buildings, a road that was actually more a track made up of loose grit and packed mud. To her left she could see a vehicle parked directly underneath the bright sun. It was some way in the distance but the orange lights spinning on the top suggested life and she instinctively moved towards it. She passed a gap in the buildings that showed a tall, steel fence, behind which train coaches were parked out on their own with no sign of an engine to move them. They looked old, dilapidated, even from here. Some way behind them a train slithered past from right to left, it was slow, squealing like the one before and with jagged sparks making scorched patterns against a backdrop of distant grey clouds.

She looked ahead to the vehicle with the moving lights. She could make it out now as a truck, the back down like a bench with a figure sat on it, side-on to her, legs swinging in tune to whatever was playing through oversized "can-style" headphones and a cigarette burning. The position of the sun meant she was struggling to pick out features, though she did see a puff of smoke in surprise where she was able to get close before he noticed her.

'Where the hell did you come from!?' He ditched his cigarette and snatched the headphones off his head with too much haste and he dropped them. The truck pitched a little as he jumped off the back to retrieve them. He took a moment to look her up and down. 'What happened?'

'I don't know.' It was all she could manage, the last word full of tears that spilled out. He stepped towards her, arms out, lips stuttering like he had no idea what to say or do and she recoiled, stepping back. 'Don't touch me!' She screamed, it burned in her throat.

'OK! It's OK . . .' The man still had his arms out, he turned his palms towards her and for a moment he was frozen to the spot. 'What do you need? I can help, OK. There's an office just down the way, a portacabin with a phone. We can't take our phones near the tracks, they get fried, but you can use that . . .' He still held his hands up.

'Where?' she said, her voice still breaking.

'It's quite a walk, but I can just drive you, yeah? That's all, just drive you there and we can get you some help. You . . .'

He stopped himself, his eyes still roaming all over her. His expression had softened, he looked a little less shocked and a lot more concerned. 'You have a lot of bruises . . . We can get an ambulance out to look you over, the police too, if you need them?' He plunged his hand in his pocket, when he pulled it back out he had a set of keys that he shook. 'Or I can just walk and you can take the truck. Just roll that way and stop when you come across it, there's always a load of blokes hanging around, you can't miss it. I'll catch you up.'

'Blokes?' Megan said. It was almost a whisper, but even a whisper can weigh heavy with fear.

'Blokes, yeah. Railway workers, construction guys, there's a lot going on . . .' He faded out, maybe he could see the fear was growing in her. She cast a look back the way she had come, her view now directly down a straight road and away from the sun for the rust on the tracks to glow a bright orange like two lines to light the way. But she didn't want to drive into a group of men. For all she knew the creep was one of them.

'Can you drive me?' It was still barely a whisper but it was enough for the man to become animated, he practically skipped round to the passenger side door to pull it open for her. He was aware enough to back away, to give her room to clamber in. He didn't close it on her either, taking the time to explain.

'I'm going to close this and it will lock automatically when you drive, but just two pulls on the handle and you're out, OK? I don't want you freaking out!' He smiled, then it dropped away like he might have said something he shouldn't.

'OK,' she managed. She was still fighting back tears but now they were loaded with relief more than fear. He was gentle when he pushed the door shut but still the silence was sudden and heavy until the driver's door popped. The engine had a dull throb as they pulled away, the central locking clunked just like he had warned and she reached out to touch the handle like it was a comforter. The road surface was more uneven than she had realised on foot and the wheels dipped and rose over its undulations. A sudden bump crashed through the interior, penetrating the layer of warmth and calm that was just starting to lay over her. The next bump had a rattle that came from the roof, like something had come loose. It got worse, quickly. He must have seen her looking up towards it.

'It's the light. It comes loose sometimes,' he said, even smiling a bit now, his teeth visible through a scraggy beard with black patches, his nose had subtle red dints like he usually wore glasses. 'I could get out and fix it back but it'll happen again the next bump I hit. The supply roads round here can shake a filling loose! I keep meaning to sort it out proper, but you get used to it.' His smile grew and she was pretty sure she managed one back. A smile can do that, especially when combined with kindness, it can bring you back from the edge of panic. There was something familiar about it too, she didn't think they had met before, more that it was like the familiarity of a kind uncle you'd never met or a mate's granddad. The tension that had been in her gut was still there, but it wasn't fear anymore, it came from her being anxious to get to that phone, to call the police and to find out what the hell had happened to her.

The man offered her a drink, told her he had bottles of water in a cool box and jutted his thumb backwards. Her thirst was suddenly overbearing and she reached back without needing a second invitation, despite the pain in her side. The man must have noticed her haste, he told her to take two from the four bottles still wrapped in plastic. He said to help herself to a Mars bar and some nuts too, if there were any left.

There were and she was so glad of it all.

CHAPTER 24

The sense of déjà vu was strong for Maddie as she came away from a block of flats for the second time in as many days having been told by an occupant that they hadn't heard any movement that might suggest a neighbour had returned home. The neighbour in question was that of Megan Laurence this time, rather than Daisy-Mae Adams, and Megan's home was in the East Cliff, a different area of the town altogether, but the feeling of having achieved nothing was the same. Her phone was ringing, she dared to dream it was good news.

'Rhiannon, what can you tell me,' Maddie said, cutting past any small talk. She had tasked the young DC with trawling for Megan's social media footprint to see if it told any part of the story of her disappearance.

'I did a search for any social media activity linked to Megan Laurence in the last twenty-four hours . . .'

'And?' Maddie barked the word just as she reached an echoey stairwell made of cold concrete and clinging to the edge of the block. Megan's flat had been four floors up.

'I found the account that matched what her boss showed you, I also found matching accounts on Instagram and Twitter that are what you might call active. Instagram is the most active.'

'How active?'

'Well, she hasn't posted for the last few days, three days ago she put some latte art on Instagram as her last post.'

'Latte art?'

'She's a barista, that's something baristas do. Looks like some sort of flower; she has quite the talent.'

Maddie's pace had slowed. 'That doesn't help us too much, does it?'

'It doesn't, but I might be able to help a little more if you tell me what this is about?'

'About?' Maddie's mind had already raced away from the phone call to start running through next actions, she'd forgotten that she hadn't yet shared her latest concerns.

'Who the hell is Megan Laurence, for a start!' Rhiannon was at least taking it in good spirit, no doubt used to Maddie making demands with little explanation. This was something Maddie had got from her predecessor; serious investigations can take you down blind alleys that are time-consuming, sometimes it's best to be down there alone. 'Only I've run that name through all the police systems and she's not known. She's not reported missing either . . .' Rhiannon faded out, her tone now questioning.

'Not yet,' Maddie said.

'Not yet?'

'Not until I get back and put the report on. She's a work colleague of Daisy-Mae Adams, Megan didn't turn up for work this morning either. Her manager doesn't seem too concerned, said she's been talking about a night out for a while so they just think she had a few too many and ended up staying over. That's happened before apparently.'

'But you don't?' Rhiannon said.

'I don't know. It could be an explanation, only no one can get hold of her. And if she's the sort to upload her *latte art* then surely a trip to London would have prompted some activity.'

'You see, this is why you should have talked to me about her and about what you were trying to achieve,' Rhiannon said and Maddie could hear the sounds of clicking and huffing in equal measure, like someone working a computer hard.

'Why, what would you have done different?' Maddie was on the ground now, breaking the cover of the building towards where she had parked the car.

'I would have asked you if she was planning on meeting up with a group of five friends in a restaurant called Dishoom at London's Kings Cross.'

'And if I said that that sounds highly likely?' Maddie walked the distance to her car in the maddening silence that followed.

'Ah, here we are. Then I would have been able to tell you that a listed friend of Megan Laurence posted on Instagram last night and how Megan was the only person tagged. It's a picture of five people who all appear in Megan's friends list and it looks like they've all agreed to do a sad face. There's a tagline too, under the photo, it says: *Sorry you couldn't make it Megs.*

'She didn't make it,' Maddie repeated back. 'She didn't make it and she was supposed to.' She added this more quietly. 'I'm heading back in. Can you start the Misper One. Also, reach out to those five people on social media for contact details, a phone number preferably, we're going to need to talk to them. Train times too, let's have a look at what trains left Folkestone last night for a trip to Kings Cross and start making some CCTV and ticket enquiries. When you ran PNC, did she have a car registered?'

'I will check.'

'Please, just in case she drove. You can't get into London without passing ANPR.'

'So we're trying to find out how she got to London, what time and if she was travelling with anyone? Just so I know we're on the same page.'

'Exactly. I'm heading in anyway, shouldn't be too long. I know that's a lot to do.'

'Take all the time you need, turns out I've got some help anyway.' Rhiannon was back to sounding good-humoured.

'Help?'

'Help, yeah. She did say that you might not know about her.'

Maddie was now the one tutting and huffing as she tried to get her phone to connect to the car. The change was sudden, the noise enough to make Maddie jump. 'Know about her? About who?' Maddie said, her focus now on starting the car.

Rhiannon came back lower, almost a whisper. 'Eileen Holmans.' There was a pause like she was waiting for some sort of reaction to that name but Maddie was pretty sure she had never heard it before in her life. Rhiannon continued, 'Says she was working Major Crime until recently when they had a bit of a restructure and it seems she's surplus. She's an intelligence analyst and, even if she does say so herself, she's the best in the force!' Rhiannon's giggle sounded strangled, like she was fighting to keep it quiet.

'Is she now. She doesn't lack confidence then.'

'Confidence, not a bit. Shoes, however . . .' Rhiannon faded out now for Maddie to prompt her.

'Shoes?'

'Shoes she is lacking,' Rhiannon whispered. 'You're not going to believe this, but she's just across the room from me . . . in her slippers!'

CHAPTER 25. SOMETHING BIGGER

I had to go for a walk, a little reset. Out of the Ugly Jug and left to walk down the steep cobbles and, for a moment at the bottom of the hill, I considered doubling back on myself, a hard left, up Tontine Street and right past the entrance to my old club. Here, a queue of memories would snake down the pavement, spilling out into the road to prompt the sound of car horns and a wolf-whistle from a downed window.

But I went straight on when those cobbles ran out and met with the road, crossing it to pass a pub called The Royal George. This had been a feeder pub for us; a last drink at pub prices. I didn't mind, we had a good relationship with Kenny McNamee who ran the place, even had a scheme where he had some discounted tickets for my place if he saw a group from out of town — and you would spot them a mile off. He ran a tight ship too, he was a man who had zero tolerance before that was even a phrase and when he kicked someone out for being a problem, he was quick on the radio system to let us know who was bad news.

Sure as sure, Kenny McNamee was there when I passed. He took a double take and a moment to wave back but he saw through what time has done to me on the outside, to his old friend hiding underneath. Time might not have been kind to me, but Kenny, despite standing outside for a cig-arette — a vice we warned would kill him twenty years ago — looked the same brittle, creased and miserable old bastard he always was. It seemed odd at first, but of course he was still where I left him! Kenny McNamee always struck me as a man who could never be anywhere else.

Nothing's changed. Everything's changed.

I carried on past the pub and straight on, up some steps and onto the harbour arm as they call it now when it used to be a pier like every other. I've walked as far out as it will take me. I like it here. On a calm day the sounds, smells and beauty can lull you, on a stormy day the rawness makes you feel alive, reminds you how we're all part of something big-ger, something that we can't control.

There are tables, a lot more are laid out on a summer's day, spread out under a lighthouse whose function is no longer to warn ships but as a feature for the Champagne Bar that fills its base. The doors would be wide open if the season was right. There is a message painted high and tall on the lighthouse side, the chosen shade of blue that of the sea at its finest: *Weather is a third to place and time.* Today, the weather is cold, but tucked in close to the locked door of the lighthouse I am missed by the worst of the wind.

That leaves just place and time. This is the place and this is the time; surrounded by the sea to keep me calm, I can write what he did.

CHAPTER 26

Everything hurt. Daisy-Mae Adams was lying down and she couldn't get up, could hardly move. She had managed to shift onto her side a little while ago but her hip was agony, her ankles too, the tenderness so bad that she couldn't lay one on top of the other. And she was cold, so cold. Her body ached from being constantly tense trying to stop herself from shivering, because a shiver was enough to unsettle the bell she still held in her hands. And she didn't think she could take another tinkle of that bell.

A noise! A door clattered open, from some distance away but the sound travelled in a space that sounded both open and empty. The footfalls were different to before, not a determined stomp towards her, but scuffed, edging closer, not directly. There was a voice too, just a squeak and a grunt, but a voice for sure. Two voices? Maybe even more.

A struggle?

Another clamour, a larger grunt, the sound of someone pushed firmly to the floor close to Daisy-Mae. Then the sickening sound of a strike landing, hitting something hard but hollow like a head or a face. Back to no noise.

Daisy-Mae was facing the commotion but could still see nothing but blackness through what she reckoned to be

99

thick tape covering her face. Her other senses were already overcompensating, meaning she could taste the dust, smell the stench of her own sweat and now she could hear the sound of someone breathing, someone other than whoever had loomed over her previously, just before the heavy blows had started. The first hits had caught her by surprise, the next few Daisy-Mae had lifted her legs for, an instinctive reaction, futile too, in trying to block a threat she could not see.

Now she did what she could to ensure there were no blows for her, lying so still and so quiet. But she was to flinch, a new sound forced her; the sound of a roll of tape pulled to expose a length. Is there a sound more terrifying? It was only the slightest movement but it meant that her bell jangled, just a tiny bit, but to her ultra-sensitive hearing it was like the ringing of a church bell.

She froze. The noises in front of her stopped; everything seemed to stop, even the breathing. She waited for a heavy step towards her, for the blows that would follow. The sound of footsteps came eventually, but it was away, back towards the door. Then there were more footsteps, too many to be one person, another thud of something heavy hitting the ground — *someone* — another body with a breath forced out by the impact.

Any movement around her stopped but now there seemed to be breathing all around her, heavy too, like people trying to recover. A groan came next, one that turned into a whimper and a heavy breath that was guttural and forced. Then came the scuffing sound of someone fidgeting against the floor, fidgeting that prompted a small bell to roll around inside a larger ball, its sound emanating out into the empty space to take Daisy-Mae's breath away.

Footsteps: determined, stomped directly towards them.

'NO!' a man's voice roared from a different place again. The footsteps stopped dead for the same voice to continue: 'She doesn't know, she can't know. You have to fucking tell her first! Here, you want a bell, have this one!' The sound of a ball shaken as hard as it could be, the sound not a gentle tinkle anymore but a clatter of solid metal smashing into plastic sides. The next sound was sickening, a blow landed hard enough to be heard over the din.

'That all you got, you fucking coward?' The ball again, shaken like a baby's rattle. The sound of more blows instantly followed, again and again until the rattling sound fell away, until all sounds of any resistance fell away and all that was left were the dull thuds of blows finding their mark.

Then those stopped too. Footsteps followed, pacing out a circle that took in Daisy-Mae and what she reckoned was at least two new arrivals.

CHAPTER 27

Intelligence Analyst Eileen Holmans was indeed wearing slippers: vanilla-yellow with brown accents. You only get one go at making a first impression and, for Maddie at least, the slippers were a big part of it. The rest came from a pair of half-sized glasses, with beady eyes peering out over the top to give off a vague air of disapproval mixed up with pride where her chest was puffed while she talked of her involvement in two murder investigations, *each occurring in the last calendar year*, she said to finish with a flourish.

'Well,' Maddie said, stalling until more words would come. 'On this team we do everything we can to avoid a murder, but you're very welcome.'

'I will take whatever I can get, just as long as I'm useful, I'm happy,' Eileen said, then clapped her hands. 'Now, this desk suits my needs best when it comes to natural light.' Eileen took two paces to the desk that was against the wall, under the window and out on its own — Maddie's desk. Maddie noted it already had a handbag placed on it, while the chair — her chair — was playing hanger to a knitted cardigan of a similar colouring to Eileen's heavy, plaid skirt. This finished off an outfit the like of which had surely never been seen inside a police station before.

Maddie was aware that Rhiannon was staring at her, one eyebrow raised and maybe even holding her breath, like the next part was going to be fascinating. Maddie just smiled. Let the old woman have the desk for now, there were plenty spare and she would worry about the seating arrangements when she knew for sure that their new intelligence analyst was staying.

'You can't skimp on the natural light,' Maddie said. 'Make yourself at home. We have a tea list, make sure you're added to it.' Eileen nodded like she approved but she didn't sit, or move away, or break away from staring at Maddie over the top of those half glasses. 'Is that OK?' Maddie prompted.

'You didn't know I was coming, did you, Inspector Ives?'

'Please, it's Maddie . . .' Maddie considered a fib, but another part of the first impression was of a woman who would see right through it. 'Not a clue, Eileen. This is a little out of the blue, but we always need good people. I've never had an intelligence analyst before. I've heard of it as a new post created for Major Crime so I'm intrigued to see what you can do for us.'

'I shan't disappoint!' Maddie had Eileen at around sixty years old but her fashion sense made it difficult to pin down a definite age. She wasn't difficult to read, that was for sure, instantly expressive; initially disapproving and maybe even a little prissy, then confident to the point of smug but with an overarching desire to impress. Maddie could work with that. When Eileen continued it was with a little melancholy. 'I'm afraid I became a bit of a problem that no one wanted. Not my fault, you understand, the inspector who took me on proved to be a bit of a magnet for chaos — in the very best way — and when they broke up his team everyone else was a round peg, except me.'

Maddie's smile widened and was genuine. If there was one thing she knew, it was being the one who didn't fit. 'All we have here are work-shaped holes, fill those and you'll be fine. Ask anyone.'

Eileen's smile bloomed with warmth. 'Sounds like my kind of place,' she said and pulled Maddie's chair out to sit at Maddie's desk. Eileen then shook the mouse and the monitor lit up to reveal that she had already logged on, logging Maddie out in the process. Maddie saw another sneaked glance from Rhiannon and there was no doubt she was fighting off laughter. Rhiannon was at last able to speak.

'I brought Eileen up to speed and she was quite insistent that she could take over from there.' Rhiannon still held eye contact and Maddie could imagine how that conversation might have gone.

'OK then.'

'So, what are we thinking? Two women abducted from the same place of work, but at different times?' Eileen said, matter-of-fact.

'I think we have to consider it. I know how it sounds—'

'Sounds wonderful!' Eileen interrupted, her words practically sang while her hands were now a blur mirrored on her monitor. 'I mean as something to work on,' she added.

'Did you ladies get anywhere with travel?' Maddie inquired.

Eileen replied, 'We've focused on train travel for now, assuming this as the most likely method for Megan. The British Transport Police manage CCTV enquiries but as I am sure you know, the hoops to jump through for footage are a little cumbersome. The footage is owned by the individual train company but we are assured the quality is good. If she did get on a train, we will know. They offer a full evidential service where they can provide information on all passengers who were on a specific train, at least those that paid for their ticket using something that leaves a trace.'

'You mean online?' Maddie said.

'Online or using the ticket machines with a bank card. The only tickets that won't have details of the purchaser assigned are where someone fed actual cash into the ticket machine. However, they seemed very proud to tell me that 97% of their transactions are now cashless.'

'I'm sure they were,' Maddie said. 'I wonder what the result would be if they surveyed only those planning an abduction.'

'I did think of that, ma'am,' Eileen said. 'If nothing else, once we identify a specific train Megan was on, we will have a list of potential witnesses. But there is an issue.'

'Issue?' Maddie said.

'Details of all persons riding a train only comes with a superintendent's authority or higher for data protection reasons. I called up to her office and unfortunately my request fell down on the criteria needed for such a sweeping breach, something I was told in rather uncertain terms. It wasn't a no, as such, it was a no for now. We would need to provide good evidence of foul play; we would need to know for sure that Megan was abducted.'

'OK, so let's work on that.' Maddie wasn't surprised, the superintendent was probably right and Maddie wouldn't have wasted her time with a request just yet. But it didn't hurt that Eileen had sowed a seed and secretly, Maddie was a little impressed. A lot of work had been done in a short amount of time.

'The problem we have with proving an abduction . . .' Rhiannon spoke now, fading out like she was considering her next words carefully.

'I know what you're going to say,' Maddie said, starting to pace. 'The moment we turn up suspicious circumstances, Megan Laurence becomes a high-risk misper. Daisy-Mae Adams too by association and then we *are* talking about two women abducted who work at the same place. At that point, this becomes a Major Crime investigation and out of our hands.'

'Major Crime are otherwise engaged right now,' Eileen offered, her expression hopeful. 'They have a murder investigation still in its early stages, I know because I offered my services and . . . well, I was not required shall we say. I think they could be amenable to a team of experienced detectives running with this for now, if it meant they didn't have to.'

'Right now we don't have anything to tell Major Crime. We're still running a misper investigation graded as low. If

105

we do prove foul play then I'll be guided by what's best for the victims, even if that means handing it over.

'So, what next?' Rhiannon said.

'Did we put Megan on as a misper yet?'

'Eileen has,' Rhiannon said.

'Good. That comes with standard actions, some stand out to me more than others, like talking to those who know her and searching her home address. You and I will do that, Rhiannon. Eileen, you need to keep on at BTP, the information they have is key. If they haven't given us anything by the time we're done with the first actions then we will head to the train station and start rattling cages in person.'

Eileen had half-turned for the conversation but she spun back to her monitor. 'Leave it with me,' she said. Maddie could tell she meant business by the way she kicked her slippers off under the desk.

It would appear Eileen Holmans was here to stay.

CHAPTER 28. THE BELL

Charles Snow used me as someone who would listen, I told you that, I think I also told you how he gave me everything, every last detail, like he was shaking them out of himself so he could function, and the impact that had on me. But let me tell you this, there's one thing to be told something third-hand, a story about a story, it's quite another thing to listen to someone telling you what happened to *them*.

Rachel Cooper did just that.

Of course there was a time before I spoke to Rachel Cooper and Charles was my only source and I remember thinking that what Charles was telling me was the worst thing I had ever heard, that nothing could ever be worse. I was wrong about that in a way I might struggle to explain. Let me try by telling you about a time when I was in my mid-twenties and I went on my first (and last) potholing trip with a friend of mine who had that as a passion. He drove me down to South Wales and I had no real idea what to expect. Before I knew it we were deep underground, deeper than I'd ever been before. Down there it's cold and constantly damp, but there's something else about it too. My mate looked at me and said: *You think you know darkness, right?* Which seemed like an odd thing to say. Of course I said I did. *Turn off your head torch*! he said and we both did it and, just like that, I knew exactly what he was showing me. I hadn't known darkness before that moment, not *really*. I remember holding my hand up two inches from my face and thinking that it could have been by my side — or even missing completely — for all I knew.

That was what talking with Rachel Cooper was like. Charles had taken me somewhere as dark as I could imagine existed, but Rachel Cooper turned off my head torch.

Rachel *knew* the fear in that empty room, she knew the sounds, the smells and the pain and I turned up thinking I wanted to know it too, that it made a difference to Christine somehow if I knew what she had been through. It didn't of course, she was as dead then as she is now but grief has a way of putting a skew on logic.

I told you that Rachel showed me in and sat me down, even offered me a tea. Then I heard her out in the kitchen, the noises of cupboard doors and running taps, then a kettle that popped and fizzed and then stopped to fizzle out at less than half done. A silence followed that, one that went on a while and I thought that was it, that she had changed her mind about the tea, about everything and I was going to be asked to leave. I even gathered my coat up to hold it in my hand and I was stood up, all ready to apologise for coming. Then she spoke, her voice sounding different and not just because it was calling out from the kitchen: 'You sure you want to know it all?'

'Every detail,' I called back and then, when she appeared, her face was different too. *Rachel* was different. I think I've said she was a good-looking woman, but that might not have been my first impression. She was tall, almost as tall as me only built slender. She was wearing one of those jumpers with a wide top to show her shoulders and also showed collarbones that stuck out to notice. That jumper hung off her like it might have been bought at a time when she was a little fuller. Her face was sucked in at the cheeks and pinched around her neck too, but this was a year or so after her ordeal, making it a year or so after the press had printed the photos of Rachel I'd used so I would know to recognise her. The hair that fell either side of her face was dark-coloured and a little straggly and even her hands and wrists were bony. She had a gold watch that slid about, clattering into her hand when she moved, again making me think it had been sized at a time when she was different.

When she came back out of that kitchen it wasn't tea-cups she was carrying and that kettle never went back on, she had a glass of whisky in each hand and handed one straight over to me, the gold watch sliding and clattering. I've worked bars for a good chunk of my life and I know good whisky; what she gave me was good whisky. She sipped at it too, just like you should.

'He took us somewhere quiet. Not together at first, you got taken alone, you woke up alone and then . . .' This was how Rachel started. Her eyes were kinda zoomed out, looking towards me but not at me. But when she stopped she did make eye contact, something like it at least. 'I've told this story so many times,' she said.

'You don't need to, if you don't want to.' I said that first and I don't know why because I sure as hell didn't mean it. That was when I still thought I wanted to know, almost to the point where I wasn't going to leave her alone until I did. Luckily, I never had to test that.

'That's not what I mean, I just mean that I've told this so many times and I still don't know the best way. The police, they always said to go from the start, to just talk it out in order. I guess that makes sense, but your mind jumps, doesn't it? And always to the worst bits.'

'I have all the time in the world,' I said and that was when I first sipped at that liquor, 'and this is fine whisky!' I remember she tried a smile but bit her lip before it could properly bloom.

'I don't really know how he got me in the first place. I was on a night out, I'd had too much to drink and I got into a taxi on my own. Only it wasn't a taxi. I didn't know that at

109

the time and I still didn't know it after. When I talked to the police, I never stopped calling it a taxi and they never put me right. Later on, the inspector running things explained that it was just part of the ruse. The way that inspector worded it, I think he was trying to make me feel better, like I never stood a chance. But he didn't have to tell me that.'

'Charles?' I said.

'Inspector Snow to me.' She allowed herself another smile at this point. 'I was brought up to respect the police, not like you get these days, it became a bit of a standing joke. He would tell me to call him Charles and I would pretend to forget and carry right on calling him Inspector Snow. We always started with that, a little joke about his name to get me relaxed enough to talk. He's a good man, kind. You can tell that. They put me with a woman officer to start with and I got why, they figured I'd just been badly treated by a big, bad man so I should sit with a woman and tell my story. But it wasn't about gender, it was about good and evil. I'd seen evil and that was how I knew there wasn't a scratch of it in Charles.'

'He is a good man,' I said to her and I think she could tell that I meant it too. I talked about him, told her my story of the blown bulb and the best lamb stew I ever tasted and Rachel Cooper relaxed right there, the sipping whisky might've helped but, whatever it was, she was ready to tell me whatever I needed.

'I remember thinking that this was it, that I was going to die. I couldn't breathe, he had big hands . . .' She stopped talking for a moment, her own bony fingers reached up for just the tips to run over her neck while she relived that moment in her mind. I was patient. 'They were just like a clamp; a perfect fit all the way round but he squeezed so tight it was like my neck shrunk. I swear he crushed it as thin as a piece of string. I grabbed him, grabbed his arms to pull them off but the moment I felt him I knew it was hopeless. His arms were like steel and . . . I gave up. That's always stuck with me, I beat myself up about that. I knew it was hopeless and I stopped fighting, I was waiting to die. I think maybe that's why I did what I did, when I woke up, I mean, when I realised that I wasn't dead I kinda decided that I was going to fight for all I was worth.'

She was hurting, I could see that, so I said: 'Charles talks about that, about you, he says he's never met anyone braver.' It was no lie either. Charles had been quite taken with Rachel Cooper and her defiance. No matter how many times the police went through what happened and even when they drove her back to the places where all her nightmares had come true, she never complained, never even broke down. He reckoned she was the best witness he'd ever dealt with.

'Inspector Snow!' She corrected me, that smile breaking out again before she could trap it. 'When he had my throat tight, there was a moment when I could see movement all around me.' She faded out at that point, her eyes still opaque where she was looking beyond me and back in time. I waited. 'At least that was what I thought: movement everywhere, like rain running down a window. That's when I gave up, when I relaxed and let it happen; it was that rain. I thought I was dead, see, I thought that was all part of what happened next, but I've spoken to doctors since who said it was more likely something to do with the blood vessels in my eyes being restricted, like when you get a floater on your eye, only there was hundreds of them . . .' She faded out again and I thought I might lose her altogether. She came back with a start. 'And then I woke up.' Her focus came back too, laser sharp and locked onto me and — somehow — she seemed even more gaunt, her skin ashen grey and puffy, like if you made a face out of clay, pushing out holes with your thumbs for the eyes.

'And then you woke up,' I remember saying back to her, I couldn't tell you why, I guess I felt like I needed to say something.

'I was in a different place,' she carried on. 'It was a room, a brick room and some of the bricks were on the floor where the whole place was crumbling down. The window was missing, steel bars crossed it but they did nothing to stop the wind. It was summertime but cold all the same like any warmth was banished. I was in the same jeans and T-shirt I had left the house in but he had taken my shoes and socks. It hurt to breathe, I know that much. I still thought I might be dead, the sun was bright through that window and it was straight at me, but there was pain and I knew that wasn't right. It hurt to breathe, to swallow, to move even. But I did move. I sat up at first, sat up to see that on the wall . . .'

She stopped talking then and that time I was sure she wasn't going to come back. She did, but I remember thinking it was only because of the defiance that Charles had talked about.

'*Don't wake up.*' She smiled out those words, not like it was funny, there was something else behind it. 'Big, black letters. Coal, they worked it out later, the police told me, those words were written up there in coal dust. The building was part of an old coal mine so I guess there was plenty around there. Useless for forensics but good for making a point.'

'Don't wake up.' Again, I was repeating back to her but I didn't mean to this time, I was just thinking out loud, my mind already picturing what that would have been like for her, but also for Christine. Alone, in pain and terrified.

'I didn't know what it meant; I just know that it made me want to get the hell out of there. So, I did. I remember a door, wide open and full of daylight and I walked out of it, half-expecting to be attacked again, for my neck to be back in that vice and this time there would be no coming back round. But he wasn't there, no one was. At least, that was what I thought.'

'So he *was* waiting?' I said, the one and only time I butted in and I regretted it instantly when she scowled.

'There was one way in, one way out. A track. I was barefoot like I said, the police think he was leaving his victims barefoot to make the next bit more likely . . . the bit where I accepted a lift off him.' She held her hand up now, a way perhaps to stop me from asking the obvious question: *why?* But I already knew the answer: *People at their most vulnerable are easy to predict.*

'I walked a long way. It was painful, the scenery was just black, like a volcano had gone off or how I imagine the surface of another planet. It was over slag heaps; you remember I said about the coal? There was a gate at the end of the track, beyond that an actual road with white markings so I knew it was public. I stopped there for a rest, leaned on the gate. My feet were pretty bad, I had a couple of broken toes that were forcing me to walk with my weight all on my heels, did I mention that? Also my feet were bleeding, enough that I could see the blood mixed up with the black dust. Then I heard a motor, an engine. Looking back now, I know I should have been scared, suspicious at least, but all I felt was relief. *I was saved!*' A chuckle this time that felt like an extension of the humourless smile she had managed a little earlier. 'There was nothing around, nothing I could see besides more falling down buildings, slag heaps and trees and yet there was a car passing, how lucky was I?'

'It was him,' I said, but low enough she either didn't hear it or it was easy to ignore. I wasn't talking to her anyway, more thinking out loud, my mind still filled with thoughts of Christine and of her waking up, struggling to walk barefoot to safety, to then be picked up when she thought . . . I can't even write it. I don't need to write it.

'He nearly drove right past, I thought he was going to at first, but then I saw the brake lights, then reverse lights and he rolled back. It was a truck, one of those with an open back and I could see chopped logs and a big axe, the sharp bit painted red but pitted, like it had seen some use. Still, I thought this guy was there to help, why wouldn't he? I was out in the middle of nowhere with nothing on my feet, I hurt everywhere and I had been attacked and . . . and he seemed so concerned. At first, I told the police that it couldn't have been the same person, he just seemed so . . . genuine. How could you do what he did to me then turn up like that and pretend to want to help? Do you know what the police said?'

I didn't, I told her as much. Charles hadn't talked that out with me.

'They said it was possible his concern was genuine, that some people are so messed up in the head that they can be different people, even forget what the other version of themselves did. In extreme cases they can act different, even talk different enough that you wouldn't recognise them as the same person. Does that make sense? It doesn't, does it?'

'Not much makes sense to me, not anymore, not after all this.' I said that then and I still mean it now. Rachel lifted her glass like when you say *cheers*, which I took as her way of saying that she reckoned the same. 'I think they were just making me feel better; Inspector Snow, he tried so hard to make everything seem like it was perfectly normal when everything was so far from it. He told me that my reaction was normal, that getting in that car was normal, that anyone would have done the same. That the way I felt then, how I still feel now, that it's all *normal*. Do you know what I feel?'

I remember that question like she's here with me right now, like it's her voice and not the sound of a million gulls chatting and cawing about the intruder at the end of the pier while waves slap and fizz against the solid stone legs. Like she's sat at the table with me, leaning forward like she did then, close enough for me to smell the whisky on her breath.

'I can't imagine' was all I could manage.

'Nothing.' She sat back as she said it. 'I should be a wreck, right? A paranoid wreck, maybe in some mental institute somewhere. But I'm not, I'm here, I'm functioning and I'm letting strange men into my flat after just a few words of introduction, how can I do that?'

She wanted an answer to this, stared at me until I gave one. 'I have no idea,' I said. 'I guess you're strong, Charles said that too, he said that you can cope where most of the world wouldn't have.' She stopped me there, shaking her head so hard her hair fell about her face.

'That's not it at all. I know evil. I know it, I've seen it and I will know it again if it ever came for me. If it was in you, I would know and guess what? It doesn't scare me anymore. I got away from this with my life because he let me, because *evil* let me.' She took the last sip of her whisky before continuing. 'If it comes for you there's nothing you can do, there's no point being scared, no point fighting even, you have to trust me on that. You can't stop it, the police can't stop it and I didn't stop it.'

That was the one and only time I disagreed with Rachel Cooper. I didn't say it, not then, that wasn't the time, but I just couldn't agree. At that time, sat in that room, full of my own version of rage and promises to avenge the death of a young woman I loved like my own daughter, I was convinced that evil could be found, it could be stopped and that I was the man to do it.

I've never been more wrong.

CHAPTER 29

There was nothing but breathing, two types besides hers, that was what Daisy-Mae had worked out. The man with the voice was breathing different, his was irregular, occasional snorts and gurgles, a scuff or two from his feet as well, which at one point got so bad he could have been fitting on the floor. Daisy-Mae had a cousin who used to do that a lot when he was a kid and that was exactly what it sounded like: snorts and moans, rushed breaths and scuffing feet. It lasted about the same time too, a minute at most and then deeper breathing: deep asleep; tired out. As for the gurgling, Daisy-Mae was sure he had taken blows to his head, he could well be bleeding from his nose or lips and if he was laid out on his back the blood would find its way to his throat.

The thought made her panic; he could choke or swallow his tongue, her situation was bad enough without lying there listening to someone suffocate. But the panic wasn't enough to move Daisy-Mae, for fear of what that meant. The man now laid out next to her had known, the few words he had shouted told her that:

She doesn't know, she can't know. You have to fucking tell her first! Here, you want a bell, have this one!

She thought more about what had happened. There was nothing else to do but sit and run over the events in her mind, from the moment that door had slammed open to the moment it had slammed shut again. Two people had been dragged in and Daisy-Mae was closer to the softer, less erratic breather, the one who wasn't scuffing and fitting. She reckoned she was close enough to talk without anyone else hearing. The burning desire to try was too strong.

'Hello.' The word was as soft as a sigh, so soft she wasn't even sure it had made it past the thick tape covering her mouth.

'Hello?' *A reply*! Spoken louder than she had, gravelly and muffled, almost like it was from a throat that had needed clearing first. A woman's voice, no mistaking.

'Are you OK?' Daisy-Mae whispered back, her eyes fidgeting against the tape, the words sounding odd where the movement of her lips was so restricted. Her confidence was now enough that she rolled slowly onto her side to be closer.

'What happened?' The woman increased in volume a little; she sounded groggy, confused and Daisy-Mae considered that she might start panicking, maybe even shout for help or try and get up and set off her bell. The words the man had shouted ran through her mind: *She doesn't know, she can't know*!

'You need to be quiet . . . *So* quiet!' Daisy-Mae breathed.

The door slammed open, the sound like a gunshot. Daisy-Mae heard footsteps, a familiar, determined stomp that crossed the floor. She was close enough to the woman to feel her move, a reaction to the sound no doubt, her movement causing a metal bell to roll around in a plastic case. Now it was the woman making a scuffing sound, but it was that of someone trying to push away, maybe lifting her legs up in defence just like Daisy-Mae had, but she knew that had only made it worse.

'Just lie still,' Daisy-Mae said, her words the loudest yet and crackling with tension. She knew she was making herself the target for a beating that would be worse than ever.

The first blow was instantaneous and felt like a kick that struck her in the thigh. Another followed quickly and pain tore through her limbs before a third kick, this one to the chest, forced phlegm out of her mouth to soak her lips behind the tape.

Then there was a shout, the woman's voice but much louder than before, clearer, like some of the fog had cleared. It was a single word — *STOP!* — and stop he did. Daisy-Mae couldn't speak, her whole diaphragm burned where she had been winded but she would recover, she could recover as the focus of the attack shifted to the woman laid out next to her. The sounds now were of body shots: legs and the chest, she thought and she soon lost count of how many. They were rhythmic at first, then a little more erratic like the attacker was getting tired. She could hear him gasping for breath, his blows now accompanied by tired grunts. The woman's cries of pain had changed too, to moaning, then just breaths pushed out as each blow landed.

Their attacker finally moved away, dragging his feet and Daisy-Mae was back to holding her breath, daring to hope it was over. Before, when he left, a door would slam, but she knew from experience that it didn't mean he was gone. There was no slamming today, just more footsteps, they moved from right to left like a caged animal pacing out the perimeter, waiting for an excuse to attack again.

Daisy-Mae was still turned towards the woman, her breathing was heavier, some gulped breaths like she was fighting a sob. Daisy-Mae was desperate to talk again, desperate to move closer, to ask a question that now burned so bright in her mind there was no way she was going to be able to hold it for long, no matter what. It was a question that had burned in her from the moment the woman had shouted out: *Megan, is that you?*

CHAPTER 30

The return to the Ugly Jug coffee shop was a return to a much calmer place overall. Maddie could see two employees flitting between tables with matching aprons and trays who were additions since this morning and the staffing crisis that had revealed itself at opening time appeared to have been resolved.

'Did you want a table?' One of the aprons spoke in the general direction of where Maddie was standing with Rhiannon just off to her side. The woman with the question was thirty-something, with cheeks flushed like she needed a break. It was another employee that Maddie hadn't seen before. 'Only, this one's just come free.'

'Then we'll take it. Could I also have a chat with Steve?' Steve Cox, the manager that Maddie had been talking to earlier in the day. Maddie had taken his details just before leaving.

'Oh . . . is there a problem?' The woman's cheeks flushed deeper, her concern enough to halt her wiping.

'No, not at all. We're police officers, we were talking to him about two young women who work here. I just wanted to talk again.'

'Did you find them?' Her face lit up in hope that ebbed away quickly.

'Not yet, I just wanted some more information if possible.'

'He's not here, popped out for something or other. He could be a while but I'll give him a call. Can I get you a drink while you wait?'

Maddie ordered two teas. The woman had readied a pad but didn't write it down, as seemed to be the way with tea. She didn't move away either, loitering instead while Maddie and Rhiannon settled in their seats.

'People are already talking about the curse,' the woman said. 'I'm Cathy by the way, I've worked here quite a while, I know the girls well. This was supposed to be a week off for me but then Steve called, told me what was going on and of course I was happy to help. We're like a family in here.' She smiled, the intensity about her had changed.

'I can imagine. Curse?' Maddie almost didn't want to ask; it was obvious Cathy was waiting for it.

'You don't know about it? About the Ugly Sisters?'

'Pretend I don't have a clue what you're talking about,' Maddie replied.

Cathy tutted, taking it as an invitation to sit down heavily at their table. Her curly hair was tied back but strands were forced loose to fall over her face and she blew them clear as part of her exhale. 'This was a nightclub once, not this part specifically I don't think, this might have been the back office or something, but before this building was all one big nightclub. Are you local?' She stopped for Maddie to answer, it was maddening.

'Not really.'

'That would explain it. People round here know all about it, people round here will be well interested to hear what's happening.' Her eyes twinkled, her face positively beaming now.

'You mean to your friends? Your family even, that's what you said about the people that work here, right?'

'Yeah, of course.' Cathy's beam only dimmed temporarily. 'So anyway, it was a nightclub called The Ugly Sisters back in the day, I was seventeen when it shut and a bit gutted to be honest, it was the only place to go for a late one. Some Swedish fella ran it and when he upped and left, no one wanted to take it on. I guess that was because of what happened.'

Maddie was resisting the urge to grab her by the scruff and shake her until she got to the damned point. She toyed with the pot of sugar sachets as a way of keeping her hands busy, instead.

'Could you get to the point? We've got a lot to do today.' It was Rhiannon who snapped first, prompting Cathy's eyes to swing to her like she hadn't noticed her until that moment.

'Of course, yeah,' she said, flustered. 'So, it was a nightclub twenty-two years ago for the Millennium right, New Year's? A couple of the barmaids finished their shift and set off home and guess what? No one ever saw them alive again.' The beaming was now at its brightest, the glee clear in her eyes at being the one to break the news, like she might have also broken the case. 'Never solved. Papers called it the Ugly Sisters Murder, it was news for months in the nationals, years round here. It will be news again if you've got two more from the same building vanished into thin air.'

'We could really do without that for now, the scrutiny, I mean. We don't know what we have,' Maddie said and Cathy made a gesture with the finger and thumb on her right hand like she was zipping her mouth. Maddie had a feeling it would unzip just as easy.

'People still talk about what happened. You know why this is called the Ugly Jug, right? Superstition. You've got some place on the other side too — Ugly Kid Joe's that sells vintage clothes, they kept the *Ugly* too. Superstition is that if you ditch it, then whatever took them girls will come back. The fact the police never solved it means that people get to call it supernatural; you know what people are like! I remember Steve laughing in my face when I told him about it, but he still didn't change the name, did he?' She sat back, her expression smug, a possible mic-drop moment if only she could resist the urge to carry on: 'The customers know about it too, see, and I suppose Steve didn't want people avoiding the place because they think it's flying in the face of something like that.'

'I suppose not—' Maddie started, but was cut off.

'Do you think it could be the same person? That he might be back and picking off staff from the same building?'

'I think that's pretty unlikely, don't you?' Rhiannon spoke again, the impatience in her voice just as clear.

'You tell me, love,' the woman snapped back. 'Can't rule it out, seeing as you lot didn't catch the bastard last time. They turned up murdered, those women, beaten to death the press said. Nasty old business. I've already called my man; he'll be meeting me here at closing to take me home. I don't take no risks. I'll be telling the others to do the same.'

'Very wise,' Maddie said.

'Now then, what more did you need to know? Only, I can't see Steve getting back here before you finish up your teas, might be an hour or more. Anything I can help with?'

Turns out she was no help at all. Despite being *like a family* in the Ugly Jug, the truth appeared closer to her being someone who took very little interest in anyone but herself. Maddie ended the conversation when it was clear that Cathy was the one with the questions, desperate for nuggets of information that she would no doubt upload somewhere by the time the two detectives had got their jackets back on.

It didn't matter anyway, the visit was about getting a list of associates for Megan so they could be added to the Misper One form, but now Maddie had a new line of enquiry: the legend of the Ugly Sisters.

CHAPTER 31. THE GAME

'So, listen to this if you really want to hear what evil is.'

Rachel Cooper said this the moment she stepped back into the room. She had refreshed the drinks, two good amounts. I should say, not only did she have good whisky, but she had the right glasses to put them in, too. Wide and heavy, thin-topped and with a mottled strip for grip. She handed my glass back and hadn't even asked if I wanted another. I did, as it happened. She'd left me stewing, the anger inside me only building and I didn't quite know what to do with it. Drowning it seemed as good an option as any.

'I've come this far' was my reply, something like it anyway. I might not be remembering what I said word for word, but mine don't matter. I remember hers.

'I had to behave,' she said, 'we all did. Behaving . . .' She laughed here, this one almost carefree, even tossed her head back as part of it. 'Behaving meant lying in absolute silence; no movement, no nothing, barely breathing. Do you know how he made sure we stayed so still?' I did, at least I thought I did from what Charles had said, but I still said I didn't. 'A kitty toy.' She stopped there for the longest time. Her whole face darkened, she'd been lifting her glass but it froze a few inches from her lips like time itself had stopped.

Her eyes were glazed, a few moments later and those lips had a slight tremble and I thought that maybe she'd stopped talking because she couldn't no more.

'We don't have to talk about it,' I said, when the pause had been too long and it felt like the right thing to say. This was another time when I remember feeling bad for making her go through it all again but I swear she didn't hear me, she can't have, she just carried on when she could.

'That's what we ended up agreeing to call it: *kitty toy*. I kept calling it *the ball, bell thing* when I was giving my story and Inspect . . . Charles, he said let's just call it a *kitty toy*. Which made sense when I got to see it. I hadn't seen it before, not really. I guess Charles had. You know these plastic balls that have a tiny little bell inside, the sort that rolls around for kittens to chase?' She waved her glass, her focus still lost, never looking for me to answer. 'That was what he used. Simple and effective, I have to give him that!' Another laugh, this time snorted out through the nose.

'Effective?' I said, but she still wasn't hearing me.

'This was bigger, though, more like a hamster's ball. Big enough that you couldn't get your hands all the way around it and it was taped real tight to my palms. The slightest movement and that little bitch bell inside, it would give you up, and that was the excuse he needed to beat on you . . . no, that was the excuse he *wanted*!'

'Jesus.' The Lord's name in vain, I remember I did that because it made her prickle, angry even, when she told me how there wasn't no Jesus, no God either. I mean I get it, that she wouldn't like the idea that there's some big force for good out there, looking over us and looking after us, because if that's the case, where was Jesus when she was in that room? After she had set me straight, she had more to say.

'I worked out a bit of a method. I would lie on my side in like a "C" shape, my body a little twisted up, but, get it right, and that ball rests on the floor nice and still; hands either side. This was the best for breathing, the best for keeping the blood flowing and the best if you happened to fall asleep.'

'You just laid still all the time you were there?' I said and she shook her head with real enthusiasm.

'He wasn't always there. He probably had errands, got hungry; maybe he had a whole *normal* life going on outside of that place, who knew, but it was all part of his game. That man came and went, sometimes he would slam the door on his way, sometimes not, sometimes he would make a big deal of coming back, shoving the door, dragging something metal behind him like he was there to beat on you and then he would wrench off the lower part of your face covering and stuff food in your mouth, a straw quick to follow. Chewy flapjack-type bars and water. I don't know how often, enough to keep the pangs from being too bad. Other times he would be back in the building and we would know nothing about it. It was all about noise, loud noise and the absence of it entirely. It was how he controlled us, how he intimidated us. It became our everything.'

'You weren't wrong,' I said, I was shaking my head, trying to get the rest of my words out but she knew what I meant, she just knew.

'Evil,' she said, in demonstration. 'No other word for it.'

'Him?' I had to ask this; I already knew the answer. 'You keep saying *him*, did you see a man? Maybe hear a man's voice?'

'It was a man who picked me up to pose as my rescuer and it was a man grunting when he swung at me. I could even *smell* that he was a man, it was mixed up in his excitement. I can't tell you much more, the police got all excited that I would be able to identify him, they asked about hair colour, eye colour, left-handed, right-handed! I didn't know a damned thing that could help. I had my eyes covered in that room the whole time and I can barely even remember being picked up. I think I had my head down the whole time, I was groggy and confused with no real memory of being taken in the first place. And I was fucking terrified! All I could see was a way home and I remember being tired . . . so tired. The police thought he might have drugged me with something that meant I couldn't remember. The tests didn't show anything up but there's stuff out there that makes you like that, then disappears like it was never there in the first place.'

'Coward.' I remember saying that for no other reason than I couldn't keep it in. She didn't seem to hear me anyway.

'He was a man and he was strong. I said about sound, how he would use it. He would stomp away, make a big deal of slamming the door and the way he did that, the way he swung that steel bar . . . trust me, it could only have been a man.'

'He was messing with you.'

'He was controlling us. We weren't tied up, don't forget, or tied down more like. That door wasn't locked, I know that first-hand. It must have been part of his game that we could walk out any time, just as long as he wasn't there to beat us back to the floor. I knew . . .' She stopped here and her focus came back like she was checking I was OK for her to continue.

'Tell me what you knew,' I said, swishing my whisky glass at her on my way to taking a sip.

'I knew there were other people there with me. I could hear breathing, I could hear tiny movements and I could hear . . . I could hear their beatings.' She stopped again, still trying to gauge my reaction that I was hiding in that whisky glass. 'I'm sorry . . . about your friend.'

'Me too.' I wanted to say more, to thank her, to tell her not to be silly and how it wasn't her fault. But *me too* was all I could manage.

'There was a time when I waited maybe ten minutes or more after I heard him leave, slamming that door behind him. It was long enough that I was sure no one could be still that long. Then I spoke. It was the first time I dared to but there's a point where you just need to *know* you're not alone, where you need some sort of normal human interaction. So, I spoke and . . .'

She broke off here, another pause, this time it was obvious why.

'He was still there.' I said and she nodded, she looked pale again too, her jaw closed up tight enough to ripple those clay cheeks.

'He made it all the way back, don't ask me how he made it back to me without making a noise because I sure as hell heard him walk away. He must have been on tiptoes; shoes off . . . He grabbed me by the throat and it just came from nowhere. My neck was back in that vice, his hands so big that he could throttle two people — me and whoever was next to me — and drag us closer together so our heads were touching and we could hear each other fighting to breathe. After that I even thought . . . I even thought that maybe it wasn't a man at all, that it was something other-worldly; a monster.' She shook her head, then muttered: 'Stupid.'

'I'm so sorry,' I said again. I know I wrote earlier how I felt bad on my first visit to Rachel because I cried: I was in *her* place, with *her* memories of *her* pain, and it was me who cried. This was that moment. I was sorry for what she went through, but mainly, I was sorry for Christine and I couldn't escape from the image I had, in which Christine was the other woman in her memory being held down by her neck.

Rachel Cooper thought I was sorry because I was making her say it all over again and she told me she didn't actually mind, that Inspector Snow had told her that talking out what happened, including the most horrible details, could be good for her and could even cleanse her own mind somehow. He told her how he did the same sometimes, how he talked out some of the horrors he saw as part of his day job and it made him feel better to do so — even just a little bit.

I didn't tell her about me, about how I was the pair of ears stood the other side of a conversation panel at the bottom of a garden that Charles Snow was using to cleanse his mind. But I did take some comfort from that; maybe I was able to help.

I need to walk again. The cold has a way of sneaking in through layers of clothes and the flesh underneath to settle in the bones. A brisk walk should see it off, for a while at least.

CHAPTER 32

Daisy-Mae had ended up turned directly towards the source of the draught. In the stillness she thought she might have heard a low hiss, a constant noise like an air purifier her mum had snuck into her bedroom once. One sound she was sure of was that of crying next to her. It was restrained, subtle, like it was blowing in on the chilling breeze. The cold was coming up from the solid floor too, seeping through her skin to settle in her bones and she needed to shift, even slightly, believing she could do it without making a noise.

She was wrong.

The bell taped in Daisy-Mae's hands rolled and chimed and she froze. She had started to feel groggy, the adrenaline left over from her beating wearing off to leave her almost sleepy but that dissipated in a moment. She was wide awake, her whole body tensed, her breath held.

Nothing happened.

She waited to try again and shift her position, her movements so slow she couldn't be sure she was moving at all. It was effective, she managed to change the side she was lying on, putting her hands down first, shifting her weight through the ball to hold it still. Another minute or two passed and, when still nothing happened, she grew in confidence, enough to consider that there was no threat left in the room.

She could still hear breathing; two types, both regular, both controlled and there was no more gurgling. The man with the voice must have recovered.

'You OK?' Daisy-Mae spoke out. It was almost impossible to whisper through the tape and she needed to speak softly, but in her head it sounded like a shout. Her question was for both, but it was the male voice that answered.

'I'm OK. Was it you who took a beating?' His voice was soft and low, like a purr that vibrated against tape.

'No. Where are we?' Daisy-Mae grew more in confidence as she spoke again. She could feel every word in a throat that felt bruised and thorny at the same time.

'Don't speak; no noise. Not yet.' The man's voice was back on the breeze to drift over her. She didn't reply, doing as he asked for a minute or more but she couldn't wait any longer. There was still a question burning bright for the other person who had been dragged in and dumped next to her and she couldn't help but voice it.

'Megan?' Daisy-Mae held her breath for the reply, suddenly fearing she had imagined it after all.

'Daisy-Mae!' The reply came, it dripped with panic and with pain but there was no doubt left now. The woman dragged in to share this nightmare was Megan Laurence, her boss and friend, a woman she looked up to, who didn't take shit from anyone. It was the closest Daisy-Mae had been to breaking down, to losing it completely and wriggling closer to a familiar voice for a tight hug and to hell with the beating that might follow.

'Quiet.' The man, in trying to shush them, was the loudest of them all, the most urgent too. They did as he asked and Daisy-Mae could hear a room holding its breath with taped mouths, waiting for a reaction. When Daisy-Mae relaxed enough to breathe again she felt something other than the discomfort and pain, something she hadn't felt for what seemed like forever: hope. It didn't really make sense, Megan was taped up just as she was, no doubt she was just as scared and maybe even badly injured, but hope was there all the same and it was something for Daisy-Mae to cling on to.

CHAPTER 33

'I do remember these now.' Maddie stood at the wall in the corner of the office, near to the desk she had been turfed out of. The intelligence analyst who had done the turfing was demonstrating a flair for the visual. Eileen had been asked to provide a summary of the Ugly Sisters case for when Maddie and Rhiannon got back and it now covered an area where two walls met.

'It's mainly press coverage for now,' Eileen said briskly. 'I didn't have much time and the press have a way of summing things up far better than case material.'

'I bet there's a lot of case material too,' Maddie said.

'And you would be right. There is an electronic case file but that only has the MG Series scanned to it, the rest is still in physical form, four hundred and three boxes in secure storage on the other side of the country. It's a lot to review.'

Maddie sighed. "MG" in this instance referred to "Manual of Guidance", and the "series" referred to the fact that they were a series of forms that the Crown Prosecution Service required to be completed for every criminal investigation — the more serious, the more forms to complete. They were the papers that would form the basis for any prosecution at court, which meant that anything appearing on an MG

Series had to be factual, backed up by evidence. The MG Series was no place for theories, hunches or opinion.

'The MG Series may not be complete,' Maddie said, thinking out loud. This case had never made it to court. Policy stated that court documentation was completed as the investigation progressed but no one really did it until they had to.

'The bones only,' Eileen said. 'The press coverage gave me a little more of the flesh, you'll have to look through the typical sensational language to find it, mind.'

Sensational language was everywhere, bold headlines jumped out of the wall: *The Ugly Sisters' Ugly Death* was one, *They Lay Dead For Days!* another and perhaps the most abrupt and simple of them all: *Bludgeoned!*

There were some snippets of case material too, Maddie read "Operation Lightyear" from the top of one document — no doubt this was the internal name that had been assigned, understandably preferred over "Ugly Sisters". Maddie walked along the wall, absorbing what she could.

'This is really good work, Eileen,' she said and her newest team member flushed a little from her chest.

'I was born Millennium year.' Rhiannon had sidled up to stand beside her inspector; she was breathy, a little shell-shocked perhaps.

'I don't think I need to talk about my age and standing when these crimes occurred.' Eileen clucked. 'Let's just say I was well into my teaching career by this time and I certainly remember the press coverage. It was constant and for a good period.'

'Teacher?' Maddie ripped her eyes away from the wall to fix on Eileen.

'Geography at a variety of secondary schools, thirty years.' Eileen shrugged. 'Now, I can take you through the material if you would like?' Said like it was optional but she had already moved to the wall and, to Maddie's surprise, she then produced a telescopic metal pointer from a pocket in her cardigan that she unfurled and *thwacked* down on a printed newspaper article on the far left of the display. 'It reads left to right like any good story,' she started and Maddie exchanged a good-humoured glance with Rhiannon before they both settled in at the front of the class.

'The coverage at the time centred on two women and the *Ugly Sisters* reference is a nod to a nightclub with the same name. Both are believed to have been abducted having finished a shift on New Year's Eve, 1999, although they finally left, on foot, at around four a.m. on January first, 2000. Both women were found dead five days later having been abducted, blindfolded and kept mostly together in a derelict location in Margate.'

'And do we—' Maddie started with a question but Eileen silenced her by moving the pointer to a different location, *thwacking* it down firmly enough to make her point.

'It is important to note that these two women are not believed to be the first victims, they were just the first to really capture the public's imagination. Their names were Denise Tutthill and Christine Matheson and we know much of their ordeal from a third woman who was kept at the same location in the same conditions.' Eileen paused for breath.

'They weren't the only victims.' Maddie was thinking out loud, giving voice to her recall rather than raising a question, but she got an answer anyway.

'They were not. The case material describes a clear pattern of escalation. It started with murder by strangulation, a female runner and a male dog walker were believed to be early victims. The woman was a GP out in a small village, the dog walker found just a few hundred metres away.'

'Found how?' Maddie asked.

'I would guess by the next person who walked the path. The terrain was woodland, both victims were dragged a short way off the path, leaving a trail as you would, then covered by a thin layer of leaves. In the case of the dog walker they even found his barking dog tied up next to its owner.'

'He wasn't bothered about them being found, then,' Rhiannon interjected.

'So it would seem. The first abduction came next, a victim taken somewhere isolated to die from injuries sustained from blunt force trauma. At this point the investigators believed they had an offender losing himself in the moment, killing his victims at the first opportunity.' Eileen paused to move the pointer again, the *thwack* this time resonated enough to make Maddie flinch where her mind was whirling with images of death — *blunt force trauma*. 'There are other possible victims mentioned but I'll skip to the Ugly Sisters as the central event of this case. This is a very disturbing story, one of abduction, strangulation and torture and, in the biggest change yet, victims kept together. Five people, as it happens, one of whom was finally able to escape and raise the alarm. Too late, unfortunately, for Christine and Denise.'

Maddie paced a little. 'So we have men and women victims, some strangled, some beaten to death and some left alive . . . why did they think it was all the same person?'

'There were signs, I'll get you a full rundown of what happened. The most obvious I have seen so far was a sort of calling card; graffiti on the wall, or a tree in one instance and always the same message: *Don't wake up.*'

'Don't wake up?' Maddie repeated.

'First thing they saw when they did,' Eileen added.

'Anything to link the victims? Age, type, ethnic group? There has to be something,' Maddie huffed, getting more than an inkling as to why this had remained unsolved.

'There were theories but overall it seems to have come down to opportunity. The two women referenced up here as the Ugly Sisters knew each other of course, having worked together. The victims also included a couple abducted from a broken-down car, again deemed to be opportunistic.'

'Opportunistic . . .' Maddie sighed back. The worst type, the least predictable and by far the most dangerous. Maddie, like all detectives, liked a sense of meaning to a choice of victim, a reason at least.

'That was the summary for the team that worked it at the time and it was the same when it was reopened for a cold case review ten years later. That review coincided with one of the survivors taking her own life. The media ran the whole story again, there was a lot of pressure and they threw a lot of resources at the review, almost as much as the original investigation. Different team, same outcome.'

'Suicide? Is there more to that?'

'I'll have to look into it. Her name was Rachel Cooper and she took on the role as a bit of a star witness it would appear. I guess ten years down the line it might have finally got on top of her. Her ordeal was recorded officially by the Coroner's Court as playing a role in her death.'

'I'm sure it was,' Maddie said, getting to her feet. 'Being the only one to walk away from that horror show . . . can you imagine?'

'There was one other, actually, survivor that is. One half of the couple, he was a long way from walking away from anything by the time they found him.'

'His partner?'

'Dead beside him, ma'am, I'm afraid to say. I will get all of their details for you but those boxes in storage will be needed to be able to tell you much more.'

'What do we do next?' Rhiannon's gaze followed Maddie as she paced. Maddie reckoned she knew exactly what was meant by that question, too. The moment they started making phone calls for Operation Lightyear case material, Major Crime would start making calls of their own, mainly to demand what the hell she thought she was doing. And the truth of that was that she had no real idea. Maddie's priority was to find two missing women as quickly as possible and muddying the waters with tenuous links to a previous investigation might just be causing an unnecessary delay.

'Who was the SIO?' Every major crime investigation had a Senior Investigating Officer. Maybe she could at least make contact, maybe there was a way of doing it off the radar.

'Detective Inspector Charles Snow. But you should know that this was his last case before he retired and it would seem he passed away shortly after that,' Eileen replied.

'Of course he did.' Maddie huffed. Already this was one of those cases where everything came with an obstacle. 'CCTV,' she said, suddenly. 'We need to go and put some pressure on BTP and get that footage reviewed. At the moment we don't have anything other than two women who have stopped communicating. If we find them, this is just a ghost story.' Maddie made a sweeping gesture to take in everything on the wall, hoping she was coming across as more assured than she felt. 'Rhiannon and I will head out to the train station. Eileen, can you get me a list of the coppers who worked the original case, put those still in the job at the top, if possible, but I could do with key personnel. Preferably someone who worked closely with Inspector Charles Snow.'

'Yes ma'am, but finding those still serving might be a challenge. Major Crime back then was different to how they seem to run it these days, they generally went for experience in their recruitment.'

'You mean long in their service, whereas these days it's whoever they can get,' Maddie said.

'That's exactly what I mean.'

Maddie turned to Rhiannon. 'The best thing we can do, then, is go find those two women safe and well.'

'And if we don't?'

Maddie shrugged, turning back to the wall of horrors. 'Then we get to see what the inside of a can of worms looks like, twenty-two years after it was last sealed.'

CHAPTER 34. DYING ALONE

I used to play football in my local park as a kid (bear with me on this one, I have a point to make and it took me as long as a walk home to work out how best to make it). I grew up in a poor area, I couldn't afford a football, not a leather one at least, but there was a boy called Wayne Townsend who could. We all used to wait for Wayne to come out so we could play and he guarded that football like it was the most precious thing in all the world and, for at least two summers, I suppose you could say it was. Wayne Townsend was a good player but he wasn't the best in our village and he was a very poor loser to boot. If he was having a bad day, or got hit with a good tackle or maybe he missed an open goal, his day would be over — just like that — and so was our game. He would take his ball home as part of his sulk, no matter how we begged, leaving us with nothing to do but kick an empty drinks can at each other or make a fire out of a stack of litter and the rays of the sun.

And this is the best way I can think to describe Ryan Saunders, the man he was, his way of thinking. Only the toy he was playing with was a steel bar rather than a football and the game was one where he was the only willing participant. So, when someone died, the sore loser in him emerged, the sulker, and he just upped and left. He didn't tell anyone that the game was over, he just picked up his toys and left those who hadn't died yet, laid out, still convinced that the slightest noise meant a whole world of pain. This was what I knew when I was sat opposite Rachel Cooper, this was what I couldn't say and another of those details that the press didn't know.

Charles told me over the conversation panel. By then we were skipping pleasantries and small talk entirely and I got the impression he had forgotten Christine, her and me, I mean, what she had meant to me. Certainly, he wasn't doing nothing to soften his words.

'He got them back to some godforsaken hellhole,' Charles started out, then paused, his eyes already glazed, already opaque and still thickening in front of me. 'An old dance hall, but you're talking falling down around their ears; a big part of the roof missing, part of the old Dreamland Theme Park on Margate seafront.'

It's been restored now — Dreamland, I mean. As I sit here and write this there will be kids whooping and scream-ing on its rides, families making memories. Back then it was wrack and ruin, crumbling under its own weight. And this was Christine's fate he was talking about now, so you know.

'Can you imagine anywhere worse?' Charles said, the layer over his eyes gone just like that and his focus on me back to sharp and intense. I knew what he meant too, there's an irony with theme parks, those family rides, with all their cheer and bright colours, are nothing more than a thin veneer that falls away very quickly. Nothing does bad feeling quite like an abandoned theme park. 'They weren't tied up, those doors weren't locked.' Charles was rarely anything other than stoic, but this was the closest I reckon I saw the big man come to crying. He didn't, but now I think maybe he should have, like it might have done him good. I still don't know how the police got to know so much, it's a wonder really, but also a double-edged sword. Charles could have done with knowing less. Then he told me more of what he knew and I guess

138

you could say the same about me. This was the conversation where Charles told me about the kitty toy, that was the first time I had heard it, my conversation with Rachel where she was to talk about the same thing was to come much later. One thing I can say about Charles was that he was thorough and he mocked up those conditions best he could as a way of understanding better. I can still picture that, Charles at his police station, his walls filled with the images of men and women beaten to death, throttled until their eyes burst red, standing out from the washed-out white that he described for their skin. Charles Snow, in the name of research, laid down holding a hollow ball with a bell in its middle, his hands splayed round it like he had just caught Wayne Townsend's football. He couldn't do it for four full days of course, nor could he replicate the terror of unsettling it, but he would have got a sense of the anticipation, the desperation even, as those people waited for the police to launch a rescue that never came. Charles took that hard, right on the chin in fact, that they never even got close. He always said that was all on him.

Charles' theory at the time was that Saunders had come up with the bell in a ball as a way of preventing escape — how could you even consider escape if your every fixation is on the thing in your hands, keeping it still and quiet? I agreed with him then but I've had time to think different. I believe that Saunders, like any true coward, wanted to beat on people, to do unspeakable acts and to murder them, but he wasn't man enough to face up to it after. After all, keep that bell quiet and you don't get a beating. Not a single person avoided the rough treatment from Saunders, survivor or not, they all got the wrong end of whatever he was swinging but the way he set it all up, you just know he would have been able to tell himself it was their own fault for the hits they got.

'You never knew when it was coming, or where from.' Rachel summed it up best to me. 'And the blindfold wasn't like what you see on the TV, some flimsy piece of material where you get to see snippets out of the bottom or little bits of light. This was thick, black tape covering my whole face, pushed down so hard it stuck to my cheeks, lips and eyelids, pulling the skin tight.'

The one thing Rachel never really talked about was injuries. Not specifics at least, she talked about getting beat a lot and there was no doubt from how she told it that there was a lot of pain, but she didn't talk specifics. I still got to know those details though, how they had laid there for days with broken bones; a wrist for one, a jaw for another.

And a shin for Christine, sheared right in half under the force of that steel bar . . .

Think of that.

Can you imagine the pain? The hit too, the power needed — the hate — to cause that damage? In twenty-two years nothing has taken the edge off the thought of a young woman laid out in pain on a decaying dance floor, the roof missing right through to the sky for the wind and the rain to do what it will; no heating, no shelter, no idea of her surroundings and where the slightest shiver was enough for the next beating.

Christine didn't die first; she might even have been last and by the time she died, Ryan Saunders had already left for good. Again, I don't know how the police knew so much, but they do know this: Christine lay in agony, desperately trying to be still, conditioned not to cry out, not to make a sound from the threat of beatings. Denise Tutthill, her friend, was dead next to her — Denise died first from a fractured skull that marked the point where she was bleeding into her brain. Denise must have done something particular to upset Saunders as this was the only significant blow any of them ever took that wasn't a body shot. I guess he knew that if you started beating your playthings around the head, well, your fun would soon be over. Or maybe Denise did something right, something he approved of and her reward was mercy, a quick end. Whatever it was, the moment the first of those people died, Saunders picked up his football and he went home.

Rachel Cooper survived because she refused to lie still and wait to die, she said it like this: *Something in me just snapped and I got to my feet and I ran.* Her eyes were still covered when she did, so inevitably she ran square into a wall, her bell ringing all the way and that wall knocked her right off her feet. She thought she had been hit at first, even brought her hands up to shield against another blow that never came. Rachel broke her nose and knocked out two teeth in that run but those were the last injuries she was to sustain — and she kept running.

If Rachel could, she would tell you the same today as she told me all that time ago: the biggest regret of her life was that she didn't turn back, that she didn't shout out that she was free, that they all were. In her defence she still didn't know she was for sure, how could she when he had tricked her so many times? She was hurting, confused and feeling a panic that can barely be imagined. Her whole focus was on feeling her way out of a series of rooms before the thought occurred that she could smash that ball against the wall and tear off the tape covering her face.

Then she ran like the wind.

Blind luck she called it and even with a hint of humour. It was a bad pun, the worst I ever heard that's for sure. Rachel ran for the sunlight, emerging into the early hours of a beautiful summer morning. She wasn't found for almost an hour and by that time she was limping up the middle of a street some distance away and with no chance of finding her way back. She could barely talk, let alone describe what had happened and where. By the time the police were called and able to work out where she had come from, Christine was dead. Medical assessments had Rachel not far from it herself.

Blind luck indeed.

It was almost ten years later that her luck ran out, or something did. Rachel took her own life. We hadn't spoken for a couple of years by that time but the last time I saw her I dared to believe I was seeing a woman getting stronger. That's not to say that I am surprised by what happened, why would I be? She had no right to get up and walk away from that room, but she did, getting up and walking away from the trauma of being in there is a whole other ball game. You can't outrun your own mind. At least Rachel's guilt, the pain and the trauma died with her. I would be lying if I said that I can't see the appeal.

My suffering is different of course and I won't sit here and pretend it's anything like the same but there are images of what I didn't see that I still can't shake. For Christine, there must have been a moment near the end where she realised that she couldn't stay there forever, that lying there meant dying there, one way or another and she wasn't going to be saved. In my mind she tried to get up just like Rachel did, maybe even when she heard the din of Rachel's escape — but her injured body would have kept her down. One thing I can't get out of my mind is the thought that Christine shouted for help that never came, her whole face taped over, her throat lined with dust and filth, her body weak, broken and useless. I know she did, I wasn't there but that doesn't mean I haven't seen it a million times, heard it even. And what I hear is her calling out for me — the father she never had — my name bouncing around in the debris and the dust. What I see is Christine dying alone, begging that I would come.

Twenty-two years may have passed but that voice is louder than ever.

CHAPTER 35

Daisy-Mae had managed to sleep, enough for a groggy wake-up in a bubble of warmth, that first wake-up in bed in the morning when you feel snug and safe. It wasn't until she tried to lift her hand to where her hair was tickling her ear that any suggestion of *snug and safe* evaporated in an instant.

The bell taped between her palms jangled.

Daisy-Mae was wide awake, her breath sucked in through pursed lips that sounded — to her at least — as loud as a shout. But then there was a louder noise: scraping, something heavy and metal lifted off the floor. She could feel the tickle where her eyelashes shifted in that direction. The next sound was of footsteps coming directly towards her.

The sound of a solid metal strike against a concrete floor was like a gun fired, narrowly missing her shoulder and instinctively she rolled away from it, the bell jangling excitedly as she did. She could feel it too, the solid ball bouncing and rolling against her palms through a thin layer of plastic. Another strike smashed into the floor, this one close enough for her to feel the air move against her lower back where she had tipped onto her side. She felt something — a boot surely — heavy on her hip, then a push rather than a kick to roll her out onto her back, leaving her facing upwards towards the sound of heavy breathing.

Then came a blow that connected.

She had lifted her legs, it was instinctive, like they might provide some protection but all she felt was a pang of hot pain that spread out like boiling fluid. Her leg clattered back to the floor and she rolled onto her side again, her breath rushed out and her hands were instinctive in their movement towards the source of the pain.

Her bell jangled again.

The next blow crashed into her left buttock. Again, the pain was immense, rushing to encompass her whole body — her whole world — where her ears were muffled by her own heartbeat and her vision was still nothing but darkness. Her mind, too, whirled with pain and nothing else. But something did make it through, a moment of clarity.

She had to stop that bell.

She was still on her side, her hands out above her, her teeth gritted while she waited for the initial rush of pain to become bearable. It was only getting more intense, increasing all the time, the stillness making it worse. Her right leg was at an angle, her instinct was telling her she needed to straighten it out to ease the pain. She tried, instructing her leg to move but all she got back was a flash of agony that ripped up through her body and left it as a silent gasp. She was going to have to move it with her hands, hands that were wrapped around a jangling bell. She could still hear footsteps circling her, waiting for the next sound, the end of the blunt weapon now dragging after them, daring her to move and invoke it again.

Amid the pain there was a numbness to her foot that was getting worse, her panic too, where she now realised that the angle had cut the blood flow off and if she couldn't straighten it, maybe she would lose it entirely. The pacing around her stopped, she felt him closer, his heavy breathing had an occasional grunt and he smelled like BO and a hint of aftershave; something sweet and cheap. It was like he could read her thoughts and was now daring her to move.

She had no choice.

She reached down. Her foot wasn't where it should be, she couldn't work out what was wrong and she couldn't get hold of it in her tied hands. She heard a scuff, the man who had been squatting over her now stood straight, the scraping sound from his weapon was different, picked up in readiness rather than dragged. Another blow was coming. It might be the last, the one that crushed her skull. Part of her even considered that it would be sweet relief.

'Why are you doing this? LEAVE US ALONE!' The man with the voice had found it again and his shout seemed to be all around her. 'LEAVE HER ALONE!' he bellowed and the ground by her ear crunched like a foot had turned, a shift of weight. The next blow came, it was solid and true and quickly followed by another, only she was no longer the target, she could hear them finding their mark. Daisy-Mae seized the opportunity, using the thuds and cries of pain to get her leg straight, resorting to pushing one foot with the other. The pain peaked and she had to fight to stay conscious, rolling into a foetal position, her face a grimace she couldn't shake.

The pain did ease, becoming bearable as the beating stopped next to her. She felt a pang of guilt that she had taken advantage of someone else's beating, someone who might just have saved her life, but it soon passed.

Daisy-Mae Adams was in survival mode.

CHAPTER 36

British Transport Police officers rarely respond well to the arrival of a county police force, worse still if the officer from that force arrives with the intention of chasing up an earlier request. Maddie was a little perverse, perhaps, in that a part of her enjoyed upsetting those who took umbrage at simply being asked to do their job and she did nothing to hide her smile as the BTP constable they had found in the small café at Folkestone Central Train Station chose to harumph and huff in reaction, rather than using words. The officer in question was dusting a fresh tea with sugar, something she never looked away from, while working her way through a series of questions steered towards avoiding the need to do anything further.

Maddie waited the BTP officer out, making it clear that she wasn't going anywhere. BTP took a little longer than most, halfway through her tea, even (and with no offer to her guests) before they set off to walk the short distance to the draughty room that housed the CCTV operating system and at least three visible spiders. BTP's huffing and harumphing built back towards a peak as Maddie fired constant questions at her, upping the pressure in a tactic that soon worked as, after just a few minutes, she straightened up and said:

'Did you just want to do it?' and with enough frustration to shake her long, greying hair. 'Honestly,' she continued. 'Is she always like this?' Her question was to Rhiannon who had been hanging in the background but was now happy to step forward and answer a little too emphatically.

'Yes,' Rhiannon said. 'She's best left to it.'

And left to it they were. The system was similar to what Maddie had seen before and intuitive enough. The stations were labelled first, then individual platforms while the CCTV for the six trains that had been London-bound that day came from a different system. The link for this was on an email that PC Huff-and-Harumph had opened up instantly, showing prior knowledge that this visit was likely. Maddie started by selecting 'Folkestone Central' as the most likely location that Megan Laurence would have started her journey and then announced that she would get them both a cup of tea, seeing as how this could well be a long job. Rhiannon took the hint and immediately slid into the vacated seat. Both women knew that operating CCTV systems was not one of Maddie's strengths.

The office with the CCTV system opened directly out onto platform 2 and Maddie was greeted by an eerie silence that seemed exclusive to empty train stations. The café was just as they had left it: a stubby room, windowed on three sides, the surrounds once white, now with that standard layer of grime that seems to coat all things train-station. The woman serving had it too, though on her it was presented as a sheen that caught in the overhead lighting as she fashioned a smile. Maddie ordered two teas and was conned into two sorry-looking toasted cheese sandwiches when she asked if there was anything hot available. The warming process took too long to justify the tepid, floppy result, but the delay meant that Rhiannon had somehow managed to find their target by the time Maddie got back.

'That was fast.' Maddie's hunger was sudden, evoked by the smell of melted cheese and bread and she tore into it with such zeal that she got some of the packaging with it. Rhiannon waited for her to pull it awkwardly from her mouth before she explained.

'The trains to London are a few minutes past every hour, the coffee shop where Megan works closes at five thirty and we know she did the close, so I assumed she would be wanting to make the 6.05 p.m. train. She did.' Maddie took in another clump of sandwich, aware that some of it fell onto the desk as she leaned forward to get a better look at the screen. Their BTP colleague who had made her excuses bustled back in, bringing a freezing draught with her.

'That her?' BTP said, the door clattering shut behind her.

'That's her,' Maddie confirmed. Rhiannon had paused the footage for confirmation, freezing Megan Laurence in the doorway of the main entrance on an elevated camera angle. She was reaching up to take her hood down. Rhiannon pressed play. After the hood, Megan stopped to fix her hair with the help of the reflective surface of a vending machine. She then scanned her phone at the ticket machine before heading up the slope towards the platforms.

'She's alone,' Rhiannon said. She already had the hang of the system, changing the cameras to follow her progress. The slope finished almost opposite the café that Maddie had just walked out of — and the same one that the grainy image of Megan now made for. The platform was dotted with people, around twenty, evenly spread out and with more emerging from the same door Megan was trying to push through, forcing her to take a step back before moving inside. There was no CCTV covering the interior but she was quick to reappear with the addition of a large coffee cup. The CCTV showed the time: 6.02 p.m.; three minutes before the train was due. Rhiannon left it playing in real time right up until the train arrived. Megan was fixed on her phone mostly, the movement of her thumb suggesting she was scrolling rather than actively communicating. She barely looked up, her behaviour that of someone travelling alone.

The train's onboard CCTV was a little more complicated and their BTP colleague slipped back into the seat to work it after they watched Megan Laurence move through its doors. There was no huffing or harumphing this time where she must have realised the seriousness of the situation. She rewound the footage of the train's arrival, counting the carriages as a way of tracing the right camera to pick up their target.

'Sixth carriage,' she said out loud and Maddie made a note. The camera on the train was better quality, clearer, the best view of Megan yet as she walked right under it for a good view of her long, dark hair falling over the back of a short, black jacket. Her hood was still down and the footage was clear enough to see it was dripping moisture. Megan was wearing a skirt that finished above the knees over black tights. On her shoulder was a cream tote bag that announced *Saving the Planet Is Sexy*. The camera was behind her as she sat at a table in a carriage that was largely empty. An older man walked under the camera behind Megan. He stopped short, a few seats back off her left shoulder to sit on the outer seat of two with his head down for glimpses of grey hair to merge with the furry trim of a loose hood. Now he was sitting, his large green jacket was pretty much all Maddie could see of him.

From the other end of the carriage another man appeared; he was late teens, early twenties, his walk a swagger and his right hand down the front of his trousers like he was cupping himself. He had oversized and bright white tongues on his trainers that dragged the eye. He swung into a seat almost opposite where Megan had stood back up to take her coat off. He stayed turned towards her, even leaned forward a little.

'Are they talking?' The BTP officer asked the question and Maddie was instant in her reply.

'I would say not, judging by her body language she's doing her best not to.'

'I agree, that twat has the whole carriage to choose from and look where he's sat,' Rhiannon said.

'Oh yeah, he's a twat all right!' the BTP officer said as the footage showed the man in question dipping further forward, his head level with his knee, his hands fiddling with his laces but his eyes lifted so he could get a view under the table. 'OK, so he's a stranger for sure. A pervert too, but not someone she knows.'

'Or wants to know,' Maddie added.

The BTP officer moved the footage on at treble speed. Megan was unnatural in her lack of movement, stiff like a plank of wood had been left to rock against the seatback, her attention down on what looked like an e-reader in her hand. The twat stayed turned towards her in his seat the whole time, his attention moved around the carriage at times, but Megan Laurence remained his focus. The footage had moved on eight minutes when the BTP officer brought it back to normal speed, announcing why.

'She's moving.'

They all watched as Megan gathered up her things then stood up to move across the aisle, sitting directly behind the older man.

'It looks like she's helping him with his phone?' BTP said and neither detective replied straight away.

'Can we find out who these two are? From their tickets maybe?' Maddie spoke next.

'I've seen it done but it takes time. It means using the CCTV to chase them back and a bit of luck with how they bought their ticket.'

'I didn't see them on the platform,' Rhiannon said. Maddie had been thinking the same.

'They could have been, we weren't looking for them,' Maddie said.

'They could have just moved carriage. The train starts at Dover, Folkestone Central is the second stop,' BTP said.

'Does this footage come off this system? Can I take it away, I mean?'

BTP was shaking her head. 'It's all in the cloud these days, too much data. But we can give other forces access to it, it's web-based so you can access it from your police intranet.'

'Can you give my analyst access?' Maddie suppressed a smile — the title suddenly seemed too grand for what was a slipper-clad woman with a home-knitted cardigan staring fiercely out over glasses. 'I appreciate it isn't for BTP to find a resource to do all that work. If my analyst can find where and how anyone of interest purchased tickets, I can come back to you with a much shorter job. How does that sound?'

'It's a form, it's always a form.' BTP was almost sounding apologetic now. 'Leave me your email address and I'll send it over, it needs endorsement from someone senior but then your analyst will have access forever, in case you need it in the future.'

'Perfect.'

'She's back on the move.' Rhiannon grabbed all of their attention back to the monitor where Megan stood back up and moved one seat forward to take the seat right next to the older man. The twat was still a few more rows forward but by now he was sitting in his seat in the traditional manner, his back to the camera and to Megan, scrolling through his own phone like he had lost interest. The older man scooted over to be by the window and conversation still seemed centred around his phone. A few minutes later and the scenery slowed enough through the window for details to be made out, including faces where people were waiting on a platform outside.

'Where are they now?' Maddie said. She wasn't answered straight away as the footage showed more movement. The old man got up first, then he reached back down for Megan who seemed a little unsteady all of a sudden and it was like he was pulling her to her feet. Not against her will as such, more like she needed the help. Her hood was back up, Maddie hadn't noticed when that had happened. The man had lifted his own hood too, his was big enough to cover any view of his face despite turning directly towards the camera. His head stayed firmly down, Megan's did too but it was more like she was trying to see where her feet were going. She moved like a drunk held up by the arm of the man who had seemed to be a stranger just twenty minutes earlier. They made for the doors; the twat's attention was still sucked into his phone and he wouldn't have even noticed as Megan disappeared from the camera's view. The BTP officer sat straighter, seemingly agitated in her movements to find a camera angle that would show their exit.

'That's Ashford International,' she muttered. Her hands faster now, the footage on the screen changing almost as quickly. 'So why can't I see them?'

'Is it covered, all of it?' Maddie inquired.

'As far as I know. I would have said it wasn't possible to get off that train without being picked up but I can't see where they've gone. It's the high speed so it runs longer than most, but . . .' She changed the footage again, her voice still a mutter. 'But they will all bottleneck . . .' The screen now showed the bottom of a set of concrete stairs where those that had got off the train were indeed bunching together, some forced to a standstill while the group stretched out up the stairs, with one punter with a suitcase causing an issue. The angle was such that Maddie could see the gangway at the top that would take them over the track to the main station building on the other side. 'Can you see them?' BTP said, louder.

'Not yet,' Rhiannon replied. Maddie didn't answer. She hadn't seen them either and she now had a feeling she wasn't going to. The crowd filed up the stairs, the bunching at the back clearing until it left no one. The BTP officer flicked through different cameras, rewinding and playing, back to huffing and harumphing where her search was futile.

'Are those stairs the only way out?' Maddie said.

'Yes. It takes them back to the station and then out through gates that are also covered by CCTV.'

'Did they definitely get off?' Rhiannon offered but Maddie was sure they had.

'They got off,' she said firmly. BTP was double-checking, flicking back through the train's internal system, searching every carriage of a train that was filling quickly as passengers poured on.

'There are some maintenance routes on that side but there's no public access.' BTP was thinking out loud.

'Locked?' Maddie said.

'Swipe card.'

'OK.' She made eye contact with Rhiannon. 'We need to get up there and see for ourselves. In the meantime, send me that form so I can get my analyst that access. I want her to look at every angle available. They went somewhere.'

'They did.' The BTP officer shrugged. 'I'll search the train again, the platforms too . . . I'm sorry, I just don't . . .' and Maddie waved her away. It wasn't her fault the cameras didn't cover every inch, or that she didn't know their limitations. But someone else did. Someone who had got on that train and then used that knowledge to remove a young woman without so much as raising an alarm.

'And I'll need to make some calls. Seems we have our sus circumstances.'

CHAPTER 37. I KNOW

'I know who killed Christine.' That was what Charles said, just like that, almost mentioning it like you might toss any old small-talk subject over the garden fence. But this was a big moment, big enough for it still to be as clear in my mind as if I was still stood there now, raking up the first signs of autumn. He even waited, watched me make my pile of mushy leaves first, two coffees balanced on the rounded top.

His casual demeanour caught me out. He would have known how desperate I was for more, to know what he did and my mind swirled up with questions like if that pile of leaves got caught in the path of a mini tornado, but I could barely get my words out. He was expecting a barrage too. He might have been casual saying it out loud to start with but he took a tight grip of that fence with the hand that wasn't holding his tainted coffee, leaning back a little too, expecting questions thrown like punches. When that didn't happen, when I still struggled, he spoke again, maybe even thinking he was second-guessing me.

'And I want to kill him.'

Charles was a man of God. I know I told you that already, I think I told you too that his faith had been tested, shaken to its core more like and he even stepped away from the church on a Sunday — his wife's church, don't forget. Betty was an active part and round that time she was more active than ever, feeling perhaps that she needed to step up and make amends for her husband faltering. She lost herself in the church just as much as Charles had lost himself in that case — and he was lost; I had barely seen him for a few weeks leading up to that conversation. I would see his car arrive home a couple of times when we were finishing up watching our television shows and pulling the curtains for bed, so we're talking late, gone ten at night, sometimes eleven. That long summer had a sudden end, the nights in particular, a cold snap rushed in, a carpet of frost fitted overnight the moment September ended and I would regularly go out first thing in the morning to scrape the car for Helen and see that Charles hadn't made it back at all. I knew he was working too hard, that the case was getting the best of him and of his time.

People talk about murder cases and they talk about the victims and their families, you see them in the documentaries they make these days where they lay it on thick about the trauma and impact for those involved, for the victims, witnesses and friends, the impact on everyone involved.

But never the police.

I'm not saying that's wrong; the victim and their family are who deserve their story told, I think I just mean that if a man lives and breathes a case, obsesses over every detail and blames himself for never doing enough . . . well, you don't just clock off at the end of a shift and leave all that at the door.

Charles had lived more than a year of people going missing, of turning up dead and of not stopping it and the longer it went on the more it was taking out of him. By the time he stopped me raking leaves he was a hollow shell, eyes made of glass, a voice with nothing but volume.

But there was something different that day, there was emotion back, something filling that shell. Considering what he had said, you might think I would accuse him of not being serious, joking even. But it never crossed my mind. Charles

Snow locked on to me and I knew right away that this was no joke, that he was *serious as cancer*. I didn't manage to get any questions out that day, we didn't talk any more at all, just sipped at those coffees in silence. What had already been said was still resonating loud enough to drown out any chance of anything more.

I know who killed Christine. And I want to kill him.

CHAPTER 38

The door clanged. It was a sound that Daisy-Mae feared more than any other, it meant the threat had returned, that it was starting up all over again. She was past it making her flinch at least, she had trained herself to suck in a lungful of air, to hold it in, to use it as her focus and it was effective. Her bell stayed silent.

This time, what she did wasn't going to matter.

Instantly there was noise, footsteps, heavy and quick, straight towards her then seemingly all around her. She was being circled, the pace still fast, the footfalls still heavy. Something loose flicked up to sting her cheek. Daisy-Mae used the din to shift her position again. It felt like a mistake at first, her injured leg was down to a hot ache, the pain just about bearable and the shift saw the return of searing pain through her calf, thigh and into her hips. The sensation threatened to catch her out and she had to fight off a sudden urge to vomit.

The footsteps slowed, then came the crunch of grit under the sole of a shoe, right next to her ear, close enough to trap a clump of her hair. Daisy-Mae couldn't help but flinch this time, but still kept that bell silent. She bit down tight on her bottom lip, scrunching her eyes shut against the pain of her hair being pulled. She knew what he wanted — for her to make a noise, to give him an excuse to hurt her more.

It must have been five minutes before he lifted his foot off, then came the sensation of fingers on her face, picking at the edge of the tape by her chin. The bottom half was suddenly wrenched clear and still Daisy-Mae didn't give him a single noise in reaction. All her focus was on her hands, on keeping that bell still. Next, she felt something pushed firmly against her lips, firm enough to push them apart, for a taste to flood through them. She was hungry, parting her lips was almost instinctive to let him push something soft, chewy and instantly sweet into her mouth. It tasted like flapjack. The lump was far too much and she wasn't allowed to finish what she had before more was stuffed in and she gagged, but was able to hold the food in her mouth. Water followed, through a straw pushed firmly against the roof of her mouth. She heard sounds of the others being fed in the same way, a bell jangled — not hers — but seemed to be ignored. This time at least.

Another chewy clump was forced into her mouth, sealed in this time when the tape was stuck back down and then footsteps away that sounded heavier still. Something solid was kicked to scrape and slide, then collided to make a sound from something wooden and hollow. A door was opened, the sound of it slamming shut was like a gunshot that reverberated to fade away. Silence took a few moments to return, but when it did, it was thick enough for Daisy-Mae to once again feel a part of a room of people all holding their breath.

CHAPTER 39

'You've moved,' Maddie Ives called out to the back of the man leaning forward, standing outside in the middle of a garden, his back to the gate where she was standing. The house was the last one in a row of cottages, the garden side-on to the road, meaning the boundary fence ran along the edge to allow a view in — on tiptoes at least.

Recently retired Detective Inspector Harry Blaker didn't even straighten up to answer.

'Obviously not far enough.' His voice was a little more than a discontented growl, it could be construed as aggressive if you didn't know the man, but Maddie did know him, just about as well as she knew anyone. Harry Blaker had been the first person she had met when she had moved police force. She had been lost, out of her depth and entirely displaced and the last thing she'd needed from her new boss was a clear first impression of someone gruff, uncaring and dismissive. But first impressions can be wrong. They had been wrong about each other, in truth, going on to form something quite formidable with strengths and weaknesses matched in a way that made them better together than they could possibly be working apart. Not that either of them would admit it. Just like neither of them had talked about how Harry had ruined their partnership with his early retirement.

But even the sound of his voice and a glimpse of his back from over the top of a slatted gate was enough to have her smiling wide, despite promising herself that she would keep any idea of missing him to herself.

'Did you bring the kettle with you?' Maddie tried again. Harry was busy with his hands, leaning forward to press down rhythmically on a clump of soil, his arse bobbing as he did. He took his time finishing up then straightened slowly. A handkerchief emerged from his pocket and he used it to dab at his forehead. Still he faced away.

'That's a gate.' The growl was deeper and ended with a sigh that she recognised as a knowing one; *knowing* that she wouldn't leave until she had said what she had come to say.

The handle was stiff and it hurt Maddie's thumb to open it. The moment she did, a light brown missile flashed towards her, lifting to collide with her thighs.

'Jock!' she exclaimed. 'My, my, how well do you look!' She ruffled his hair, then did as she was told when he rolled onto his back to demand a belly rub. Jock was a King Charles Spaniel that Harry might say had forced himself upon him as part of a previous case, though Maddie knew the truth and it was clear even in the way Harry told the dog off, sending him strutting back across the garden where cushions had been laid out for his comfort.

Harry had turned to face her. He finished dabbing at his forehead, missing two lines of sweat either side of a face that might have weathered a little more since she had last seen him. The right sort of weathering, however: filled out, less tension than she remembered and possibly even a little tanned. The run of sweat on the right skewed a little when it reached his cheek and caught in a deep scar part-concealed by a thick beard that went a little ragged on his neck. Harry's broad shoulders were present and correct, his large shovel-like hands and thick limbs too, pushing against the material of a checked shirt that was untucked over mud-splattered chinos that narrowed into welly boots. The checked shirt was open enough to show a white T-shirt underneath, gone part see-through from his exertions.

'Well, Harry, looks like a meadow threw up out here. You used to be good at all this, I remember flowerbeds you could set your watch by!'

'It's wild, Maddie.' Never one for more words than necessary, Maddie was a little surprised to even get her name.

'Are you talking about your lifestyle or your garden?' Her grin now so wide it was making her face ache.

'I know a bit about police officers, I know they never turn up for no reason.' Harry was refusing to bite, just like she knew he would. 'You're lucky, I thought it was Avon calling. I was just about to tell you to fuck off.'

Maddie was a little taken aback. 'Who is this Harry Blaker that says *fuck* and what have you done with my old friend?'

'It's amazing what a visit out of nowhere from someone you really don't want to see can tip out of a man,' Harry growled. Maddie's smile held, but it was waning.

'Are you talking about Avon now, or . . .'

His face broke into a smile that highlighted the new wrinkles. 'Who is this Maddie Ives,' he said. 'And what have you done with the version who knew when I was joking?'

'Very good.'

'I've been working on new material. Now, what do you want?'

'Actually, I was just passing and I thought I would pop in and tell you about these great jobs they've got back at our place. *Civilian Investigators*, they're calling them and the idea is to get a load of civvies in to do a lot of the shitty work that proper detectives don't want to do, for half the cost and with none of the rights or pension benefits. It seems to be attracting a lot of miserable, clapped-out ex-coppers who retired and realised that all they had left to do with their lives was talk to daisies while dressed like a lumberjack. Not sure why that made me think of you . . .'

'Tickseed.' Harry Blaker's growl was deeper than ever and it only made Maddie's smile broader.

'Tickseed?' she repeated back.

'Tickseed. Not daisies,' he replied.

'Noted. So these jobs, I can send you a link if you'd like, it's an application online, very easy and—'

'I know I don't look like I'm busy . . .' Harry fixed on her now with something she thought was the beginning of a smile. Sure enough, it broke out a little with his next word: 'Ma'am.'

'Ah yes, I'm an inspector now, Blaker, and still serving, that puts me in charge.'

'Temporary Inspector, last I heard,' Harry said and Maddie held her first reaction. She had been the one trying for a bite but had very nearly been caught out by the master. 'And in my garden I'm always the boss.' There was a pause like he was considering his next words closely. 'Which means if you want a tea, you'll have to make it yourself.' He went back to pushing down on fresh-looking mounds of earth like a chef kneading dough.

'Do you remember anything about the Ugly Sisters?' Maddie said and Harry's bobbing up and down stopped. This time he straightened a little quicker.

'I remember I never liked that name. They weren't ugly, far from it. Two young women taken off the street at no age. They were murdered, part of a bigger picture, we were never even sure how many victims there were. The press summed up the whole case with that name and it stuck. Did you get him?' Now his look was earnest; a flash of hunger that had once been so familiar when he was leading Major Crime.

'Him?' Maddie said.

'*Him*, the bastard responsible all those years ago. I assume that's why you're here with that smug-looking grin, *temporary* inspector?'

'No, if that was why, I would have made a far better entrance.'

'What about it then?'

162

'Twenty-two years ago those women were abducted on their way home after working a shift at the Ugly Sisters night-club. Right now I have two women gone missing within a few days of each other, they both work at the Ugly Jug coffee shop, it's part of the old nightclub building. I've just watched the CCTV footage of one of the girls and she was abducted. It doesn't give us much of the suspect, but enough to know he could be old enough to be repeating a trick he pulled more than two decades ago.'

'Trick?' Harry locked on to her, his tone disapproving.

'You know what I mean. From what I've been able to find out, what he did back then was in two parts. Part one was abducting, torturing and murdering. Part two was disappearing without a trace. I'm just hoping we're not already at part two.'

Harry broke away, his eyes to the floor like he was searching for something. He seemed to find it, taking a few paces to pluck a gardening fork from the earth.

'Sounds like a fresh team working the case is exactly what is needed to me. I wasn't too involved, if that's why you're here. I was a skipper at the time, of a robbery team. We were diverted to work that case like everyone else but we just did some case material. We got statements from those that were on the periphery and I'm pretty certain we didn't get anything that made a damned bit of difference. Not that anything seemed to make a difference to the outcome of that one. Fella by the name of Charles Snow was the SIO, he was a decent detective from what I saw, he would have kept good records of who he tasked with what. There will be people able to offer a lot more than me.'

'You're right, he did. He wasn't the only one who kept good records. Charles Snow died soon after that investigation was closed—'

'It was never closed,' Harry growled.

'Became inactive, then. When DI Snow died, The Job seemed to accept that the Ugly Sisters case—'

'Op Lightyear, if I remember right. That name is disrespectful,' Harry cut in.

'Op Lightyear . . .' Maddie said, taking her ticking-off. 'The Job figured that it might have left an impression not just on him, but on his family too. They took the unusual step of assigning a FLO to his widow.' Maddie paused now, she had come here with a strong suspicion, but Harry's reaction was confirmation. 'It was you, wasn't it?'

'That was never official. They were informal visits.'

FLOs — Force Liaison Officers — are specially trained officers assigned to the families when a victim has died in traumatic circumstances. This is a vague description on purpose, allowing cases to be considered on individual merit. The family of a murder victim will always have the offer of a FLO, child deaths and road traffic collisions are other common areas, but the wife of a retired police officer who died from a short illness was not something that should come close to the right criteria. FLOs were in short supply, used sparingly.

'It was formal enough to be recorded in the case notes. Turns out I've picked up an incredibly thorough intelligence analyst, somehow.'

'Intelligence analyst? What the hell is that?' Harry scoffed.

'Some newfangled role, a bit like those civilian investigator jobs I was talking about. Anyway, when I was learning the ropes as a detective I worked with someone who taught me the value of looking beyond the material that was written down for a file. That same person told me how a case file is made up exclusively of facts and how a courtroom is no place for opinion. He also told me never to forget that *facts are just proven opinions.*'

'Sounds like a very wise detective indeed. What's your point?' Harry said.

'Charles Snow worked that case as SIO for years, the one person who knew it best. Only he never had an opinion, or a theory, proved right. He never got a conviction.'

'And you think he might have had a theory that was right after all?' Harry said.

'If anyone did.'

164

'And you think he might have talked these opinions out with his wife?'

'And I'm not the only one. Whoever decided she could do with a visit from a FLO was thinking the same. That's why they sent you, isn't it?'

Harry's grin took a while and even then it wasn't fully formed. 'I was fresh out of training. Maybe they just saw it as a good example for me to get some practice while looking after one of our own?' Maddie held his gaze, it didn't take long. 'Fine, I see you've lost none of your sharpness. Or your cynicism. They might have been thinking along those lines. Charles, towards the end . . . he became a little distant. He worked that case hard, he was obsessed and then he asked for a move out of nowhere. Did his last few years in some admin role in a broom cupboard out in Cranbrook.'

'And did you find anything out? Anything of interest?'

'I did exactly what I was asked. I documented it too, all that was said is there for you to find and no, there was nothing of interest. Charles' wife was a difficult woman to speak to, it took a few visits to even get in the door.'

'Even with your levels of charm?' Maddie quipped. 'From what I can see, you're just about the only officer she did speak to.'

'She was angry at The Job for what happened with Charles.'

'Would you talk to her again?' Maddie said. 'Now that we have two more women missing, now that she might have the chance to help us, to help solve the case that hung over her husband's life — and death — for all that time. If he said something, anything, no matter how silly or insignificant that helps us . . . DI Snow could still be the key, the man who cracks this case and—'

'All right!' Harry cut her off. 'I assume that's the speech you've prepared for the wife, I don't need to hear it. You'll be wasting your time.'

'There was a serious case review ten years down the line. A whole new team reviewed every document, they spoke to everyone who was involved: *fresh eyes*, just like you said and they got nowhere. If we're going to have to do that again, if *I'm* going to do that again then I need to think different.'

'By going to see the widow, just like I did all those years ago,' Harry said.

'Yes. But now it's possible it's happening all over again. She has to listen to that, to respond to that, but I need to get in and make her listen. I think you can get me in the door at least.'

'This serious case review, did they speak to her then too?'

'She refused.'

'We weren't exactly close, Maddie. It's just as likely she'll slam the door on me.'

'So say no. All I need is for you to come along and to bring your face . . .' Maddie paused enough to look him up and down. 'Maybe wash it first.'

'OK,' Harry said.

'OK, what?' Maddie said, her surprise adding an octave to her voice.

'I'll help. We'll go and see the widow and I will introduce you. You're right, I am your only chance of getting through that door.'

Maddie huffed. 'But I had this whole argument ready for you, it was really persuasive, I even did a little role play on the way over here with me asking and you growling.'

'Did you still want to do it? I'll finish up with my daisies while you do.'

Maddie had gathered herself together enough to grin. 'Tickseed,' she corrected him.

CHAPTER 40. MURDERER

Well of course I wanted Ryan Saunders dead too, but Charles saying it sparked all sorts of fantasies as to how. I enjoyed them fantasies too, I can't lie about that, I think we've all done that at some point, played out some diabolical revenge on someone in our minds. I have to say, I really went to town. I even said them out loud to Charles, stuff about taking him off the street, terrifying the man, taking him somewhere and slowly breaking bits off like stripping down an old car. Charles let me talk, let me talk myself right out and then, when I did come to a stop and with anger racing my heart so fast I could feel it in my feet, he looked right at me and said:

'Could you do that? Could you really?'

Charles knew I couldn't, I guess he'd seen bravado before, almost every weekend when he was a uniform cop. But he also knew that, in the heat of the moment and with hate in his heart, a man can be capable of more than just words.

I guess the time has come for me to talk about that.

This is the first bit that really feels like a confession: I killed a man. I stabbed him to death with a knife and I looked him right in the eye as I did.

The blood is what I remember most.

The blood, the rain and the panic. But mainly the blood. It was everywhere, like when I lifted that blade I cut the sky itself to turn the rain red. I got Ryan Saunders in the chest first go. I had to twist it too, to get it back out. I could feel gristle and bone as I did, I hadn't been expecting that, but it came free, bringing more blood as it did.

Ryan Saunders didn't die straight away. Movies were all I had to go on and they had me thinking that the moment I stuck him, his struggle would stop and he would slide to the floor with his eyes wide, clutching his wound, maybe a request that we tell his mother that he loved her or a few words to repent his sins. But life is nothing like the movies. I understand it better now, what happened I mean, time has a way of making you understand the simple elements of a complicated act. Now I know that Saunders was *dying* from the moment I opened up a wound in his chest but, because he was a full-grown man maxed out at five litres of blood, it was always going to take a while for him to lose enough to bring him down. There was a lot of adrenaline too and that didn't just keep him up on his feet, Ryan Saunders came back fighting.

So I stabbed him again.

This is the part when I can tell you for sure that I am no psychotic, cold-blooded killer. I know that may sound strange here, following on from me talking about wrenching a knife out of a man's chest to plunge it back again. But I was panicking, that's the truth. A cold-blooded killer waits out a man fighting for his life, or lunges again to speed it up, knowing that is what he has to do, but the reality for me was panic. I thought he wasn't going to die and all I had done was make him angry. I was so panicked that I very nearly missed altogether. He was fighting hard like I said, we never truly had Saunders under control; he was a big man, strong and broad; arms like trunks, fists like hammers; easily the sort of man who could hold down and throttle two people at once and that first blow hardly registered. I might have doubted it had happened at all if I couldn't see it clear as you like. In the struggle his shirt got wrenched right off his back leaving him bare-chested, his wounds out on show. His skin was soaked in rain and blood to make him difficult to get hold of. He was being held from behind and in the moment he folded forward, his head pushed towards me like a trussed bull, my panic had me lashing out with that blade again. I aimed for his head but I got him in the shoulder, then the upper back as he got one arm free and tried to take me out at the legs. That one didn't stick where I reckon I must have bounced off his spine. Saunders reared up at this point and this is the image that my mind conjures up still, sometimes at night, to wake me up in a cold sweat, breathing like I spent the night running for my life: Ryan Saunders leaking blood from everywhere, his eyes two blocks of shadow where the only strong light is behind him and the raindrops hitting so hard as to leave an aura around him tinged red, like a brake light lit through mist. When I punctured that hole in his chest it unleashed a demon whose visits have been nightly since.

I lashed out again and this was the one that I got right, the one that got the reaction I wanted: the demon's roar fell silent and its movements were suddenly clumsy. Saunders was let go so he could step away, it was more of a stumble, his left hand reached for where I'd stuck him while his eyes chased the floor with no focus. That roar was now replaced by grunts on every outward breath.

I moved forward and this part you could take as cold, there's no way to write it otherwise: I stuck him again, in the side of his thick neck.

I got a good bit of flesh, I felt something contract around that blade, like I had stabbed him in the hand and he'd made a fist around it, tight enough for me to let it go and, sure as sure, that knife stayed put.

His whole left side slumped, his arm first and I knew he was going down, his fall like an internet video called *Demolition Fail!* where the explosive charges only work on one side of a tall building. It still goes down, but the disturbed side drags the rest so there's no control and more of a mess.

169

Even Saunders' expression — when it changed to that of a man who seemed to know he was done for — only filled half of his face.

If I could have talked to Saunders after he might have told me that I had the exact same expression, or maybe I didn't, maybe in that moment I really did feel avenged and I looked smug, even with a big, stupid grin. I hope I did. I hope that was the last thing he saw.

I know now how I should have felt. I've had twenty-odd years to replay that moment and I've been here for what has happened since, enough to realise that from that moment on, I was done for too. I do wonder if Saunders knew that. I doubt it I suppose, he was probably too busy trying to work out how to stay alive with a major nerve to his left side severed and most of his blood already merged with a puddle thundering raindrops at his feet.

This is a confession, like I said; only not of being a killer, but of making a mistake. My mistake wasn't killing another human being, or whatever you call a man like that, my mistake was thinking that once that act was completed, it would be over.

It wasn't over, it couldn't be.

The murder of Ryan Saunders was the autumn of the year 2000: the Millennium, when the world was supposed to stop and planes were supposed to fall out of the sky.

Nothing stopped. Everything changed.

PART TWO

CHAPTER 41

Debbie Rix smiled, she had to work hard but it came. Her smile was projected out through her kitchen window towards a seven-year-old girl who just didn't seem to feel the cold, certainly not while she was fervently bouncing on her trampoline, red-cheeked and ecstatic, showing off her best seat drops and swivel hips while she knew her mother was watching. She was good too, her coach had said so, but then practice wasn't an issue, she would be out here every minute of every day if she was allowed. Mia Rix always seemed at her happiest when she was on the trampoline, like it set her free and cleared her mind.

Debbie wished she had something like that.

She allowed her eyes to drop and the squeal was instant: *Mummy, watch*! And Debbie did as she was told. Her smile had dropped too, her face now flinching to the sound of something falling to the floor with a thud in the living room. Staring out that window had her facing away from the noises, obediently. He didn't like it if she watched.

Michael Rix was in there and this day had been coming for a while. His mood had been building, his hostility like a kettle on a hob turned low. The fact they had been married for fifteen years, together for seventeen, meant that she could recognise the signs, even if she still couldn't do anything to head them off.

The only thing she really knew was where it had all started: twenty-two years ago, before they had even met, when Michael Rix had been abducted along with his girlfriend of the time and kept in a room as one of a number of people who were blindfolded and beaten for daring to so much as move. Michael was now the only one of those people left alive, left to endure the years since of being told how lucky he was, but Debbie lived and breathed the dark periods that were left and *lucky* was not a word that came to mind.

Another thud, then the hiss of expelled air like a cornered cat and Debbie knew it to be a hiss of pain. He would tire himself out eventually, get to the point where he had taken enough and she would go in there to find a wreck of a man, exhausted, bruised and sobbing. Sometimes he would beat on himself so bad there would be blood — even broken bones in the past if fingers, his nose and knocked-out teeth counted. The therapist had explained his self-harm as a man acting out, punishing himself for being the only survivor when so many others had died. But he blamed himself for more than just surviving, it was more that he had allowed himself to be abducted in the first place, surrendered all control to another and was unable to do anything to stop the murder of his girlfriend as she lay beside him.

The same therapist had also told Debbie what she knew already, that the silence from the police, the people charged with finding the person responsible and bringing some sort of closure, remained the biggest obstacle to Michael moving on, to having the chance of a normal life.

Mia's love of the trampoline had started as a reaction to her father's Post-Traumatic Stress Disorder. Debbie had bought it specifically as a thing to usher her outside the house to use when he was coming to the boil. At least something positive had come out of it; Mia had found something she truly adored — perhaps she wouldn't have otherwise. But her father was getting worse, the eggshells on which they walked were now ever-present, the time between episodes shrinking to the point where one could even run into another.

And Debbie's anxiety was only growing, a feeling that had started as a niggle was now a full-blown certainty: something was coming that was going to tip Michael so far over the edge that there could be no pulling him back.

CHAPTER 42

The top end of Folkestone, almost out of the town altogether and Maddie turned off a main route into a quieter, more residential road. A family pub with an impressive array of child playthings in its garden passed to their right, then an entrance to a slab of land cut out of the estate and occupied by any number of allotments laid out as brown strips lined by plastic tunnels and plastic chairs. Maddie could see hardy gardeners moving about between them with woolly hats for heads and damp patches for knees. The daylight that had never really fully arrived was already starting to leave.

'Any of this looking familiar?' Maddie glanced over to where Harry was turned away, seemingly transfixed, out of his window. The street was typical of estates built in the 1930s: two rows either side of a wide, straight road. The houses were built in twos, constructed like a giant mirror ran down their middles and with gardens that were sized before a time when planners were intent on fitting homes together like Tetris.

'Doesn't change much around here,' Harry summed it up and he was surely right. Besides front lawns being carved up for herringbone-patterned drives, an always increasing number of parked cars and a scourge of satellite dishes, this estate would have the same look and feel overall as when the bones were first laid. The address they wanted came up on the right to back onto the allotments.

'Nice place,' Maddie said, taking a moment to take in the frontage. Betty Snow did not have one car, let alone two. Nor did she have a satellite dish or a herringbone drive. She did have a slab of crumbling concrete, a garage door hanging lower on one side than the other and a parcel of unruly grass beneath the bay window, with bare borders; something Harry noticed too, straight away.

'She was a keen gardener, I remember that.'

Maddie grinned. 'If anyone would. We've checked voters, no doubt she still lives here.'

Harry was thoughtful. 'She was late fifties when I saw her last, I guess she might not have the mobility anymore. It's harder than people think.' Harry then shook his head, no doubt responding to Maddie's smile growing wider. 'Go on, chip in with your standard gardening comment.'

Maddie didn't have one. Instead, she made for the door, knocking without hesitation. 'Seventy-seven,' she said. She had read Betty Snow's actual age in the case file. There wasn't enough time for a reply. A woman considerably younger than seventy-seven tore the door open to stare out, her hands bright blue in loose gloves that rustled like paper. Everything about her said *furious*. Maddie lifted her warrant card.

'Good afternoon, sorry to bother you. My name is Detective Inspector Maddie Ives and this is . . . this is Harry Blaker. We were hoping to be able to speak to Betty Snow. Does she still live here?'

The woman's livid face was podgy, the expression bunched up into the middle of it. It shifted quickly to incredulous.

'Live here? Yeah, we have a Betty Snow here.' Her anger may have dissipated but the smile she attempted seemed more like a snarl. 'Did you need to speak to her?'

'Would that be OK?' Maddie said and the woman shrugged.

'Fine by me.' Her gloves rustled as she rubbed them together, stepping back for Maddie to step in. The smell arrived like a blow, a combination of stagnant air, microwave dinners and something far less pleasant. A hacking cough emitted from the door to Maddie's left. There were stairs to her right but Maddie made for the noise, arriving in what was surely meant as the living room. Now it was dominated by a large bed, there wasn't room for much else, save for an ancient television on a stand pushed into the bay window. Everything about the room looked like it had faded, the blue carpet, the yellow walls with white touches, the bedsheets and even the bedside cabinet. On top of it was a jug of water and a stack of colourful magazines topped by an oversized copy of the Bible. The cabinet looked to have been pulled just out of reach of the woman propped up in the middle of the bed. She looked faded too, the colour in her skin, the white in her hair, the light in her eyes. She took a while to focus, then gathered up a confused look while her palms pushed down on the mattress so she could sit straighter; again, the sound was akin to rustling paper. Directly above the woman, in the centre of the wall, Jesus Christ hung from a cross, a spider's web thick with dust drifting out from his thorny crown.

'She just had a change, I need to . . .' The woman with the gloves pushed back past Maddie and reached down for a yellow bag marked *Hazardous*. It seemed to be the source of the nastiest part of the smell that got worse as it was walked right under their noses. Maddie heard the front door, then sounds of a wheelie bin slammed shut.

'Hello Betty, my name is Maddie Ives. Sorry to disturb you, I was rather hoping you might remember talking to my friend Harry Blaker?' Maddie gestured to where Harry had stepped into the doorway behind her. The woman returning from the bins was back to answer, talking downwards as she shed her gloves.

'You'll be lucky if she remembers what she just ate. How long ago did you talk with Betty?'

'About twenty years ago.' Maddie sighed and the woman seemed to be delighted at that.

'Well then, good luck with that!' She moved into the room proper, stopping beside Betty and taking hold of a pale hand to talk loudly. 'You've got some people come to see you, Betty! That's nice, isn't it. They just want to see how you're doing.'

'Doing?' Just one word from the woman Maddie was counting on as being a witness was enough to show her fragility, confusion and more than a little fear. Maddie didn't want to be upsetting anyone, she certainly didn't want to be striking fear into the elderly.

'That's all!' Maddie beamed, stepping closer too, where Betty was starting to squint. Her breathing now had a rattle where the rate had increased. 'We used to work with your husband, with Charles.'

'Charles?' Her face changed, the fear dropped away and her eyes shifted to the door. 'He'll be home soon. He's a good man, you know, not for us to judge . . .' She gasped like her breath had run out and she had forgotten how to take more in, her thin lips bumped together and she forced a swallow that moved her whole head. 'So much pressure. It can crush a man. He'll be home soon.' Her focus sharpened, her watery eyes a little less faded as they searched the doorway.

'Charles Snow last came home seventeen years ago,' the woman muttered for Maddie's benefit, clearly feeling that clarification was necessary. 'Cancer; he died right here in this room. Betty put the bed in here for him, converted their lounge with the intention of changing it back when he recovered enough to be able to manage the stairs. He never did. Can't say if she converted it back before she started going downhill herself. I tell you this, though, the human mind is a funny old thing.' The woman looked at Maddie with a new intensity. 'They were very much in love, you see, and when he went it broke her heart and you know what they say about the heart and mind: you can't break one without the other.'

'I guess not,' Maddie said, her next breath shallow as her own heart took a hit.

'She says some strange things about her Charles sometimes, some days she's full of stories of how he proposed, how he looked after her and how he's a good man, next she'll be thrashing around like she's fighting him off! Calls him all sorts! Who knows what's going on in there, you would think I would be used to it by now, I've been a carer all my life and I tell you this, every one of them is different.'

'She has two children, are they local?' Maddie asked.

'The daughter is, she's fairly regular. The son definitely isn't, I think he might even live abroad. Did rather well for himself, pays for us lot, I know that much. She has carers covering twelve hours of the day, has done for years now. I'm the only permanent, the rest are agency that I organise. I couldn't even guess how much that's cost over time. He doesn't visit much. I reckon paying for her care is how he deals with the guilt.' The carer looked back over at Betty who had given up on the door. 'When the son does visit he always seems to me like he's sizing the place up, even asked us for the code to the safe, like any of us would know! Can't even get to the blasted thing down there. You find that with people who have money, don't you? Always thinking what more they can get, only interested—'

'Do you have a phone number for them?' Maddie cut her off, accepting she was now wasting time and desperate to limit it as much as possible.

'Sure. Is there something wrong? Something you think they can help you with?'

'Probably not,' Maddie admitted. 'I'll just take their numbers in case. It's what Charles knew that we could do with, really.' Maddie was thinking out loud, her voice travelled enough for Betty to pick out at least one word.

'Charles?' she said, again. 'He'll be home in a minute. You shouldn't judge . . .' Another pause to gasp at air. 'Even good men, with good hearts . . .' Her lips smacked, the strain clear as she swallowed again and that rasping breath seemed worse. By the time she had recovered enough to speak she had lost her trail of thought and those eyes had dimmed back to nothing.

Maddie followed the carer through to the kitchen at the back of the house, to where she kept a contacts book in her bag. Maddie was really clutching at straws now; the idea that Charles would have spoken to his children about an investigation he was running was verging on ridiculous. But maybe Betty had talked about it later, when they were older, before she had lost the ability.

The carer tutted and scribbled to try and get a pen to work and Maddie took a moment to look around. The *faded* theme was still present, not only in here, but out into a rear garden that looked ragged at the edges. The lawn was mowed but patchy like it had been allowed to grow tall before being cut back. The edges had messy hedgerow for the first half, then nothing but fence for the rest. Some of the panels were starting to pitch over, it was worst where a row of conifers in the garden next door looked to be trying to force their way through. Maddie found herself wondering how long it might have been since Betty had sat out there just to enjoy the sun on her face.

'Is that OK?' The carer was talking to Maddie and she snapped out of it. 'I've put my number on there too, in case you need a general point of contact.'

'Oh, that's great, thank you. Sorry again, you know, if we caused any confusion or upset.'

The carer shrugged. 'I'm not sure poor Betty can get more confused. And she likes company, she likes the idea that people still want to visit her. The daughter does try but even she's coming less and less. I get it, I mean it's not nice to see your mother like that.'

'I'm sure it isn't.'

'Losing your faculties is hard enough, but it's the COPD that takes the award for drama. They call it the death rattle for a reason.'

'COPD?' Maddie said.

'Chronic Obstructive Pulmonary Disease. Breathing, basically, her lungs are packing in.' There was a silence. There was very little to say to that.

'At least she has you, I'm sure that makes all the difference,' Maddie said.

'We try!' The carer came back brighter. 'She keeps us on our toes does Betty, she still has the occasional surprise for us.'

'Surprise?' Maddie said.

'Yeah, don't be fooled by the bedbound look! Seems sometimes our Betty likes a walk and she'll set off for the shops in her nightie. Never gets far, just enough for us to send out a search party. Not for a while now but I still reckon she's got one in her!' The carer's smile brightened further.

'Well, she's lucky she has people like you looking out for her.'

'As best we can. We leave every night and just hope that she stays asleep for one thing, then wakes up for another. Sometimes I think she understands what we do for her, appreciates it even, but she'll probably have forgotten I'm here already. The only people she seems to remember are Charles or the vicar who still comes in every Sunday. Oh and the man who lives next door that she's taken a real disliking to!'

'Oh really!' Maddie smiled. 'Do we need to knock and ask him to keep the noise down?' she quipped.

'We never hear him, to be honest, but it's a bit of a standing joke. Betty often asks if he's still there but she can get quite vicious. I think she would actually be gutted if he moved away, who would she hate on then?'

Maddie shared the woman's laughter and thanked her again. She picked Harry up on her way out, being sure to lean in to the living room and thank Betty for all her help. Betty took a moment, like they were meeting for the first time again, then insisted that she should wait for Charles, that he was a good man and how they shouldn't judge him.

The carer was far from discreet as she rolled her eyes.

CHAPTER 43. THE GRAVE

Betty Snow appeared where I was digging the grave and goodness me, did she look just like a ghost herself. She sure must have floated down there like a spirit because I didn't hear a thing and you should trust me on this, your hearing is never sharper than when you're burying the body of the man you just stabbed to death in a frenzy.

Betty wore a nightdress that night; long, white cotton, the tails catching in the breeze of two a.m. to add to the vision of a haunting and one that I saw out of the corner of my eye first. The moment it took to focus was enough for my heart to skip, to consider that Ryan Saunders had stood up out of his body as an apparition to face the man who was now putting him in the ground. I could be forgiven for such thoughts with his body a few feet away, wrapped up in a bed sheet and with my hands still showing his blood as a stain.

'This is over now?'

Charles was with me in my garden, with me in that hole in fact and those were the words that Betty said. She was talking direct to him. Her voice was fragile and strong at the same time, fragile enough for Charles to step towards her like he might need to stop her collapse, yet strong enough to stop everything for me: the breeze in the trees and the twinkling of the stars high above. She stopped my breath too, all the while I was waiting for the next thing to be said.

You see movies with murder, with graves being dug out as a perfect rectangle, all sharp edges and dug deep enough for a man my size to stand up and not see out, but it was nothing like that for us. We dug down four feet at the most and then we had to turn our man on his side and pull up his legs to bunch him up where it was deeper in the middle. To get the size and shape like you see at funerals, or in them movies, would have taken us to the middle of the next morning and, by then, the whole world would have been looking in from their back windows. As it was it was bad enough that Betty Snow appeared, apparition or not, to stand over what we were desperately trying to hide.

But Betty Snow already knew. I didn't know that at the time of course, I might have if I had taken to thinking deeply about what she chose as her first words to her husband, but I wasn't in the right frame of mind for thinking deeply.

This is over now?

That was what she said. Not *what the hell are you doing* or *who the hell is that!?* Because she already knew.

'It is over,' Charles replied in the way that, when I did get a moment to think, told me that there had been a conversation. But he was lying. I don't know if he meant to or if he actually believed what he was saying, but nothing felt like it was over to me. That night in my garden was another part that I had played out before it happened, another part of the fantasy. In that fantasy I dug a deep, crisp hole and I kicked Ryan Saunders' rotting body into it. I covered him over and patted down the dirt, then I dragged the compost heap back over the top of him because I liked that as a final message, a final *fuck you!* Then I stepped back and I felt avenged and satisfied and it drew a line under what had happened to Christine and I could get back on with my life.

The reality was nothing like that. Betty Snow weren't supposed to be there for a start.

When she was done with Charles she locked eyes with me and time seemed to stop all over again. Still a ghost, she held me in a spell; the light from a high moon flaring her dress a frigid white, even her skin had a sheen and seemed just as pale as the last glimpse I got of Saunders when I was rolling him up in that sheet. I remember thinking, in that moment where Betty and I stared at each other, that maybe she might even approve, that she had talked this out with Charles and agreed it as the best outcome.

That was not a consideration that lasted long.

'This is one of God's children.' Betty still held me with her eyes but her words were for both of us. 'No matter what he did.' She looked back at Charles for the next part. 'You play your part in the judgement of people in life, that is your job, but only God makes a judgement in death.'

'Well then,' Charles said with a cold determination, 'now he will have his chance.' There was another moment of total stillness, the breeze was gone, the stars drawn on a blackboard rather than burning in a three-dimensional sky.

'He will have his chance with us all,' she said and those were her last words that night. She lingered long enough to look down at the child of God wrapped in a bloody sheet, made the sign of the cross over her chest and then she was done. I didn't know what Betty Snow was thinking as I stepped out of Saunders' shallow grave to watch her float away, the breeze returning to toy with her nightdress. I knew what I was thinking, of course, I was thinking how that would surely be the end of Betty Snow's involvement and how, in time and despite the magnitude, it would become one of those things that no one is sure even happened.

But I was wrong about that. I was wrong about her.

CHAPTER 44

Michael's noises had stopped, thankfully the bouncing hadn't. Mia was now onto star jumps and she waved back as Debbie held up two fingers in a gesture that meant she would be back in two minutes. She got a wave back and then, with a perfect hip-twist, Mia was facing away and lost in her sport.

Debbie turned to face the living room and the shadow that was filling the door, the white surround like an open mouth and the silence beyond it ominous. This was always the worst part, the part where she could never be sure what she might find.

'Mike?' she called out, not expecting an answer. She knew he would hear, his hearing was just about his sharpest sense after his eyesight had been damaged as part of his ordeal. Michael had almost lost one eye completely; the blows he sustained to his head distorted his eye socket to the point that part of his skull was pressing on the eyeball and, for a period, his ability to see was the least of their worries. Michael had talked of a painstaking operation — ground-breaking, apparently — from which the doctors had emerged to boast of new techniques and lessons learned. She didn't know much of the detail. They didn't meet until a few years afterwards and Michael was clear from the start that he was done talking. Debbie had respected that then, and still did. She'd respected his decision to quit his therapy too, something she was now being forced to regret.

'Mike?' Are you OK in there?' she tried again, desperate for him to reply, to say anything. Even a grunt or a moan that would tell her she could step inside that room and not find him dead. She might not want to live with him anymore but that didn't mean that she wished him harm, or even that she didn't still love him. She heard movement; it was encouragement enough for her to step in.

The shadow spread out from the door to fill the room. The curtains were drawn and black objects littered the floor, the closest she could make out as a cushion pulled from the long sofa. The single-seater armchair was beyond it, tipped up on its back and Michael was sat on the floor beside it. He had his back to the radiator that ran under the window, his shoulders brushed in white light where the curtains were leaking a little. His head was bent, it lifted to the sound of her footsteps.

'I'm sorry.' His voice was an empty whisper. As terrifying and upsetting as it was to see him in a rage, fighting himself, trying to tear open his body to get to the demons that lived inside, it was no match for this state. The emptiness, the despair and the sorrow formed a layer that nothing could penetrate. She was careful where she stepped as she moved to sit next to him. The metal of the radiator was cold against her back when she used it to slide to a sit. She was already accustomed to the poor light, enough that the doorframe opposite glowed a hot white that stung her eyes.

'Don't be silly,' she said as part of the same exchange they'd had a million times before. She knew where it would go from here too, with a little cajoling Michael would be able to get to his feet and take himself up to bed. There, he would find an uncomfortable sleep, careful to position himself around any new bruises, sometimes with a new whistle to his breathing where he had broken his nose or chipped a tooth for the umpteenth time. His rest would last anything from three hours to three days and then, on his emergence, the first thing he would do was wrap up their daughter in the warmest, biggest of hugs and try and hide the fact that he was sobbing into her hair.

Mia had been a surprise, unplanned for sure, Mother Nature having her own say when she and Michael had agreed that they would never cope with the extra strains a child brought. It had been tough too, tougher even than she had considered, but when she watched that hug, Debbie recognised the only time she ever truly saw Michael Rix at peace and she wondered where they would be if they didn't have Mia. She was the only force strong enough to pull him back out of the shadow.

CHAPTER 45

Maddie considered she had done OK with her first meeting with Harry Blaker. At least she thought she had. She'd wanted to play it cool, to hide her true delight at seeing the grumpy old bastard again and she reckoned Harry had done the same, both playing the game of burying their true feelings among the tickseed in his garden gone wild. It was a game they had been playing for some time; in truth, maybe even from the moment they had realised that they complemented each other. A mutual feeling of fondness and respect had grown from there and how Maddie had missed that; she had missed him.

Vince Arnold, on the other hand, was not a man who was capable of playing anything cool.

'Harry Blaker!' Vince was in the Domestic Violence Investigation Unit flirting for a cup of tea, his face now entirely consumed by the widest smile as Harry appeared in the police station looking like a man slightly out of sorts. Harry had once summed up Vince by calling him a *slobbery Labrador* and he was certainly playing up to that now — the excited beast whose master has just returned home.

'Vince,' Harry replied, simply.

'No one told me you were coming back! Yet here you are, bold as brass!'

'I'm not back, Vince.'

'Harry is just going over some old case material, another pair of eyes to see if I'm missing something.' It wasn't just the old case material Maddie had planned, she had every intention of tweaking his interest with her live missing persons investigations. She'd asked if he would come back so she could sound out what she had with someone who could spot a gap. He hadn't committed but he hadn't refused outright either, something she had seized on, calling Detective Chief Inspector Julian Lowe on the hands-free to ask his permission for Harry to enter the building and look at the material. DCI Lowe was someone she had chosen on purpose, knowing he would grant it without a second thought.

'You look back to me. And is that a tan!?' Vince was positively singing.

'Antigua,' Harry growled.

'Antigua!' Vince sang back at him. 'Check out the boss, doing retirement properly with some winter sun!' Maddie saw a realisation register with Vince, it was enough to change his whole demeanour. 'So, you're back, only not as a guvnor? Does that mean I can call you Harry now? Or Hazzah? Or H? What about *newb*!?' Vince's excitement surged back, peaking even, like his master had not only returned home, but was now headed straight for the biscuit cupboard. Maddie watched on as Harry Blaker fixed Vince in a stare that was still talked about as part of his legend and, sure enough, she'd never seen Vince reduce so much in size, so quick.

'I guess I'll stick with "boss" then, you know, out of respect,' Vince muttered, his smile dropping away but reignited when Harry reached out for the firmest of handshakes. Harry smiled too, no doubting it was genuine.

'Good to see you again, Vince, you remember what I told you about Detective Inspector Ives?'

'She makes a shit cup of tea?' Vince blurted back, then grimaced. Another part of Harry Blaker's legend was just how much he disliked foul language.

'Not that part, I told you not to hurt her. I assume you've been keeping up your end of the bargain?'

'If anyone's going to hurt anyone, boss!' His grin consumed his face again. 'I know you've seen her in a fight.'

'Good point.' Harry's smile was now directed at Maddie. He was in his clean shirt and a fresh pair of chinos, or at least a pair that weren't mud splattered. He was missing the tie that was part of his DI days, but still, the last eight months without him dissipated in a moment. 'So, what are we doing?' Harry said and Maddie had to snap away from the warm glow of nostalgia to realise that she was the one supposed to be giving the directions. She reached down for her daybook.

'Oh, yeah. I forget you've got a rock 'n' roll lifestyle to get back to! My intelligence analyst said she would have something ready for us. She should be back any minute . . .'

'Are you not having a wet? I didn't come in here just to make the office better-looking, you know!' Vince was now doing indignant.

'Well, I'm a DI and Harry's a guest, Vince, so mine's white, no sugar.' Maddie grinned.

CHAPTER 46. BETTY'S BOMBSHELL

Betty Snow had a bombshell for me. That was what it felt like when it was delivered in that way that she had: righteous and level. She was an arrogant woman if I may speak the truth, in the way that those who see themselves as a mouthpiece for a higher power can be. She'd prayed on it she said, and God had told her what she must do. She told me how marriage is a sacred vow and that she saw *love-thy-neighbour* as the same. Then she told me how she knew that my heart was pure.

I think that was when I knew I was in trouble.

On the day of that conversation she was every bit the attentive wife at her sick husband's bedside. It was late in Charles' illness, late in the year too and I'd left footprints in the frost on my walk there. He wasn't just sick in truth, he was dying and quick, fading in front of our eyes like when you used to shake out Polaroid photos, only in reverse. That day was my first visit in a week but he'd aged a hundred years. It was noticeable too that they were still talking about him coming home for Christmas but it wasn't as a place for him to recover anymore, it was as a man who didn't want to die in hospital.

Prostate cancer. It wasn't so long before that moment that Charles had first told me how he had pissed blood. His big eyes were full of fear and that was just about the only time I ever saw that. I've seen people with far worse symptoms, a far worse prognosis even, rear up to the challenge, bullish for the fight, but not Charles. He knew from that first moment what was coming for him and I've never seen a more marked change in a person.

When he first told me it was in the middle of the summer months and we had warmth on our backs and were stood out in that gentle hum that comes with summer, the type that so often lulls you to take a nap. It should have been pleasant, but nothing about Charles was pleasant that day, or what he had to say.

'That evil we buried in the garden, we didn't stop it at all,' he'd said to me soon after, his eyes all wild by now. 'It's spread out, it's come for me and now it has me.' Charles Snow, a man as level as a patio slab, came right out with that. He believed what he was saying too and I wanted to tell him to stop being silly, that it was just a bit of colouring to his piss and it could just as easily be a kidney stone. I did, in fact, I said all of those things but I didn't believe it in that sunny garden, I didn't believe it later in that hospital ward with the heating up too high while the frost clawed at the window and I don't believe it now.

Charles was right.

You can murder a man consumed by evil, you can bury him in the ground and hide what is left under a compost heap for twenty years and try and forget he is there at all; but that doesn't mean he isn't. A shadow is not something that rots and dies and the blackness I saw as Saunders' eyes in the moments it took to take his life was not the trick of the light I first thought, it was my first view of what that man really was. That blackness reached back for Charles first as a cancer that grew, then Betty as a rot in her mind. Even my Helen sensed it as a bad feeling that chased her out of her own home, taking our Jessica with her.

But before that, when Charles was laid out in his sickbed and when Betty's mind was still sound, that was when her bombshell came — or her ticking time bomb, more like. She fixed me with those righteous eyes over her heavily sedated husband and she spoke with the arrogance of a priest at a pulpit:

'The secret that lies buried in your garden is mine as much as yours.' I couldn't speak, nor look away, just like that night under that bright moon. You need to remember this too: we'd never talked about that night, not once since. Our relationship was different after, of course it was, we didn't speak much at all, truth be known, we didn't see them for dinner and we would never again be two families just passing the time of day. But there was something she needed to say and she chose that moment: 'And it is not a secret that can follow me to the afterlife. When I stand in front of our Lord I will be washed pure. I ask for His forgiveness every day and He has granted it, Paul, but there are terms.'

'OK.' I had to squeeze that word out, I reckon she released me from her spell just enough to say it. There were others swirling around in my mind but they just wouldn't come and that hospital ward suddenly seemed hotter, drier too, so my voice had a little rasp to it, that word more like a cough.

'I told Charles my plan.' Betty Snow took hold of her husband's hand, breaking away from me to look at him with something that might have been anger as she did. 'When I pass into the arms of our Lord, my last will and testament will include the delivery of a letter from where it is currently held in a safe place. This delivery will be to the relevant authorities, addressed to Operation Lightyear. This letter contains details of what I saw that night, Paul.' And this was where she leaned in a little, not that she needed to, she already had all of my attention. '*All* of the details. The same letter also contains a full confession written by Charles' own hand, so that he may be free to beg for his own forgiveness.' She stopped there. There was more to come but she was taking her time. Charles' sleep was so deep and so still it was like he had passed already and she looked down at him, head to foot, and I have to tell you this, despite what she was saying and what it meant for me, I still remember thinking in that moment how that woman loved that man with all her heart. I even felt a pang of jealousy for that. I think the fact that she loved him so much was what stopped her conscience tearing her apart, it was how she had been able to support Charles, all the time he was alive at least, but she would not offer me the same courtesy.

'OK,' I managed again. My mind was still whirling, it had switched to survival mode, throwing up options and next moves — self-preservation. But Betty Snow, before she lost her mind, seemed able to read mine. It was like she could see every option and idea moving behind my eyes and the next thing she said was designed to smash them all.

'You can't move away, Paul, not now and not ever. You can't run. Forgiveness and repenting your sins are your only option. I will pray for you but you must choose your path yourself. You cannot dig up what you did either, the soil is tainted; *dust to dust*. Any movement or concealment will bring forward the revelation of that letter and would do nothing to help you anyway. Charles took the knife and put it some-where else, he never told you where.' She was still looking at me, she paused here, studying my reaction. She was right, of course. I never even asked Charles what happened to the blade I used, I never wanted to know; out of sight, out of mind. She must have been satisfied as she started up with talking again. 'Charles told me the whole story of what you did, of what you both did and it only needs that knife for the police to know it to be true.'

I must have looked every bit like a man who had just had the rug pulled out from under him because she moved round to where I sat, dragging her chair noisily with her, over the beeps and hisses of the machinery keeping Charles Snow some sort of alive. Suddenly she was the nice old lady from next door with the lamb stew in a crockpot. She took my hands in hers and I remember the warmth like she'd just stepped out of a hot bath.

'You need to repent what you did, beg for His forgiveness and He will grant it. Sins and secrets are heavy for a reason, they will drag you down if you do nothing. But He can free you, Paul.'

I think I nodded. I know I was back making trails in the frost soon after and I know that was the last time I spoke to either of them. Charles did make it home for his final days but there was nothing of the sharp detective left, nothing that I could appeal to, that's for sure, even if I had wanted to — and I didn't. By that time it was Charles who was being stalked by the shadow of death and it was so close he would surely have felt its breath on his neck. A man in that situation clings to the idea of forgiveness in the next life, he wasn't about to take pity on me and risk it all.

Even a man like me who doesn't believe death to be anything more than a slow rot back to the dust I came from, when I am facing the end, I will pray too. Hope is always the last thing to die.

CHAPTER 47

Daisy-Mae's whole right leg was numb. The coldness of the floor and the lack of movement meant that it wasn't just her leg that was without feeling and she would need to move — ever so carefully — to promote some blood flow. But it didn't seem to matter what she did, it was like it had been removed completely. Initially she had been glad when the pain had died away to be replaced by a combination of pins and needles and flashes of heat, but she would give anything for that to return — for *something* to return. The absence of feeling was far more concerning.

A scuffing sound. It was right next to her, like a heel dragged over the stone floor, then the same noise repeated, another heel dragged, feet dragged together, someone sitting up, perhaps.

'Daisy-Mae . . .' A voice, low, muffled by a gag but not whispered. Then a silence that was absolute and thick. It was a voice she knew too, a voice that she desperately wanted to reply to but terror had her frozen still, waiting for the sound of determined footsteps leading where a length of solid steel dragged behind.

It didn't come.

'Daisy-Mae . . . I think we're alone but you don't need to talk, that's OK. I just want to know you're OK, that you're still with me here!'

'You can't speak, don't speak!' A different voice, male, the same voice that had been silenced by a beating previously, the same voice that had called out to save her when the next blow might have been the final one. His voice sounded different, weakened by his treatment perhaps.

'I'm hurt, but I'm OK.' Daisy-Mae had meant to whisper but a sob had been waiting for its opportunity and it took her by surprise to rush out. Then silence; three people again waiting for the consequences.

Still nothing.

'We can't just stay here, we can't just lie here in silence and do nothing; we'll die,' Megan said.

'Megan . . .' Another sob escaped with the name of her friend. 'Why?' It was the only word Daisy-Mae could manage. She had plenty more, but this one summed them all up.

'I don't know, Daisy-Mae, I don't know what's going on. I was on a train, the police were looking for you, they spoke to me, but I had no idea . . . How badly hurt? Can you walk?'

'Walk!?' Daisy-Mae repeated. The very idea had never been more terrifying. She was already conditioned not to move, let alone stand up and walk.

'We can't stay here, we just can't. We have to go.'

'I can't!' Daisy-Mae breathed, the true seriousness of a leg she couldn't even feel, let alone put weight on suddenly becoming apparent. She hadn't thought about what it meant, she hadn't thought past trying to ease the pain and stay quiet. But leaving, *escaping*, that wasn't going to be possible. 'I think my leg is broken!' She was louder still, made louder by a desperate whine that she could do nothing to stop. 'I think it's broken and I don't think I can move.'

'I think I can.' Megan's voice had a grim determination, like it came from a mind made up.

'But if he *sees* you!' Daisy-Mae said.

'He'll beat you to death.' The male cut in, his tone flat, matter-of-fact and saying what they all knew. Whoever had them under their control had been looking for reasons to hurt them from the moment they had woken up there. Ringing a bell taped to the palm of their hand was enough for a beating so bad as to break bones, what would he do if he found Megan standing upright, *escaping*?

'He's going to beat us all to death eventually. We have to try,' Megan said in that same determined tone.

'I'll go.' The male voice, still flat, still matter-of-fact. Resigned perhaps.

'I said I'll go, so I'll go!' Megan replied, angry. Daisy-Mae knew her friend could be formidable when she wanted, she'd seen her deal with problems in the past.

'You need to look after your friend,' the male voice replied, 'and then, when I don't make it back, you'll have every chance to take your turn walking to your doom.' The last word had a grunt of exertion, then scuffing like he really was pulling himself to his feet. His bell clanged and rolled too. 'I'll get help and bring it back,' he said, his tone now a little less flat, tinged with his own version of quiet determination that was enough to stoke hope in Daisy-Mae.

His footfalls away were quiet at first, as if he were on tiptoes, but then something loose, like a rock, skittered and rolled where he must have caught it with his foot. The footfalls stopped, but he was quick to get going again. Daisy-Mae listened to them fade, the sound of his bell rolling against its plastic housing did the same.

Then there was another noise; closer, it came from behind her and she jerked a reaction as she felt something touch her hip.

'It's going to be OK,' Megan's voice purred almost right into her ear. The touch was hers, she moved in tighter; as close as she could. With both their hands tied up, thick tape over their faces and Daisy-Mae with a leg worse than broken, this was as close as she could get to a comforting embrace, but she would take it.

Suddenly, hope had found its way back.

* * *

He got to his feet then stopped, feeling the floor with his toes so he didn't step onto the two women that he knew to be somewhere at his feet. The plastic ball in his hands skittered and rolled, then settled to more of a tinkle as he stayed still for any reaction. There was nothing. The other two were so quiet they must have been holding their breath.

It was time to move.

He had come through two doors on his way in, bumping into both, the first the hardest where the surround came down at an angle to catch him on the shoulder. He made for them now — or at least the direction he thought they were in. He held his arms out in front of him, waiting for the ball to bump into something solid. The wall was further away than he had anticipated but it did come and when he was at a half step, so he hit it harder than planned, and the sound the hollow plastic made was loud in the empty interior. It was enough to freeze him solid and for a suppressed gasp to come from behind him where he had left the two women.

He let the silence build for another few moments. Then he opened his eyes to look out over the scene.

The two women had moved together, the younger one the little spoon for the older — *Megan*. He was going to have to teach her a lesson, that one, she was growing in confidence or in desperation — either of which was dangerous. Maybe he should have snapped *her* leg out of the two. He shook his head silently, that wasn't necessary, his thinking at the time was right, *Megan* would not be leaving without *Daisy-Mae*.

And *Daisy-Mae* would not be leaving.

He closed his eyes again. It was essential to move like he was blindfolded just like they were, he knew how closely they would be listening. He was barefoot the same too, because you walk different when every step is over the painful grit or chunks of masonry that he had spread out over the floor.

He felt his way along the wall, running his hand flat to be sure he was making a noise the two women could follow, stopping when he felt the raised wood of the first door surround. The wood was coarse and chipped and he let his fingers curl round it to pull himself through the opening. The next room was smaller, his first step into it caught a piece of something that skittered and bounced ahead of him; *perfect*! The sound was like the first ivory key pressed on a grand piano, a note booming out and then fading slowly to capture an audience who were apprehensive for more. Daisy-Mae and Megan were his audience, the sound of his footsteps moving away was the performance they yearned for and he would give them what they wanted. He was sure to drag his feet a little so more shrapnel scraped and slid. More ivory keys. Each sound would be more beautiful than the last to an audience who would be baying if they could, cheering his every step closer to his escape and subsequently to theirs.

He opened his eyes to find something sizeable, bending down to scoop up a piece of grey stone and rolling it underarm with a flourish, watching it skip, slide and then bump into the far wall. He nudged another with his foot, his movement now more of a dance, with twists and drags. The noise in that tight space, with its low ceilings and thick walls, would surely be the most beautiful music his audience had ever heard; the music of *hope*!

False hope.

He made the far end of the room, the angled doorway, and took a moment to rest on a raised step. It was time for the grand finale, for the sound those women had been waiting for and, like any good musician, he would make them wait. The first part was to throw away the ball he had been holding in his hands, it bounced and rolled. His hand lingered on the door handle while he waited for silence again, he could feel the chill from the metal through the thin material of his glove and he allowed his eyes to shut again while he breathed in, long and deep as the room returned to silent. The air was dusty, layered with stillness and fear to the point that it was stifling.

How he adored that.

He pulled the door wide open, the springs yawned to add to the finale that came when he pushed it shut again.

Silence.

Megan or Daisy-Mae sobbed, his money was on Daisy-Mae, sobbing because her rescuer had made it out. Only he hadn't, he'd made it to the other side of the room then opened and closed a door, falling to a sit in the same movement and now he was facing back the way he had just come. He wasn't sure what he would do next, how long he would leave it before the door would make its noises again and Daisy-Mae and Megan would know that someone was back. Their hope would burn so bright that he reckoned he would see the glow from here. But if that were true, it would fade far quicker, right about the moment the wicked end of the crowbar started its drag across the stone floor he had just crossed; doused completely by the time he made it back to that room, to stand over them and to vent his anger that one of them had dared to leave.

He reached out to carefully lift the weapon now from where he had left it leaning close to the door. The weight felt good in his hands, maybe it wouldn't be long at all, he could barely contain himself.

CHAPTER 48

Maddie walked into the meeting room that her intelligence analyst had been prepping to the point that it was starting to look like an incident room. The walls were busy with material like her office, though it was noticeable that, this time, the emphasis was on case material over press coverage. A VOWS assessment was a new addition too, started on a flipchart, a simple and effective way of putting everything known into visual categories of V-Victim, O-Offender, W-Witnesses and S-Scenes. Maddie read out the first name from it that she hadn't seen or heard before.

'Michael Rix?' she said. This was the first entry in the "Witness" box. Eileen was working intently on the room's only computer, her head leaning forward like the monitor might be a window she could climb through and she made a gesture that she needed a minute. Maddie shrugged at Harry who was sipping from a mug of tea, possibly to hide any reaction he had from his first sighting of the elderly woman now commanding the room.

'Michael Rix,' Eileen said, finally. She clicked her last click, straightened up and fixed Harry with those beady eyes over her glasses. 'And I don't believe we've met?' She stepped out from behind the desk to get closer.

Maddie stuttered to life. 'Sorry, yes . . . this is Det . . . this is Harry Blaker. He was the inspector in Major Crime until his recent retirement.'

'Inspector Harry Blaker!' There was a rise in her voice like she was delighted. 'I saw your name on the list I provided Inspector Ives, but you have a reputation that precedes you. That is something I have come to learn is not uncommon in police stations — what makes you a rarer breed is that your reputation is rather excellent.'

'Glad to hear it.' Harry seemed a little taken aback.

'Eileen Holmans, intelligence analyst,' she announced and thrust a bony arm out from her thick, knitted cardigan. Harry took up the offer.

'Are those slippers?' he said and all eyes dropped to what were unmistakably vanilla-yellow slippers complete with brown accents.

'Comfort and productivity go hand in hand.' Eileen had a smile that was gone in a flash as she got down to business. Harry's gaze seemed to stay with the slippers as she kicked them off into a pile and walked, barefoot now, to a digital whiteboard that came to life. Harry dragged himself away from the slippers to make eye contact with Maddie, who shrugged, suddenly feeling the need to add some background.

'Eileen's just joined us; a surprise bonus having worked for Major Crime when it was centralised. That didn't work out, so—'

'That's not quite true. It was working just fine if you ask me.' Eileen spoke out of the top of her glasses. 'But some of the methods employed made some senior people rather uncomfortable, people who would rather sit in their office while others get the results, preferably without the slightest of fuss. I may not be a hardened murder detective with the reputation of an Inspector Harry Blaker, but even I know that results do not always come from fighting clean.'

'I think you're going to fit in here really rather well!' Maddie couldn't help a giggle.

'Michael Rix,' Eileen announced, taking back the room, 'is the only survivor left that we are aware of. I have to give a caveat at this stage: this briefing is a rushed summary, the case material is extensive and involves five forces and I would love to tell you that I have read and assessed it all, but of course that has not been possible, yet. The witnesses alone number more than a hundred and fifty. I know we talked briefly about what is in archive, ma'am, unfortunately it looks like it is everything we will need. I still haven't made the request as . . . well, it would come with a number of questions that I may not have an answer for at this time.'

Harry looked over, questioning what this meant. 'We're a DV team,' Maddie started in explanation. 'I'm OK investigating these women as mispers. I'm using a tenuous link that one of them was once a victim of domestic violence but the moment I start requesting archive material from one of the largest investigations the force has ever undertaken . . .'

'It will go somewhere else,' Harry finished.

'It might. It probably should, to be honest. If there is a link, that is.'

'You seemed convinced there is.' Maddie had learned to interpret his growls, this one was a subtle warning.

'Gut feeling.' She shrugged. 'Which is not something I can articulate to Major Crime. We haven't got anything that I can say for sure links the two. That link, if it exists, will be in one of those hundred and fifty boxes . . . I guess we just need to work with what we have.'

'Which is not much,' Eileen added. 'Michael Rix, for example, was not keen to assist the first time around. Categorised as a key witness due to the fact that he was a survivor rather than him providing any actual key evidence. He gave a scant account and, from what I read, even that was difficult to extract. The poor man was rather understandably traumatised but the other witness fared better.' Eileen was standing in front of the VOWS assessment, in one slick movement she unravelled the same pointer she had produced before out of her pocket and *thwacked* the end down on the next name down: *Rachel Cooper*.

'I remember her, she was in the paper a lot,' Maddie said. 'Did you ever meet her?' Her question was to Harry who was already shaking his head.

'Like I said, I was tasked with peripheral witnesses. The name came up in some of the briefings I went to but she always spoke to the same interview team, as you would with a witness like that. You would want a good relationship, someone she would be comfortable talking to and you wouldn't change that.'

'Detective Inspector Charles Snow,' Eileen said. 'You're right, all the material with her name on it, and there is a lot, mentions him as the lead interviewing officer.'

'ABE?' Maddie said. Police-speak for Achieving Best Evidence, this references any witness statement taken by sitting someone down and capturing their story as video footage, rather than writing it out. It's always been a preference to ABE a victim of a serious crime, it allows for a smoother recall, takes far less time and can be massively impactive further down the line if played in a court of law for a jury to watch.

'Yes, but some poor typist has transcribed it for the used material. I've skimmed that, I can watch the many hours of footage if required?'

'No, there isn't the need,' Maddie said.

'The Cold Case Team did sit through it and they produced some rather handy summaries. Rachel gave a very detailed account of the treatment these poor people had but what she couldn't help with is *who*. She knew it was a man, she described him as strong, described a vehicle that was used to pick her up when she was abducted for a second time—'

'She was abducted twice?' Maddie said.

'It was all part of the same abduction,' Harry cut in, his tone low and flat. 'The offender took these people somewhere remote and he strangled them until they lost consciousness. We found bodies of other victims, those that never regained consciousness, but those that did found themselves somewhere remote, run-down buildings mostly, but not locked up or tied. They could leave and they did. They were barefoot, injured and weak and they were looking for rescue. We know from Rachel that she was picked up by a passing car just a few minutes after she made the road outside.'

'It was the offender?' Maddie breathed.

'It was.'

'I don't remember that part,' Maddie said.

'A lot of details never made the press. Rachel did some media interviews but always with a police officer present, information was very tightly controlled.'

'Makes sense.' Maddie nodded.

'I actually thought it was a bad move at the time,' Harry said. 'This was someone who wasn't going to stop doing what he was doing and we had an opportunity to warn people via the media and we didn't take it.'

'Warn people. You mean that if they wake up somewhere remote after having been strangled, that they shouldn't rely on being rescued by the next person that passes?' Maddie could hear the shock in her voice.

'Sounds ridiculous, perhaps, but turns out it would have been good advice. I was just a DS at the time, not a major crime DS either, so it was nothing to do with me. Now I can see it was a much more difficult decision.'

'That fine line between catching an offender and stopping anyone else becoming a victim,' Maddie said.

'A fine line for sure, one where the focus on one can ruin your chances for the other. Charles made his choice. This offender had a clear MO, one that we knew very well because we had Rachel Cooper. If the offences continued, became a series even, Charles wouldn't have wanted to force change, he would have wanted predictable.'

'But it didn't become a series?' Maddie said. 'He just stopped.'

'He did. And now you think he's started up again, twenty-two years later. From nowhere.'

'And you don't?' Maddie snapped.

'I don't know what you know. I do know that Operation Lightyear was huge, still the biggest investigation I've ever seen and the review ten years later was almost as big. No one solved it, no one got close as far as I know. If you have two women missing right now, linked or not, they need to be your focus. Looking back won't give you answers fast enough. You can worry about links and being the one to solve Op Lightyear later, but—'

'You think that's what this is? Some vanity project? Some opportunity to make a name for myself?' Maddie's tone carried more of her anger.

'You would.' Harry shrugged again. 'Make a name for yourself, I mean and, for a *temporary* inspector looking to get back to Major Crime—'

'Don't even say it,' Maddie spat. She spun away too, paced to the back of the room where the door was hanging open. She considered continuing her walk but pulled it closed instead, taking a deep breath as she did. She paused to organise her thoughts. 'This is not about me trying to make a name for myself. There is a link here, there *has* to be. I know twenty-two years is a long time for someone to lay dormant, I know this is just a standard misper investigation on the surface, but this is linked. We don't have any missing person lines of enquiry left, not really, so looking back might be the only way I can go forward, I just need to look at different elements.'

'Different how?' Eileen said.

'Not the case material. At least not solely. I still think I'm on the right lines with Charles, with what he knew, with what he was *thinking*.'

'But we can't know that.' Eileen again.

'Maybe we still can. We need his daybooks, his hand-written Post-it reminders, his diary, bits of fag packets . . . anything that he wrote down as part of this investigation. Ten years ago that review you talked about, Harry, they would have read every word of the case papers.'

'Almost certainly. I've led reviews myself for other cases and that's what you do,' Harry agreed.

'But not the daybooks, not the unused material, because that's not so easy.'

'The same reason you went back to see Betty Snow.'

'A huge investigation, then a huge review of that investigation . . . I have to think different,' Maddie repeated back.

'The only reference to theories and DI Snow concern him debunking one,' Eileen cut back in. 'I'm not sure if that helps any? I need to write another name up, actually.' She picked up a marker and walked to the board, her pen squeaking as she made the first entry in the *O-Offender* category.

'Ryan Saunders?' Maddie read out loud. 'They had a suspect?'

'Not for long.' Harry's growl cut across where Eileen was starting to speak.

'Quite right, Mr Blaker. Ryan Saunders was the only suspect that was ever named. It was a name that got as far as the press but Charles and his team were very adamant to move the investigation away. He was released without charge. DI Snow wrote his reasons out extensively.'

'As you would,' Harry said.

'Have you looked into Saunders?' Maddie directed her question at her analyst.

'I've only just found the reference, literally as you came in. I will get you a summary intel package around him,' Eileen clucked.

'What do you remember about him?' Maddie directed her question to Harry.

'I didn't meet him. We all knew he was a convicted murderer, convicted as a juvenile, killed a little girl when he was just a boy himself. There was a lot of backslapping when he came through the door, a lot of people fancied him as their man and his record played some part in that. The victim, the little girl, she was strangled and found covered in leaves in woodland—'

'Just like in this case!' Maddie was trying to quell her excitement, waiting for her bubble to be burst.

'Like some of the early victims, sure. But Charles ruled him out.'

'Why?'

'Like I said, I was never close to the investigation. I just know that Charles was respected, everyone said he was the right man for the job. He was obsessed too, no one wanted someone through the door for this more than he did. So when he moved away from Saunders, we all did. He wouldn't have done that lightly.'

'Did this Saunders stay local?' Maddie's question was meant for her analyst again but Harry answered.

'I sincerely doubt it. The press got hold of his name somehow and they went with it. These days you couldn't print half the stuff they did about him, I remember there was a lot of panic that we were going to get someone mobbed out there; killed even. Last I heard, Charles himself was overseeing Saunders getting relocated. Renamed probably.'

Maddie huffed. 'Someone must know where he is? Relocation has a duty of care, it means—'

'It does if Witness Protection do it. Charles might have taken some advice from them but it was never an official police-backed move. Charles just helped him disappear. It might have been a reputation thing, senior management worried about how it looked for us to hide a man who murdered a child. They did a lot of work on him, wasted a lot of time on Saunders—'

'And you don't think I should be making the same mistake again? Was he spoken to again by the Cold Case Team?' Another question Maddie aimed at her analyst. Again it was Harry that answered.

'They couldn't find him. I guess he took the advice he was given and managed to keep his head down. Can hardly blame him, I suppose, suddenly he was thrust into the limelight as murdering a child and people made up their minds that he was responsible for the deaths of two pretty young women too.'

'We don't have time for another misper investigation.' Maddie sighed. 'If Charles and all his resources ruled him out, I have to respect that. A hundred and fifty boxes . . .' She was mumbling now, pacing too. 'There's something in there that helps, there has to be.' Her mind was racing, talking this out wasn't helping at all, it was just muddying the waters if anything.

'Maddie.' Harry's voice, only softer and she turned to it.

'A standard misper investigation comes with a list of actions, actions that you know. Stick with those, for now at least. Those will keep the investigation going forwards.'

Maddie felt herself flushing at the chest and neck, she didn't know if it was anger or embarrassment. She cussed internally, annoyed that the sudden block as to where to go next had coincided with the return of Harry Blaker. This had been a bad idea, bringing him back here.

'Eileen,' Maddie said. 'You were chasing up BTP?'

'I was, ma'am. I had a call back from them too. Megan Laurence booked her ticket online using an account she has with the Southeastern Train Company. She booked a return from Folkestone Central to London, St Pancras.'

'And then got off at Ashford,' Maddie said, still pacing.

'The suspect she walked off with bought a ticket from Dover Priory, the beginning of that particular route, but two days earlier, using a ticket machine at that station. BTP were also kind enough to grant me access to their CCTV, which shows him paying by cash, same jacket, same hood up that gives us nothing identifiable. On the day he abducted Megan he got on the train at Folkestone Central; hood up the whole time and he seems very aware of the camera locations. I also think he waits for Megan Laurence to move onto the train, then follows.'

'There were two people in the carriage with her, what about the other male?'

'I found him on the CCTV. He also got on at Folkestone Central but there's nothing to suggest he was following Megan. I have some bad news if you want to speak to him, it would appear he didn't buy a ticket at all.'

'Of course he didn't,' Maddie groaned.

'This man, do you think he was following Megan specifically? This wasn't just an opportunist picking someone from a platform?' Harry asked his question of Eileen. Maddie was interested too, she'd seen that both women were from the same workplace and just assumed that this was part of how they were chosen. She hadn't considered it merely being a coincidence.

'Where he stands in relation to Megan, the timing of when he moves and his behaviour overall, I believe he was there for her.'

'And then he took her off that train at Ashford for them both to disappear off the face of the earth,' Maddie added.

'Is that possible? Ashford's a main hub, surely every inch of it is recorded?' Harry said.

'Rhiannon and I went up there, we got a Southeastern employee with an access card to test it out and it is possible. The platform isn't one hundred percent covered. The route is covered, assuming you head into the station like passengers should, but there are maintenance routes with swipe card access that can keep you off the cameras.'

'Swipe cards are logged,' Harry challenged.

'They are. They're just not always logged against individuals. A card was used at the material time, no doubt it was our offender, but it's a pool card. The railways are maintained by a mess of agencies and external companies so they keep a stash of cards to ensure they have the access they need. It's a terrible system. I left Rhiannon there when I came to see you, she's getting a list together of anyone who might have had access. It's going to be a long list.'

'And our offender might not even be on it,' Harry said.

'There's also a code you can use if you've forgotten your pass, can anyone guess what they're using?'

'Four zeroes?' Eileen chanced.

'You're on the right lines. It's 1,2,3,4. All the doors are.'

'How many people would have been told that over time?' Harry's growl was one Maddie recognised as frustration.

'Exactly. We need something else. Like how a stranger leads a young woman off a train at a stop she didn't want to be at without a fight, or so much as a whimper.'

211

'We know she didn't fight?' Harry said.

'She stumbled a little from what we could see. And there were enough people getting off that train to form a bottle-neck at the steps, that's a lot of eyes and ears. If she was asking for help someone would have seen or heard. Stepped in, even.'

'Maybe he had a compelling threat, gave her a strong enough reason to stay quiet and obedient,' Eileen offered, glaring out over those reading glasses.

'Would have to be a hell of a threat,' Maddie said. 'I talked to her, only for a few minutes but I wouldn't have her as an easy target.'

'Drugged,' Harry said, his voice at its most guttural yet. 'Another thing we took from Rachel Cooper's account was the possibility that she was drugged, that they all were. She didn't remember anything about the first abduction, or much of the second for that matter. There was nothing in her system but she wasn't found until four or five days later and back then . . .'

'That wasn't released to the press either, was it?' Maddie said.

'No,' Harry conceded. Then, when a thick silence fell over the room, Harry finally broke it. 'Where do we go from here?' he said.

'We?' Despite herself, Maddie grinned. 'You need to go home, Harry. I just wanted a second opinion from someone I respect and when I couldn't find one, I thought you might do!' She felt better, she had a sense of direction now, next steps at least.

'I haven't helped,' Harry said, ignoring Maddie's teasing.

'It's not your fault Betty Snow isn't a competent wit-ness, any more than it's your fault the security at Ashford International is lax. I've already mentioned this job to Major Crime. They weren't convinced at the time, but I will get them down here to listen to what we have.' Maddie looked over at Eileen and got a nod in acknowledgement. 'Megan is a high-risk misper, no doubt about that, Daisy-Mae is the same by association. Major Crime will take it, I'm sure, and then I'll see if they need me to do anything more. The likelihood is that I'll be back up to my eyes in Domestic Violence case files by the end of the day and you, you can get back up to your eyes in tickweed.'

'Seed. Tickseed.'

'They looked like weeds to me, Harry.'

'That's always been your problem, Maddie, you can't see the flowers for the weeds.'

CHAPTER 49. ANOTHER NIGHT

Wednesday, 9 November 2022

There is an ambulance that has arrived for next door, their truck pulled across the frontage of both our houses with lights left to pulse through the last of the darkness and straight into my living room. It is cold in here, cold and empty and not just because the sun is yet to rise on a new day. The radiator is long since switched off and this door wedged shut; another room stripped of all its life and warmth — radiator or not — another room I can't bear to use. Even the carpet has a crunch to it under the sole of my shoe where dust has settled on dust.

All I can do is watch the flickering lights, an awkward sit on the arm of a sofa that used to take me laying down with my baby daughter sleeping peacefully on my chest, constant delight as she murmured and sighed. That is not a comfort I have ever found again. Certainly not as I sit here now with this ledger balanced on my thigh to note the latest activity involving next door.

Last night a car pulled up outside at dusk, two people with it, a man and a woman. Both coppers. They weren't in uniform but they might as well have been. I've met a lot in my time, I'm not talking about Charles either; spend any time running a nightclub and you'll get used to the way they pull up in their cars, the way they step out, their heads always up; surveying. Last night two coppers were surveying Betty Snow's house and I still can't think of a reason why.

It was enough to keep an old man awake wondering. I gave up on sleep in the end, chose a strong coffee and an early start in favour of getting more and more frustrated that sleep wouldn't come. I thought I would be able to get on but instead I am stood in the shadows of a desolate living room, watching for an ambulance crew to reappear, totally unaware that they carry my fate just as much as that of Betty Snow.

The timing is not lost on me of course, it is the page before this one that contains Betty Snow's promise scratched out in pencil, although it now feels like it wasn't me that wrote it at all, or at least not willingly. It is almost like Betty Snow, as the apparition in a nightdress, wrote it for me, like maybe the ambulance is too late and an already dead Betty Snow and her unfinished business passed through the thin layers of brick and mortar to write out her promise again, to remind me of the contents of her last will and testament. Like I could ever forget.

Last night I waited for the police to leave while standing right here, the carer showed them out. Then I timed a walk to the bins when the police were gone but the carer was still out the front, taking long breaths of fresh air before returning to the stagnation of Betty's home. I was in time for a *hello!* Cheery as I could muster, something I've done a million times so she wouldn't have thought much of it and she said hello right back. Then she took my question about Betty getting a visitor without a hint of suspicion to tell me it was old colleagues of Charles' checking in on her. I left knowing two things: Betty Snow was still alive and kicking and I had been right about who her visitors were.

As disconcerting as an ambulance is, it is at least self-explanatory at the residence of a sick woman. Their attendances are regular, enough that I no longer panic at the sight but the early morning visits are the most concerning as Betty is left alone overnight to sleep off the rigours of another day inside her own mind. Plenty of time to fall from her bed or to choke on her own tongue. I can't tell you how many times I have stood right here, waiting for the crew to reappear with their heads shaking; making the most of the fresh air where death has tainted it black.

The crew reappear as I watch but their heads do not have a shake, their demeanour is not downbeat or defeated, they are cheery, both dressed in a dulled green from head to toe, bags matching, the breath of the man who is first out erupts as laughter that the accompanying carer copies like a mirror held up. I'm good at reading people, it comes from a lifetime working out the troublemakers from the party-makers in a crowded club but anyone can see that the paramedics are relaxed. When they do shake their heads it is reassuring, their hands held out palms-first, they're telling the dumpy little carer (who always has treats in her bag for any local cats she sees) that she shouldn't worry, that it was nothing this time and that she did the right thing. *Better safe than sorry*, I can almost hear those words through the double glazing, the half-tipped blinds and their layers of dust. The dumpy carer waves them off, already scouring the streets for a cat to pet. By the time the ambulance pulls away, the passenger returning her wave, she has two at her feet.

The sun is suddenly in the room, it lights a layer of frost that covers my front lawn. Betty Snow has survived another night. And so have I.

CHAPTER 50

A coffee shop, just a normal coffee shop at nine a.m. on a normal day, surrounded by normal people for a normal conversation. But then, sitting in this environment telling yourself everything is normal is a contradiction in itself. It has to be.

Debbie Rix can no longer remember *normal*.

Debbie had dropped Mia at school less than half hour ago, watched her every step across the playground, right up until she stopped at the door and twisted for a last wave. Just like every school day. For Mia at least, there is something like normal.

'That's why you need to just leave. Yes, he has his problems and yes, they are ruining his life, but they are ruining your life too, babe.' Debbie's attention snapped back all at once to a sharp focus on bright red lipstick. Debbie was also in a conversation with her friend, Mandy Adams-Wright, sitting opposite her. Newly divorced, the Wright part should have been dropped in exchange for the settlement but Mandy didn't want to, she liked the double-barrelled surname, thinking it made her seem more sophisticated. It's an accessory, just like the bright red lipstick and her outfit that complements it. She's always done up, always makes an effort. You have to be done up to pull off that shade.

Debbie was still fixed on her lips when they formed more words. 'You're still young, there's a happy, normal life out there for you somewhere!' There was a chuckle too, carefree; more so, it seemed, when it fell from bright red lips. Debbie broke away to look around, to where any number of carefree conversations were going on, other girlfriends talking about the partner in their life, or weekends away, or how shitty their boss is. *Normal*; that word again.

'I can't . . .' Debbie said, knowing she has said that a million times before. She used to follow it up with reasons, with an explanation that Michael couldn't survive without her, that she might as well put the noose around his neck before she left (if she was feeling a little dramatic). Actually, she didn't think he would choose a noose, far more likely a knife to his wrists, maybe even to his own chest. She shuddered. Michael had cut himself before, it was rare, but on that day he sliced his thighs like he was carving a turkey, sat so his lap had filled with blood.

'Did you want that or what?' Mandy gestured at the donut oozing its jam innards and left untouched on Debbie's plate.

'Sorry, Mand!' Debbie tried a smile. 'I did say I probably wouldn't eat it . . . I had breakfast.'

'Yeah, what was that? A spoonful of dust? You're wasting away; I mean, I reckon I could do with a go on the stress-and-anxiety diet, you'll lose a good few pounds without even trying on that shit, but you're starting to go too far now, babe, you need your strength. It's gonna be hard, but you've talked about it now, it's out there and that was the difficult bit.'

Talked about it. Debbie caught herself to stop a huff. She'd told Michael she couldn't go on like this, that it wasn't fair on Mia and that she could do with some space, some time apart. She'd expected a fight, yearned for it almost, she wanted Michael Rix showing some emotion that wasn't just rage at himself. But she had got nothing; just a man agreeing that it might be for the best, saying he was sorry but with words that had nothing to them. His was an emptiness that

218

she had lived with for too long, one that, if she ever did leave, would surely consume him until there was nothing left.

But Mandy and her red lipstick was right, this was *her* life too and she hadn't been happy for a long time now.

But more than that, more than everything, there was Mia.

CHAPTER 51

A Post-it, two words and a set of initials: *Call me. JL.* It was starting to peel away from the monitor, caught in the constant breeze of a desk fan that Eileen Holmans must have left on the previous evening to cause an irritating ticking noise that made it even harder to ignore. Not that Maddie could anyway.

JL: Julian Lowe. During her time working with Harry Blaker on a Major Crime team, Julian Lowe had been the DCI overseeing the team — their boss, effectively. Back then, a Post-it note flapping in the breeze at 7.10 a.m. would have been concerning, though not entirely unexpected. Now it was just concerning.

'Ah, Inspector Ives.' Maddie spun to her intelligence analyst. A new day came with a new outfit and Eileen was adorned in a thick sweater with a roll-neck over navy trousers. The slippers were a change too, a pale blue with some white details chasing across the toe. She was carrying a mug, bone china, the spout making up the tail of the cat that was drawn on the side. Maddie didn't think she had ever seen anyone look so at home in a police station.

'Morning.'

Eileen gestured at the Post-it note. 'I assume that is for you?'

'Yes. Julian Lowe. He was my DCI in a previous life. Not sure what he might want from me now.'

'Did you need me to find a phone number for you?' Eileen said.

'No, thank you. I have it.'

'Fine then. I'll leave you to your call. The kettle's just boiled, I'll pop back and make you a cup.'

DCI Julian Lowe picked up on the first ring to heighten Maddie's anxiety. Her first words bounced around the empty office. 'Morning, sir, seems you're not the only one who wanted an early start. Is the note from this morning?'

'Good morning, Maddie, we didn't really have time to speak yesterday, how have you been?' Yesterday: Maddie had called Mr Lowe to get Harry Blaker clearance to access the police station. This had to be linked but she still couldn't think why. And the fact he was now trying out small talk meant her sixth sense for danger was now in overdrive.

'Keeping my head down, learning what I can. No one told me there were so many meetings at the next rank up!' Her laughter was forced too, the whole conversation now bristling with tension.

'Very wise. Although I'm not sure that investigating the most famous — or infamous — murder investigation in the history of this force would count as *keeping your head down*!' The DCI snorted. And the reason for the call was revealed. 'Yesterday, you suggested to me that Harry Blaker might be able to assist with a misper who might be suffering at the hands of an abusive partner . . .' He paused like Maddie could interject if she wanted to. She didn't. She might have fibbed about that.

'I would hardly say I am investigating it, sir, rather that we are making ourselves aware of any similarities this might have with any previous cases. I spoke to Major Crime last night and—'

'You spoke to Major Crime and they spoke to me.' Lowe cut her off, the tone suddenly much more familiar. 'A DCI Mark Hall, someone I believe you met?'

'I did.' And she wouldn't mind if she never met him again. He had reluctantly come down at her request, then spent the entire briefing rolling his eyes and shaking his head. He hadn't asked any questions either, something she had taken as a clear sign of arrogance.

'Mark Hall is concerned about the case that you have.'

'So he should be, sir.'

'Yes . . . Only his concern is more . . . political than you might be considering.'

'Political?'

'You and I go back a little way now, we've got each other's back for sure. May I talk frankly and off the record?'

'Please.' Maddie was still standing but she braced herself with a lean against a desk.

'He doesn't think for one moment that two missing women who work together in a coffee shop are linked to any number of victims who were murdered more than twenty years ago. Those were his exact words, Maddie, if I may be so candid.'

'OK.'

'Look, I can understand his point. He can't think of a reason why someone like the Op Lightyear offender might fall silent for twenty-two years and then start offending all over again. That goes against the grain of everything we know.'

'It does.' Maddie couldn't disagree with that but she wouldn't even if she could, she didn't want to delay the DCI getting to what he wanted to say.

'But now you've made that link, it is on record and Major Crime feel they are duty bound to take that seriously.'

'I agree, they are,' Maddie snapped.

'As do I.' A sigh, a play for more time to think of his next words, perhaps. 'Major Crime have been structured and restructured over the last few years, centralised, localised and generally messed about. The result of that is that they've lost some good people and a lot of experience. They're short of bums on seats and they've been forced to recruit those that previously might have been sent away for . . . for further development.'

'Haven't we all, sir.'

'Quite. Ultimately, they do not have the capacity to take on an investigation of this type, of this magnitude.'

'Sir, I get the feeling you're beating around a bush here. What do I need to know?'

'Mark is aware that Harry Blaker is involved, I assume you mentioned his name. You also said you would be happy to continue the misper investigation — and all that comes with it — and Mark is open to this. I think it solves a problem for him. But . . .'

'But?'

'He is not happy that it is you leading the investigation. He is aware you are not a substantive inspector and I know how that sounds, but we're talking reputational damage here, Maddie. Mark called me because I have a relationship with Harry, to request that I speak with him and ask if he will step back in to run things. Just until . . . Well, for now. Until we get this whole thing bottomed out.' Maddie had a reply but she held it back, waiting out a pause where she could almost hear the DCI squirming. 'I know,' he said, eventually. 'It's a tough message and I don't want you to take it as a personal slight on you or your abilities, we all know that—'

'Harry won't,' Maddie cut him off. 'That means he comes back and what, just steps into his old suit and dusts off his desk?'

'He will. He is, Maddie. I spoke to him late last night, then to Recruitment and it would appear he can just about do just that.' This time the pause was simply because Maddie was lost for words. 'Let me tell you he said no at first, of course he did, but then he started asking questions . . . They were all about you.' Still Maddie didn't have a response. 'He said he would only even consider it if you were working with him, if it were a team of people you selected personally and that was after he went through just about every alternative he could, where you still led this investigation. And I said to him what I will say to you now, Harry comes back as the head of this investigation, with your assistance, or this investigation goes elsewhere. Likely into the CID arena but with assistance cobbled from wherever we can . . .'

'So . . .' Maddie managed, but she couldn't get any more words out. DCI Lowe helped her out.

'He said no, Maddie. Until I made it clear that the only way you could continue looking for those women is if he agreed to return. This counts as the one and only time I have heard Harry Blaker swear!' A chuckle, quick to come, even quicker to go. 'He said that you had the bit between your teeth, that you want to find these girls and that you were the best person for them. He said that if it was the only way, then he would do it. But you would have to agree.'

'Did he.' Maddie was now a swirl of emotions, nothing that would stick. She had been caught out and surprised, then angry. Now she didn't know how she felt.

'He's coming in at ten. I think the three of us should get together, how does that sound? We can talk this out, see how this might work.'

'OK.' Maddie ended the call, certain that any more words could only get her in trouble. But she couldn't guarantee she would have anything better to say, come ten a.m.

CHAPTER 52. THE BAD GUY

I came back to the coffee shop, back for the buzz of other people and away from the constant anxiety of what might be happening through the wall and into next door, like an ache that is getting worse.

I was absent-minded when my coffee came, flicking back through what I had written, stopping to read sentences, paragraphs, a whole page at one point and I got lost, lost in my own storytelling. Strange how that can happen considering the story is mine, what I remember, what I carry around like a constant weight that drags behind me. I looked up and my coffee was there. It comes with a glass of water in here, a small bowl too for oddly shaped lumps of brown sugar — more than you can carry in two hands. I was just in time to see the dough-faced woman moving away, an empty tray in her hand. I don't know how long she was there, I don't know what she read, I don't know if she read anything at all.

Maybe I am getting lax. Just a day ago, in this same place, I was far more protective, gripping this ledger tight, even writing with one hand holding up the cover so no one could see in from the side, despite there being no reason anyone might care to. I think it's the ambulance, I think it's knowing that the secrets that have fallen out of me and into the pages of this book will soon be free to be written all over again. By the *gutter press* no doubt, as police reports too or, the worst of the lot, in the sewer of social media. I thought about this when I walked here today, even considered that I might as well throw this book away, the contents with it. But I don't think that's right. The fact that I killed a man and buried his body will come out, I have known that for some time now, but the truth is more than the facts.

I know what will happen from here. I can see my future as clear as though I am watching it live on television: it is me, sat across a scuffed table in one of those windowless interview rooms at the police station, the solid walls holding the air so still that it thickens, develops a taste almost. From where I sit I will be able to see my own expression, washed of all colour and personality, it will be on the small screen of something the size and shape of an old VCR. It makes a gentle hissing noise to remind me that everything I say and do is being recorded as evidence. There are two police officers — always two — and they sit opposite me and they are stern, one sits tall and stiff to stare straight at me, the other is bent forward, his eyebrows rising, his head occasionally shaking from side to side while he is flicking through this very ledger.

He is skimming it too, there are just a few parts he needs, just a few key sentences and he will stop when he finds them, jab a finger to save his place so he can look up at me. He will disregard everything else, he will have found his *fact* and he will not care for the truth. Not there, not at that point in time. All he will care about is that he has a slam dunk sat in front of him: a murderer with a confession.

Writing this out will still count for something and I cannot stop now. That last will and testament from Betty Snow will lead them to the facts but what I am writing will lead them to the truth.

That prediction, that sight into my future is not plucked from nowhere by the way. I was arrested once, hence my glimpse of what to expect. I was dragged into a violent alter-cation in the toilets of my nightclub. Two coked-up fools

226

needed ejecting and it was necessary to meet excessive violence with excessive violence. A room full of unreliable and or plain disinterested witnesses meant it was never going anywhere — that and the fact that I did nothing more than my job — but I still had to go through the rigmarole of police questioning and earning myself an entry on their database as part of the fun. The fact I didn't fight to wash my name entirely clean didn't feel like much at the time, but it would be everything soon, it would become part of the *facts*: a murderer with a confession and a violent past.

None of this matters. I have no intention of talking to them, not to a solicitor either, not to anyone, which is another reason to get it all down right now, while the coffee is good, while the only sounds are tables of people laughing, where no one is here to twist my words and tell me I didn't see what I know I saw, or do what I know I did. They'll do their best to make me out to be the bad guy, a cold killer who buried the evidence with his own bare hands, maybe even skirting over the fact that one of their own helped me do it (let sleeping dogs lie — or dead dogs more like) to try and avoid their own negative press. But, if I do make it to that room, there will be nothing more for me to do than to point at this ledger, to tell them to read it all and to come to the only conclusion that they can.

Ryan Saunders was the bad guy.

Today I want to tell you about him, what Charles told me about him. Ryan Saunders was no stranger to a police interview room himself. He was first arrested when he was just twelve years old and not for what you might expect of some errant boy — shoplifting or some dumb assault on a smaller kid — but murder. That's right, you read it here first (unless you read any of the press from the time of his arrest), Ryan Saunders was a convicted murderer and still a child when he earned that moniker. He held down an eight-year-old girl by her neck because she threatened to tell on him. He'd tried to get her knickers off, see, it wasn't rape, but it mighta been had young Sally Andrews not been a determined little girl who had lashed out, promised to tell her dad what he had done and made a run for it. But Ryan Saunders had been faster; stronger too.

Saunders said that he didn't mean to kill her, said how he couldn't get hold of her arms or legs because she was flailing all over the place to fight him hard, so he just grabbed what he could to stop her moving. He said he was just trying to calm her down so he could say sorry. She did stop moving, that's for sure. Sally Andrews died in a small section of woods that backed onto her garden at the time, the same woods she always played in and she was less than twenty metres from her own bedroom window when she took her last breath. She kept her collection of dolls propped up in a line across her windowsill, their faces pressed against the glass, she liked to think they were watching her play. That day they watched her tiny body go limp, then they watched it dragged into the thickest bush that the twelve-year-old Ryan Saunders could find to be covered in a layer of crispy leaves.

I found some coverage of the trial, there wasn't much because of reporting restrictions but they did let a statement come out from the victim's mother. I read it over and most of it was what you might expect from something like that but there was part of it that stood out, some lines I didn't expect: *My little girl's killer might just be a boy himself but one day he will be a man. There is a darkness to his heart that you can see in his eyes, locking him up can only darken it further. He should never step out into the sun again. He didn't get a whole-life sentence here today but Sally did. We all did.*

Twelve years later, at the age of twenty-four, Ryan Saunders, dark eyes and all, walked out of a minimum-security prison as a qualified and well-practised carpenter. He was in his prime as a physical specimen too, little else to do but lift weights after all. The state had ensured him a new name (Ryan Saunders was what he changed it to), a place to live and conditions managed by his probation officer. Hardly a man taught a lesson, hardly a man who had paid for what he had done.

But I will pay. In my future I can see myself clear as day, in that police interview room where they will skim all these words until they find their fact: *Paul Morgan: the bad guy.*

CHAPTER 53

The distant sound of a door forced open was instant and thundered through the stale atmosphere, carried on the constant draught that swept over Daisy-Mae Adams to keep her chilled. In contrast, Megan's breath was warm and came as a gasp that tickled the back of Daisy-Mae's neck.

Then there was silence, the silence of someone standing still. Daisy-Mac clung to the hope that it was a rescuer surveying the scene, working out how to pick their way through the loose ground she had heard the man kick and scuff his way through as part of his escape. Surely it *had* to be a rescuer, their returning attacker would just sweep straight through, maybe with that sound of dragging metal that seemed to follow his every move.

But there was still just silence. She felt a chin nuzzle into the back of her neck, took it as Megan telling her that she should stay quiet, play it safe. If it was a rescuer then they would find them soon enough. *God, she hoped so.*

The man who had left to take his chances, to alert others, had been gone overnight. Daisy-Mae had no way of knowing that for sure and yet she did know that. She reckoned it must have been early evening when he had got up, ripped away his ball and bell and made for the door. The temperature drop from that point had been marked, enough to cut through the general numbness, but that wasn't the only way she had known; night wasn't just the darkness you could see, it was a feeling, a sense of the world asleep. Especially if you weren't.

Daisy-Mae had dozed at best, she would continually wake from a dream about being stabbed in the leg, only the pain was real. They had managed a conversation after the man had left, her and Megan, bolstered by the fact that his escape had been far from noiseless yet he had still made it away without being intercepted.

Megan had talked first, asked how Daisy-Mae was, then was forced to wait out her tears at the first sound of a friendly voice in a most unfriendly place. In contrast, Megan seemed so calm. She talked out a plan, the first part of which had her taking off the only piece of clothing she could, a skirt she said was far too short to wear again anyway, to wrap tightly around Daisy-Mae's ankles. Megan only had her fingertips exposed where her hands were restrained so it was tough going but she managed to get her injured leg tied up against her good one in a sort of splint. The pain had rushed back from the disturbance, bad enough to have Daisy-Mae retching again, but overall it was better, more manageable. Megan had talked endlessly about how it was going to be OK, how it wouldn't be long before they were rescued now the man was outside the building where he would head straight for help, for a phone or a passer-by. She said they would have to be somewhere quite remote but how remote was anywhere really these days? Daisy-Mae had listened, she knew Megan was doing her best to keep her calm, to keep her positive and it had worked enough for Daisy-Mae to feel hope blossom. But the hours had passed, the temperature had dropped and that blossom had drifted away a petal at a time until there was nothing left.

Until now.

The silence was crushing, like a weighted blanket thrown over them both where they lay. Megan pushed herself in closer and tighter and was now holding her breath, just like Daisy-Mae was holding hers. Both were waiting for the next noise, for the sound of someone calling out, a voice explaining that they were the police, that they had been sent to help, been told that two women were here and how it was all going to be OK.

But the next noise was not someone calling out. The next noise was a scrape of metal against concrete, distant, but distinct.

Dragged towards them.

PART THREE

CHAPTER 54

He had never left. The tie helped, but the final piece in the Harry Blaker jigsaw was the return of his waxed jacket, black with four square pockets making up the front, faded and battered at the elbows and cuffs. Faded and battered overall, in truth, but Harry just wasn't complete without it. He'd had a shave too. He had kept a beard since suffering a scar on his face — Maddie had been sitting next to him in the moments that scar was forged — but it was trimmed shorter, the edges sharper. His fingernails were back to pristine, maybe even trimmed too. But there was also a look behind his eyes that was instantly familiar, a hunger, a look she had missed for sure and one that helped shape her reaction.

There had been a few hours since the call telling her that this moment was happening, that Harry was coming back to take over her job, that she was being replaced. She'd been angry about that, enough to take herself away on her own, to take some time to think about it.

She wasn't angry anymore.

The most important thing right then was finding two missing women who, if she was right, were in a lot of danger. Despite herself, she knew their best chance might well be stood in front of her with a trimmed beard and a battered

234

jacket. Harry looked a little awkward, DCI Julian Lowe did too and Maddie didn't speak straight away, dragging out that moment for as long as she could, enjoying it too much.

'Harry, what are you doing here?' she said and his reaction was priceless, both men exchanged a glance and then he even stuttered a bit. She grinned to let him off the hook and his face flooded with relief. 'So then, *boss*, what do we do next?' she continued. 'I brought a team for you to meet.' She turned to where they had filed in behind her, managing to stay silent. Eileen Holmans was standing at the front — of course she was — Rhiannon just off her shoulder and Vince Arnold hulking behind, his expression full Labrador that was just missing a lolling tongue. Each one of them looked delighted. She couldn't blame them, she was delighted too.

'What we always seem to do next,' Harry said, that authoritative growl of his leaking humour like a sieve. 'Put the kettle on.'

CHAPTER 55. INSUFFICIENT EVIDENCE

Ryan Saunders was never going to see justice. Those were Charles' words, he was a serious man overall but that day he really was *serious as cancer*. He believed that with all his heart and it was tearing him up in front of my very eyes. Saunders was an official suspect for a time, the only one the police ever had and it did look like they might turn him into a life-serving prisoner at one time. CCTV from my club put him there on New Year's Eve, but alone, silently drinking soft drinks in a booth where he had the best view over at the bar where Christine was working. It was where she always worked. We had two main dance floors and that night we had trance classics from the last decade in one room and disco-cheese in the other. Aside from those main floors we had areas for a quieter experience; chill-out bars we called them and Christine worked the one we called "The Funky House". It was high-backed leather chairs (wipe-clean, always), concealed fibre optics, a lower volume to the sounds and a higher price for the cocktails. Christine ran it like it was her own and she was good at it, to the point where she had her own regulars. What none of us realised in time was that Ryan Saunders was one of them.

He had a talent for blending in, despite his size. He would order his drink from another bar and carry it through so he never really got close enough for Christine to notice him. He certainly noticed her. That night he barely moved for the last hour and a half of trading, he just sat facing out in her direction. He left the club before close, before it thinned out too much — again, the action of someone who knew a thing or two about blending in — but he stayed in the area. Police knew that he filled his car at a petrol station three miles away on Cheriton High Street, that his home address was a right turn off that forecourt and the main road back to the club was a left turn — and he took a left.

That was the last CCTV sighting. There were witnesses who might have seen his car, at least two taxi drivers gave statements putting a gunmetal-grey BMW 3 Series coupé in the area of the club for kicking-out time, its lights on but dipped to look like two rings scorched into the freezing darkness. Ryan Saunders drove a gunmetal-grey BMW E36 with aftermarket (and over the top) circular xenon lights. A similar car with a man fitting Saunders' description had been seen at various dogging sites in the months before, there were witnesses (wanting to remain anonymous for some reason) who came forward as part of police appeals for information. There were people who bore witness to that car on the night in question too, at least one who saw it driving slowly up the town on roads that Christine likely took, others who saw it driving up Tontine Street to pass the main entrance to the club and another who saw it at the top of the Old High Street, pulled over untidily on a pedestrianised area. Where it was empty.

The police knew that Saunders had a history of sexual violence and they were building a picture up of someone with who been unable to change his spots.

They don't change, a sexual predator is a sexual predator, these men are broken, led only by desire and a spate behind bars does nothing but increase that desire.

Charles' words to me after he was forced to let Ryan Saunders go. Charles told me how, for the most part, Saunders answered the questions in his police interview. He

237

said he knew who Christine was, not by name but when showed a photo of her, he said he knew she was a barmaid at a nightclub where he liked to drink. He admitted to thinking she was attractive: *That's not illegal, is it?* Charles told me how Saunders said that with a big smile and how it took every ounce of strength Charles had not to take him down there and then.

Insufficient evidence. Charles practically spat these words when he told me that Saunders had been released. Forensics was the big hope, seems it often is when it comes to murder, but they couldn't put Saunders at any of the places where they had found death. They couldn't link him to any of the other victims either, not in any way, Christine was the only one they ever proved that he even knew existed.

Christine on her own was not enough.

The appetite for Saunders waned. He was a pervert for sure and he was in the area around the time Christine and Denise left work but they couldn't even prove that she was abducted on her way home, let alone by whom; not *beyond reasonable doubt* at least. Saunders' car was located and a fine tooth used for anything that might help, only to come up clean — his home address got the same treatment with the same outcome. That was the time when Charles — leading the investigation — was told to cast a wider net and to release what he knew they already had: a stone-cold killer.

When I say that the appetite had waned, I didn't mean Charles. He was angry in a way that I hadn't seen before or since, it was all-consuming and it didn't take too much conversation over that fence for it to consume me too.

I had wanted Saunders dead even before he had a name, but Charles was willing to trust in the justice system right up until the point it failed. He had done all he could. It wasn't enough.

After that we had to be a little patient, I did at least. The irony of those next few months was that it was the time needed for Charles to go big on Saunders' innocence, to really take him out of the picture. Charles went as far as personally moving Saunders away from the area as part of his plan to make sure *Ryan Saunders* was no longer a name on anyone's lips. Charles took it a step further, somehow that man steered a whole police force to the point that it fully expected Saunders, if he had any sense, to disappear and to stay disappeared. It took longer than I would have liked and the process was painful, but Charles was able to provide the perfect outcome.

We had Ryan Saunders all to ourselves.

CHAPTER 56

The scraping stopped close enough for it to nudge Daisy-Mae's hair. She felt Megan move against her from behind, a subtle movement to try and get closer, protective perhaps. But she was in no position to offer anything, let alone protection.

There was breathing. Heavy and long. Sighs, one after the other. A man surely contemplating a gap, a missing captive. Even with her mind consumed with terror there was time for logic and for realisation to puncture Daisy-Mae's brain; their would-be rescuer was dead, discovered trying to escape. She knew that from the fact that the man now looming above her was taking his time, surveying the scene, considering the level of punishment for those who had remained.

The sighs stopped, the breathing a little more normal. Then the sound of a metal bar clanging to the ground like it had been thrown. Daisy-Mae slammed her eyes shut behind the tape but all her other senses lit up at once. Megan was wrenched away from her. She screamed, kicked out too to catch Daisy-Mae in the ankle.

'Get OFF ME!' Megan's voice settled to words, they were shrill and sounded odd where they vibrated against the tape. The sudden separation left Daisy-Mae with a chill down her back. Then she heard a dull thud — a strike finding its target — and Megan gave another scream. The scream ended with a scrabbling, scuffing sound like she was pushing out with her feet, trying to push herself away. More dull thuds, like someone beating a mattress for dust, then another dragging sound, all the while the bell was clamouring and rattling in Megan's palm. She was dragged from right to left, across Daisy-Mae's feet, in the direction where she had heard the solid metal bar thrown. That awful scraping noise told her it was being picked up. Then a sound far more awful as her friend screamed panic and pain. Megan formed more words: *No!* over and over, *no, please! Please! You don't have to do this! I was quiet, I wasn't doing anything, please!*

The first strike of the weapon hit the floor to make a stinging sound that whined like an oversized tuning fork. It was scary. Every sound was designed to be, but the next was the worst one yet. A changeable whistle, the sound of something long and heavy being swung through the air over their heads, at pace and in a circle, swinging faster and faster, louder and louder, dipping close to Daisy-Mae at times where she still held her eyes scrunched shut, waiting for a strike to land.

Megan took the hit and this time there was no scream, or even a moan, just a sound like expelled air from a sack of skin.

'Stop it! STOP IT!' Daisy-Mae roared, trying to lurch towards the noise but only just managing to sit up. Her leg shot with pain that threatened to take her back to the floor. He did stop. All the noises stopped. No more whistling through the air, no more scraping of steel against the floor, no more begging from her friend. Daisy-Mae was at a clumsy half-sit, leaning away from the pain in her leg, off balance with her two legs straight out, tied together with Megan's skirt, waiting for the assault to move onto her. But this time Daisy-Mae had her eyes wide open. She was past cowering on the ground, determined now to meet whatever was coming face-on.

But the only sound was of a steel bar discarded once again, then of footsteps moving away and a door opening to be roughly pulled shut.

The silence, when it returned, was more complete than ever. The stillness too and she twisted to face the direction where she had last heard her friend, reaching out to nudge an obstruction with the plastic ball in her hands. No response.

'Megan?' Daisy-Mae whispered, then again, louder. Nothing. She held her breath to really listen and again there was nothing but silence. No movement, no moaning in pain or the gurgling, laboured breathing of someone unconscious.

There was just nothing.

CHAPTER 57

Maddie stepped out of the car, her head up, taking in the frontage of the new-build semi-detached house in front of her. It was part of an all-new estate made up of solid-looking red-brick fronts, broken up occasionally by the odd house half coated in weatherboarding. The homes were practically built on top of each other and at obscure angles to make it difficult to tell one footprint from another. Maddie knew it was the way of the world these days, a way of getting as many houses as possible into a too-small space, but it wasn't for her. The gardens were small too, their target property had a garden just large enough for a six-foot trampoline with one side resting against the fence. This she knew for sure as the higgledy-piggledy layout meant they had approached their target property from the side, allowing a decent enough view in. It had been enough for Maddie to know that someone was in.

She stepped away from where Harry seemed to be hesitating. 'Come on, you're in charge now. You haven't forgotten how to knock a door, have you?'

Harry hadn't, his knocking was just as competent — and as firm — as she remembered. The door still took a while to open, long enough that Harry's huge fist was raised again when there was finally some movement.

'Hey, I'm . . .' Harry paused long enough to sound unsure. 'Inspector Blaker. Harry Blaker.' The woman looked a little stunned. Harry did too.

'We were hoping to talk to Michael Rix, if he's here?' Maddie added quickly, burying her amusement.

'Mike?' The woman could hardly have looked more terrified.

'Mike, yeah. Is everything OK?' Maddie moved a half step forward to move in front of her gruff looking colleague.

'Fine. But he isn't here, sometimes he . . . he isn't here.'

Maddie took a moment to show her a smile while the woman's fear still seemed to be on the way up. 'Debbie, right?' Maddie had read the summary that Eileen had been able to provide in a hurry.

'Debbie,' she repeated back.

'There's nothing to worry about, no one's in any trouble. I thought you might even be used to speaking to the police!' Maddie tried a chuckle and it got her nowhere.

'We don't speak to police anymore, Mike, he doesn't. He did, I mean he helped all he could . . .' Her eyes flicked from Maddie to Harry and back again. 'That was all a long time ago.'

'We're not here to upset anyone, Mike might be able to help us again.' Harry was back in his stride and Debbie Rix fixed on him.

'He can't. Trust me on that. Mike can barely help himself these days.'

She was a slight woman, twitchy too, seemingly using the doorframe to keep herself upright. She had mousey brown hair with streaks of blonde that looked natural. Her make-up was subtle, her top a little dressy in a way that was not a match for her casual-looking tracksuit bottoms. She looked like a woman who had been out earlier, then gone straight for the comfy slacks on her return. A life spent policing came with a good feel for ages and Maddie had her in her mid-forties.

'Any chance we could just have a chat inside? I'm sure you would like to be able to see your daughter,' Maddie said and the woman snapped to her like she had guessed her pin number. 'I assume that's who I saw on the trampoline?' Maddie added in explanation.

The woman took a moment then stepped backwards into a bright hall. Maddie took the lead, following her through to a kitchen at the rear. It was a room that pushed out sideways, the living room accessed from a door that came off it. The door into it was open to give a snippet of a darkened room with curtains pulled shut. It wasn't the first time Maddie had considered that Michael Rix was at home, just preferring to stay quiet.

'She's really good at that.' Maddie gestured out of the window at the young girl showing no signs of stopping on the trampoline. She was twisting and turning, her eyes closed at times — despite the considerable heights.

'She loves it. I can't get her off!' A smile, or at least a turn-up of Debbie's lips either side. 'I couldn't even get her upstairs to change first.'

'She's home early,' Maddie said and Debbie's smile faded to nothing.

'She gets stomach aches. I talk to the school a lot, we've been to the doctor's and they've got the records so they all know—' She stopped at Maddie's raised palm.

'It's OK!' Maddie said. 'I wasn't having a pop, I'm sure you're doing a great job.'

'I know how it looks. They come and go, she just gets anxious, that's all. It used to be a sickness thing, she would just throw up, now it's stomach aches. It's rare she needs to come home but today . . . today I got the call and I thought I would give her a sunny afternoon in her favourite place.'

'Does she like school?' Maddie asked.

'She does. She's bright too, I don't know where she gets that from, not me I tell you that much!' Another flicker of a smile, this one seemed to last a little better.

'How's Michael doing?' Maddie said, watching for a reaction carefully, noting that Debbie's eyes flicked to the living room at the mention of his name.

'How do you think he's doing?'

'It was a long time ago, Mrs Rix.' Harry spoke now, he had a growl that could seem harsh at times and this was one. 'I was hoping he had got the help he needed, he seems to have made a nice life for himself here at least?'

'We have a life, yeah. A nice life for sure. Nice things, a nice house for Mia . . .'

'But Michael is still struggling?' Maddie said, deliberately softer.

'I don't blame him for that. We never put a deadline on his recovery, you can't do that, that's not how trauma works.' It felt like Debbie was repeating a tagline, regurgitating a counsellor's words maybe.

'Would he talk to us?' Harry said.

'Why would he do that? Why would he need to do that? What happened to Mike is coming up for twenty-three years into his past, so unless you're here to tell us that you finally got the man who did it . . . ?'

'No,' Harry said.

'Of course not. So why would you even be back to drag all this up again?'

Maddie stared at Harry as a warning, a reminder of their conversation on the way where they had discussed the need to be careful. Maddie had talked about how they couldn't know what they might find and she wanted to be sure they understood Michael Rix and his mental state fully before introducing the possibility that something like what he had gone through could be happening again. Harry had stayed quiet at the time and she was about to find out why.

'There might be something similar going on. We don't know for sure, but speaking to Michael might help us work it out,' Harry said. And there it was, laid bare, unable to be taken back and Debbie Rix took a moment to form a reaction. Her eyes burst with fear first, then her mouth fell open, hanging like she might catch a fly.

'It's OK,' Maddie said, trying to limit the damage. It was already too late.

'You can't tell him that, you can't!' Debbie stammered and Maddie sensed they were about to lose her altogether.

It was about to get worse; a single word froze them all.

'Mum?' Mia Rix, red-cheeked and still panting from her exertion. 'Who are these people?'

'Just some of Dad's friends, love!' Debbie turned and crouched down to her daughter.

'Dad has friends?' Mia looked confused at that. 'Can I have some water?'

'Of course. But take it up to your room, please. We're just talking in here.'

'OK. Can we still get takeaway, if Dad comes back?'

'We'll see.' Debbie's voice was wrung out with tension, something that Mia seemed oblivious to. She even hummed a little to herself as she walked through to the stairs.

'Where is he, Debbie?' Harry was quick to put the pressure back on the moment he could.

'I . . . I don't know, really I don't.'

'Does he often disappear?'

'He needs his space, we all do, right?' Debbie said.

'That must make things difficult for you, though. Bringing up a child is tough when one half is unreliable.' Maddie kept the pressure on.

'I never said he was unreliable,' Debbie snapped, angry.

'You can be unreliable through no fault of your own. I don't know what he went through, not like you do, but—'

'No one does!' More anger and Maddie gave her a moment to get it under control.

'How long does he disappear for?'

Debbie shrugged. 'You tell me.' She sighed, back to resigned. 'More so, recently. There was a time when he would never go out at all. I thought that was hard but this . . . this is harder. It's not like he comes back any better; more stressed out if anything.'

'Stressed out?' Maddie said, her eyes suddenly scanning Debbie for bruises, contusions, scrapes — any physical signs

247

of abuse. Debbie must have picked up on it. 'What does a stressed-out Michael Rix do?'

'Nothing to me! He's a good man, angry, but only ever at himself. Sometimes I wish it was at me, anything to give himself a day off.'

'Does he self-harm?' Harry's bluntness again, the last eight months had done nothing to soften his edges.

'He hurts himself, yeah. It was under control for a long time, might even have got better, but then . . .'

'Then?' Maddie prompted.

'It's hard, you have to understand that. Living with Mike is hard . . . So I told him I didn't want to anymore.'

'You've split up?'

'No . . . But I have told him that I'm leaving, that I need space, that Mia and I can't stay here all the while . . .' She ran out of words, gesturing instead, a raised hand that slapped back against her thigh. Maddie followed it, stepping towards the door and the dimly lit living room beyond. Maddie found the light switch on the wall and strong, white downlights erupted to show up a room turned upside down. Maddie turned back to where Debbie's chest had a visible rise and fall. 'I've stopped straightening it up for now. He seems to have contained it in there, he doesn't go anywhere else.'

'He's got worse since you told him?' Maddie said.

'Yeah. Not towards me, I can't say that enough. He would never hurt me or Mia, he loves us, he loves his daughter. She's the only reason he comes out of this room.'

'But her anxiety?' Maddie said, referencing the little girl who couldn't not be aware of her father breaking himself — and their furniture — in a fit of self-loathing. 'And her stomach aches?'

'He doesn't . . . I haven't told him that . . . He wouldn't hurt Mia!' Debbie stammered.

'But he is hurting her,' Maddie pressed.

'When did you tell him?' Harry said.

She lifted both hands to her temples. 'First? A few months ago we talked about it, not seriously. A week or so since we had a proper chat and he knew I was serious, it's happening.'

'How much has he been here since then?' Harry pushed, a little too hard perhaps as Debbie scowled.

'Why are you asking that?'

'We're trying to catch up with him, I just want to know if we're going to find him here.'

Debbie's face went white. 'Please! You can't come back here! If he knows the police . . . if he knows it might be happening again . . . He can't know!'

'What if it is happening again and he could help?' Maddie tried. 'There might be some peace for him to find in that.'

'He can't. Please, he can't even help himself.'

'Please, Debbie. Think of all you've been through, that's all I'm asking. If there is someone else out there who can be stopped from having that experience, wouldn't you want to help?'

'Of course I would.'

'Where might he go? You've been married a long time, long enough to have some idea, surely?'

She huffed, slumping forward, and Maddie knew something significant was coming. 'He has an older sister. She's the other side of the town. He doesn't trust people, doesn't really have any friends or any other family to talk to, but he will go there. He never stays long though, I tell you that now, she'll be lucky if she gets half an hour.'

'Thank you,' Maddie said softly.

'What does he look like, these days?' Harry said, again prompting a scowl of suspicion. 'In case we see him on the way.' There was another sigh as Debbie opened up her phone and took a moment to find a picture and swing it round. Michael Rix was an older man to the one on file, his features still true only they had slipped a little. His hair was longer, thinner too, to merge with a beard that had gone the same way. The picture showed him standing outside in an expanse of green grass, though directly underfoot looked like the black, rubber type stuff used as footings for children's play areas. He was holding Mia tight in his side. Maddie grabbed Harry's arm, it was involuntary. In the photo Michael was wearing a jacket; olive-green, long and quilted, with an over-sized hood that had furry edges.

The jacket from the train.

CHAPTER 58. MICHAEL RIX

I've never seen anyone like Michael Rix. Not before and not since. I knew who he was, and more important than that, I knew *what* he was: *the other survivor.* Charles told me that before the three of us met up for the first time. But I didn't have to spend long in Rix's company to know that this was a lazy description of the man. In truth, he was just what was left after Ryan Saunders had finished with him and I can tell you now, that wasn't much. I only met Rix twice. The first time was a meeting Charles set up and was adamant should happen, although the whole vibe was odd — awkward and strained. Charles himself was odd, awkward and strained now I think about it and I suppose it could have been Rix himself who had insisted that meeting happened. Maybe he wanted to size me up a little, work me out. I can understand that, of course, seeing as the three of us were about to do something that would change everything.

The next time I met Rix was the day he played his part in the murder of Ryan Saunders.

But before we ever set eyes on each other, Charles talked about him, told me his first impression was that of *a pair of eyes on a stick.* I remember this seemed unkind at the time but, as was often the case with Charles, he was more right than I could know. More than twenty years since and I still don't have a better way of projecting a first impression of Michael Rix into your mind. At that first meeting Rix was nothing more than an observer, not even a nod when Charles went through the plan that he had — Charles was always the man with the plan. Rix mighta been there in body but I don't reckon there was much of him there in spirit. He held himself the whole time, his arms across his chest like a kid caught out in the cold and he never looked at me, not in the eye at least, not that first time.

The next time he was a man for sure and a different man altogether. Years back, there was a story came out of a zoo further up the county, about how they expanded and took on a lion. He was special to the keepers because he was the first, but even more so because he turned out to be so docile. Nothing like what they were expecting, I guess, and over time they all got close, the thing treated like a pet. Some idle weekday this lion was sunning himself on a flat piece of rock and a keeper was cleaning a window and, in a moment, the lion was on her, tearing and ripping with jaws and claws. That keeper should never have been in there, not with a lion loose and there was all sorts of criticism after. I remember the zoo tried to defend itself and I remember how that defence was torn apart just as quick as the back of that poor woman. The zoo's people said that Raya (the lion's name, it just came to me) was docile, non-aggressive and that plenty of keepers had walked through that compound, cleaned those same windows, even hand-fed the brute. But the zoo was found to be negligent, forced to close down completely when the judge awarded the keeper a big payoff and he might have summed up the case the best: *The zoo has no defence; it was always a lion.*

Michael Rix was always a lion.

That first meeting he was sunning himself on a rock. The next time I saw him he took hold of Ryan Saunders with a grip alone that was enough for him to shout out in pain — and I think I said that Saunders was a big man himself — then Rix spun him towards me like he had just taken hold of a toddler making a scene in a supermarket. This was the one time we made eye contact by the way, Rix held Saunders tight from behind, he bunched his arms up tight together behind his back to thrust the man's chest out towards me.

I'm struggling to think how to describe the next bit but all I can say is that in that stare, in that moment, Rix was communicating with me better than he ever had. Maybe I'm imagining it now, maybe it was just the way he was holding him that dared me to do what I did next, to stab and to keep stabbing, or maybe my recollection is right and via that eye contact Michael Rix told me to do it, made me do it even, and he wouldn't release me from his spell until I did.

Charles was angry with how it went down at first. He was the man with the plan like I said and it was a plan that included time for a little Q&A session. Michael Rix was supposed to get hold of Saunders so I could *show* him the knife, maybe cut him a little bit so he knew we weren't messing (I wanted to do that anyway, I wanted to make him hurt some). But then Charles wanted a talk. It wasn't for a confession, we were a long way past that, but Charles wanted details, he wanted to know his victims, how many and where. There were families out there waiting for answers and Charles, like the good detective he was, wanted to be the one with them.

But the only thing Rix needed from Saunders was his death. I guess we were on the same page with that one. Don't get me wrong, I'm not saying that Rix lunged the knife forward, it was in my hand for sure, I can't even say that I stabbed Ryan Saunders in the chest *because* of Michael Rix. But there was something in his eyes, something about him and his change into a fierce and powerful lion that had me lunging soon as I could, before Charles could even get a word in. I don't regret it, I said I was sorry to Charles after but I didn't mean it then and I don't mean it now. I'm not sorry I gave Ryan Saunders the justice he deserved.

You shouldn't be either.

Michael Rix changed again when it was done. From cold and powerful he was back to the beast sat still on a rock. I remember being a little bit jealous of that, how he had got what he wanted in one moment then seemed to be at peace in the next. For me it was different, there was a magnitude to what I had just done, a realisation. I panicked then and I've been panicking since. But not Rix. I'm not sure that's a man who *can* panic. Charles and I were stood out in that deluge, unable to tell blood from rain, sodden and covered, the easy part done and already fretting about the next part, but Rix was a picture of serenity, a modicum of calm among the chaos. He was supposed to assist us further, the man with the plan had included using Rix's strength to shift the body, it was Rix who had the truck with a flat back that was perfect for the job and then he was to be the third shovel digging behind my conifers (more hands and all that). But in the moment Saunders lost his life, we lost Rix. The man walked off into the storm, into drops of rain so large I could see each and every one with the naked eye and I watched him go, didn't even bother to call out because I knew he wasn't listening. And let me tell you something else about that rain, those big drops, they were bending around him and I saw it with my own eyes. His fingertips dripped, but bright red with blood, not clear drops of rain. There was an aura too, a protective glow that was clear as day. Sure, you will say it was the distant hue from street lights reflecting off soaked clothes and skin that had a trick for my eye, that gave him the false impression of an aura but I said it about Betty Snow and I will say it again: righteousness has a power that we cannot understand.

Righteous or not, that was the last time I saw Michael Rix.

CHAPTER 59

Daisy-Mae was back to still, back to a foetal position on the floor, measuring her breathing and listening intently for the sound of the door. But this time it was different. This time she wasn't lying still to be compliant, she wasn't listening for the door out of fear, this time she was preserving energy for his return. This time she would not lie quietly while he paced around her, teasing her with the sound of a scraping weapon, this time she would sit up to face him again, this time she would roar out her name and the name of her friend he had left for dead next to her.

The waiting was killing her slowly and she couldn't stand it anymore.

CHAPTER 60

Eileen Holmans was quite obviously in her element. The meeting room that had been booked for an hour slot by DCI Julian Lowe in order to allow Maddie time to come to terms with a difficult message and for Harry Blaker to be brought up to speed was now block-booked indefinitely with the DCI's endorsement to act as a makeshift incident room. An incident room that Eileen had ensured was quickly filling with boxes of historic case material wheeled in by an overalled and constantly perplexed man who had driven overnight from a secure storage facility. He was wearing his fatigue all over his face, enough that Maddie had fast-tracked an action to get the man a strong coffee.

'There's still two more pallets,' the man said, the coffee steaming up his glasses while he rested on his set of hydraulic wheels.

'Boxes NZ22 and NX28?' Eileen bustled over, her eyes sweeping up from the documentation to the overalled man, fixing him in a stranglehold. 'Pallets three and four?' It was a question, only asked accusingly.

'Three you have, I just dropped it in the corner, four is the next one up.'

'Very good,' Eileen replied and bustled away. Maddie made a face at him, in which she tried to communicate that he was doing well and that they appreciated his efforts. As it was, he left his coffee untouched and dragged his wheels back out to meet Eileen's demands.

'One of those boxes contains the majority of material we have on Michael Rix. I have a summary that should include all that is significant but I want to be sure their "significant" is the same as mine.' Eileen had come back over, feeling, perhaps, like she owed an explanation.

'Fresh eyes.' Maddie shrugged her agreement.

'The other box has all of DI Snow's daybooks, handwritten notes and correspondence. I know this was your priority when we sent for them . . .' She suddenly looked a little awkward. 'Has that changed? I mean, it's not for me to tell you how to do your job but should I assume that Michael Rix is now the priority?'

Maddie couldn't stop a grin breaking out at that. 'Finding him is a priority for sure, that's what we need to do next. The inspector's written material is still important, I want to have a look through that myself so when we have it identified can we put it to one side?'

'Of course,' Eileen said, then lingered.

'Is that OK?' Maddie prompted.

'Just that that material was about looking for a link with what we have today and with what happened twenty years earlier, the thinking being that Charles had an idea who the bad guy was but couldn't back it up with evidence . . .'

'That's exactly what it's for.'

'And now we think that Michael Rix is highly likely, that he might have been the offender that Charles was looking for the whole time . . .' She fizzled out but her question was obvious.

'We don't know until we know,' Maddie replied, a grin breaking back out again. 'Someone very wise told me that once.'

'Inspector Blaker?' Eileen smiled back.

'Don't ever tell him I called him that,' Maddie said.

'You have my word.' Eileen was quick to scuttle away again, back to the only computer in the room, her update to a spreadsheet that was still in creation, visible up on the big screen. It looked like the beginnings of a system that ensured no boxes were missed. Probably unnecessary but Maddie never had a problem with thorough.

'Do we know any more about Michael Rix?' Harry Blaker had returned without Maddie noticing to make her flinch. It was Eileen that answered.

'I have a summary, nothing to add from my own findings yet.' Eileen's frustration was clear. 'For someone so important, it would appear he was not given too much time or effort first time round. I expect two competent detectives such as you to bring me a lot more to work with, however.'

'We'll try.' Maddie grinned at Harry, who looked like he was just about to have his own reaction. 'Best we try the sister again, then.' They had been unsuccessful earlier, knocking there immediately after leaving Debbie Rix. A neat house in a neat row, but no answer and suspicious neighbours had them leaving empty-handed. From there the only place that made sense was the police station to get every available detail on the man who was now at the centre of their investigation.

'Michael Rix,' Eileen started, her voice loud and carrying as much authority as she could muster. 'Not known to police prior to 2000, meaning he has no real criminal record to talk of. Not much to talk about at all really. His medical records are provided in quite some detail but the focus is on the physical injuries he sustained.'

'What about his mental health? Is that covered?' Harry asked.

'Summarised for court as part of the impact statement but nothing for twenty years, so no way of telling if he is still suffering,' Eileen said and Maddie's mind flashed with the image of a living room turned upside down.

'I think we can assume the trauma hasn't gone away. His wife was very adamant about that. His medical records, were they just for the injuries sustained as part of Op Lightyear?' Maddie said.

'No, actually. The application was only for 2000 onwards but they seem to have responded with the lot. We know he suffered an injury as a child, for example, a damaged eye socket that also damaged his eyesight—'

'How?' Harry cut in.

'Biking accident, pushbike. We're talking of an injury when he was a twelve-year-old boy. He has had reduced vision in his right eye since then. Social Services had a record on the incident, they interviewed the mother at the time of the accident when it was referred to them from the hospital. The specialist was not entirely convinced that a fall from a bike could have caused the injury, but it was never taken any further.'

'The police never investigated?'

'No. The referral was filed at source for intel purposes.'

'Just in case it ever happened again,' Maddie said, knowingly. There was still a similar system in place for child injuries or any injury to any person where domestic violence could have been the cause. A hospital or GP would generally make the police aware for the incident details to then "sleep" on the system in the event that something else happened and a fuller investigation might be needed.

'Reduced vision. Victims with bells tied to their hands . . .' Maddie was thinking out loud about the case details she had read up on. No doubt Harry was thinking the same.

'If we're really considering him as an offender, are we also taking into account that his injuries were appalling? He was beaten just about as badly as anyone, diagnosed with Post-Traumatic Stress Disorder after.' Eileen spoke with her hands lifted to rest on her hips.

'We need to rule him out,' Harry said, despite Maddie believing that he was much further along the scale than that.

Again, her mind was filled with the image of the living room and Rix's wife's frustration at how he *beats himself up*.

'Did you manage to print those stills?' Harry said and Eileen clicked her mouse, the screen changing to provide the answer. The big screen was ideal. Eileen had taken a still from the CCTV footage that showed the man on the train who had accompanied Megan Laurence off at Ashford International Station — and his olive-green jacket.

'We should have seized that photo,' Maddie said, referencing the photo on Debbie Rix's phone. It was the first thing she had said when the front door had shut behind them and Harry was consistent with his answer.

'We can't have him spooked. He can't suspect he's anything more than just a witness or he could become a lot harder to find. Him and anyone he might have under his control.'

'I'm not sure that's going to make a difference. He disengaged with the police last time and was just as difficult to find as any wanted man, even with knowing his home address. It was a big reason why they stopped trying.'

'We won't stop,' Harry growled. 'Did you speak with uniform?' Another question barked at Eileen, another question she was more than ready for.

'I spoke with Acting Sergeant Vince Arnold, as you requested, who said, and I will quote, *I will add it to the list of jobs we've got that you lot can't be bothered to do yourselves!*' He then said something about how a Labrador has its uses after all and then, when expressing how much he has missed you, Inspector Blaker, he used a profanity and I think I rather scolded him.'

Maddie giggled. She couldn't help this one.

'You have my blessing to pull that man up on his language, Eileen, trust me on that.' Harry's tone suggested he had seen the humour too.

'I thought I might. Uniform are continuing with all the address checks for both missing persons. All family members for both Daisy-Mae and Megan have been spoken to with no significant updates. We have a missing persons appeal that has gone out on all social media outlets and local press, we have also contacted the nationals but they are very choosy. We're not likely to get any coverage as it stands. Of course, if we were to—'

'No.' Harry cut Eileen off, something she clearly didn't enjoy.

'Making a link to the Ugly Sisters case officially, to the press, would create a storm that would just muddy the waters, it could hinder us rather than help us out,' Maddie offered, taking the edge off Harry's blunt response. 'For now at least.'

'As long as you appreciate that without that link, the national press are not interested. They're just another missing person,' Eileen said.

'Noted and thank you for trying,' Maddie said.

'Megan's family are running their own campaign. They might make the link themselves,' Eileen persisted.

'They might but that's a spark that only really takes hold if the police agree. Right now, we don't need to be doing that,' Harry added.

'Right now we need to be heading back out to speak to the sister. Maybe grab a tea on the way and sit up on the address for her to come home or even for him to turn up there.' Maddie searched the table for where she had put her car keys, then reacted to Harry who had the start of a grin. 'What?' she said.

'We might have to sit still for more than ten minutes, so *best get a cup of tea*. Some things never change!'

CHAPTER 61. SHADOWS

I know how this is going to sound, which is why I left it 'til now, to a point when you have a good understanding of how I got here, to this time and place, and so you would know I'm not crazy. I couldn't just sit down and start talking about shadows and how you can't bury them to rot down like a body, or how you can't kill a shadow. You would have written me off as crazy from the start and to be honest, you still might. Nothing I can do about that, it's like my Helen used to say: all you can do is tell someone a story best you can, it's up to them if they believe the ending.

My ending is coming. I've known that for a little while, I know what it will look like too. Charles was my preview, see, a vision of what happens when you realise that a part of that shadow is growing inside you. I was assured a front-row seat for all his suffering and don't even bother saying to me how that was just a coincidence.

We buried Saunders in my garden, naïve enough to think that everything he was would rot like the compost. It didn't. Shadows don't rot but they do stretch as the sun allows, easily far enough to reach for Charles and to show itself clear as day on a printed X-ray. Charles knew exactly what that was and now I do too.

Every day that shadow does the same, brushing against the back walls like a tease then covering the houses completely, seeping in through the windows to fill the rooms behind.

You can't kill shadows. You can't run from them either.

CHAPTER 62

The trampoline was the only sound, a rhythmic pattern, three jumps, two-footed, one fall onto seat with twist, then three jumps, two-footed. It was a sound Debbie Rix knew so well — even deadened as it was, through double glazing. Her daughter's routine on the trampoline was just about the only thing constant in her life; the only thing she could rely on.

Her case was packed and at her feet, Mia's too. They were the reason she was standing with her eyes closed. She couldn't think about the next step and whether it was the right one or not all the while those suitcases were in her vision. But the fact she had packed them at all was a very clear indication that her mind was already made up.

This is going to kill him.

Those words swirled in her head. She had told Mia they were going away, a holiday, and that was kind of true. She'd booked at a caravan site a half-hour's drive away, chosen specifically because it offered the use of trampolines. It also had a clubhouse and a swimming pool, all that you would need for a good holiday. But the caravan she had booked was not for a week away, it was a three-month initial lease she had negotiated with the site to "see how she would get on". The moment that call was over it was official, she was leaving Michael, it was all planned.

He hadn't been home since. It wasn't unusual for him to disappear for days at a time. She knew he slept in his truck, even if he had somewhere else to stay, he wouldn't, preferring the solitude. He certainly came home looking like he had been sleeping rough, or at least sat upright in the passenger seat of that rattly old thing. She'd gone out to try and find him the first few times, told Mia it was just a drive that would help her get off to sleep — despite her never struggling — and then having to wait until she did before she could head to the really scary areas like the beach or the top of the cliffs, never knowing if she was going to find him asleep in the truck, or a pile of clothes nearby with a note saying *sorry*.

She never did find him. Now she didn't even bother trying.

Suddenly she found herself hoping he stayed away. Her decision to go had been sudden, her movements while packing the suitcases fervent, verging on panicked. He had been resigned when she had talked about leaving but seeing the bags packed, seeing this was real, that would surely spark somewhere. He was losing Mia too, the more Debbie thought about that the more panicked she got as to what his reaction was going to be.

'Mia!' Debbie called out. 'We're going!' She heard a cheer in reaction. Mia walked a big grin back in through the door, a grin that dropped away to confusion when it was only her mother stood over their cases.

'Where's Dad?'

'He's meeting us there,' Debbie said, praying she sounded convincing, putting back the difficult conversation planned for the journey, for when they were out of the house.

'Then who's that?' Mia pointed to the sound of a key working its way into the front door. The sound was distinctive when it was Michael, he always left his glasses in the truck and would have to rest his finger and thumb against the lock first as a guide for the key to find its place. Debbie froze, her breathing shallow and her body tense, not knowing what to do. Her sudden fear caught her out, the realisation of the mistake she had made in still being here. She hadn't seen him angry at anyone but himself for a long time but she still remembered what it looked like when she had got a glimpse of it being directed at her. It had taken her breath away. That was so long ago that she had managed to convince herself that it could never happen again, but the sound of that key was the jolt she needed to know that she was wrong.

She should have gone, thrown a few essentials in a bag and not hesitated. She could still have talked to him, but later, when some time had passed, when his anger had passed. It was still part of him, dormant for so long, but dormant wakes up.

Like a sleeping lion.

CHAPTER 63

'Esme Rix?' A woman peered out from the sliver of her front door, just one fearful eye visible. It widened, then flickered down to the floor and back up again like she might be sizing Maddie up. She wouldn't have been able to see Harry Blaker, who was just off Maddie's right shoulder.

'No, sorry. Not here,' the woman said in a far-from-convincing tone. Maddie already had her toe in the door, something she did as second nature these days (as was pointed out on a recent visit to an aunt) and she felt it squidge against the leather of her shoe. 'Could you . . . ?' The woman flashed angry but it was fragile, Maddie might only need a word for her to break into pieces.

'Sorry, habit!' Maddie let the door close then met eyes with Harry, his concealment behind the door hadn't been planned but it had been lucky. One glimpse of the hulking, scarred and sombre Harry Blaker and Esme might have folded completely. 'We're worried about Michael, we're police officers and we just want to find him to make sure he's OK.' Maddie raised her voice, her mouth so close to the door that the words bounced straight off the solid wood to make her lips tingle. There was no reaction.

Maddie allowed a moment for contemplation where Harry had lifted his fist in a clear gesture that he wanted to start hammering. That wasn't the way to get in, not here. Esme really would fall to pieces and Maddie reached out to stop him. It might have been as long as half a minute until she was proven right. The door clicked then pulled open, the sliver of face that appeared was even smaller but Maddie was closer, close enough to stare directly into a big, brown eye that shifted nervously in a watery surround.

'Police officers?' the woman said.

'I'm Detective Inspector Maddie Ives, Detective Inspector Harry Blaker is just off camera there.' She nodded to her right, fixing a smile that contrasted with the ultra-serious expression on the warrant card she held up to seal the deal. It worked enough for the door to open a little more, enough for Maddie to see the woman in full at least.

'He goes missing, always has.' She shrugged painfully thin shoulders, her shoulder bones threatening to cut through the flimsy material of a plain white T-shirt. She had brown hair tinged with grey, the impression overall was of someone older than Maddie had considered at first, mid to late fifties perhaps. She had a tight ponytail, her hair long enough to wrap around itself and act as its own tie. Maddie reckoned those eyes could be spectacular if she cut loose, or at least relaxed a little. A little more flesh around those high cheekbones wouldn't hurt either.

'Are you OK?' Maddie said, switching the emphasis from her brother.

'Me?' Clear surprise in her voice. 'I'm OK.'

'You look a little upset?'

'My brother's missing, I'm concerned.'

'Can we step in? We could do with your help to find him so we all know he's safe and well.' Maddie waited out a long pause, her question was worded for no wriggle room. There could be no refusal.

'My . . . My other half has gone out but he will be home soon . . .' the woman said. 'He won't like it that you're here.'

Her fragility seemed to peak and Maddie leaned in to press home an advantage.

'Well, your missing brother and the fact that it is my job to find him is none of his *fucking* business now, is it? I'll tell him that too, if he needs it explained. We just need a minute.' The woman stepped back, perhaps perceiving Maddie's determination as aggression, but whatever, it worked. Maddie moved forward, aware that Harry was close behind her.

The home opened up, a large hallway with white walls and light carpet. The walls had a smattering of pictures, every one of them of the couple that lived here, every one of them showing a stout-looking man, younger by ten years at least, with a shaven head and arms tight around the tiny waist of the woman who was still edging away in her own hallway.

'How's Scott doing? I didn't know he was out of prison,' Maddie said, turning to take in Esme's reaction. The woman's eyes flared again, then they snatched away to the picture Maddie had last looked at. 'You know about his prison stretch, right?'

'Of course.' She was lying, no doubt.

'I know his last girlfriend, his ex-girlfriend at least. I met her at the hospital just after she had her jaw wired.' Maddie lifted a finger to tap on the photo of the stout man. 'Scott Harkness beat her so bad that she still gets headaches and she can't close her mouth up tight. The surgeon said that might improve, but it might not. He definitely has a type.' Maddie now made a show of looking Esme up and down.

'You said something about my brother?' she snapped.

'I did, but now I'm worried about you both, Esme. Are you married? Is that how come I got your name wrong?'

'You don't need to worry about me. I don't have much time either, can you just ask your questions?'

'His wife says Michael Rix comes here when he goes missing.' Harry spoke, his voice filled the space. 'Is he here?'

'No!'

'Can I check?' he persisted.

'You don't believe me?'

'You shouldn't take that personally, do this job long enough and you stop believing anyone,' Maddie said.

Esme gestured, it might have been permission, Harry certainly took it as such to push past and make for the back of the house. He was instantly noisy opening doors and rattling handles. 'Just make it quick!' Esme called after him.

'Where might he go if not here?'

Esme shook her head. 'You tell me! He's not like other people, not like anyone. Most people move in patterns, they're predictable. I never know where he is, what's going on inside his head. He doesn't turn up here anymore, did Debbie tell you he did? Since I . . . for the last year at least he's not been here and even before that it was only ever a coffee out the front. You get twenty minutes with him on a good day.'

'So that's how long you've been with Scott, a year?' Maddie's inflection made it a question but she already knew the answer. Esme just shrugged but it was one of confirmation. 'He would have moved in fast, on the back of a real charm offensive. I bet you couldn't believe your luck, he's a good-looking guy after all, spends a lot of money too at first, wining and dining, probably a holiday in there, too. How long until you realised you're not allowed to see your friends? That you're not allowed a job or a Facebook account either?'

She stiffened. 'You don't know what you're talking about.'

'We both know that's not true.' Maddie softened her tone and stance. 'I don't want to meet you the same way I met his last girlfriend. Promise me you'll look after yourself.'

'Michael won't come here. We've never really been close,' Esme said, not promising anything.

'Since what happened?'

'Since ever. There's thirteen years between us, I was a teenager when he was born, my mum had a new partner and we didn't get along at all so I was spending as little time in the house as possible. I moved out first time when I was fifteen, I was back for a few months and then I went again. Sixteen

270

years old and living with my boyfriend and his family. I never went back after that.'

'So he's your stepbrother?'

'Same mother.'

'Is he close with your mother?'

Esme huffed, she seemed to lose some of her tension with it. 'Their relationship was complicated. The whole thing was complicated.'

'Tell me about it.'

'I thought you wanted to know where he might be now, not where he was thirty years ago.'

'Thirty years ago, that would have made him what? Ten years old. So where was Michael Rix when he was ten years old?'

'He had it tough, OK, we both did but he got it worse. My mum, she isn't a bad woman. It wasn't her fault, I really think she did what she could.'

'What wasn't her fault, Esme?'

'Is this relevant?'

'Yes. You're wrong about him, we *do* all have patterns, they're set by who we are, by what made us. What was it that made him?'

'Michael was an accident. I guess that's as good a place to start as any. His dad never wanted kids, Lord knows he didn't want me and I was already there when he moved in. He was an arsehole, to me, to my mum. I saw him do some pretty bad things, but the worst was when she fell pregnant with Michael. He drove her somewhere to get him aborted, made me wait in the car. The next thing I know she came back on her own. He got arrested that day, kicked off when she stood her ground. You know the bad thing?'

'Go on?'

'She will always say that she saved Michael's life that day, which I guess you could say is true, but he might have been better off never being born.' She lifted eyes that were filled with water and panic in equal measure. 'I don't mean . . . that sounds so bad, doesn't it! I just mean that he was never wanted, from day one. Mum tried but it was hard work, babies are hard enough but when Michael wasn't wanted, wasn't welcome even — Sometimes I think . . .'

'What?' Maddie said as Harry swept past, his heavy foot-falls now up the stairs beside them.

'That I could have done more. I couldn't wait to get out of that place and when I did go, Michael was only two. I knew it was going to be hard for him, even at that age I knew, how could it not be? I could have stayed and . . .'

'And what? That's not fair, to have something like that on your shoulders. I can understand that a fifteen-year-old girl needs to look after herself, I reckon Michael does too. It was your mum who was responsible for him, she should have looked after him. If she was with someone like that, someone abusive, a bully, she should have left him for everyone's sake but especially for her own.'

Esme's smile was sudden and she looked to be at her most fragile yet. 'You don't give in easy, do you?' And Maddie knew that her hint had been strong enough.

'I see it a lot.' Maddie shrugged. 'Women who were once kids seeing their mum getting treated like a piece of dirt, it normalises it, they think it's OK. Maybe they even start to think they don't deserve better. It still amazes me how many incredible, talented and beautiful women think themselves lucky to be locked in a tower.'

'He doesn't lock me up!' She huffed, like it was ridiculous.

'So you're free to leave, whenever you want?' Maddie said and Esme baulked, then fought to hide it. Maddie took her warrant back out, reaching for the stack of business cards she kept in the back. These were a special order, they gave her first name only, then details of a dry-cleaners' underneath. The company was real, run by a domestic violence survivor who knew how to handle enquiries when someone called for the *Maddie* that worked there. 'If you want to be free for real, you can call me anytime. There are so many things I can do to make it happen and it's easier than you think. There are women getting free every single day.' Esme hesitated but she did reach out with slender fingers to take the card.

'Dry-cleaners?' she said.

'In case Scott searches your purse and I bet he does. If he were to call, the woman knows what to say. It's a place I use, it has to stay between us of course. If ever you need to talk but you don't want to call me direct, or come to a police station call this number and ask for Maddie. You'll get an appointment. Bring some dry-cleaning with you. She has a room out the back where we can talk. And the best bit: great rates on the cleaning!' Maddie tried another smile, Esme flickered one of her own.

'I'll get my colleague to leave you his real details, in case Michael gets in touch. Will you call us?'

'Of course. I still worry about him. He does this a lot, I know that, but one day . . .'

'One day, what?'

'He just always seems close to the edge to me. I just wish . . . they couldn't have chosen a worse person to pick on, he was just starting to get a life, there was hope for him then.'

'They?'

'He was abducted, you know all about that, right?'

'The basics, what happened?'

'Michael had a girlfriend. She was a little older than him, not ridiculous and it was a good thing that she had a little life experience, she seemed to know how to handle him. It was his first meaningful relationship and I really thought it was going to be good for him.'

'Callie Marshall,' Maddie said from memory. That name had been included in the summary as the woman who had been found lying dead next to a barely conscious Michael Rix twenty-two years earlier.

'Callie, that was her. She was nice, poor thing didn't deserve what happened that's for sure. They were volatile, though, it wasn't all plain sailing. They were taken right out of their car, her stuff was still in there, her bags packed like she was leaving. That wasn't unusual, they were a bit off and on around that time. I really wanted him to be happy and to find someone who made him happy. When I was at home . . .' She faded out again for Maddie to prompt her.

273

'What is it?'

'You live in a house like we did, growing up, and you start to think that the world is not a happy place. That no one is. *Normalise*, that's what you said, isn't it? Then I got away, I remember moving in with my boyfriend and this whole other family and it was just . . . it was night and day. They *were* happy and I realised that most people are, aren't they?'

'Most of the time. Life isn't easy, Esme, not for anyone, but the right choices are what make it easier.'

'I don't think Michael has ever been happy. Never truly and that breaks my heart. Please find him.' Her eyes were watery again, this time enough for tears to leak down her cheek.

'We will. You're right too, he needs to find his happy,' Maddie said, lifting a packet of tissues from her trouser pocket that she offered. 'Just like you need to find yours.'

* * *

Maddie made her way back out to the car, starting the engine but staying put with the car idling, staring out through glazed eyes. Harry picked up on her hesitancy.

'What are you thinking?' he said.

'That Michael Rix is a damaged man about to be abandoned by his family and that twenty-two years ago, his first girlfriend tried to abandon him too.'

'And you think that could have been a spark?'

'I do. I think he killed her for it.'

'And not just her?' Harry said.

'Not just her. Strangulation is about control, isn't it?' She was thinking out loud, she already knew the answer.

'Popular opinion.' Harry shrugged.

'What if, twenty-two years ago Michael Rix realised he was losing control, losing the one bright light in a life that had been full of terrible violence and it brought something out in him.'

'Plausible,' Harry said, not sounding entirely convinced.

'And now he has a daughter,' Maddie persisted. 'A whole life. And what did Debbie just tell us?'

'That she's leaving him.'

'Another spark, Harry. He's losing control all over again. Daisy-Mae and Megan are in a lot of danger and they will know it by now, but Debbie and Mia . . .'

'They may not,' Harry said, now sounding far more convinced. 'Let's go.'

CHAPTER 64. CHARLES FIRST

Charles was first and I guess this makes sense. Charles was the man charged with hunting down Saunders and then he betrayed his own beliefs to seek out a very different version of justice. It seems logical that what was left of the man he put in the ground would come looking for him first. His wife too was in easy reach and so much a part of Charles that there was virtually no separation. Only they are separated now, one dead and the other held in a sort of living death, trapped in her own mind, their reunion in the afterlife delayed indefinitely — a final *fuck you!* for sure.

I think I said that this was no coincidence, that I would get to watch what played out with Charles and Betty before it turned on me. There's nothing worse than a slow death and I've had the slowest on record, I'm a tree rotting from the inside out so you wouldn't know it, some days I can barely stand on my own steam. We get our strength from the joy in our lives, people do I mean, so all my strength left the day my family did.

So why am I only talking about this now? Again, if I had started with that, if I had told you from the start that Ryan Saunders was more than a man, that I stabbed him to death and buried him but there was a part I couldn't kill, a part that has come for its revenge in the form of his shadow, what would you have thought of me? You would have thought me crazy perhaps, driven mad by this old house. But I can tell you now because you know the story better, you know the order of things enough that it has to make sense to you the same way it does to me.

Charles first, Betty next, my family after that to take my joy, my strength with them. Charles' illness was quick, a jog that turned to a sprint the moment it was spotted (and wouldn't evil react like that?) to spread out and steal his retirement, his *happy ever after*, a time that the Snows had talked about at our table, plans that included little more than freedom, a camper van and passports.

Instead, they got a sudden funeral for one with the other sentenced to spend the rest of her days in her own living room.

Betty's disease is usually reserved for those that are older and her decline has not followed the usual pattern. Sure, they say every case is different but hers is a disease with clear phases. The first of these might even be the worst and it was where Betty lingered for the longest time. Phase one starts the moment of the diagnosis; from this moment on, Betty was painfully aware that her mental capacity was due to fall off a cliff and there was nothing more she could do than look over the edge, wondering what the fall was going to be like. Betty and I had one meaningful conversation after Charles died, just one and it's too important not to mention.

Betty was at the point of meeting carers, not her idea by the way, something her son arranged. I knew him as James but when he knocked on my door, a year or two had passed since I had seen him and he seemed to want to be someone different, he was quick to tell me how *people call me Jim, now*. So, Jim it was. He was wearing a labelled shirt, chino trousers that seem to come up short, with pristine shoes and no socks and a pair of sunglasses that he lifted to rest on his head when he came inside.

'I want you to know that Mum's having carers in, as much as she needs for as long as she needs and I'm paying.'

He said this proudly, stood right in this kitchen and trying to stifle his reaction to the décor. I remember the silence, me waiting him out, thinking there must be more to it than that, that he must want or need something from me, but that was it. Then he thrust a hand out, the one that wasn't holding a mobile phone buzzing and whistling, for a shake that was as firm as he could manage and he was gone. I saw through him straight away of course, in his expensive trappings, with his silver Mercedes parked right across his mother's empty drive so everyone would know it was his. All he really wanted me to know was the *he was paying* part, so I would know that he could.

My meaningful conversation with Betty was just a few minutes after that Mercedes left. It was a visit that started out all sorts of awkward. We stumbled over a greeting on my doorstep, then I asked Betty Snow in and she made it more awkward by hesitating. But she did come in, giving me as wide a berth as my porch would allow. She loosened up a little when the kettle was on to make a coffee she insisted I did strong (telling me how she wasn't allowed caffeine anymore, not with her medication) and a reaction that told me it was far too hot when she made a start.

'James said he had come round,' Betty started and I didn't answer. It wasn't just that it wasn't a question, it was her expression, her eyes frosted like a bathroom window. 'He was talking out his plans with me, he's a good lad, you know, under all that bluster and bullshit that he seems to have brought back with him. We all knew everything when we were his age, right?' There was a focus, a switch pressed to clear her vision just like that, a focus right on me. I should say, that was the one and only time I ever heard Betty swear.

'We thought we did,' I said and that clouding came back like a switch pressed again, though there might have been a smile beneath it. I talk about this as a conversation but she wasn't there for me to talk, it felt like another occasion when I had been sought out purely as someone who would listen.

'She's round there right now, the woman who'll be caring for me, in my house. It will be just her to start with but there are others she will call on, when . . .' Betty ran out of words and I thought I should try and help.

'When you need them?' I said.

'We always know what getting older can mean. It can mean getting weaker, getting sick. I saw that with Charles and we have to accept God's plan. I've never been afraid of dying, I know what is waiting for me.' That switch flicked again for her to stare right into my eyes with enough force that it felt like it might push right through. 'But a slow death, losing my mind, my memory of Charles . . . my faith.'

I said something here, at least I started to. It was going to be something about how you can never truly lose those things but she cut me off and I remember I was glad she did. We would both have known it as a lie.

'I've spent a lifetime renouncing evil in all its forms and yet, here it is. I'm going to get sick, very sick, but I will not die. Not soon. I will be held in that house, a place that positively glows with the warmth of memories, but it will go cold long before I do. Charles is waiting for me, he told me he would and, my love, I am coming, but not before . . .'

Turns out I wasn't there just to listen, turns out I was there to do something for her, something that would stop my breath, my heart, the clocks too, it seemed.

'Kill me. Like you did that man.' Betty's focus was again unflinching, even more intense, pushing me back so I had to take a lean. 'Be merciful, deliver me to my husband and to my Lord before . . . before I am set in for the long wait.'

Another silence. This one not awkward, this one shocked and heavy, this one two people not knowing how to react. Betty must have known what I was going to say, though, she cut over me. 'And don't say you can't!' She dared me. 'Because I know what you can do, I know what you . . . I know what you're capable of.'

There you have it. *Serious as cancer*, Betty Snow wanted to die and she wanted me to do it. She came round to *beg* me to. I didn't have an answer for her but she reacted like she had got one. She stood up, clumsy enough for her half-finished coffee to slop over the sides and she leaned forward, her palms flat on this very table, the right one trapping a slip of paper and a key firmly enough to leave a scratch on the soft surface that you can still feel with a fingertip.

'But, if I did . . .' I said and I'm not proud that in a moment like this, when talking with a friend of many years about her deepest fear, that all I could think about was mine. 'Your will . . .' I said. 'When you die, the world will know what I did and then my life . . .'

'Will be saved! Along with your soul.' That was what Betty said and I tell you for sure, her belief was unflinching. 'I will forget this conversation, just like everything else. I will forget you and, when you use this key to enter my home at night, awake or not, I will forget what you have come to do. There will be no fear, no pain and no more delay.' That focus again, that stare to hold me tight. 'This piece of paper has the code for the safe, what you find in there is yours—'

'I don't want your money.' I still regret that this was my answer. It was true of course but she took those words and twisted them in her mind into an agreement. She heard me agree to murder her while she slept, I'd just refused to take her money.

'Thank you, Paul, for delivering me to Charles.' Her last words to me. It was also the last time I ever saw her smile. Betty Snow had a wonderful smile. She was a woman of great warmth and that glow she talked about in her own home, I can tell you now that it started from her.

I watched her walk away, watched her walk right out my front door and I found myself considering what she had asked, even considering that maybe I did owe her this. Betty Snow's deterioration was quick from there. The single carer became two on a rolling shift before the season changed to steal the colour from the gardens and the winter darkness that followed gave me plenty of opportunity to sit at my table, hands in gloves that reached right up above my elbows, toying with a kitchen knife like a baddie in a slasher movie. I would always sit in the dark too, like the world might know what I was contemplating if I turned a light on.

I did get as far as entering her home, twice in fact, both times to stand over her while she toiled in a restless sleep, her mouth contorting through scowls like she was in pain. Her chest thrust upwards a couple of times towards me, daring me perhaps, daring me to make that cut and release a soul yearning to get out and take its place next to her husband, back in the warmth. I remember holding that knife just like I had held it once before, both hands on the hilt, one overhanging the butt so I wouldn't slip when pushing it deep enough to reach her big heart. I can't tell you how close I was. Both times, my mind intervened, it flashed with what was in that will, with what it meant for me and my life.

And I didn't.

I told myself that I couldn't do it, that I wasn't a murderer, at least not the sort that could kill an old woman in her sleep. But the truth was that I was saving myself, my own skin. I was selfish, not wanting to bring forward the point where I would have to face up to my past.

But that time was always going to come. That time is now.

CHAPTER 65

'Just hold on to me, that's it.' Debbie pushed herself back further, Mia held so tight under her arm that she squealed in pain.

'What's happening, Mum? What's he doing?'

'It OK, it's going to be OK, everything's OK,' Debbie breathed, hoping she was sounding reassuring. But they were stuck, trapped, there was no more distance she could put between them and the noises coming from inside the house. This time it wasn't contained in the living room — Michael wasn't contained in the living room — the noises were everywhere and shattering glass was the latest to make them both flinch and squeal as the kitchen window exploded outwards from something thrown. That something landed a few metres away with a dulled thud on damp ground, the same damp that was seeping through the seat in Debbie's trousers. It was cold, freezing cold, enough that she considered Mia's shaking wasn't just out of fear.

They couldn't stay here.

They were under the trampoline, crammed in a space six foot by six foot. The base had a curtain of crinkled blue tarpaulin that concealed them, its reach enough to brush the mud patch left when the grass had died.

Michael was a sleeping lion no more. He had walked in, his head bent, his demeanour familiar as the same empty shell she had lived with for almost as long as she could remember. But a glimpse of the suitcases and he was empty no more, his whole form had filled with rage and too quick for him to hope to control it. Michael had taken a step towards her, his eyes full of hate, his hands lifted like he might be reaching out for her throat and she had frozen to the spot, locked in by those eyes. She couldn't describe it, only that she couldn't run, couldn't defend herself, couldn't do anything but wait.

Michael had stopped himself. His internal battle leaking out as a grimace, then a cuss before he had spun away from her like an invisible force had reached out from the living room to pull him back in. The first smashing sound was just a moment later, glass smashing, but with bass — more like a pop — the sort of sound that only came from penetrating a double-glazed window.

She had fled through the back door, meeting Mia on her way in to see what the noise was about. Ushered her back, told her they needed to leave, almost being overcome with panic when Mia had refused, insisted they go and see that her dad was OK with that stubborn streak that Debbie so adored.

'Hide-and-seek then!' It had been a desperate move, the only one she could think of. Michael was now expecting her to leave, he would see the back door wide open — see the gate a few steps away that she wrenched open too — and think they had gone that way. The trampoline offered the only solution, so many times it had been a safe space for Mia, that day it was to be more literal. Debbie had dived under, holding the skirt for Mia who had still hesitated, then grinned a little at the idea. 'We need to be so quiet, OK, we can't get seen!' Debbie said, while searching her pockets and turning up empty-handed. Her phone was on the kitchen side, she had known that already but desperation made her do it twice.

Then Debbie had stopped, suddenly aware of the lack of noise. Silence was the part she dreaded, it might mean an episode was over but she never knew what she might find. It was different this time, she remembered the last time he got angry at her well enough to know that it had been different, that the silence had marked a change in tack. Debbie waited; they both did. She could hear her own breathing, Mia's too that mingled with the breeze ruffling the trampoline skirt to make a ticking sound where a safety label flapped around the netting above.

'Can we go in now? I don't want to play anymore, I'm cold!' Mia's whining voice was low, barely audible, fearful. Debbie's hand shot out to grab her daughter at the top of her arm and to force a squeal that was far louder.

'You have to be quiet, I told you!' Debbie begged through gritted teeth. Her fear, her urgency, something had the desired impact and Mia rushed a nod then slunk away, her back against the fence to sulk quietly, any notion that this was a fun game now long gone.

Debbie crawled slowly to the far side. She reached out to lift the canvas skirt and get a glimpse back at the house, to assess a route to the gate, now that Mia might be more agreeable to using it. But their route was blocked and Debbie exhaled her own squeal, throwing herself backwards to recoil from the thick legs and soiled boots that were so close as to fill her view.

CHAPTER 66

Two more turns. Vince Arnold was driving, the siren howled, darting ahead to bounce off the tight streets of the new-build estate and back over the bonnet of the surging patrol car, the blue lights picking out weatherboarding on a house in the distance.

One more turn.

The tyres had a squeal, the sound more prominent where Vince's colleague had reached out to kill the siren from where she was sitting in the passenger seat. She left the blue lights on, the flicker now caught in the fragmented front window of the home address of Michael and Debbie Rix. Vince thumped the dash-mounted button to give an update on their status. 'Control, TA me please.'

TA: police-speak for *time of arrival* so the control room could note it on the call log and start to monitor the attending officers. The call had come in from a neighbour reporting a possible domestic violence incident next door; a disturbance at least. The informant said they had heard bangs before but today was the worst yet. They said that a family lived there, including a young daughter around seven years old. *Mia Rix*, the Force Control Room had confirmed. Then they had found that the address had been tagged by Major

Crime, the tag read that the male occupant — Michael Rix — was wanted by ADI Maddie Ives and attending officers should be aware of his warning sign: Violent.

The smoked glass ornament laid out on the footpath in a mess of window fragments was already enough to warn Vince of that. The front door was insecure, it pushed open with a dip of the handle.

'POLICE!' Vince bellowed, pausing momentarily for a response and getting nothing. 'WE ARE ENTERING THE PREMISES!' Another bellow, this time with no waiting, this time with a quick movement forward. The stairs to the first floor rose up the left side, his colleague made straight for them while Vince headed for the back of the property, finding a kitchen that took on the width of the house at the back. A door to the garden was hanging open, there was more broken glass and a darkened entrance to the living room. He stopped on the threshold, aware of a figure sitting silently in its middle, the sound of a passing car pushed through the hole in the living room window, ruffling the closed curtain as it did. The figure had movement, rhythmic, an outline inflating and deflating like it had just sat down after a huge exertion.

'Michael Rix?' Vince said into the gloom. It prompted a half-turn and eyes that caught in the weak light. 'You're under arrest for murder.' The light switch was on the wall, Vince found it without having to take his eye off the seated man. The light was sudden and harsh, washing a scene of devastation in white. Devastation that didn't end with the upturned furniture, toppled television and burst window. Michael himself had taken a hit or two, his nose ran with two streams of vivid blood, though that didn't explain the sheer volume of the stuff staining his top and running down his fingers.

'Murder?' he said, now turned fully, his eyes morose and empty and his head sunk to his chest like it was weighted. 'Is she dead?'

CHAPTER 67. HELEN MORGAN

I told you I was no writer and I can't even start to describe my panic when I realised what we had unleashed, what was reaching back for us concealed in that shadow. It was so much worse that I couldn't tell her, my Helen or my Jessica — who was grown up by that time — so they would understand. There was a breaking point — isn't there always? That was what Helen called it at least. Jessica was in her room, it was dusk, the sun just about to slip out of sight and I was doing the last checks that all the curtains were drawn. Jessica's wasn't and we argued. I told her every night to do that small thing for me. I know she called me crazy, I know she thought I *was* crazy, but I shrugged it off as a superstition and said how I was only trying to protect her. She argued with me and I'm ashamed to say that I lost control, that my panic took over. I only bumped her on the hip when I made for the window. I could see the sun sinking out of sight beyond her, the last of it visible through the gap in two houses on the other side of the allotments. Her bedroom had an elevated view out onto the row of conifers that marked the halfway point in our garden giving her the best view from the house of their shadows reaching back like long fingers.

I knocked her over. I didn't mean to hurt her but her fall was onto an upturned shoe and it made her cry out. Helen came up the stairs and demanded to know what the hell was going on.

No harm done.

That's what I said but I couldn't have been more wrong. She wasn't hurt, Jessica I mean, but the harm done was more than I could imagine. That fall opened up a wedge wide enough to split a family in two. Helen and Jessica on one side, me on the other.

'You don't understand.' I said that too, looking like a crazy man no doubt, I know I was still trying to get them curtains shut, I know I was panicking.

'Make me, then!' my Helen screamed back. 'Because I've had just about enough of this.'

And I tell you now, I very nearly did, right there and then I was ready to tell her everything. Every day I wonder how different it would be if I had told her then like I'm telling it now, only as a walking tour that would have started at the shallow grave in our garden.

But even as I write that down I am shaking my head. My Helen . . . I know how she would have reacted, I know she would have been disappointed; gutted even, maybe even scared. I couldn't take that, not her looking at me with all those emotions whirled up inside her and knowing that I was the one that had caused it. That was another reason — the biggest even — for starting this in the first place, for writing it down in order and in full, so one day Helen will understand and I won't have to see her face in the moments before.

Helen will see this now, she will see these words, read them in the order that they were meant to be told and she will understand; she'll have to. I know Helen felt *something* when she was in that house. It might have sounded crazy at the time but it will click, it will all make sense. She talked about moving — all of us — about leaving that house, how there was an atmosphere there, something about it that she couldn't put her finger on. We got as far as looking for somewhere new, Helen walked us around a show home when the swathe of house building was just starting out. Can't say I liked it. I remember thinking it was like a pebble on a beach. The site had been cleared, the bones of the first places were in, but only the one we walked round was complete. It was immaculate inside, all smooth, white and tactile. But when we stepped outside again it was back into a flat and dusty landscape — pebble on a beach. I was just kidding myself anyway, I couldn't move there, I couldn't move anywhere.

Betty Snow was deteriorating by then. She had fallen off that cliff and I thought maybe I could run, sneak out from under her nose. But then I would make small talk with the carers and that answer would come with a roll of the eyes: *She still asks about you, you know! I think she likes to know you're still next door. You two must have been close.*

But Helen could leave and Helen did leave, taking Jessica with her and there was not a damned thing I could say to convince her to stay. Nothing that made any sense. Everything was so simple for Helen, she gave me an ultimatum that made it sound like it was for me too: *stay on your own, or go with your family.* To this day she still thinks I *chose* to stay.

I remember watching them go. It was the evening and I had cooked a meal. By that time we only really ate together on a Sunday and this was the middle of the week but I laid the table out, made an effort with setting places. Things had been getting bad and I wanted us all to talk over a meal at our family table. I knew I wasn't going to be able to tell them what was going on but I *could* tell them how much I loved them.

I thought that might be enough.

They left before the food came out. The night had set in by the time I got back to the table, the food had burned, the shadows were as thick as they ever got and all that was left of the cheery flames of the burner was a layer of cooling ash.

The last of the light had gone.

CHAPTER 68

Debbie's lunge backwards was into her daughter, her elbow connecting with Mia firmly enough to make her squeal again. She kicked her legs out too, towards those legs, towards where the boots changed angle, where Michael was bending down and Debbie waited for those dead eyes that she had seen fill with rage in front of her.

What appeared wasn't her husband at all, it was a stranger's eyes, bright with concern and lit up further by a radio pushed upwards from where it was strapped to the chest of a man who looked uncomfortable in his squat.

'It's OK, I'm a police officer. You're safe.' A hand reached out; *POLICE* written on the top of the sleeve. 'Let's get you out of there, shall we? I'm Vince, is anyone hurt?'

No one was. Debbie stepped out into a weak sun that was dappled through trees and hazy through a low mist, adding to the feeling that the whole thing was unreal, like the end of a movie. She was still holding tightly to her daughter, feeling the warmth and a strong sense of relief wash over her.

'Mike?' she snapped at their saviour, interrupting where he was talking into his chest radio, saying how he had found the family, how they were OK. 'Is he . . . ?'

'He's going to be OK.'

'Is he still in there?'

'He is, but he will need to come with us. There's something we need to talk to him about.'

'He didn't . . . We're fine. He gets angry, loses control, but we know just to stay out of his way. I'm not pressing charges or anything, you don't need to take him away, just . . . Maybe you could just stay here while we get our things together. We're . . .' She looked at Mia, her hand flushed white where her grip had tightened on her mother. 'We'll still go on our holiday, yeah, give your dad a little space?'

'He's been arrested, Mrs Rix, for something unrelated. Detectives will need to speak to you, they are on their way. Is there anyone that can sit with young Mia?'

'Arrested . . . ?' Debbie broke away from Mia's fearful face. 'I . . . I have a friend; she works but she might be able to come along if I say it's urgent, but . . .' She glanced to the back door, flicking to the smashed window and the roller blind that had been pulled down at an angle for one end to rest on the windowsill. 'Is the house bad? I can't have her here, I don't want people seeing this.'

'I can have Mia dropped wherever you need but we do need to do this now.' He must have reacted to Debbie's change in expression, to the panic that was rising up again, because he continued. 'She's safe now; you both are.'

CHAPTER 69

Rabbit caught in headlights. An oft-used term in policing but rarely could Maddie have applied it more effectively than if she was asked to explain Debbie Rix left to wait in a police station. Things were moving quickly all of a sudden, Harry had gone to Ashford after receiving a call from the search team who had been tasked with moving outwards from that coded door off platform 4 of Ashford International Train Station. An earlier update had all but sunk their hopes entirely, the sergeant leading the search had compared the opening of that coded door to opening the wardrobe to Narnia, only swapping snow and forest for a huge area of railway maintenance buildings stretching in both directions. Some of which were still used, some were locked up and forgotten, some were derelict and falling down; but searching them all could take weeks depending on the level of scrutiny required — and what they were looking for. That last part Maddie had struggled to answer. It was Eileen who had pointed out the derelict building element, how that had echoes with those crime scenes discovered more than twenty years earlier. Maddie had agreed, confirming what they were looking for: the body of Megan Laurence.

When the call from the search team came she held her breath for the news. The sergeant had been quick with his assurance that they didn't have a body but he did have something a detective should see — and Harry had been dispatched.

Rhiannon was still out at the Rix address. She was tasked with talking to the neighbour who had called in a disturbance, trying to get clarity on what they had meant by *it happens regularly*. She would also be leading the search at the Rix family home, a key task that needed doing urgently in the hope of turning up a lead on where he might be keeping Daisy-Mae and Megan.

The remaining *key task* was the rabbit in headlights sat in front of her on the third floor of Folkestone Police Station, a room known internally as "the rape suite" because it was the only one kitted out with soft furnishings and, as such, was where they brought victims who needed a more sensitive approach than an interview room.

Debbie Rix looked like she was going to need more than a comfy place to sit. The comfy place in question was a three-piece suite and, in truth, it wasn't that soft. It was synthetic leather, black — a colour choice hardly adding cheer — that crinkled and squeaked with the slightest movement. The room had its own kettle and fridge, the milk was on the turn but it would do, the taste disguised by two sugars that Maddie hadn't asked if Debbie took. She looked like she could do with it.

'How are you feeling, Debbie?' Maddie started. There was a low table between them, Maddie was sitting on the single sofa of the set. Debbie was a slight woman, even more so with her shoulders hunched forward, her head hanging between them and with the larger sofa as her backdrop.

'Murder?' She lifted her head, it looked like an effort. 'That's what you said, right? About Michael.'

'What do you think about that?' Maddie replied.

'No.' She shook her head too, doubling down on her answer, two versions of *no*. But Maddie got the feeling it was more to convince herself than anyone else.

'I spoke to the patrol that found you, that went out to your house and found Michael too. They described your

293

house to me, what Michael had done to it. Sergeant Arnold found you and Mia, he told me he found you cowering under a trampoline in your own garden.' There was no question, Maddie was sure it didn't need one.

'I know how it looks.'

'How does it look?' Maddie said.

'Like Michael's violent, like he's out of control, but . . .'

'Your house is destroyed, windows and televisions smashed, upturned furniture, broken plates . . . He was out of control, Debbie, you can tell me what you want about him in general, but today he was out of control.'

'OK,' Debbie said, a flash of annoyance, not agreement. 'He came home and my bag was packed, *our* bags were packed. I'm leaving him, his family are walking away from him and he got angry, you can't blame him for that . . . It's almost nice to know he still can . . .'

'What do you mean?'

'Michael, his problems . . . he's just like an empty vessel. It's been getting worse, it's like there's no emotion inside him and then it all comes at once to overwhelm him. That's when he punishes himself, but he takes himself away from me, from us both.' She lifted her eyes for the last few words, sure to make eye contact.

'Your neighbour told us it's a regular occurrence, the sounds of banging, smashing—'

'They need to keep their nose out of other people's business! They don't understand, they can't understand,' Debbie snapped.

'What about Mandy?' There was a reaction to that name, one Debbie swallowed after a moment's consideration. 'She was quite happy to declare herself your best friend. Sergeant Arnold dropped Mia to her, she was happy to speak to me on the phone. She's a nice woman, good for you, very supportive.'

'Is she?' More anger.

'You do feel threatened by Michael, you told her that. You told her that he takes it out on himself, that it's a form of self-harm linked to his PTSD, but you also told her that some-times the way he looks at you, you're not entirely convinced he wouldn't lose his control enough that you might get hurt.'

'He doesn't hurt me! You don't understand what that man went through, either, what happened to him . . .'

'What did happen?' Maddie was softer, she sat back too, showing her willingness to listen.

'You should know better than me!'

'Not the impact it had on him, I can't know that. You've been with Michael every day since, you've seen what it's done to him.' Maddie got no response. She would need an easy question. 'You got together a short time after he was abducted, is that right?'

'Years,' Debbie snapped, then seemed to calm herself down. 'About three years after.'

'What happened to him? What do you understand?'

'He was abducted.' Another snap of anger, then a pause to come back softer. 'He was taken from his car. He'd parked up with his girlfriend, he was young but old enough to be in love, to know that he was. They both were. They were grabbed and knocked out, drugged he reckons, then taken somewhere. They were tied up, blindfolded and beaten if they made a noise.' Debbie's anger was building again. 'Oh, and they had bells tied to them, you know, just to be sure that being quiet was impossible. Michael laid out there for days, freezing cold, waiting for you lot to work out what was going on and come rescue him. But you didn't. His girlfriend was beaten to death a few inches away from him and he got to hear *every single blow*. He was beaten too, left for dead himself, beaten so bad his eye socket collapsed. It's a miracle he can still see at all, it's a miracle he's alive at all . . .' She seemed to run out of steam, her eyes suddenly watery, the tears more likely fuelled by anger than sadness.

'You have every right to be angry. What happened was unacceptable, it was before my time doing this job but that doesn't mean I don't know about it, anyone in this station will tell you it's the worst case to ever happen on our patch.'

'And you never found him! The man that did it, he got off scot-free, didn't he? Have you any idea the damage that did, the damage that *still* does?'

'I can only imagine. But what if we have found him, Debbie, and what if Michael knew what had really happened all along?' Debbie's head was shaking, it stopped. She had been breathing heavily and that stopped too, like she was holding her breath. She lifted her head to study Maddie closely, her eyes narrowing.

'No,' she said, leaning in to get a closer look. 'You're saying Michael? You're saying my Michael—'

'Michael wasn't strangled,' Maddie cut in firmly and Debbie stopped, sat back a little like she might be ready to listen. 'Not like his girlfriend was, not like everyone else was. We think the killer had a sort of criteria and strangulation was part of it; a key part.'

'But that doesn't . . . so what . . .' Debbie flailed.

'He broke his eye socket when he fell off his bike, aged twelve,' Maddie continued. 'But he told you it was done as part of his abduction, when his girlfriend was killed?'

'That . . . he told me . . .'

'She was leaving him, she told him on the same day she was abducted from her car, did you know that? Did he tell you that?'

'They were in love . . . he said.' More flailing, this time it didn't look like Debbie was going to make it back to proper words, this time it looked like she might fall apart completely.

'Biscuits,' Maddie announced, snapping her fingers and standing up. 'I left them on my desk. Let me just grab them and we'll carry on.' She stared down the lens of a GoPro camera on a stand that was silently taking in the scene. Debbie had given her permission, but had hardly cared. 'Witness Interview with Debbie Rix paused . . .' Then she smiled over at Debbie before finishing her piece to camera. 'Because I think we both could do with a pause for thought.'

CHAPTER 70. THE FINAL VICTIM

When I lost my family, Rachel Cooper had been gone a good few years already but I found myself missing her more. I know why Rachel spoke to me, why she kept letting me back, why we got on so well; she was using me just like Charles did, giving me all the detail she could as a way of ridding it from herself, passing it on in the hope that it might dilute the taste of those memories enough that she could swallow it down. I take comfort from that. I felt guilty for finding her but maybe I was good for her, maybe I helped.

I can't tell you how gutted I was when I realised that there was a day when she had not coped at all, when everything must have come on top of her at once, when she had given up.

The coroner's report into Rachel's death was put out into the public domain and, by that time, it was all that I could get. That was frustrating; I had been spoiled, see, got used to being kept up to date with everything by the detective inspector leading the investigation, almost like I was part of the team. But Charles Snow was gone too, my direct link long broken and I had to make do with finding the report hidden in layers of the internet. Most of it was flimflam, flowery words saying the same, not much at all. I read it all a few times over to see if there was anything I was missing, anything between the lines that I might be able to take a little more from. There was nothing. That report, for all its flim-flam, had just two words of real information: *Verdict: Suicide*.

I went to Rachel's service, I wanted to, out of respect for sure, but another part of me wanted to find out *how*. I chickened out of asking the question of her gathered family and I am glad that I did. *How* would have changed nothing, *why* was all that mattered and I already knew the answer to that: Ryan Saunders. Rachel was just another of his victims. The thought of that, ten years after he had been wiped off the planet, made me so angry that I considered digging him up, just to desecrate him again.

The police reopened the enquiry when Rachel took her own life, something that made the press again, the media still referring to it as *The Ugly Sisters Murder*. Ten years on and they still knew nothing about respect. By then the police were calling it a cold case, which made me think about Christine, about her body at the end and the coldness that only comes with death. If Charles had still been alive for the case being reopened I know he would have worried. It meant fresh eyes looking into it all, asking questions when they couldn't find Ryan Saunders to triple-check his alibis. A man like Charles doesn't worry easy either, so it might have been catching, I might have found myself worrying too. As it happened, I barely gave it a second thought. The police were never even close. Charles made it his life's work to make it clear that Ryan Saunders was a man who intended on disappearing once the investigation was complete, even making it seem like it was the best thing for everyone if he did. In different circumstances or with a far darker sense of humour, we might have laughed when Charles told me over the fence how he had put himself forward to be the officer per-sonally helping Ryan Saunders disappear. There was a reaction, it wasn't laughter, more a stunned silence where those words forced us both to consider what *disappear* meant.

Sure enough, the cold case stayed frozen solid and the story fizzled out, replaced completely when some politician got caught with his pants round his ankles and his face in a trough. The *gutter press* couldn't resist and got back to their sneering and leering. Charles was right a lot, but perhaps never more than when he said: 'It's about boredom. People are outraged and determined for answers, until they are bored. Then they go looking for something else to be outraged at.'

That made me think again about Christine. The idea that the world would get to the point where the way she died wouldn't matter anymore was not something I could understand.

But he was right. And I am glad he was.

CHAPTER 71

Debbie wasn't prepared for the voice that answered. She called Mandy Adams-Wright the moment the detective left the room, desperate to check on Mia who had been so upset the last time she had seen her, still crying out to see her dad despite all that had happened. It had been enough to break her heart. And then, just one word was enough to break it all over again.

'Mum!' Mandy must have seen who was calling and handed it over. Mia's voice was shrill, fragile and excited all at once.

'Hello, my baby!' Debbie breathed. 'I was just calling to see how you were. Is everything OK there?'

'Yes! Aunty Mandy made me chicken nugs, I've got beans too but I think they must be different beans to what we have, they're OK, but I think I prefer our beans. How long am I staying here? Mandy said she didn't know. She said she'll make me a bed up just in case but I want to go home with you and Dad.'

'I know that.' A tear slipped down Debbie's cheek, catching on her lips that were upturned in a smile prompted by the chicken nugget and beans story.

'So, when can I come home?'

'I don't know right now. Me and Dad are just helping the police out, Dad might have to stay and help them a little bit longer, he's very important.'

'The policeman told me they were angry because Dad broke the TV but I told them that's been broken for ages and that I didn't even mind.'

'That's great, honey, I told them that too. It's nearly bedtime now, I'll ask Aunty Mandy to make that bed up for you, make it all nice and comfortable so you fall asleep nice and fast and by the time you wake up, I'll be in there with you!'

'Oh, well I don't know how big it is, I think you will fit, I'll make sure I sleep right over on the edge. Don't forget to wake me up when you come in, I want to see you.'

'Oh, Mia! I want to see you too. I love you so much and I am so sorry. I didn't mean to hurt you today.'

'It's OK. Aunty Mandy said it was starting to bruise. She said I'm going to look like a rag of muffin. I don't know what that is, but she said all the kids will think I'm cool!'

'Of course they will!' Debbie couldn't manage any more words, she could feel herself losing it, tears stinging her eyes were one thing but her daughter hearing her cry was another. The thought of her daughter bruised as a result of her elbow — accidental as it was — was enough to push those tears out. 'Could you put Aunty Mandy on if she's there, please . . .' Debbie said, finally, getting herself back together just enough. Mandy came on the phone.

'Ragamuffin! That's what I said, bless her!' Mandy sang, then instantly her tone changed when Debbie gave in to her tears. 'Oh, Debbie . . . I'm so sorry. You've had quite the day. Anything I can do, you know that, just say the word.'

Debbie sobbed openly, no longer feeling the need to stay strong. If she couldn't fall apart in front of her best friend — hell, her only friend — then who else was there? Mandy waited her out with the occasional tut. She spoke to Mia too, Debbie heard her tell her daughter to eat up all her dinner and how she was just going into the next room to talk to Mummy.

301

'What the hell, Debs?' Mandy said, the words laden with sympathy but still expecting an explanation.

'He's been arrested.'

'I got that. He smashed the place up again, I hear. Did you call the police?'

'No! A neighbour must have heard him. But that's not why he got arrested, he's . . .' She couldn't say it all of a sudden, the words just wouldn't come. Mandy told her to take her time. 'Murder.' It came out as a whisper, Debbie wasn't even sure her friend had heard it at first as there was no response.

'Murder,' Mandy said back, her speech distorted to project an image Debbie could almost see, an image of Mandy Adams-Wright hunched over, her bright red lips pushed against her phone, a nervous eye on the door in case Mia came close enough to realise the trouble her dad was in.

Debbie suddenly felt sick.

'Who?'

'I don't . . . all that happened all those years ago, when Michael was beaten, when his girlfriend died . . . they're saying he wasn't the victim.'

'Wasn't the victim? What do you mean?'

'I think that's what they're saying! My head hurts, Mand, my head feels like a washing machine, all these things just spinning round and round.'

'But he was beaten badly, they smashed his skull! We know what happened, don't we?'

'I don't . . . I don't know. Something that they said about his injury, something that he told me. I just don't know.'

'Did he go and see Paul? That's the name, isn't it? When this happened before, I mean.'

Paul. Mandy was right. It was bad now, the last time it had been this bad was a few years earlier, a period where he would come home having seen *Paul* and he would be agitated, nonsensical, even frothing at the mouth on one occasion where he was talking so fast. He would be talking about how this man had told him that he knew what happened, who was responsible but she could never get any real sense out of him. He never wanted to talk about it. He was so changeable, so unpredictable, his emotion coming all at once and then gone just as quick, like a dropped rock in a still pond.

'I haven't even heard the name Paul for a while. The police didn't mention him either, they were talking about twenty years ago, about those girls, about his own girl-friend . . .' Debbie was fighting herself again, fighting not to break down.

'Is Paul even real?' Mandy said, voicing a suspicion Debbie had carried for a while. 'Did you even get that bottomed out?'

'I don't know, Mand . . . I just don't know anything when it comes to Michael. How can we be married for fifteen years and he still feel like a complete stranger?'

'But a *murderer* though?' Mandy said.

Debbie's breakdown was complete when she realised that, really and truly, she just didn't know.

CHAPTER 72

Maddie knew exactly where to find a packet of biscuits, the packet she had told Debbie was on her desk. A white lie, but she wouldn't waste any time concerning herself over that. She was back in the same "Refs Room" where she had previously been greeted by PC Gibbons inhaling noodles off a spoon. He was missing but the older-looking PC who had snuck out behind her last time was present and correct, laid out on the sofa that she now realised to be identical to the one she had just left Debbie Rix sitting on. A job lot, no doubt. The officer's feet were up, his eyes shut but the tables were turned as this time Maddie would need to be the one doing the sneaking. She even went up onto tiptoes until she was in reach to pull open the only cupboard with a padlock hanging open.

Bingo.

The cupboard was labelled *Team 5* and several packets of biscuits presented themselves. Team 5 must be those currently on shift, and the sleeping policeman would be a — rather ineffective — part of that team. She took the rich tea fingers, figuring they might not be so missed as the custard creams or chocolate hobnobs.

Her phone was shrill enough to drown out the noise of the television that was playing to the dozing member of

Team 5. He fidgeted, coming round, and Maddie bolted out of the room with a big smile she couldn't help that almost bubbled over into laughter.

'Harry,' she said into her phone, her sugary contraband rustling where she had stuffed it into her armpit.

'We have a crime scene.' Maddie pushed through her second set of double doors, far enough away from the scene of her own crime to be able to pause, noting the anxiety in Harry's voice.

'We do?'

'Don't wake up,' Harry said, like he didn't need to offer any more explanation.

'Written in the places where victims were found dead, or where they regained consciousness . . .' Maddie recalled, out loud.

'In spray paint up on the walls in one of the unused maintenance buildings; bold as brass. Fresh too.'

'No one knew about it, it was kept out of the press at the time and never released,' Maddie said, still airing thoughts out loud while it sunk in.

'It wasn't. I made a few calls. Seems this has a lot of people very excited for that very reason. The only person who should know that calling card is the only victim still alive, or the killer himself.'

'Assuming they're not the same person,' Maddie said.

'And right now, with all that we know, that's becoming a better theory all the time,' Harry said.

Maddie agreed, and she said so, her eyes fixed on the stairs that led back to Debbie Rix who was waiting three floors up. 'This also confirms that we know what those women are going through, Harry, I can't stop thinking about that. Twenty-two years ago, the Ugly Sisters were dead in four days.'

'They were,' Harry said.

'For Daisy-Mae Adams, this is day four.'

CHAPTER 73. JUDGED

You will be judging me by now, that's what people do. It's all the easier these days too, seeing as how people put their whole lives out there to be judged. And yet we are still no better at judging ourselves. I guess it's easier to look out than in; even me, with all that I've done stabbing, killing and burying, I still find myself tutting at someone parked badly on the street or a stranger cussing out loud in a coffee shop. I am the last person right to judge anyone for anything and I bet if you were to think long and hard about yourself, you would see that you shouldn't be judging me either. But we still will, you and I.

Good people can do bad things, see — evil things, you could say — and, depending on who's telling the story, that doesn't make them a bad or an evil person. It can't, or this whole human race is nothing short of doomed.

CHAPTER 74

'Where does he go, Debbie?' The woman detective barked the question, reinforcing it when she dropped a packet of biscuits heavily onto the table in front of where Debbie was still balanced on the edge, hurriedly wiping her eyes. Something had changed in DI Maddie Ives since she had left the room and Debbie cursed herself for flinching. She wouldn't be intimidated, if that was now her plan. She hadn't done anything wrong.

'Michael? I don't know, I already said that.'

DI Ives didn't sit back in her place opposite, she paced instead, fidgeting with a ponytail tied high. When she spoke again, her aggression was a little more dialled down.

'It's happening again,' the detective said. 'I want you to think about that. You know as well as anyone what those people went through all that time ago and I want you to hold that in your mind, I want you to think about that before you answer me. Two more people are missing, Debbie, two young women, one of them wasn't even born when this happened the first time over. If you can help us stop this, if you can help us find him, you have to.'

Debbie was shaking. She didn't know why, she wasn't scared or cold but it was bad in her hands, enough to be visible. Adrenalin perhaps, the whole day getting on top of her more like. Any anger she had at listening to accusations about Michael, any desire to defend him, to shout and scream about how she knew her husband and she knew he wouldn't do that, any anger about being here in the first place when she hadn't done anything to deserve it, it was all gone, dissipated into the wind with that one phrase: *It's happening again.* She tried to speak, it was supposed to be a question seeking confirmation that the police believed Michael was responsible for this, that he had been responsible then and he was responsible now. But all that came was a confused mumble.

'Where does he go?' the detective asked again. 'Because those women could be at one of those places, right now they could be tied up, blindfolded, beaten and terrified. If you know—'

'He has a sister. She—'

'Esme. I spoke to her already.' The detective cut her dead like she already knew that Esme would be no help. 'Michael doesn't go there anymore, not since she got a new partner. Even when he did, it was never more than a twenty-minute thing, a cup of coffee on her front lawn because he didn't like going in. He doesn't like other people's houses.'

'I don't know where he goes . . .' Debbie felt another tear rush her cheek. She wiped it but another was quick to follow, her hand soaked enough that she could see her tears drip from her little finger. 'Fifteen years married and my husband can be gone for days at a time and I have absolutely no idea . . . And you wonder why I want to leave!'

'Days?' The detective sounded surprised. Then she said, 'And when he comes back, you must talk about where he's been, maybe you ask him or maybe he just tells you. He must say something that gives you an idea?'

Debbie was shaking her head. 'I know how that sounds, I've had this before, I talk to Mandy about it all, about what happens and she sounds just like you, she can't believe it, that's just not how relationships — marriages, even — how they work. But it's how we work. It's how we've always worked. I knew I was marrying a damaged man but I fell in love with *all* of him. Damage included.'

'Does he sleep rough? When he comes back home you must be able to tell if he's had a wash? If he's been missing for days then surely—'

'In his truck. He has a truck,' she blurted, she knew she was blurting. She'd forgotten about it.

'What truck?'

'I don't know! I knew you would ask that. Big, three seats in the front, a metal bed behind. He uses it to feed the animals.'

'What animals?' The detective jumped in with her question instantly, Debbie knew it was coming.

'Farm animals. There's somewhere he goes on the Alkham Valley, I don't know any more than that. He gets a few bags of animal feed and he takes it up there. He likes animals, always has, feeding them calms him down, gets him away from the world.'

'And you've never been there?' the detective snapped.

'No. He's taken Mia a couple of times, but not recently, that's dried up. I don't mind, I don't like him driving. I'm not . . .' She suddenly realised she might be saying too much, getting her husband in trouble. Then she considered that her husband was already in trouble. 'He doesn't have a licence and with his sight . . . He has his glasses but the doctor said he shouldn't be driving, not really.'

'So there are no documents for the car? Nothing you've seen at home that might have the registration on it?'

'No. I don't have anything to do with it. I don't know if he has insurance or anything, I don't know how he would, really. I know he sleeps in it, when he disappears, when he goes away he sleeps in that truck but he doesn't keep it at the house much. I don't know where it is most of the time.' The questions had been relentless but there was a pause now. The detective thinking over what had been said, maybe. Her next question was very different.

'I said *murderer*, Debbie, about your husband and you didn't tell me how ridiculous that sounds, did you?' The inspector sat back down, opposite Debbie. Her expression had softened, there was even a sort of smile when she leaned forward like she might be looking to take hold of Debbie's hand.

'Didn't I?' Debbie said. 'I'm confused, my head's a mess. I'm just trying to catch up with it all, trying to get what you're saying to sink in.'

'You're not surprised,' the detective said and it didn't sound like a question.

'I'm tired, it's been a long day, I want to get back to my daughter, she was so upset. She needs her mother.'

The detective seemed to soften further. 'OK then, we've kept you long enough.'

CHAPTER 75

'How's it going?' Maddie had a viewpoint overlooking the rear yard of Folkestone Police Station. She was still in the "rape suite" though Debbie Rix was leaving in the back seat of a marked police car that Maddie could see from her position. Harry sounded a little out of breath on the other end of the line.

'I'm just leaving,' he said. 'I'm going to secure the scene for tomorrow. We're losing the light and there's not much else that can be done. CSI are coming first thing but it's not a good environment for them.'

'How so?'

'Big, open buildings that are mostly insecure. The door was literally hanging open. Inside we don't have much in the way of hard surfaces or touchpoints.'

'So very little where you might leave a trace and a lot of ready-made excuses if you have.'

'Exactly.'

'Just like Operation Lightyear, when they never found anything to identify a suspect.'

'I remember the forensic summary from the time. The only contact traces they ever got were from the victims.'

'Which included Michael Rix,' Maddie said.

'What did his wife say?'

'It was what she didn't say that interested me.'

'Which was?'

'She didn't say that there is no way Michael Rix is a murderer.'

'Do you think she knows something?'

'I think she knows what he is capable of — and she can't rule out murder. I was close to losing her completely at the end so I called it. I'll speak to her again when she's had time to think about who she's protecting.'

'Makes sense.'

'She did mention a truck that Michael uses. She also said she doesn't think he has a licence, something I have confirmed on PNC.'

'We know the sort of people that make sure their cars aren't registered to them.'

'His eyesight might explain it in this case, his doctor might have denied him the ability.'

'Wouldn't that be on his PNC?'

'Not if he has never had a licence, you would need a record to put it against.' There was a pause, both officers thinking the same thing, no doubt. It was Maddie who articulated it. 'These are all things that we need to speak to Michael about. Did you get a message from Vince?'

'To call him back, I was just going to.'

'I did speak to him. Vince booked Rix in and got turned away. Custody skipper's concerned that he has a head injury and some cuts to his chest that will need checking over at A&E before anyone can interview him.'

'That's not ideal. Head injury?' Harry said.

'He was bleeding from both nostrils. It's probably just a whack to the nose but Vince lost the argument. He was very apologetic.'

'They'll always err on the side of caution.'

'I can't see us interviewing until tomorrow,' Maddie said.

'Have you heard from Rhiannon?' Harry said; hopeful, no doubt, that she had turned up a smoking gun.

'They're going room to room. The property search will mostly be done tonight but they're seizing computers and phones, interrogating those devices will take a lot longer.'

'Seems like we might be done for the day,' Harry said. 'Maybe that's not a bad thing. We should get some rest. Tomorrow could be quite a day.'

'Rest,' Maddie huffed, 'asleep in our comfy beds while those women . . . it doesn't bear thinking about.'

'It doesn't,' Harry said firmly. 'So try not to.'

CHAPTER 76. SOMETHING BAD

The night is here. Thick and heavy, the lights choked out, the garden a thick slab of black having started out as the smallest of shadows around the bottom of those conifers that has grown, reaching back to merge together and into something more.

I've been walking, pacing I guess you call it, agitated by something; anxious. I don't know what, I get that way sometimes and I'm pretty sure we all do without knowing why. You can read a lot into that, think that something bad is coming your way, hell, you can think it might be here already. That was a feeling I used to ignore as nothing, but not no more.

Now I know better.

CHAPTER 77

The noises had stopped, the creaking and squeaking that started out sounding like it was coming from the other end of the room, to then move directly above. She was being toyed with again, that was how it felt at least, someone revelling in making sounds that would have her cowering on the freezing cold floor. The draught was gone, it had been a constant she was used to, a nuisance that had stiffened her limbs and neck, prompting shivering that threatened the bell in her hand. Now its absence added to the feeling that something had changed, that something was different and that could not be a good thing.

Daisy-Mae was back to sitting up and still needing to lean heavily on her good side to stay there. The draught wasn't the only thing missing, the silence seemed thicker too, like there had been a noise that she had only noticed now it was gone. Just something else to add to her disorientation. She was frustrated too. She had been trying to work the tape free that was wrapped tight around the back of her hands, then over the ball to keep it in place. She had managed to work her index finger and thumb free on her right hand, just enough that she could move them both but only to press them together. She had been doing it constantly, praying that the tape was loosening with every movement and that she might be able to get that pinching movement clear enough to grab the tape that was so tight over her eyes. If she could see, if she could only get part of her vision back, who knew what was possible from there.

But she needed to stop, for a moment at least. The movement was causing a pain in her hand and it was threatening to cramp. Her frustration increased, threatening to bubble over into panic that she wasn't doing enough, that it was never going to be enough and she was never going to work those fingers free and she would never see anything in this world again.

Suddenly, smashing the ball on the floor didn't seem like such a bad idea after all. Daisy-Mae might not have seen what her hands were pushed up against but she had been holding it long enough to know its make-up. The shape of the ball splayed her fingers to render them useless and smashing it would surely give her more movement. She didn't know if it would work or how loud it would be when it broke, but if she was heard and her actions discovered it would surely bring forward her end.

Daisy-Mae was feeling ready for that, getting to the point of yearning for it. Her pain was worse and spreading now she was holding herself differently to compensate for her injuries. She couldn't just stay here, waiting. Megan had done that; she'd been talked out of leaving and now she was dead.

Daisy-Mae rocked to get a firmer base. The small bell rolled and tinkled, a sound specifically designed to be pleasant, the irony not lost on her in a space that seemed to mute anything cheery. She moved her arms out to one side, grimacing at the shooting pain from her damaged leg still tied off against her good leg, roaring up from its centre and into her midriff like a sucker punch. She stopped the movement, hissing quietly while it died down. It made her angry and it helped her make a decision. Something had changed around her, she could sense it and now she needed to be the one driving change. She needed to be helping herself out.

She jerked the plastic ball down into the solid floor, the force as hard as she could muster. The noise was like a dropped firecracker but there was no give, no change to the position of her hands, just a painful vibration that travelled up her wrists. This wasn't the time to stop, to wait and see if someone came in while the ball was still solid and she was just as defenceless. She had to assume they were on their way, that the final fight for her life had started.

This was it.

She raised her arms again, roaring from behind the sealed tape as she brought it back down hard against the floor.

CHAPTER 78

Maddie's ringing phone tore her away from the quaint-look-ing house on the screen of Vince's laptop. It was a front view, there was a garden path cutting through lawn to a modern front door and an established and pretty tree off to the side that shouldn't block any light to the big front window. It was beautiful overall and yes, she would like to go and see it. Vince would too, she could tell how much from the excite-ment in his voice as he described what they could do with it, bringing up the floorplan to show how the kitchen could be opened out, exclaiming at the size of the bedrooms and the room for a garage.

'I have to get this,' Maddie said, the name *Eileen Holmans* burned bright on her screen, just underneath the time: 8.17 p.m.

'Inspector Ives.' Eileen spoke instantly before Maddie could offer her own greeting.

'Jesus, Eileen, I don't like you calling me that at work, let alone at this time of night when none of us should even be thinking about that place.'

'Here's the thing, I didn't leave,' Eileen said.

Maddie had walked her phone into the living room where the fire was down to embers but still hot as hell judging by the feel of Alfie's fur when she reached down to scuff his head. 'Didn't leave, what do you mean? You're not still there?'

'There was a lot to do—'

'There's always a lot to do, there's also a time to do it and a time to make sure you're rested.'

'I know, I am sorry. It's just . . . I wanted to stay on and get your conversation with Debbie Rix transcribed.'

'Really, Eileen! That can definitely wait.'

'I just thought I would have a look at how long it was, how big a job it might be. That was when I noticed that there was a period of time when you left the room, when Debbie was on her own and the camera stayed running. She made a phone call. She was pacing, wasn't always in front of the camera but the audio is good enough.'

'She said something, something important?' Maddie's question was rhetorical, she already knew the answer from Eileen's tone, from the fact she had called at all.

'She called her friend, Mandy Adams-Wright, the woman we left her daughter with. Debbie spoke to her daughter first, then to Mandy. This was when she mentioned *Paul*. It's a bit difficult with only half of the conversation—'

'Paul? Paul who?' Maddie's impatience got the better of her.

'Debbie didn't use a surname,' Eileen said.

'But you have someone in mind?' Maddie prompted, certain that Eileen wasn't calling simply to tell her one of the most common given names in the United Kingdom had come up.

'This was a big investigation with any number of witnesses. There was a Paul who saw a vehicle that matched with a suspect vehicle that was put out, there was a Paul who was an ex-boyfriend of Denise Tutthill, there was a Paul—'

'Eileen, it's late and every minute it is getting later. You didn't call me just to list Pauls.'

'Quite, Inspector Ives. I called you to talk about Paul Morgan.'

'Paul Morgan. Who's that?'

'Paul Morgan was part-owner of the Ugly Sisters Nightclub, the place that two of the victims left prior to their abduction on Millennium night. You asked me to go through all of the written notes that Inspector Charles Snow made as part of this investigation, I should tell you, there are fourteen handwritten daybooks, he was an extensive—'

'Eileen!'

'I scanned those daybooks for that name and Paul Morgan is the only Paul to have made the cut. Charles Snow has written the following note: *Paul Morgan, part-owner of the Ugly Sisters Nightclub.* This note is circled firmly enough for it to have cut through the page a little.'

'OK?' Maddie said.

'The rest of the page is missing.'

'Missing?' Maddie was repeating words back so much it was likely becoming tiresome.

'Torn out. Quite crudely. The rest of the page.'

'Charles tore something out of his daybook in a major investigation?' Maddie said. She wasn't having that and her tone carried her disbelief. There are major no-nos in police investigations, actions that can lose you a case and perhaps the simplest example is tearing a page out of a pocketbook or daybook. Forget Major Crime senior investigating officers, that's day one stuff for brand new officers, something that continues to be hammered home for the rest of a policing career. Daybooks are evidential, tearing a page out is akin to the destruction of evidence, an offence on its own as a worst-case scenario, even the best case is that you provide the defence solicitor with what they need to ensure a jury can never reach the promised land of "beyond reasonable doubt": *I put it to you that this missing page is, in fact, key evidence, a realisation that my client was innocent all along but your investment of resources combined with the pressures from the press and the community were such that you were too far down a path to consider a different one, to consider doubling down, so you simply tore out this new line of enquiry, this doubt that you had and continued pushing my client as guilty of crime you suspect yourself he did not commit. Without all of the available evidence I have no choice but to call for a mistrial and for my client to be released immediately.*

Maddie didn't have Charles down as someone lax with any rules, let alone something of such significance.

'Someone did, that's all I can say. I don't know who or when, but the tear mark is clear, there's half a page missing.'

'And you think Paul Morgan is the Paul that Debbie Rix was talking about when she made that call?'

'I can only say that I was looking for the name *Paul* in Charles' notes and Morgan was the only one I found. Then I noticed the tear and I thought you would want to know.'

'You were right, that's good work, Eileen.'

'Also, I looked into Paul Morgan a little more and I think his last known address might add to your interest.'

'How so?'

'You've been there, almost at least. Paul Morgan was Charles Snow's direct neighbour.'

CHAPTER 79. LOOKING FOR TROUBLE

You can always tell police officers. I think I said it in here before, the way they drive their cars, the way they step out with their heads up already looking for trouble. I don't blame them and there has been a number of times in my life when I was happy to see them arrive if my club boiled over. I never called them for something going on inside the club but two drunks wrestling in the street enough to stop the passing traffic would have my phone in my hand, putting my call in when I knew other people would be too so I was sure to look like the responsible club owner.

I can't say I was happy to see them tonight, not out of the blue, not stepping out of their car with their heads lifted towards <u>my</u> house. They moved forward, that stride they all have, always somewhere to be, somewhere to get to. I never knew Charles to ever go out for a stroll, not even with Betty, every step that man took had a purpose.

Tonight, they had purpose too and I didn't have long to react. I made the front door first, sliding the catch, twisting the key, even dipping the handle so I knew the door would open easy. I just had the time to hide myself and wait them out. I felt a little pleased with myself for my own quick thinking. Unlocking the door meant they could push their way in and see a house that had been empty for some time. There could be no mistaking the feel of an empty place dominated by the darkness and the cold and there would be no need to come back.

They did feel it. I know that, I heard what they thought, I heard the confusion in their voices and then I heard them call out my name.

Had I called back, they would have heard confusion in my voice too, confusion about why they were here in the first place and what they might possibly want from me.

CHAPTER 80

This was it. Daisy-Mae heard the door pulled open roughly enough to smack off its housing and she flinched. But it wasn't fear that forced her reaction, it was tension, readiness for what was surely coming. The ball had broken, only not like she had imagined. She had hoped it would pop inwards like a blown egg, shattering into tiny pieces that would fall through her fingers, giving her full use of her hands back. But the ball had stayed mainly whole, the integrity held together by the wound tape. It had been enough to release her finger and thumb a little more, enough that she had been picking at the tape covering her eyes and she could feel a piece starting to lift away. Now it was a race, winning meant removing the tape before the logical part of her mind won over, the part that was telling her how there was nowhere near enough power in that grip and this was never going to work.

But it wasn't going to matter anyway. She was out of time.

The door slammed in a hurry, the footsteps towards her were fast — as fast as she could ever recall — anger powering them, perhaps? Good. This would be over quickly. That was all Daisy-Mae could hope for now, for a quick end.

Still sitting up, she was facing the approach, still picking at her cheek, desperation had her digging so hard it hurt. The raised piece budged a couple of millimetres to pull at her skin and she surely wasn't imagining a slight increase in the light. She still wasn't going to have a chance in a fight but she might at least be able to stare down her attacker, to force him to look at her properly.

'Come on then, do what you gonna do, you *fucking piece of shit*!' Her words were squeezed out, they were muffled, incomprehensible against the thick tape that still made her lips tingle. She was still clawing at her face, the tape seemed to be everywhere and she got a hold in a pinch, using the longer nail on her index finger against her thumb, squeezing as hard as she could muster. The tape came away a little further, this time there was no imagination necessary as she uncovered part of one eye, enough to see a shadow lurching towards her.

She lashed out. The movement throwing her further off balance, the tape flapped against her cheek and she struck nothing but air. Part of her vision might have returned but nothing like enough, the world was still a blur, just movement across blocks of shadow. She was desperate to get one strike in at least, just enough to count as going down fighting.

It wasn't to be. Her takedown back to the floor was easy, though not with the punch or kick she had been expecting but a firm grab over her mouth and nose that led her to the floor, the grip tight enough to hinder her breathing. The panic that had been pushed away by anger now surged back and the vibration against her lips was constant where she was trying to scream. She was back on her side, trying to roll away, still gripped tight, tape flapping away from her uncovered eye, still struggling for focus.

'Quiet!' A single word injected directly into her ear as a hiss and it stopped her screaming for at least the time it would take for a breath. 'Or he'll hear you and that's when he hurts you!' She was almost being cradled, that was how it felt at least, her head laid like it was on someone's lap, her mouth covered tight. The man — it was a man's voice — lowered her head all the way to the floor, gently. Then he changed his position, using his weight to keep her mouth covered, one hand on top of the other as a pile where she now lay flat on her back, his weight shifted so his stance was that of someone giving compressions. Only he wasn't moving, he wasn't looking down either. His head was turned, his attention straight up to where Daisy-Mae heard the sound of a squeak and a thud. Her exposed eye was watering and still not focused, the room was dark overall. She could only stare straight up, the ceiling was little more than a black slab but, in an instant, two lines of white appeared, like slits either side of a long, straight shadow. The white slits widened, closed and even moved in time with the noises above her. It was light, a light turned on directly above that was strong enough to bleed through cracks. *Floorboards?* It had to be.

The increase in light was enough to put some detail on the man holding her down, though he was still turned away, peering up at the same slits of light. She could see the fuzz of facial hair and part of a collared shirt that moved with his breathing. His hair was pushed down and out by a woollen hat that was dark red in colour and pulled down over his ears. She could smell him too. His hand had a smell that she knew — diesel mixed with something, she thought; she had smelled it before, in that room. The voice was distinctive, just as familiar and then it all fell into place: the man who had been laid out next to her, who had left to get them rescued; *he was back*! He had come back to hold her down, to tell her to be quiet after gently taking her to the floor. Daisy-Mae was so confused, her mind ran with scenarios, how it might be possible that a man she thought was dead, who had left for help to then take so long to come back. But he *was* back and he was helping her, protecting her from the noises above, from the danger that came with it. There would be time for questions, time for answers, but right now it was all going to have to wait.

The sounds above her increased, her eye shifted back to the ceiling, to the slits of light that still danced and moved.

She still couldn't see much else, the strong arm still pressing down firmly on her mouth was also blocking her view out. She heard voices, not enough to make out words, a shout — one word, a name, she thought — followed by more words that were lower in volume. She could hear two voices at least, one higher-pitched enough to mark out as different; a woman's voice, the pitch able to penetrate the layers between them a little better but still not good enough for Daisy-Mae to make out words.

She sucked in a deep breath through her nose, it was loud, loud enough for the man to snatch back to her, to lift one of his hands from her mouth and to make a shush signal with one finger against his own lips. He shook his head too, his big eyes were filled with something — fear for sure, melancholy too, she thought. Then his free hand moved to her cheek and she recoiled, instinctive, but the next sensation was a gentle tugging movement where he was pulling away what was still left of the tape. It pinched and nipped at her skin, at her eyebrows and lips, but in a few moments she had both eyes uncovered, able to stare into his better. He was holding his breath too and then, in response to the loudest thump yet from above, his eyes burst wider and a breath seemed to have been forced from him. They stayed staring at each other, exchanging silent fear in the darkness but also communicating to the point that Daisy-Mae was sure they were both praying the threat from above would just go away.

She knew she was, at least.

CHAPTER 81

The two houses where Betty Snow and Paul Morgan lived were the same in style and outward appearance but there was a difference that Maddie hadn't noticed the first time. That said, she hadn't paid much attention to Paul Morgan's house at all. Like most coppers, Maddie had developed a sort of sixth sense for houses and what was inside, based only on a view of the front. Betty's house would contain just her by now, the last of the carers would have left for the night: *We leave every night and just hope that she stays asleep for one thing, then wakes up for another!*

It looked like a house regularly visited by caretakers. One of the glass double doors that granted entry to the porch was pushed in slightly, enough to have a shake in the breeze. The porch itself was tired, the doors were trimmed in aluminium — something not practised for a quarter of a century — and the once brilliant white of the wooden surround was now peeling bare. The look overall was worsened by an exposed bulb, its light under threat of being choked out by a mass of spider's webs. Maddie could also see a neat stack of post next to a mess of a few weeks' worth of charity bags. No doubt a fit, mobile and aware Betty Snow would have cleared the porch, replaced it probably, but pulled the doors shut at least, as part of the last checks before bed.

Paul Morgan's house had a whole different feel to it. Something else the carer had said (and with a giggle) came to Maddie: *The man who lives next door that she's taken a real disliking to . . . I think she would actually be gutted if he moved away, who would she hate on then?*

The man next door. Maddie focused on his house, her extra sense screamed that it wasn't in use and hadn't been for quite some time. It wasn't just the obvious things like the lack of a car on the drive or a light visible from anywhere inside, it was the curtains left wide open in the upstairs bedroom to shout *empty*, the blinds too, on the ground floor that were tipped, not shut for the night. The whole place was cold and uninviting. The moon, which was making a battling appearance between the obvious rain clouds, threw a silvery light that didn't seem to touch it.

'You sure he lives here?' Harry said, voicing his own extra sense.

'No,' Maddie said, across the roofline of the car where they had both taken a beat to pause. The silence that followed was punctured by the sound of a distant train and a fox cry further up the road. The side of the house had a garage with a flat roof, sudden movement dragged Maddie's attention and she watched a cat stride across it with the nonchalance only a cat can manage. She made for the front door.

The knock got just the response she expected: none at all.

She knocked again, bringing her phone out, dialling Eileen for any other addresses or contact numbers for Paul Morgan, now fancying this as a waste of time. Eileen cut across her question.

'Michael Rix is available for interview! I was just going to call.' Her words were blurted, a loss of composure that didn't fit with how she had presented so far. 'They were able to get him assessed and there's no sign of concussion. He says he doesn't want a solicitor and has asked to be spoken to as soon as possible. He'll be ready for you first thing in the morning for sure,' she continued when Maddie didn't respond straight away.

'First thing? What about tonight?' Maddie said. 'If he wants to speak to us?' Maddie had been caught off guard, airing her thoughts as they came to her.

'Tonight? I didn't think . . . I mean, I don't know. Nights will be on soon, it will be a different custody sergeant, so . . .' Eileen's loss of composure now seemed more like excitement.

'He's due a rest period, but a prisoner can waive that if he wants to get on with it. Let the skipper know that we will speak to him tonight,' Maddie said.

'Of course, ma'am . . . You called me for something?'

Maddie had almost forgotten, her focus snapped back to the darkened door in front of her. 'We're not getting any answer, it doesn't look like anyone lives here at all, to be honest. Did you get any other addresses or contact numbers for Morgan?'

'I'm sorry, I didn't. That is his last known address but that dates back to the Operation Lightyear investigation. I ran a check through voter's, which still lists him there as the sole occupant, but that can be unreliable.'

'Dammit. OK, don't worry. That Michael Rix interview is the priority now, anyway.' Maddie reached out, pushing the door handle, habit perhaps, whatever it was, the handle dipped, the door swung inwards. 'Shit!'

'Ma'am?' Eileen said. 'Everything OK?'

'Sorry, yes, I'll come back to you!' Maddie stammered. 'It's open.' She spoke to Harry now, who was pushed up against the front window and on tiptoes to see into the room he had already called out as *living room*.

'There's a camera in the window looking out but it looks old. I don't reckon it's in use, it's pointing away from the front door,' he said with a shrug.

'I guess we'd better make sure everyone's OK inside, while we're here,' Maddie said and Harry gave a knowing grin that Maddie took as agreement. They moved inside.

Her first impressions of the interior were the same as the exterior: cold, dark, empty. It was also sparse, the only sign of a homely touch was a worn rug laid down the middle of the hallway that dulled her footsteps, while the exposed floorboards squeaked a little underneath. The dim light that was able to force its way in was perfect for highlighting patches of dust. Maddie saw the outline of another camera above a doorway that led into a kitchen at the back. The style was that of early commercial CCTV systems; bulky and out of place. Stairs led away up the left wall, on the right was a closed door, but with glass panels, so she could see through into the shadow-ridden living room. Inside was a long sofa down one wall and a small television set on a dusty stand turned at an angle like someone had needed to get behind it and had never turned it back.

A white flash was bright and sudden, accompanied by a thumping sound as a trip switch fell and a *tink* sound where the bulb over their heads blew.

'Dammit,' Harry said, his face turned up. 'That's what happens when a place is allowed to sit in the cold.'

It was cold too. Colder than somewhere sealed to the elements should be. 'I don't reckon this place has been heated in years,' Maddie said, a shiver leaving her body with perfect timing. Harry was already on his knees, his face in the first cupboard door of three that made up the underside of the stairs. She heard another *thump* sound and a beep from the kitchen somewhere that confirmed power had returned. Harry stood back up out of the cupboard to speak.

'Let's try switch number two,' he said and the word *two* was accompanied by a burst of light from the porch, still bright enough to have Maddie blinking. 'POLICE!' Harry then bellowed to assault her ears at the same time as her eyes.

'Jesus Harry!' Maddie said. 'There's nobody here.'

'Habit.' Harry shrugged.

'The carer seemed to think someone was here recently,' Maddie said and she made for the back of the house and into the kitchen. The ground floor was a mirror image of what she had seen in Betty Snow's house. Here, the moon through the back window was the only source of light and it lay on everything as a strip of bright silver, instantly banished when Maddie found another light switch. Harry trudged up the stairs behind her, the ceiling quickly developing a squeak. She moved to the fridge first, revealing a scant supply of food and a funk to suggest it wasn't fresh. There was a row of kitchen cupboards beneath an empty run of work surface that contained tinned goods and packets of cereal, all in date but some pushing it close. The dust was present and correct on windowsills and patchy on the work surfaces, but noticeably missing from a kitchen table that seemed to be laid out for dinner.

Maddie stepped to it, running her fingertips over chips, scars and even a cut in the wood. There were three empty plates on placemats, two with their back to the garden and one on the opposite side. The cutlery was laid out formally, there were name tags too, the one she could see said *Morgs*. Her eye was drawn beyond it to a wood burner with its door ajar. She pulled it open wider, the handle loose enough to come off in her hand and she cussed, then fiddled trying to get it back on. Opening the door had caused a swirl upwards that had agitated Maddie's sinuses, but it was dust she could taste and smell, rather than ash.

'Nothing upstairs.' Harry's voice cut through the kitchen to make Maddie jump so hard she dropped the solid handle to clatter against the floorboards.

'Jesus!' she said again. 'I think I might have got too used to working alone. The burner's been out of action for some time I would say.'

'The beds are all made but they don't look like they've been slept in for a while. There are some clothes in the master bedroom but they're stiff with dust,' Harry added.

'Someone is here, though, some of the time at least.' Maddie's last test was to feel the kettle, there was no heat at all and the gauge showed it to be empty. 'And there seems to be a dinner party planned.'

'Paul Morgan?' Harry said, picking up the name tags one by one while Maddie was pulling open drawers, moving along the work surface as she went.

'I assume that's his nickname but I can't find anything to put him here for definite: no post, no documents or bills, nothing at all formal.'

'We can get confirmation. The council tax system, DWP or—'

'I know that, Harry. I want to talk to him now, to get some clue on what the hell is going on. Paul Morgan might have nothing at all to do with anything, but I just . . . I just feel . . . I can't explain it.'

'You're following a hunch, Maddie. That's what we do.'

'And we're close to something, *I'm* close to something, that's what I can feel. But not close enough. What am I missing?'

'Who says you're missing anything? Last I knew you had someone in custody for abducting those women.'

'Michael Rix,' Maddie said and saying his name out loud fuelled her agitation. 'We might be able to speak to him tonight, Eileen said so on the phone. This is a waste of time, we need to get back.' She set off with a determined stride, forcing Harry to step out of her way where he was standing in the doorway to the kitchen. 'I'll send a patrol back here to talk to Paul Morgan at some point, there's nothing here . . .'

'But it could have been everything,' Harry was calling out after her, still from the kitchen where she now strode down the hall. It was enough to slow Maddie down almost to a stop as she considered her response.

'What if we find those girls dead, Harry, and all that's left is could-have-beens?'

'It happens. This game we play is always stacked against us. Surviving this career means learning how to lose.'

Maddie did now stop, the handle of the door leading out to the lit porch in her hand. 'How can you say that? How can you just be flippant when you know what losing *actually* means?'

'I'm not being flippant, not for a moment, Maddie, I know better than anyone what losing means. All I'm saying is that setting yourself up to win at *all costs* can be a larger price than you realised.'

'Is that what retirement teaches you?'

'Yes. And if they taught it to us earlier, then maybe less of us would have retirements like Charles Snow's.'

CHAPTER 82. FOOTSTEPS

Here I was thinking I was all out of confessions, but life isn't like that. I reckon Betty would tell you the same thing, that's why people of faith have to keep going back to ask for their forgiveness. Life comes with things you don't want to do, bad things even, but that doesn't always make you a bad person.

I am protecting someone.

That is not my confession, that sounds like a good thing done by a good person; my confession is that I cannot let them leave.

And I cannot protect her for much longer.

CHAPTER 83

Daisy-Mae was alone again. The draught was back, the blind-fold too and the darkness that came with it; everything back as it was. She and her rescuer had both waited out the sounds from above. She didn't know how long for but the noises had held her attention while she had held her breath, watching slits of light dance under footsteps that had moved away for a few minutes — long enough to take a breath. But they had come back all at once as a determined stomp, followed by lighter steps like the first person had a reason to be upset. There was conversation, mostly from the deeper voice, but still she couldn't pick out a single word.

She knew when they had left from her rescuer's reaction. It wasn't relief, more a slight drop in his agitation. Before her rescuer's appearance she had got herself to the point where she wasn't scared anymore, it came from desperation, from thinking she had nothing to lose, but his return meant there was something to be quiet for, a reason to hide.

She had a reason to be scared again.

His fear had been catching too. Daisy-Mae had whined a little when he had finally taken his weight off her mouth and told her he was leaving. She had begged him to take her with him but all he could do was promise to come back.

I will come back but you have to stay quiet. You don't understand what will happen if you don't.

Then he had given her some water, a chewy bar too, the same as what had been forced into her mouth as food before. He said there was a whole stack of them in the corner, even pushed another one into her pocket when she had said she'd eaten enough.

It had made her feel better.

When he left, there was a sadness to him. The fear and panic seemed to have drained away and she took it as a reaction from a man who desperately wanted to take her, to save her, but couldn't, not right then. But he would, just as soon as it was safe. She listened as he explained that he needed to stick the tape back down over her face, then wrap a fresh reel of tape over her hands and wrists — something he did tighter this time — to trap her hands against the broken fragments of the ball, covering over the finger and thumb she had worked free. She let him do it all, knowing that this time it was just for show; temporary. Her rescuer had got out and he'd come back for her, but it wasn't safe to move yet, she could see that from how panicked and anxious he had been to protect her; to keep her quiet.

I will come back. He said it again, leaving her clinging to those words. She refused to consider that she was back as she had started — her blindfold back in place, her movement even more restricted with her hands even tighter in their restraint — even if it could seem like that on the surface. She had taken a giant leap closer to getting out of that place.

She had to believe that.

CHAPTER 84

The first impression of Michael Rix was that of a disappointment. Maddie was purposely standing in the doorway of interview room three in the bowels of Folkestone Police Station, leaning out to prompt eye contact with the prisoner as he was walked towards her, but it didn't happen. Rix studied the floor the whole way, his custody-issue daps with their rubber soles squeaking out his progress.

She had been expecting more. She had seen the pictures taken of him when his injuries were documented as part of the original investigation, read descriptions too, all of which had portrayed a man who was tall, strong and determined. One description had him as *athletic* and *not a man who could easily be overpowered*, a note made when the narrative was that of Rix the victim. She could accept that twenty years had passed since then and that muscles can waste but she had still been expecting a spark in him, a defiance for sure, something that fitted with a man capable of such atrocities. What she really wanted was arrogance, a goading smile and a strut through the heady mix of cleaning chemicals and body odour that was a permanent fixture of any custody block, something to back up the idea of him being a calculated murderer who had been waiting more than two decades to even be accused.

Instead, it was a squeaking, scuffing sack of emptiness that lumbered towards her; eyes down, hands cuffed to the front to bump him in the groin with every step. Maddie spoke to the jailor bringing him.

'You can take those off. I reckon we can handle him without,' she said. The jailor rattled a bunch of huge keys, sifting through them to get to the smallest. Rix rubbed at his wrists the moment the cuffs fell away, his eyes still down, his shoulders still rolled forwards. He was in a custody-issue navy blue tracksuit, the material loose to the point that she could make out the shape of his spindly legs as he stepped towards her and took his place on the edge of a seat without being asked. The jailor shrugged his shoulders like he might have been disappointed too, then closed the door to seal them in.

Maddie slowed her movements from that point on. The air in a room too small for the purpose thickened even more, the sounds of her ripping open the DVD that would record sound and vision and throwing the case on top of the unit seemed unnaturally loud. The machine took its time "initialising" and Maddie used it to stand over Rix, not wanting to sit opposite him; not yet. It made no difference, Michael Rix didn't seem aware of anything external, let alone intimidated by it. Still his gaze was down, now on the tabletop and Maddie changed tack, taking her seat and leaning forward for a reaction.

Nothing.

At least it gave her a moment to size him up, to study him up close in detail. Rix's forehead and one of his nostrils were stained with dried blood that was flaking, a clump hung from one of his nostrils to shiver as he breathed in and out. His lank hair was pushed apart into a sort of side parting and long enough to conceal his ears. His forehead carried deep creases, his eyebrows raised; the impression was of a constant effort being required to keep his bloodshot eyes open at all. His facial hair was a mess — turning white where it lined his jaw — but with an orange tinge that was darkest around his mouth. The facial hair ran onto his scrawny neck to merge with mottled skin. He had a pair of glasses tucked in his top, one lens thicker than the other to the point of almost being cartoonish.

The door pulled open for Harry to make his entry. He'd been dealing with paperwork, wanting to be sure they had all the right permissions to interview a murder suspect who had displayed clear signs of mental health issues and who was still bearing self-inflicted injuries. Maddie had been surprised that the custody skipper had agreed to the interview that night at all, and Harry had flat-out refused to believe it. Harry's return came with a shrug that told her he had now been satisfied and he took his place beside her.

The questioning could begin.

When Harry sat, it was on his own hands, a stance that leaned him forward enough for his chest to brush the table. Every part of him looked restrained and Maddie cussed internally for not considering what this might be like for him. Harry had been the SIO for a case like this before, a killer that Michael Rix could turn out to be just like. That offender had taken the lives of the innocent purely for the thrill of it, he had revelled in the pain and the misery caused and had then made it personal by targeting Harry and his family directly. The results were still unspeakable. They had caught the killer in that instance but the interviewing part and the chance of any sort of closure had been taken away from them; from Harry. It had been for the best, there was no way on earth they could have put Harry in the same room as that man, but the parallels with this case hadn't even occurred to her. She found herself hoping that Harry stayed sat on those big hands.

Perhaps it wasn't such a bad thing that Michael Rix wasn't showing signs of arrogance or an intention to goad his interview team. Instead, his rising chest and the slow-motion mashing of his palms together were the only sign of life at all.

'Michael,' Maddie snapped with the intention of making him jump but getting nothing more than eyes raising up to meet with hers in slow motion. 'Are you OK?' It was a strange question, not normally the sort she would open with for fear of powerful scorn: *Of course I'm not OK*. But here it was instinctive, it felt right, a concern that there might be something deeply wrong with the man sat across the table.

'Yeah.' His first word. His head dropped with it. There was a subtle grimace like the movement had hurt somewhere.

'Your date of birth makes you forty-four . . .' Maddie said, another thing she might not have said otherwise. This got a reaction, not a smile but something close and it was clear he was ahead on what she was thinking.

'Hard to believe, eh?' he said and he was right. She had needed to check.

Maddie started the recording then ran through the formal bits to get one-word answers back, increasing to three words when she asked why he had refused a solicitor: *Don't need one*. He would need to be more fluent with the main part of the questioning, she was going to need to open him up a little.

'You look like a man suffering to me, Michael, like a man with the whole world on his shoulders. Today can be a good day for you, the start of shrugging some of those burdens off. Where is Megan Laurence?' She leaned back in, expecting those eyes to lift and reveal something, even when the answer might not. His expression did shift, but to confusion, a deeper furrow across the brow of a man she would have put twenty years older if they had just met on the street.

'Who?'

'Do you not bother to learn their names?' Maddie said. That should have been an angry question, she should be angry — furious, even — but it wasn't sparking, she might even have been veering towards sympathy, such was the pathetic nature of her offender.

'I'm sorry . . .' he said and Maddie waited for him to continue, for his confession to begin. 'That isn't a name . . . this wasn't what I was expecting?'

Now Maddie flashed angry. She spun away, reaching down for a large evidence bag with a vivid blue seal. She dumped it on the table. Harry took his cue, freeing up his hands to slide a piece of paper over. The evidence bag was clear, the thick, olive jacket with a furry trim to the hood laid out inside. The piece of paper was a printout showing two full-colour stills from the train's CCTV. The first showed a man wearing that olive jacket, sat next to Megan Laurence in a train carriage, the next was a short time later, when both persons were walking up the middle to leave. Megan was at the front, almost blocked out completely by the jacket that was now on the table. The man wearing it had a clear hold of her arm as he led her away in what was the last image they could find of Megan.

'This is you,' Maddie spat. There was no question, she didn't feel like she needed one. A solicitor would surely have stepped in here and demanded a question, maybe even asked one of their own: *How do you know that is my client?* And then gone on to point out the fact that the jacket in the bag was not a one-off by any means. But there was no unruffled solicitor. There was just Michael Rix, his bloodshot eyes almost completely hidden in a squint.

'I don't see so well,' he murmured.

'You have your glasses.'

His reaction was that of a man who had forgotten. He plucked them from his jumper and put them on, his movements cumbersome, taking two goes to get them straight, not what you would expect from a man who had worn glasses most of his life. The prescription was actually strong on both sides, they made his eyes look like they were being pulled out of their sockets.

'On a train?' The first sign of any animation but it was fear that she picked out from his words. 'Oh no, I don't use trains.'

'So that isn't you?' Maddie said.

'I don't use trains.'

'We seized this jacket from your house, your wife has a picture on her phone of you wearing it. Is this your jacket?'

'I do have that jacket.'

'It's the same jacket you are wearing in this picture,' Maddie said, quick as a flash.

'I don't use trains,' Rix said, his tone still devoid of any real emotion.

'Do you abduct, torture and murder women?' Harry's first interjection, his voice rumbling with menace that resonated in the small space.

'No.' Rix's reply was instant, unfeeling. 'But I've seen it done.' He lifted his gaze to fix on Harry — the first sign of any sort of defiance. His lips curled a little and for a moment Maddie considered that he might break out into a sneer. Harry rocked back onto his hands.

'Tell me about that,' Maddie said.

'I think that has been done enough, don't you?'

'You're talking about twenty years ago?' Maddie pushed.

'Twenty-two years, ten months,' Rix said. 'When *I* was abducted, me and my girlfriend. When *we* were abducted, when *we* were tortured, when *she* was murdered. And when *you* did nothing about it.'

'I can see you're angry about that,' Maddie said.

'Not anymore.' He shrugged and any sense of emotion seemed to be shrugged off with it.

'How *do* you feel about it now?'

'I don't feel. I don't feel anything, not for ages, months sometimes and then all at once . . . And then all I get is anger, it's only ever anger.'

'What is it that you're angry about?' Maddie's tone was marked in its change, veering back to sympathetic.

'You really need to ask that?'

'At us? Because we failed you and all those others? Or at your family maybe, because they can't understand how you feel—'

'You don't talk about them!' There was that anger, and there it was *all at once*. 'This is nothing to do with them, this is about me. Any anger I have is about me, towards me, *at me*!' He thumped his chest hard enough for a hollow sound to fill the room, there was a rustle too, where he had a dressing over a superficial wound on his chest. The clot of blood quivered in his nostril, effective in backing up his point.

'Why would you be angry at yourself, Michael? I've read a lot of what we were told at the time, a lot that Rachel Cooper said and there was nothing anyone could have done. The only person to be angry at is . . . well, the person who put you through that, the person who killed Callie.' Maddie leaned back in, studying him as close as she could. His eyes lifted at the point she mentioned his old girlfriend. They were wider, the effect of being pulled out on stalks even more prominent. But there was no other reaction. Maddie pushed harder. 'Unless that was you. That's the sort of thing that would make forgiving yourself very difficult.'

He fixed on her now, both nostrils flared, the blood again had a shiver. 'Callie . . . ?' He said, the word seemed like it had needed to be forced out. 'You think I hurt Callie?' There was something building in him now, Maddie wasn't sure what.

'Are you telling me you didn't?' Maddie needed him to say it, she needed a direct lie.

'I would never have hurt her.'

'And yet she's dead,' Maddie said. 'Her abduction on the very same day she told you your relationship was over. We found her packed cases in the car you were both taken from.'

'I would never have hurt her.' Another spark of something, still it wouldn't catch.

Maddie leaned away a little, crossing her arms to tell him a story. 'I work in a domestic violence section for most of my time and I see a lot of violence towards women — too much, I can tell you that for nothing — and you know what is always a pinch point, when the violence is often at its worst?' Maddie left a gap long enough for him to answer if he wanted. He didn't. 'When she finally has enough and tells him it's over. When the man has to face up to the fact that he is losing her for good.'

'I didn't hurt her, I would never hurt her!'

'What about Debbie? What about Mia?' Maddie threw herself forwards, her words like an assault.

'I TOLD YOU!' There it was. He was out of his seat, only just, enough to hover, to take his weight through his thighs, the strain quick to show on his face, flushed red. She waited him out, until he lowered himself back into his seat, back onto the edge. 'Please . . .' he said, lower, softer. 'Please don't mention my family.'

But Maddie had every intention of pushing her point. 'We found them cowering under a trampoline, laid on sodden mud, close to broken glass where you'd smashed the back window. That's violence, however you want to dress it up or explain it away. Have you any idea the damage that sort of thing can do to kids, to your kid, to Mia? So don't tell me you would never hurt those that you love, because you did it earlier today, didn't you?' A longer pause, this time for as long as was necessary.

'I get angry, I don't even see them, I don't even know who's there. We have a plan when it happens, a coping mechanism so my family stay safe, stay out of my way.'

'So they're not safe if they are in your way? Is that what happened? Did Callie get in your way? Did Daisy-Mae get in your way; or Megan perhaps—'

'NO!' His cheeks were suddenly as bright as sunburn, the loose skin encircling his eyes still white to give him a curious look overall. Maddie sat back, intending on another silence that Rix would need to end. Instead, it was Harry.

'What did you mean at the start? My colleague's first question seemed to catch you out. You said this wasn't what you were expecting. What did you mean by that?'

Those pulled-out eyes shuffled from side to side behind the lenses, like a man suddenly searching himself for an answer. He still wasn't looking at Harry when he replied. 'I don't know, I guess I didn't know what to expect.'

'But not that name, not Megan Laurence?' Harry pressed.

'I . . . I don't know that name.'

'So, there is a name you were expecting to hear?'

'I don't know, I don't . . .'

Harry was onto something, Rix was on the back foot and Maddie sat back, making it clear that this line of questioning was set to continue. Rix's eyes on stalks shifted to the noise of Harry slapping a piece of A4 paper onto the table between them.

'PC Arnold, the police officer who arrested you at your home address, he noted the first response you made to him. He wrote it down and offered you the chance to sign it as correct, as your words. And you did that. Do you remember?'

'I . . . I wasn't in a good place.'

'*Is. She. Dead.*' Harry read from the sheet, a photocopy of Vince's pocketbook. Maddie got a glimpse of Vince's messy handwriting as well as the initialled signature next to it, complete with a dried swipe of blood across the page: *MR*. 'That is what you said, isn't it?' Harry pressed.

'I said that.'

'Now you're telling us you've never heard of Megan Laurence. That wasn't who you were talking about . . .'

'No,' Rix confirmed, his voice almost a whisper.

'Michael, we only want the truth and let me tell you something from a lot of experience, only the truth will help you. Lies will trip you up, they will destroy you and they will destroy any chance you might have of going back to your wife . . . to Mia.' Rix now stared directly at Harry. '*Is. She. Dead.*' Harry said again. 'Is. Who. Dead?'

There was hesitation but Maddie could tell it was weak, she could feel the silence hacking away at it with every passing moment. It took another thirty seconds.

'Betty Snow.' It was another whisper, Maddie had leaned back in, she locked eyes with Harry in response, he was straight-faced where she could feel she was leaking her own reaction. *Betty Snow?*

'Did you murder someone called Betty Snow?' Harry asked. Rix's head was slowly moving from side to side before he could even finish the question.

'No, I said I wouldn't.'

'To who, Michael? Who asked you to murder Betty Snow?'

'Paul.' Lower still. 'I don't know his other name, I don't know . . . I don't know anything else.'

'But he asked you to kill someone? He can't be a complete stranger, that would be rather foolish.'

Rix's hands had been under the desk but he took them out now, resting them on the table to fidget with them. 'He knew I wasn't going to get him in trouble, he knew . . . he knew I wouldn't want to.'

Harry sat back, Maddie had worked with him long enough to know he was after a change of tack, a change in the questioning officer, too.

'There's something you want to tell us, Michael,' Maddie said, her tone at its softest yet. 'Maybe even something that you've been wanting to tell us for some time.' She paused, awaiting the eye contact that took just a moment. It was all the confirmation she needed to know she was right. He still needed a final push. 'What you went through, what Callie went through and all those others, you should know that it is happening again. That is why you are here, that is why you were arrested. We have reasonable suspicion that you were responsible twenty-two years ago, which means we also suspect that you know where two young women are, right now. If that isn't the case, but you know something that can help, you can quite literally save their lives.'

'I don't know anything about that!' Rix whined.

'We're missing pieces, Michael. We know someone called Betty Snow, I might know who Paul is too and we're here to understand who you are. What I don't know is what brings you all together. That's what you need to tell us.'

'I . . . B-Betty . . .' He stammered, then shook his head, more violently this time. 'I don't even know where to start.' His face creased in frustration. There were other signs there too, signs of someone shutting down, shutting off to the point where she might lose him altogether.

'We can break this down, keep this simple,' she said. 'Start by describing Betty Snow for me.'

'Betty . . . She's old . . . just some old lady.'

'How old?' Maddie said, setting him up for a question that really mattered.

'I don't know . . . eighty, maybe?'

'Eighty years old. So now help me understand why anyone might want to hurt an eighty-year-old woman?'

Michael's chin now rested against his chest, he had scrunched his eyes tightly shut but he lifted them to peer at her over the top of those thick lenses. This was the angle that first highlighted the scars running down the side of his nose and along the top of his eye socket, underlining the eyebrow on one side. It was a slightly different shape too; she could see it now.

'Mercy . . .' His voice barely above a whisper and Maddie leaned closer.

'What does that mean? When is killing someone mercy?'

'She's sick, she's really sick.'

'Why you?' Maddie's tone was low, still soft, matching with Rix.

'He said I owed him, for what he had done for me.'

'What did he do, Michael? If Paul has a hold over you, this is your chance to be free from that. We can help you.'

'He found him. It was supposed to make everything better, it was supposed to be better . . .'

'Who did he find?'

'I can't say any more, I won't say any more. I want to go to bed now.' Rix suddenly sat straighter. 'I want to go to bed, the man out there at the desk he said I could ask at any time if I needed to rest,' he finished through gritted teeth. The spark was catching, it was panic.

'You didn't do it, you didn't hurt Betty.' Maddie was careful, like talking to a child who was upset about monsters under his bed. 'Paul still has a hold over you.'

Rix was back to shaking his head, his chin rubbed against his chest as he did. His eyes down, shifting from scrunched tightly to wide open, his mouth a grimace. 'He had a key, said she had begged him to do it. He said I owed him, that I could have what she had put in her safe for him as some sort of reward.' Those eyes lifted to fix Maddie in the most intense glare yet. 'Killing what needs to die is one thing, but I don't kill people for reward.'

PART FOUR

CHAPTER 85. THE END

This feels like the end. I started out by saying that I'm no writer, that I only know a few of the basic rules, starting at the beginning is one and I reckon you also need to know when you're at the end. I don't want to be going on and on when there's nothing left to say, there's no need to be explaining the same things over again. I can't say I'm not relieved to be at the point where I think people will understand that we didn't kill Ryan Saunders. We killed the man, the flesh and muscle, that sneering smile of his and that lumbering walk he had like he was always stumbling away from a fight, but we didn't kill what was inside him. Not good enough at least.

All we did was bury it under the compost heap in my garden, close enough that it could reach back to show itself as the shadow in Charles' prostate, to rot his wife's mind and to push my Helen and Jessica away. I can't say I expected to get away free and easy but I thought its plan for me was different, not an ailment like the others but a grip instead, a vice that won't ever let me leave this house and won't ever let me be anything but cold and alone inside it. But just recently it had me pissing blood. I remember Charles knew; the moment he told me what he was seeing in the pan, he knew. I said how it could be a kidney stone or an infection, but he didn't listen, couldn't listen, because he knew. Just like I do now. My suffering will be the worst of them all. Charles' illness lasted just less than two years and Betty was standing at the edge of that cliff, looking over at her fate and waiting to fall for the same length of time. Then the fall was fast, angst and pain now overridden by confusion — her real punishment now is the delay.

But what of me? I can't say why I have been picked out as the one to suffer the most, the one to watch everyone else and to know so well what lay ahead. I can only think that my fate was sealed the moment I agreed to let it be my garden that concealed him. Maybe you wonder why I agreed to that in the first place and the answer is real simple, it was Charles' idea — the man with the plan — and he called it *separation*. Charles was sure the spotlight would fall on him at some point. I guess he'd lived a lifetime of seeing the police get to the right answer eventually. He said that he just needed to make sure that the spotlight, when it came, wasn't bright enough to show up any cracks. I guess that was where my garden came into it: *separation* doesn't have to be very far at all, just the other side of a conversation panel will do it.

Charles wrote the story that everyone could believe, only his story was contained in a file marked *case material* and in those A4 hardbacked books I saw him with a lot. Sure, others played their part in that same story, Rachel Cooper with the biggest part of all, but they were all just side actors to Charles. He was the man taking the words off them, he could control the direction, even where it began and where it ended. He could also control who was involved and he cut me out, almost entirely. I was just some guy on a list of people that didn't matter: the guy who happened to be the owner of the club where two of the victims worked. Nothing more. And Michael Rix? He told us everything we needed to get to the name *Ryan Saunders* but Charles played Rix's part right down to a man who refused to help: silent, damaged and of no use.

Ironic as it might be now with hindsight, but Ryan Saunders might have been Charles' finest hour. I might have buried that man in the ground but Charles buried him as a suspect in the minds of those around him and those that were to come after. That whole case file was nothing more than a trail of breadcrumbs, every one of them placed so it led away from the truth. It was perfection.

Perfection, that is, right up until Betty Snow and her billowing nightdress. What I didn't realise at the time is that from that moment on, this story became hers. Charles could lead his colleagues on a merry dance away from the truth for years, decades as it turned out but Betty, with her last will and testament, was always going to be the one laying the final crumbs in the trail.

A trail that leads back to Paul Morgan: the bad guy.

CHAPTER 86

Daisy-Mae had been still long enough for the hope to have begun to ebb away as the cold ebbed back in. She was back on her side, back facing the wall and away from where Megan was still laid out beside her. Daisy-Mae hadn't managed to get a glimpse of her fallen friend when her tape had been removed for a short time and she considered that her rescuer had faced her away on purpose. She thought back and remembered being sat up for the tape to be pushed back down over her face and being turned to the left when he had done so. Her rescuer knew they were friends, he must have been protecting her, not wanting her exposed to the trauma of what the poor woman must look like having been beaten until dead.

But Daisy-Mae had been left long enough in the darkness to consider that he should be back by now, that something had gone wrong. She had got a hurried view of some of the room, at least, a snapshot of the left side when her rescuer had shifted his weight and she had seen something against the wall she reckoned she was now facing. It had been a rack of shelves, metal-framed, the edges of which had caught in the weak light like silver teeth. It was the sort of edge that could help free up her hands, that might slice through tape no matter how thick it was wrapped. She had been trussed back up so that if the man who meant her harm returned, he wouldn't see any difference and would have no excuse to harm her further. But he had barely needed an excuse so far and besides, the ball she still held was in pieces, the bell stuck fast between her palms, that would surely be all the excuse he needed.

She needed to be rescuing herself.

With the bell restrained, a sideways slide was now possible in relative silence. Progress was still slow, however. Her legs were still trussed together, her damaged side little more than a dead weight to drag, sending shoots of pain up into her torso and beyond. She managed a couple of feet before meeting her first obstruction, lifting her hands together to confirm it wasn't the shelving unit but something that felt like a solid box just about low enough to roll over.

She took a moment, battling to control breathing that was suddenly heavy from the exertion so she could listen for noises. There was nothing.

The roll onto the obstruction forced her face-down into it. The sensation through her nose and forehead was of something padded, her nostrils flooded with the smell of old leather. Her numb leg suddenly felt like it had been dipped in hot ash and she pushed with everything she had to continue her roll over and off the other side, banging her head off the floor in the process. She hissed out her pain but there was no time to rest and recover. She pushed her hands out together, getting almost to a full arm's length when she hit something solid. She pulled the ball back and thrust it forward harder to gauge the noise it made: metal. She had made it. She shuffled closer, stopping when her shoulder bumped up against it, then felt for the lowest shelf, pulling herself up using a bent elbow. A little more feeling around in the dark and she found the edge she had seen. It made the right noise at least, a sawing sound, encouraging her to go faster.

The whole unit rattled, the sound far louder than she had considered so she slowed down, pressed lighter and was quieter. Still there was the shake and rattle of loose items, still there was noise, but it no longer felt like it was making too much difference.

'Fuck it,' she mumbled into the tape that had stuck to her lips since her roll over the padded obstruction. There wasn't the time to be worrying about noise, not anymore, she had to get her hands free to stand any chance. She couldn't rely on a *rescuer* anymore.

CHAPTER 87

'I told you it was buried!' Betty Snow's carer said, seemingly satisfied, standing hands on hips, watching Harry's exertion at trying to clear a path to the safe in the basement. It was a dumping ground down there. Harry's latest struggle was with a rocking horse and he growled away Maddie's offer to *cop the other end*. It was the final large item, the rest was small enough to be booted over to one side.

The safe was floor-standing, ground-anchored. Maddie had seen some like it before and reckoned it to be halfway up the scale as to how secure, maybe she would award an extra notch taking into account that it was in a basement that was well concealed. The short, sharp, steep stairs that spiralled down to it started in a shoe cupboard under the main stairs and had come as a total surprise.

Maddie supposed she would have to mark the security score back down considerably, however, when taking into account the fact that the owner had given out the code as part of an agreement that would see her murdered in her sleep.

If Rix was to be believed.

One thing she had to react to was the idea that Betty Snow was in danger. They had bundled straight out of custody to carry out a welfare check and security assessment that couldn't wait until the morning. The carer had sleepily disagreed on the phone, Maddie could hardly blame her for that. She had disagreed again when Maddie had said that she needed to check the contents of the safe while they were at Betty's home. If it contained an envelope stuffed with money then it might add weight to what Rix had said. Although Harry had a valid point when he said, *it's a safe, that's where you put money*.

Betty Snow still slept soundly. They hadn't woken her, all agreeing that it was best not to. The basement spread out to make a large space and, judging by the harsh light bleeding through from above, it included the space right under Betty's makeshift bedroom.

Maddie's attention shifted to straight forward, lit up in the end of her torch beam. The safe's steel surface glinted, the keypad too, with a mirror shine and she stepped towards it, punching in the code written out on her hand.

'Nineteen sixty-nine.' The carer was watching closely. 'The year they were married.'

Maddie had no reply. Hesitating at the final key press, the moment of truth. A clunking sound confirmed at least something Michael Rix had told them was true.

Maddie and Harry exchanged a glance, Harry's eyes with a glint from the torch.

'Money,' he said, having said the same thing numerous times on the way over. 'Has to be.' And Maddie pulled the door, letting the torchlight flood the inside.

'It's not money,' Maddie said, instantly.

CHAPTER 88. ONLY DEATH

The shadows lie thick in this house to keep it cold and dark. I am sick, running-out-of-time sick and I cannot leave. There is still hope, hope at least that my family can return to me, that we can be a family again, even if it's just for one last time. I've thought this one over, taken my time and still there is no way I can put into words what I would do for that to happen, for one more night in the warmth of my family, one more night like it was.

So I put it into action.

You're here now, you've come this far with me and you're still here and that has to mean something. I think it means that you will understand when I say that I didn't want Megan Laurence to die, not like that, with a steel crowbar popping her skull like how Jessica would open a chocolate egg at Easter and I certainly didn't want to be there to see it. The shadow always fills the basement first, it was how I knew where to bring those women for him.

I know what you might say, that I *snatched* those women off the street and you might compare me to what has gone before, to the very thing I swore to wipe off the face of the earth, but time changes everything.

Twenty years has changed everything.

There are some things you cannot defeat, time has taught me that for sure and realising it is actually quite liberating. Get over yourself and your own ego and you can start thinking different. That was what I did. To get what I want one more time, I needed to let Ryan Saunders have what he wanted — *one more time.* Saunders took two women from the Ugly Sisters nightclub twenty-two years ago and there was I, in the coffee shop made up of the leftovers from my old club, with two young women buzzing around, talking out their plans to anyone who would listen. It wasn't even an idea when I left that place, it was nothing, sat in my subconscious until the night when the shadow came to fill the basement, bringing a message with it. Two more was the only way, two more as close as the first time round, two more and he might finally be appeased.

I know I was right too, because the first time Daisy-Mae Adams made a noise he was here to take over, to react just like he had when Christine and Denise had made their noises, with a swinging steel bar and lying between them to savour his moment. I would know when he was done, he would walk me out of the basement and I would close the door to the cupboard under the stairs to realise that I was bare-chested. There were knife wounds in my chest and neck too, the same place where I had stabbed Saunders. Only my wounds were not as serious as his, enough to bleed, a sign that I was on the right lines. I do remember the cutting, the knife was left in reach, hanging on protruding nails by the doorway.

There is a mirror in my porch. The last place Helen would check her outfit, hair and make-up before she went out into the world; Jessica did the same too, when she got old enough to care. I never took it down, I never would. I walked to it when Saunders left me and assessed those wounds. I was covered in sweat too, that basement always gets so hot and it doesn't make much difference that I put a fan down there to run over those girls where Rachel Cooper told me about a constant draught. I stood in my hallway mirror soaked through, the time just right for the sun to come through the frosted glass of my front door and it made me shine. That aura I talked about before, I think I called it righteousness, it was there, wrapped around me. The final sign I needed that what I was doing was right.

A good man doing a bad thing.

I should tell you this too: it's a mirror no more. That glass wasn't reflecting Paul Morgan, not in those moments; it was a window through which I could see Ryan Saunders. The last time I saw him alive he had his shirt ripped off and he was soaking wet, with knife wounds leaking blood down his front. That was what I could see, that was what had been in my basement lying with those women, waiting for an excuse to beat on them with a steel bar.

I know that you will understand this by now.

He might have used my flesh and muscle, my sneer and that lumbering walk I sometimes have, like I am stumbling away from a fight. But it was not me, it was not my will.

Helen and Jessica will return here, to this house and before Betty Snow has the end to her story, I will have the end of mine. I had hoped that something might change when Megan Laurence died; Rachel Cooper told me how she got up and left because she sensed she could, because something dark and heavy in that room was suddenly gone and she said she felt it go. She also said she felt silly saying them things out loud and how I wouldn't understand, but I do. That same thing is here now and I will feel it when it leaves.

There can only be one reason why Saunders remains. This time the first to die is not enough. This time he means to kill them both and you might think that I will have played my part in that and that's why I wanted to write this before he does. I think you'll understand by now, I don't think you'll be reading this thinking that I could stop it all, that I could walk down into that basement, banish those shadows and save that girl from her fate. Sometimes I want to, all the time I want to, maybe, but then I remember what Rachel Cooper said, that one phrase that I know won't become a memory, no matter what, destined to repeat in my mind day after day.

If it comes for you there's nothing you can do, there's no point being scared, no point fighting even, you have to trust me on that. You can't stop it, the police can't stop it and I didn't stop it.

We didn't stop it either; Charles died trying. Now I am dying too and I can only hope that when it takes what it wants, there is mercy enough in that shadow for me to get what I want.

The only thing I have ever wanted.

CHAPTER 89

The tape gave all at once. Daisy-Mae's arms ached from the sawing motion, from the constant pressure needed to turn the upturned edge of a shelf into an effective cutting tool. She didn't know how long it had taken but she didn't think she could have kept it up for much longer.

There was no time to rest. Her hands were apart, coaxing out her right hand entirely was suddenly easy, the weight of the plastic practically pulled it away. She got her left hand free before making short work of the tape covering her mouth and eyes. This final action had her gulping air, then coughing where the dusty interior met with a throat that felt like it had been scrubbed dry. She was still thirsty, despite her earlier drink, the hunger pangs, too, were a constant backdrop to pain consuming her torso, flaring out from her damaged leg. But it didn't matter that she was tired, hungry and weak: she needed to move.

Her eyes were quickly accustomed to a dim room. There were two light sources, both weak, neither of which had been present when her eyes had been briefly uncovered before. The largest came in the form of flat panels lit up in shades of white at the far end, the other was a bulb almost directly above her, yellow like a hazy sun.

She took a moment to look around. There were bare, brick walls either side of her and the two ends of the room were painted a filthy white. The space was divided up into two rooms and Daisy-Mae was in the middle of the largest. The smaller room was directly in front of her, it was the space that held the lit panels, visible through an open, internal door that also revealed the bottom of a set of stairs. To her right, Megan's body was laid out on bare concrete, positioned just right to be saturated yellow from above, its hue filling eyes that had died open.

'Jesus, Megan,' Daisy-Mae said, out loud. She ripped her eyes away, chasing along the floor, searching for obstructions or something she could use. The stairs at the far end had to be the only way out. It was a long way to drag herself. Her eyes fell to the squidgy obstruction she had rolled over, a thick leather pad on a worn, wooden base.

'A pommel horse?' Again, she spoke out loud, the shake in her voice as clear as the cracking feeling as she worked her jaw. She'd used one just like it in a gymnastics class at her old school. This one was lower to the ground than she remembered, smaller overall. Studying it closer, she could see any number of fresh-looking scrapes and deep dents that she explored with a finger. 'No! No way!' She snatched away, jerking her hand back like a scorpion's tail. She started her search of the room again, this time it was frantic, more specific and she found what she was looking for almost immediately. Against the wall, leaning at a drunken angle so the shelving unit to her left was holding it up, was a steel crowbar. It took two shuffles to get to it, now easier with hands free and able to push off from a flat palm. She took a firm hold of the cold steel and spun back to the pommel horse, focusing on getting the best balance she could, then closed her eyes tight. Her next movement was to swing the bar as hard as she could muster downwards. She heard the *swoosh* through the air, oh-so familiar, but then, so was the next sound.

The steel end struck the pommel horse, the leather took the blow with a dulled thud; *just like the body blows she had heard land to her left, when her rescuer was taking a beating!* She had heard the shouts in pain at the same time and, with eyes covered, it had added together to create an image in her mind. It was a lie. The mark that had appeared on the pommel horse was identical to the others. Realisation came like nausea.

He had been lying right next to them!

Daisy-Mae was tired. Physically, every part of her that wasn't shooting sharp pain ached down to her bones, but mentally she was in knots, her exhaustion now at one with her confusion and her desperation. She was alone again. And she had been this whole time.

The footsteps! Her tired mind turfed another realisation out from its midst. Those footsteps could have been real help, real rescuers. Why else would he have held her still and silent?

Daisy-Mae found a tight grip on the marked leather to wait out the feeling that surged through her, trying to manage her breathing so as not to succumb to a full-on panic attack that would have her screaming as loud as she could. Time passed, long enough that she could start coaching herself.

'You're better off, Daisy-Mae, look what you did. Your hands are free, you can see and talk . . . and you can move.' She pushed the crowbar away and performed a clumsy roll onto her front. The pain was horrendous, the broken leg still sending searing hot jabs outwards. She waited it out, peering back at where it now trailed behind, still tied against the other.

The distance to her only escape route looked further away somehow, but it might as well have been a mile. She wasn't sure she was going to be able to move forwards at all. She waited out another wave of panic, it subsided enough for her eyes to settle on the stud wall that made up either side of the internal door and the black, tool-shaped silhouettes that were flat against it. Something she could use, perhaps? It fired her determination.

'One step at a time,' she said through gritted teeth, a grunt too, where she started moving forwards. It was slow going, her arms had never been her strongest asset and they struggled to drag her weight. She lifted her chest higher, clawing at the bare stone, her elbows scrabbling for purchase, kicking out with the heel of her good foot and disturbing her dead leg as she did. She could make out a cutting tool halfway up the wall, a hunting knife even, as she inched closer. The teeth on the perforated edge were large enough to cast their own yellow-tinged shadows. A broom, too, was leaning by the doorway and her mind hatched a plan to use one to get the other — she just needed a few more metres.

She threw another elbow out, grunting again, using her right arm to sweep the concrete of bits of brick, stone and grit that seemed out of place, scattered like someone might throw birdseed. She edged forward, fighting her own body screaming for her to stop. She only allowed herself a few seconds' rest when she was close enough to make a grab for the broom. Not quite close enough and she clipped it with her flailing hand, causing it to slide down the wall, clattering onto the concrete for the loudest single noise yet.

This time she got a reaction. It came from above: *footsteps*. Daisy-Mae froze, her neck ached where she was craning upwards and she had to roll onto her side to keep looking up at floorboards that burst with white light. The slits widened in a pattern that told her that the movement was directly over her and towards the stairs in front. The distinctive sound of a door pulled open at the top of those stairs was instantaneous.

Someone was coming.

Daisy-Mae scrabbled for the broom again. It was just out of reach, her fingertips bumped the bristly end that was closest and she lunged for a better reach, ignoring the pain that came with it, to get a handful. It was coarser than she had imagined, the bristles almost sharp and they dug into her forearm as she lifted it, scraping the handle end up the wall. It was just too short, the silhouette of the hunting knife tantalising. She prodded upwards to pierce its shadow but nothing moved. She tried again, straining to gain the inch she needed, but it was no good. Her desperation peaked and she threw the broom upwards to make up the distance. It was a good shot, a direct hit to change the angle of the knife slightly but not enough for it to fall. The broom clattered back down to land well out of reach. The stairs clunked, the sound of heavy footsteps descending slowly, coming closer, each one heavier; still her captor was revelling in sounds.

And it was her captor. Rescuers don't walk like that; ominous and slow.

Daisy-Mae couldn't give up, not now. She had got free and crawled the length of the room, what more might she be capable of? She spun on the spot, hunting for something else, anything else. Her eyes rested on the steel crowbar she had discarded by the shelving unit. Even in a moment like that she was able to stand outside of her panic long enough to appreciate the irony. The idea of beating him to death with the same weapon he had used on Megan prompted a grin that would have looked crazy for sure, coated in that orange haze.

She started for it, using her hip to pivot round, then flattening herself back on her front, throwing her elbows out again to drag herself forwards.

The footsteps reached the floor behind her, the sound changing from the clunk of hollow wood to a slap on concrete. She would be able to see him if she turned, but there wasn't the time, her progress was as fast as she could go but it was not to be fast enough. Her tied legs were an anchor dragging uselessly behind her. Then came a noise that did make her turn, a flat-palmed smack on the partition wall, both sides, firm enough to topple the hunting knife she had unsettled with the broom. That was a weapon that might give her a chance. She spun back but couldn't see it where it had been absorbed into a clump of shadow.

'No, no, no, no, NO!' The man filled the doorway, his voice strong, if a little strained, arms out like a star jump with both hands out of sight. The same man — her *rescuer* — only everything about him was different. There was no woolly hat or plaid shirt, his hair was free and unkempt, clumped together like it was wet, long enough for the ends to catch in the draught she now knew to be caused by a near-silent floor fan. He was bare-chested too, running with sweat, with hacks to his chest and neck that she knew to be fresh from the runs of blood that fanned out from them and down his front, soaking into his waistband to darken his jeans. He looked wild as he stepped in, moving towards Daisy-Mae who was now stranded between two weapons and unable to reach either — not in time.

His clumsy, lumbering walk arced round her and she could only watch as he made for the shelving unit. Here he stopped, facing away, his right hand rested against the wall, his head forward, his back rising and falling like he was breathing heavy. He dropped in a sudden squat and, when he turned to face her, he had picked up the crowbar for it to hang in his grip.

'You can't stop it,' he said, his tone different again, no longer dripping with fear, it was now . . . *excitement*. 'No one can.'

'Please . . .' Daisy-Mae uttered. All that was left now was desperation; the anger, the determination, the fight was all gone, all of it stolen by the utter hopelessness. 'Please!' she begged again. But she got nothing more from him than a shrug and the same excited words:

'You can't stop it!'

CHAPTER 90

Daisy-Mae had one chance and no time to take it. She threw herself back onto her side, back towards the shadow that she knew to be holding the hunting knife, her elbows taking the impact on the solid concrete. The man stepped after her, the dragging steel noise came with him, but it was slow, like he was giving her a chance — toying with her, more like.

She made it back to the stud wall, still couldn't see where the knife had fallen. The shadow did give up two black sacks overflowing with clothes and she pushed her hand into the closest, scrabbling helplessly, desperate that her fingers would wrap around the hilt of the weapon. They didn't.

She pushed the first sack out of the way so hard that it tipped and spewed its contents, one of which was a tote bag that fell in a way to reveal its slogan — *Saving the Planet Is Sexy*; a mobile phone, too, that she might have recognised as her own were it not smashed to pieces. Instead she reached for the next sack. She never made it.

A blow landed on the back of her injured leg just below her buttock. There was still feeling in that part and it was the worst pain yet, the shock wave travelled to concentrate at her knee where it rested against the floor. The man grunted with the exertion. She rolled her forehead against the solid floor, side to side, her eyes scrunched tightly shut, trying to cope with the pain. She retched a little, her mouth and throat suddenly burned with bile that she spat out in clumps. The steel dragged, the sound grabbed her attention, the source bumped her in the ankle and she twitched away. It continued round, moving up her side and coming to a rest against her head. Even when he lifted the crowbar up from there he was sure to run it up the side of her head, pausing for a moment against her ear like he was marking out his target.

Daisy-Mae was out of time.

'What?' The man's exclamation was sudden, out of place, his tone heavy with upset. 'Can't be! No, not now!'

Daisy-Mae dared to open her eyes, rolling a little onto her side to where she could see the man looming above her, the crowbar swinging in his grip, but his attention was back through the doorway, back towards the stairs he had come down. He stepped away, a half step really but she could almost see the internal battle dragging him away against his will. He took a full step this time, enough to take him out of sight and Daisy-Mae moved, pulling herself to the door to peer round. The man had one foot on the bottom step, but his attention was fixed on the flat panel that was closest to him. She was close enough to see that it was one of a bank of monitors and they seemed to be showing CCTV. She could make out a digital clock that ticked like it was live. It was just gone eleven p.m. and there was movement on one of the screens. The view was of somewhere outside; a large, flat-sided, dark-coloured van was backing onto a driveway. The camera position was such that it filled the screen as it rolled backwards, coming to a stop so that the words PRIVATE AMBULANCE were clear down its side and on the double doors on its rear.

'Not now!' The man seemed desperate now, beside himself, even. 'Not NOW!' he roared, stumbling as he threw himself up the stairs.

CHAPTER 91. FROZEN NAILS

The sound of the rain washed over Paul Morgan a moment before he felt the torrent. The thundering rain was mixed with icy balls of hail like frozen nails tipped out above his front door. The sensation might have been pleasant in other circumstances, nostalgic even, to remind him of the first day he and his wife Helen had taken ownership of their family home, but Paul was lost to sentiment just as much as he was lost to feeling. Paul was lost entirely.

Betty Snow was dead. The undertaker's van backing onto her drive was all the confirmation he needed. He had known it was coming, just not yet, he had an agreement and he had kept his side. This wasn't right.

Paul stumbled over his own doorstep, the overhang must have been giving him some shelter as that single step made the sensation of the rain stronger, pinching and stabbing at him all over. The wound to his neck was the deepest by far and was still leaking blood that mixed with the water. He moved across his sodden front lawn to hop over the low wall, his direction towards the Snows' front door.

The rear doors to the black ambulance flashed open together and the movement through them was instant, the shadow that emerged was shaped like two men as it burst outwards, roaring voices came with it and thicker shadows jerked out to point straight for him. Paul knew who it was, he knew what it was. Everyone owes a death and his time was up. The relief that flooded his body might have caught him by surprise had it not been so intoxicating.

'Drop it! DROP IT!' Two words repeated over and over emerged from the confusion and Paul realised he was still holding the steel crowbar. He did as he was instructed, the sound of the steel hitting the gravel of Detective Inspector Charles Snow's drive came at the exact same time as he was hit from the side by more shadows; hip-level, a blow that took him to the ground and forced the air from his lungs in an *oomph*!

The gravel was hard and sharp, just like those frozen nails from above, then came the sensation of strong hands all over him where his limbs were entwined in shadow and he was forced onto his back for a view of the night sky, the moon choosing that moment to offer a fleeting glow of light.

'Safe!' Another roar, this one from close to Paul's left ear and he snatched to it.

That was when he saw her.

Betty Snow was there. At least, her apparition was. She was floating above the roaring, bucking shadow that was holding him down, her face older than he could imagine, but unmistakeable. She was in that same nightdress, made bright white by the moon, the ends flapped and shuffled in a breeze Paul hadn't noticed. And she was smiling, beaming even. In a moment of clarity Paul knew exactly why.

It was over for her. Charles was waiting.

CHAPTER 92

'What if this doesn't work?' The vehicle lurched as if in response to Harry's concern. The driving was erratic, the urgency clear from the moment Maddie had briefed the team on what she had, on what was at stake and just what they had to do. She'd done her best to appear confident, to disguise the fact that her hurried request for resources was based on little more than a theory thrown together from pieces of a far from complete puzzle.

'It has to,' Maddie said. They were slowing, maybe even to a stop. Confirmation of their arrival came in the form of two firm slaps against the tuneful metal walls of the hast-ily borrowed coroner's vehicle. Its next movement was far slower and it was backwards. She felt a bump through the rear wheels that might have been a kerb.

'CONTACT! TARGET EXITS PROPERTY, WEAPON, WEAPON, WEAPON!' The shout came from the front, the brakes were suddenly rough, another lurch, this time to a complete stop and the team of firearms officers sat between her and Harry and the back doors all got to their feet. Dressed in standard-issue "firearms black" from boots to helmets, they merged with the thick shadow making up the rear until the back doors opened like they had been kicked. The night had cleared up, a thin drizzle remained to mingle with the light of the moon. Maddie heard a shout that cut through everything: '*Police*! *POLICE*! *GET ON THE FLOOR, GET ON THE FLOOR NOW; DROP IT, DROP IT OR I WILL SHOOT!*'

Maddie had strict instructions to sit still until it was clear but there was no way she was going to stay still. She moved to get a view out. The view she got was of Paul Morgan. He was bare-chested, with a solid-looking crowbar in his right fist, leaking blood too, from the top of his chest and the side of his neck. He looked like he had come out for a fight but the will seemed to leave him as she watched. Granted, he was facing up to a firearms team, two of which appeared from the side to take him to the ground, holding his arms and legs while a taser weapon showed its presence with a red dot on his chest. She hadn't known what to expect from Paul Morgan, but one thing she hadn't expected was this amount of fear — terror, even. The emotion shaped his whole face, leaking out like the blood from his open wounds as he was hurriedly searched, the absence of any other weapons confirmed with a shout of *SAFE*!

'Jesus!' Maddie said. 'Betty!'

Harry was pushing past her already, making for the elderly Betty Snow who had appeared from out of her house, the carer who had agreed to stay after being called earlier in the night was flapping at the doorway, like Betty had some-how given her the slip. At least Betty Snow was smiling, standing out in a freezing breeze but beaming down at the commotion like how a mother might look at her child who had just been polite.

'Betty, hey, let's get you inside!' Harry got to her first to gently coerce her back to the furious-looking carer behind them. Betty's smile seemed permanent, her eyes lifted to flicker between the two detectives.

'You shouldn't judge him.' Her voice seemed stronger, her breathing lacking the rasp from their earlier visit. 'Even good men with good hearts can be tempted by evil.'

'OK, Betty. Inside, in the warm.' Harry stayed with her while Maddie turned away, moving quickly around where Morgan was still restrained on the floor, still ignoring their rules as she moved into his house, aware of shouts of *CLEAR!* bawled from inside to accompany at least two shuffling torchlights. But Maddie wasn't interested in the main house, she was interested in what she had seen next door, knowing the houses were a mirror image of each other.

The third — and largest — door under the stairs was ajar and, sure enough, she found stairs right behind it. Maddie peered down them, swinging her own torch into the murky depths to where a set of eyes peered back. A young woman, laid out on the floor, now twisting onto her side, squinting blind, her hand out, a blade held in it that moved like a warning to catch in the bright torchlight.

'Police!' Maddie called out. 'Put the knife down!' she shouted, then found herself needing to get her elbows out to stop two firearms officers pushing past her, weapons first. Maddie shifted her torch so it wasn't quite so in the young woman's face, to try again. 'Daisy-Mae, is it? Daisy-Mae Adams. I'm Detective Inspector Maddie Ives, it's over.' Another couple of seconds passed and then came the sound of a knife blade clanging onto a concrete floor. Maddie continued down, fighting herself not to rush. 'Is Megan here too?'

'Dead!' A rushed whimper rose up from the filthy, sobbing mess of limbs still squinting up at the light. The woman's legs were tied together, lying straight out, and there was prominent bruising on her neck, face and arms but she managed a point that Maddie followed with her torch until it rested on a lifeless figure.

'OK, Daisy-Mae,' Maddie said, 'you're going to be all right.' She reached for a crude-looking light switch hanging from the wall. The reaction was an eruption of light so bright it was painful, leaving Maddie feeling for the switch to turn it back off, taking her back to torchlight. A firearms officer added more light and Maddie took a moment to assess the area. Under the stairs and off to the left side was a filthy camp bed directly under where the eruption of light had come from. She ran her torch over food receptacles and water bottles but she stopped on the child's dolls: five of them, all stood in a line against a partition wall where a crude slit was cut out like some sort of bizarre viewing gallery into the larger room.

'What the hell was he doing down here?' Maddie breathed.

PART FIVE

CHAPTER 93

Paul,

Thank you for your time today, for listening. I think I talked at you a lot and I had a lot to say, so I thought I should write down the important parts, the parts I need you to understand. Time can fade words and their meaning so I put them here, where time cannot find them.

All that is left of my husband is my memory of him. He lives on in our children and grandchildren, of course, but they never saw him like I did; no one sees a husband like a wife.

But I do not write this letter as a tribute to Charles, there will be another place for that, I write this letter so you will understand that as my memory of my husband fades, I fade. As my memory of my children fade, I fade. Money, belongings, my mother's old clock, even this house, these are nothing more than circumstance, trinkets of an existence. What we really are is in the people that we love and that love us back. Forget them, we forget ourselves.

I will forget them and I will forget myself. I will become nothing and no one. A sack of skin with a team of carers intent on keeping my cells alive, but I will be dead already. I may even forget the Lord who made me.

By the time you read these words you will have already sent me back to Him. I will be with my husband too, smiling down at my children until they take their place by our side. I considered that you would feel bad, conflicted perhaps, so I left this letter for you to find when you had done what I asked of you, so that it may provide you comfort.

I want to thank you, Paul Morgan, with all of my heart. For freeing my soul and returning me to my Charles. My mother had a core belief and it was this: one good turn deserves another.

You told me how you felt when that black ambulance turned up for Charles, for his body at least, you told me the sadness and the sorrow you felt and I know that was true. I know you truly loved Charles as a friend and neighbour. You said that when that black ambulance returns for me that it will be harder still, that there will be sadness for me and my passing, but it will mean so much more: the end of your own life as you know it. I know that weighs heavy on you and I know that this is a power I wield over you.

I listened, Paul. I listened and I prayed on it and I made a decision with His blessing. It is not my place to have such power over another. I have changed my last will and testament, removing the instruction to the police with regards to Charles' written confession that includes the role you played. My passing, the arrival of that black ambulance to remove my body and return it to the dust of God's earth, will now be nothing to you, just like it will be nothing to me. For my soul will already be free. This is my thank you, my gift.

The copy of Charles' confession is attached to this letter. It is the only copy. I left it for you so you will see that it existed, that this was not a serpent's trick. These next words, Paul, I beg you to contemplate them: do not be hasty. The temptation to destroy Charles' words may be strong, but pray on it, I beg you, ask of Him what you should do so that you may find your own forgiveness.

But I want you to know that you have mine.

God made forgiveness for people just like you, Paul, for good men with good hearts, tempted by evil.

Thank you, Paul. Do not feel bad for what you have done, I know that I asked a lot of you. You told me how you once counted yourself as a good friend to us all and I want you to know that you remain so, that this will never change.

Your neighbour and your friend,

Mrs Betty Snow

Helen Morgan sat back to signify that she was done reading, her hands made a squealing sound as she dragged them backwards over the table's surface. Maddie had noticed how she hadn't physically touched the letter, it was a photocopy anyway, the original seized as key evidence the moment it was removed from Betty Snow's safe a week earlier. Jessica, her daughter, had either skimmed it or read it in record time before moving away to sit on the arm of a sofa chair in the living room behind them, choosing to sit facing away with her legs brought up and her arms wrapped tightly around them.

'But he didn't? He didn't murder Betty Snow, I mean?' Helen said, her face contorting like she was searching for a suitable expression.

'He didn't. Based on what he wrote, he couldn't bring himself to,' Maddie said.

'And I can't see that, what Paul wrote, I mean?' Helen was a brusque woman, unimpressed from the first moment. It had been hard to get her to agree to a conversation and Maddie had needed to give her something to even get through the door. Betty's letter had been it.

'And you can't show me what Charles wrote, either? This so-called confession where he talks about someone that my husband *did* murder?' Helen sniffed.

'No. But soon . . .'

'But you want me to talk to you? To tell you everything that I know?' Helen said.

Maddie shrugged. She'd tried the nice approach, time to use a little shock factor.

'Yes, because I'm a police officer who has just discovered a murder victim buried in your garden at the time that you were a resident—'

'You don't think that this has anything to do with me, do you?' She bristled and Maddie left the question unanswered for just a beat.

'If I did, this conversation would be in a police station and you would be under arrest for murder. That can still happen, if you would rather the protection of a solicitor, or—'

'You can't arrest me, I haven't done anything wrong!'

'I absolutely can, Mrs Morgan, I don't know who's done wrong until I talk to them. That's how investigations work.'

Helen's chair caught the floor as she shoved it back, the noise like a lost whale, loud and sudden enough to make Jessica jump in the background. Maddie stayed seated.

'I didn't offer you a tea,' Helen mumbled. The kettle was just a step or two away and in front of a window that she stayed facing out towards for the whole time the kettle took to boil. 'Helen,' she said, eventually, before twisting round back into the room. 'Please, call me Helen. That Mrs Morgan rubbish is all a bit formal.' Her stern mask had slipped, her lips fidgeted and she huffed, like there was some sort of argument going on inside her mind. Whichever side wanted her to return to the table won through and she landed heavily back in the same chair. Another huff, then she barked 'Jessica!' and her eyes jerked away from where they had been skimming back over the letter. 'You're going to be late for work. We'll talk this all out later but right now . . .' Jessica was mumbling before she even got to her feet, it was still going when she passed behind Maddie, but the lack of any argument told its own story.

'Talk to me about Paul,' Maddie said, deliberately leaving it open-ended. 'I really only came here to get an understanding of him from someone who knows him well.'

'Knew him well!' Another huff. 'Paul . . . Well, he's sick, did you know that? He hasn't been well for a long time, truth be told. But this . . . I mean, *murder*! That's not my Paul, that's not the man I knew, the man I *loved*. Everything changed when those women were taken, when they turned up dead. Paul, Charles; they were never the same after that.'

'What happened, Helen?'

'Oh, you tell me . . . Paul's big, stupid heart, that's what happened!' She waved out her arm, suddenly animated. 'He took it personal, Paul did. He might have been the last person Christine Matheson saw alive, ask Paul and he will tell you he was for sure. He waved her goodbye that night, probably a kiss and a cuddle knowing him, he kissed them all!' She quickly raised her eyes, concern chasing away what might have been a smile. 'There was never anything in it. Christine was younger, a lot younger and a very attractive woman for sure, but Paul's the protective sort, always has been; the father-figure type. You ask anyone that knows him and they'll tell you. I think he was drawn to working security for that reason.'

'Security?' Maddie said. That was something that was missing from the picture she had of Paul Morgan.

'That was how he started out, working the doors at a nightclub as part of the security team. Soon he was pretty much running the place, then he borrowed a lot of money in our name to make it official. I never minded, I never doubted he would make something of it, once he sets his mind on something . . .'

'So he felt protective of Christine?'

'And Denise, no doubt, but she was a little older, a little less naïve of the world. We're all a bit stupid at twenty, aren't we?' Maddie nodded her agreement. 'And Paul had just become a dad, having his own little girl made him ten times worse about the world and the arseholes that are in it. He became protective to the point it was an obsession. He took on more than he should have with Christine, I know he sorted out a couple of lads who hadn't been treating her too good, he gave her money too, nothing major, just stepped in when she had a problem with the rent. He said it was an advance but I bet he never took it back. I only stepped in when there was talk of him going guarantor for her, that felt like asking for trouble.'

'So he took it hard, when she was one of the victims?'

'I didn't realise how hard, not at first. I mean, he was upset when we got the confirmation but it was like . . . it was like he already knew. I thought there would be a massive reaction but there was nothing like it. I remember feeling a little bit relieved that he took it so well.' She smiled, it looked a little inane and fell away quickly. 'I knew he was talking to Charles a lot, they became close and I was glad, I thought it was helping, but . . .'

'But it wasn't?'

She shrugged. 'I don't know. It was when Charles died that Paul really seemed to start losing himself. That was when he stopped listening, to me, to reason and logic; to anyone. But . . . but *murder*? And Charles too? I mean, that man was so clean he squeaked . . . They were good to us, Charles and Betty, right from the first day we moved in. Betty was big with the church, part of the team even and Charles was involved too. Real pillar of the community types, you know what I mean?'

'I think so.'

'I knew something was going on with them two.'

'Charles and Betty?'

'Paul and Charles. You can always tell when men are plotting something. Normally it's a game of golf or a trip to the pub but I guess . . . I don't know what I thought. I knew Charles was having a tough time at work and I thought they were helping each other through it. Paul would never talk about his mental health, it's just not a thing a man like that would ever consider.'

'When did you start noticing there might be something off?'

'It was gradual, it snuck up on us all. He said some odd things but I didn't pull him up on it at first, I guess I was scared of his reaction. When he started being off with Jessica, both of us really, that was when I first considered there was a problem. I remember one evening, coming up the stairs to find Paul sat on the landing with just these big . . . these wild eyes . . .' Helen started her head shaking, her eyes glazed over and her face made an expression like she was seeing something she didn't like. 'He said he was guarding our daughter from the shadow, or something just like that. You tell me what the hell that means?'

Maddie took a moment. She'd put this visit off as long as she could, hoping the legal elements would be resolved by the time she sat down with Paul's wife. They still weren't at the point where she could talk openly but she would say more than she should. It was the reason she had been sure to come on her own. This wasn't a case that was ever going to make trial and it wasn't just his guilty plea that would ensure that. Paul Morgan's mental health assessment had already made it clear that there was no way the judicial system was going to be right for him. Harry had still advised Maddie not to give anything up, to continue kicking that can down the road until it was all tied up, but that simply wasn't fair. There were things that Helen was going to need to know.

'He's been quite descriptive, Helen, about a lot of things in the memoir that he has written. He talks about shadows a lot and when we found where he had been sleeping, it was . . .'

'Bonkers?' Helen offered. 'I knew he was going to get worse when we left, I knew it . . . I think that was why . . . why I didn't ever go back to that place, to our home.'

'He was sleeping in the basement. There was lighting set up that we now think was designed to banish darkness completely. Spending his nights there would surely have meant very little sleep. Insomnia and a mental health condition not addressed, that could explain some of the things that he has written, his thoughts . . . They're all over the place.'

'All over the place?'

'It's his version of events. It covers what happened twenty-odd years ago and what has happened since. We have been able to verify much of it. We know for sure that Charles told him too much about the police investigation, far more than he should. Paul did some of his own investigating too, he befriended both of the survivors enough that he was able to tap into their misery. Paul had to keep everything that he knew secret of course, taking away an essential coping mechanism. Police officers only survive the career we have by talking it out.'

'He could have talked to me!' Helen said.

'No, he couldn't.'

'Why? What was in that thing?'

'You can see it, you have my word. It's clear he wants you to see it but don't expect only answers. It's . . . It's jumbled.'

'What does that mean, *jumbled*?'

Maddie tutted, trying to tip an example out of her mind that explained it best. 'Paul talks about going out for a coffee, for a walk in the area that he used to work but his own CCTV shows that he only went out twice and both times it was likely to . . . to abduct those women.'

'OK, so he didn't go out when he said he did. We all have fantasies, ways we would rather spend our day.'

'We do, but it appears Paul believed in his fantasies. In one entry he waved at a man called Kenny McNamee, he was in the harbour, stood outside the pub he ran . . .' Maddie paused for a moment, tapping her pocket for her notes.

'The Royal George.' Helen finished the sentence for her. 'I knew him too, Paul and I went to his funeral. He died an old man, he would be ninety years old if he was still around.'

'Had he not died eight years ago. Eight years and three landlords ago.'

'Paul's confused, seeing things wrong, I saw it start myself and I told him it was going to get worse unless he got some help.'

'That wasn't all that Paul mixed up. He described in a lot of detail what those women went through twenty years ago, what Christine went through, specifically, how she had her shin broken when she was beaten with a steel bar—'

'Jesus Christ!' Helen's head fell into her hands.

'It didn't happen,' Maddie said, leaning forward. 'Not like that, not Christine. She was badly beaten, no doubt about that, but no broken bones. Paul, however . . . he did break a young woman's leg with a steel bar. We found her in his basement, the leg snapped almost completely in half.' Helen covered her mouth, started rocking slightly. 'It's possible that a case that he obsessed over every day for twenty years and reality . . . I think they mixed themselves up in Paul's mind to the point where he couldn't differentiate anymore. He was torturing people, killing them even, down in that basement, then going upstairs to sit at his kitchen table and write it down like it was a memory of what someone else did. In truth, he still believes someone else did what he did to those women in his basement; some*thing* else at least.'

'I don't understand . . . That's just not . . . I don't believe it!' Helen still had her hands clapped over her mouth, her words distorted.

'And when we arrested him, Paul thought it was raining frozen nails and Betty Snow was a ghost. Something like when you first moved in?'

'Hail . . .' Helen whispered. 'It was a bit of an in-joke for years, how we should have seen that as a sign, I always said it was like God himself was tipping frozen nails over us that night, his way of telling us something. It was funny then, it's not funny now, is it?'

'I'm sorry, Helen, I can't imagine how difficult this is.'

'He was funny though, Paul was.' Her eyes glazed again, she was back inside her mind, this time it seemed a happier place and her smile was genuine. 'We had a good run. Ten years or more together, all of it happy. Jessica came along and those first few months were the hardest and happiest of all, she made us even stronger, but then . . .'

'Parenthood changes everything, it changes people.'

'It was Christine that changed everything. He was so angry and that's what I don't understand. The things he said he would do if he ever got a hold of the man responsible! *Scum of the earth* he said. And now you're here telling me that he did the very same things?' Helen's demeanour switched back to the woman who had refused to let Maddie in, who had refused to listen at all.

'He did find the man responsible. Then he did those things that he had promised when he was angry, then he buried what was left in your garden. But Paul didn't get his peace from that, or whatever it was he was expecting, I think it just added to the pressures on him.'

'How could he keep that from me? How could I not know? Right in my garden, all that time . . . I was living with him!'

'You'd be surprised what secrets people can keep. Was there a time when he stopped talking about it? About Christine, the case overall?'

Helen rubbed at her face. 'I guess so. I guess I never really thought about it, we were just trying to get on with our lives. The case was reopened, I remember that, it was back in the papers and that made things more difficult.'

'How so?'

'Pressure! I said, he doesn't cope with pressure, with anger!' Helen snapped.

'Did he ever mention a man called Michael Rix?' Maddie said, watching carefully for a reaction.

'Michael . . . I remember the name from the press. His girlfriend was with him. She died, if I remember right.'

'Did Paul talk about that, about him?'

'No. He didn't actually talk about it much, never any names,' Helen said, then fixed on Maddie like she had detected something in her reaction. 'What is it? Something about this man?'

'They knew each other, Paul and Michael.'

'Knew each other? How?'

'It's complicated,' Maddie said, already knowing she was going to have to explain better.

'Complicated?'

'You'll understand better when you read Paul's words. Michael Rix seems to be the only element that he has been deliberately misleading about. He has written that they only met twice but we now know that's not the case. Paul and Michael have been in touch for years. Paul stepped it up in the last year or so. We think . . .' Maddie was again hesitant, unsure just how much she should share.

'What? What do you think?' Helen demanded.

'We think Paul had a plan to deflect any police attention when we were looking for the missing women. Michael Rix is more than a little messed up himself and Paul seemed to want to use that to his advantage. He bought the same clothes as Rix, wore glasses so thick it must have given him a headache, grew his hair a similar length and even rented a pocket of land with some chickens on it, having got to know that Michael found them calming. Paul bought a truck, too, that was similar to the one used to abduct the victims in 1999, a truck that he loaned out to Rix so he could go have his moment of calm feeding the animals. It was a way of giving Rix a link to that vehicle.'

'Paul bought a truck? He doesn't even like driving big cars?'

'We found it in his garage . . .' Maddie said but not as a way of proving a point. That wasn't necessary, Helen was already lacking conviction, already doubting everything she thought she knew. When she spoke again she was back to a whisper, her head shaking. 'His own CCTV shows him leaving in it on two occasions, but there was another when he drove it out late at night but just stayed pulled across the front of the house. It looked like he might have been using it as a place to think, maybe to write those thoughts down . . .'

'Renting land . . . a truck and a new hair style? I just don't think I understand any of this.'

'It's a lot, I know that and I'm not explaining myself well. Paul had the semblance of a plan with some sense to it at first, but I think everything ran away from him in the end. He intended on setting Michael Rix up. There were flashes of straight thinking in there, he updated one of the girls' social media from her phone but not with anything that would stand up under any scrutiny. We found it in that basement, it was smashed, again that might have been in a moment of clarity.'

'And you're sure this was all Paul? Maybe this Michael Rix was manipulating *him*, did you think of that?'

'There's nothing to suggest Rix had anything to do with abducting those two women, Paul was working alone and he was too disorganised, too frantic and too paranoid to be working with anyone else. Michael was supposed to deflect our attention, but he was Paul's undoing. When Paul couldn't bring himself to murder Betty, he asked Michael to do it. Rix identified the man responsible for his ordeal and his girlfriend's death and Paul buried him in your garden. He tried to use that to convince Rix that he owed him and Betty's death would make them even. He told him there was cash in the safe from Betty, reward for showing her mercy.'

'So this *Michael* was part of it, then? This skeleton in my garden?'

'According to what Paul wrote — but I'm sure you understand how unreliable that will be on its own. It looks like he supplied the name of the man who murdered Christine but he gave that to a serving police officer, he has a clear defence. I'm pretty sure he knew what they were planning to do with that name but proving that will be a very different matter.'

'But you can prove Paul's part? And I don't just mean what a sick man wrote in a diary?'

'Some of what he wrote is very relevant. How he was buried four foot down and on his side with his legs pulled up, for example, we found that to be true. The knife too, Paul said he didn't know the whereabouts, that Charles had hidden it. Charles' letter told us where and I don't think I need to explain whose traces we found on it. There was more. The knife had snapped, Charles led us to the handle and part of the blade, the rest was in the same grave.'

'Why would Charles do that?'

Maddie shrugged. 'Maybe he had a plan of his own. A plan B at least.'

'And how did Betty know?' Helen's head was back to shaking like she was struggling. There was so much information it was hardly surprising that it was coming back out in snippets.

'Betty saw them. On that night when Paul was digging up your garden with Charles she came out, she must have been disturbed and she saw them. It was much later, when she got her prognosis, that she asked Paul to take her life, to put her out of her misery. It seems she was convinced he was capable of it. She gave him a key to her house and the code to her safe for his reward, which he assumed was money.'

'But it wasn't. His reward was this letter telling him he was off the hook, that she was keeping his secret?'

'A change of heart,' Maddie said. 'I've seen her last will and testament and she was as good as her word. She changed it when she was still able. The solicitor confirmed that she removed a section that directed the authorities to the location of a handwritten letter.'

'You would never have known.' Helen wore a fragile smile. Her seat did a second impersonation of that lost whale as she stood up and went back to staring out of the window, reaching out with her left hand like she might need steadying, her wedding ring clunked against the work surface. 'And that pressure that drove him mad . . . maybe it wouldn't have been quite so bad, maybe . . .'

'Never is a long time, Helen.' Maddie spoke to her back. 'We can't know what difference it might have made. At least this way we get answers for all those families.'

'They got the right man then, you know for sure that the man Paul killed and buried . . . He was who did that to Christine?'

'Looks that way. There's a lot more detail in Charles' letter and this Michael Rix that I mentioned is suddenly a little more talkative.'

'Paul never was any good at pressure . . . Can you imagine?' Helen spun on her heels to lock on to Maddie with eyes that had turned watery. 'No matter his bravado, Paul would have felt guilty for murdering another person. Add to that the pressure he was under from believing his life would end in prison and Betty Snow got sick, real sick. He couldn't leave that house, he told me that and now I know why. He couldn't talk to me, to anyone and he had to watch us leave without him . . . It's enough to drive anyone mad.'

'He'd convinced himself he was dying too, that there was a shadow in his own prostate, just like Charles.' Maddie shrugged.

'Cancer? Is there?'

'No. A few days after his arrest he passed a kidney stone. A man thinking straight would have gone to the doctor a long time ago.'

'But *torture . . . murder . . .* !'

'He was lost, Helen. I don't make excuses for people who arrive at murder, that doesn't mean I can't understand the journey that takes them there.'

'He can't have meant to kill those women.' She was shaking her head resolutely, but it was noticeable that she broke eye contact and spun to face out the window again.

'Daisy-Mae Adams is just nineteen, she was the one who survived. Despite her age she's proving to be a good witness. It took a few days for her to be able to talk to us, but she's doing well. Paul killed her friend down in that basement, Daisy-Mae was there when he did it and he was going to kill

393

her too. It might not have been the Paul Morgan that you know and loved who stood over that young woman with a steel bar, but it was Paul Morgan.'

There was a far longer pause where Maddie was letting Helen be the next to speak. 'Did you hurt him?' she said, eventually.

'Hurt him?'

Helen turned back to face Maddie. 'When he was arrested. He's unwell and confused but he's capable of . . . who knows what. You knew that too, so did you have to hurt him?'

'No.' Maddie gestured at Betty's letter that was still lying between them. 'We found that first, Charles' own confession was attached but it was the letter that gave us an idea what to do next. Betty mentioned a black ambulance a couple of times and in a way that stood out to me, something that might get him out of the house far enough that we could get hold of him. I realised those houses had basements when we saw Betty's, that was when I first considered that we might know where Daisy-Mae was. We had seen cameras in Paul's home and it had seemed strange, stranger still that there was one angled to cover Betty's drive. Then I saw that letter and it made sense to me. He's been waiting for that black ambulance to turn up for a long time, I reckoned he would come out and meet it. The firearms team wanted to take the door off and do a full armed entry but Paul would have got hurt if we had gone down that route. We didn't know his mental state then, of course, but now I think that his levels of confusion, his paranoia . . . A full entry would have forced a very severe reaction, it would have put him in danger; Daisy-Mae too. They listened to me with the ambulance and . . . well, sometimes you get lucky.'

Another long pause, a woman trying to take it all in, no doubt. 'Lucky,' she said, eventually. She moved back to the sink, her hands tripped over an upturned cup and she ran a drink of cold water that rushed over the sides. She was still clumsy putting it down on the table, her hand with a clear shake. 'Is that what I should tell Jessica? That her dad is *lucky*?'

Maddie sighed. 'I honestly don't know what you can say to your daughter. The press coverage for this is going to be significant, they'll unearth every detail and soon, so she is going to need to be told before that happens. I will do it with you, if you want? We can tell her together.'

'I don't know . . . I don't know if that'll work, what you must think of him, you've seen first-hand what he did, I don't see how you can sit in front of his daughter and be anything but delighted he's in jail. Maybe I should be too . . . I just don't know how to feel!'

'People see police officers and assume we think in clear terms: *right* or *wrong*, but life is never so simple. This job teaches you that before anything else. Paul might have been a good man once, a good man driven mad by grief, by guilt, the loss of everything he cared about and by fear of his own mortality. But those two young women, they are innocent and my job is to protect the innocent. Think about it any more than that and it can drive you mad just the same. Paul killed an innocent young woman, changed the life of another and I don't forgive him for that, not for any reason.'

'Everything he cared about,' Helen said quietly, repeating back the only part she might have heard. 'I left him. I made it worse. Maybe this is even . . .'

'Your fault? Definitely not. Paul Morgan made his own choices and he couldn't live by them. We're here now because of what guilt can do, there's no need for you to set off down the same path.'

'You're not very good at this.'

'At what?'

'The part where you make me feel better.'

Another smile. 'I didn't come here to make you feel better. In fact, I came here knowing I was going to change your life for the worse.'

'Are you done now?' Helen tried a fragile smile of her own.

'There is something else, something I don't want coming out later that you didn't know.'

'This gets worse?' Helen whispered, both her hands lifting to cover her mouth.

'There's just one more detail you should know. This was all an escalation because Paul saw himself as running out of time to do one last thing.'

'One last thing?' Helen said, her watery eyes had lost their focus and shuffled side to side.

Maddie tutted, trying to find the words. 'When we were in Paul's house the first time, it was empty . . . not empty, discarded. Like someone had picked up some essentials and left some time earlier. There was a good layer of dust, all the doors shut up, but . . .' Maddie hesitated again.

'But what?'

'The table was set. There's a big kitchen table at the back. Clean plates, cutlery, the works and there was no dust, not there, it had all been wiped down. Even nametags . . . homemade.'

'That was—' Helen exclaimed, her head snapping back, her focus too. 'That was when we left!' She looked at Maddie now, her expression like she was in pain. 'It had got bad, I told him we were leaving but he wasn't listening. He went and made a special dinner while I packed, laid the table like we did at Christmas . . . it was *fucking* March! We never did eat what he cooked, I took Jessica and . . .' Her face flushed, the closest she had been to finally breaking down. 'And this was about that dinner? That was what he wanted?'

'I think it was. But he describes a feeling to that house that started from the grave he dug and he could only have you back when that feeling was gone — only, in truth, it was guilt. That is a feeling that will only get worse and Paul got desperate, looking outwards for the cause when he should have been looking at himself.'

'Outwards?'

'Paul convinced himself that the evil intent that was in the man he killed and buried in your garden wasn't dead, that it lived on in the shadows.' Maddie paused a beat, still trying to find the best way to explain herself. 'I know how that sounds' was all she could manage.

Helen sat straighter in her chair, looking like she was pulling herself together. 'You know, he said to me once . . .' Helen's eyes were down, fidgeting from side to side, her voice just above a whisper. 'We had a row of conifers across the garden, about halfway down and the way the sun sets casts their shadows back towards the house and he said . . . he said they were the fingers of the bloody devil! Or some rubbish like that. I told him to stop being so damned silly . . . I did check in with him after we left, phone calls to ask if he was getting the help he needed. I always said that if he could get himself better then we could come back, not just for dinner either, for bloody good! Do you know what he said?'

Maddie had an idea, but still prompted her anyway. 'Go on?'

'He said that we *should* stay away, how it was safer. I got angry, I never really forgave him for that to be honest, for thinking that his family wasn't reason enough to try and get better. And all that time . . . all this . . . all to finish a *fucking* dinner.'

Maddie moved her hand to rest it on the back of Helen's. 'I think he really believes he was keeping you safe and he was willing to live in his own version of hell to do it.'

Helen snatched her hand back, the stern mask fell back over her face, chasing her tears away.

'Well, now he can burn in it, can't he?'

CHAPTER 94

Maddie's next stop was more comfortable, in terms of the seating arrangement at least. From a solid kitchen chair to a sofa, battered and worn, but aren't those always the most comfortable? The conversation she was there to have, in the back room of a dry-cleaner's on a side street in the medieval city of Canterbury, however, had the potential to be every bit as uncomfortable as the one prior.

But at least this time, there was a chance she could make a life better, not worse.

Esme Rix was the first to push through the door and cross the exposed floorboards that amplified her careful steps. Everything was matched with the sofa, everything was old, battered and worn but some places just suit that and this was one of them.

Esme managed to look even more slight than when Maddie had first met her just over a week earlier. She looked more nervous too, avoiding any of the soft chairs to remain standing, having gently placed down a bag for life overflowing with clothes — Scott Harkness's clothes — between her feet. The oversized jumper she was wearing would belong to Scott, too. It was big and shapeless, a way of smudging her edges, of trying to force her beauty to merge until it was hidden. Maddie was pretty sure the previous girlfriend had been wearing a men's hoody when she had first met her. That was when she was trying to discharge herself from hospital, battered, bruised and with her head bent while she just tried to get home, to get back to *him*. Maddie had refused to let her leave, even put her under arrest at one point, cuffing her (illegally) to a piece of furniture so they could talk. And talk they did, until Maddie had got a spark out of her that no fist could extinguish.

Maddie was delighted to see something just like that in Esme already. This was a woman who had called the number to make an appointment of her own free will, who must have recognised the situation she was in. Maybe she wasn't going to need too much persuasion to take the next steps. Maddie had her handcuffs in her bag, just in case.

The door opened again and Maddie stood up to greet the third woman with a lingering hug.

'I assume you two have met?' Maddie said.

'We . . . I . . . We spoke on the phone, I think?' Esme said, her voice brittle enough that it might crack at any moment.

'You would have done,' Maddie said. 'But I should do a more formal introduction. This wonderful woman is Grace Hughes. Grace is a survivor, just like you, and one day she might tell you her full story, but just let me assure you it is nothing short of incredible. But there's more than just surviving and Grace is the poster girl to prove it. She's now in a very healthy relationship with her own business here. Not satisfied with that, this little side hustle was her idea, something she wants to do, to provide women with a safe place to make the first step to a better life—'

'Or just a cup of tea!' Grace cut in over Maddie, who took the hint.

'Or just a cup of tea,' Maddie said, aware that she could launch into her full *let's-get-you-safe* speech too early and cause nothing but panic. Grace was so much better at this. 'I tell you what, how about I go make it?' Maddie added and made it to the point where that old, worn door was creaking at her before she stopped to the sound of a voice.

'Thank you, Inspector Ives. For all this.' It was Esme, sounding a little stronger.

'For what?' Maddie said.

'For giving me a little push to face up to this, to what's been happening. Otherwise, these things can fester, can't they? No one else knows what it's like in that house, behind that closed door. I've tried to talk to my mates but I get the impression that people don't have the time, they don't really want to know unless you've made the perfect family home like they have.'

Maddie was still holding herself back, suppressing the police officer inside that wanted every detail, every happening from behind the closed door Esme had just referenced laid out in a signed statement so she could go and arrest the piece of shit she knew Scott Harkness to be.

Patience.

'You're right, you never know what's going on behind closed doors, Esme, but trust me on this, there's no such thing as the perfect family home.'

THE END

READ AN EXCLUSIVE SAMPLE
OF MADDIE IVES BOOK 8

Don't miss the new Maddie Ives thriller, coming January 2023. We are delighted to bring you an exclusive preview of the first two chapters.

* * *

CHAPTER 1

Tuesday

Lynn Hathaway knew fear. Even when it was just a breath pushed out hard enough to cause distortion down a phone-line. Real fear can freeze a hardened call-taker in their chair, it can stop the world for just a moment, sucking all the noise, movement and air out of a busy room of blinking call boards and banks of chatting emergency call-takers.

This was one of those calls.

999 police, what's your emergency?

A line Lynn had delivered a million times to a million responses. This time the reaction was another breath that tailed off into a whimper. It was enough. Lynn Hathaway knew voices too and this was young, a child for sure, the desperation thick enough to clot in her ear. Lynn ducked her head to focus, her right hand lifting to push the headset more firmly against her ear so she wouldn't miss a thing.

'Everything's OK, my name is Lynn and I'm here to help you.' She was off script now, there were other things she needed to be saying but fear needs one thing: reassurance. Lynn fixed on her two monitors, they were close enough for the green text standing out from the black background to hurt, she held her breath for the next words as if they were all she had been waiting for her whole life. There was just breathing at first, then a muted knocking sound: knuckles on wood perhaps, but distant. The bright green font glowed with a mobile phone number; it wasn't a number that had called before or her screen would be populated with linked information, something that might help.

'Can you tell me if you're OK?' Lynn's cursor flew across the screen, a trail left behind it where she had turned the function on in a moment of boredom. She was regretting it now. She clicked to send the phone number for fast-track subscriber checks. Someone in admin support would receive it as a request and start making enquiries with the phone company that had issued the phone. If it was on a contract, they would have the details in around twenty minutes or so, which, in the world of emergency assistance, was an eternity.

A muffled cry. This was distant too, then another knocking sound, finishing with a scuff and another cry that faded back to loud breathing.

'If you cannot speak to me and you require emergency assistance, press five-five on your keypad and we will respond.' Lynn was back on script, her words very deliberate, her eyes shut briefly, silently begging for those tones — anything. There were more gasping sounds, then scraping like the phone itself was being dragged against something.

Two tones.

The screen also confirmed the keys had been pressed. The BT Operator who had passed the call to the police had made the same request but not got a response. As per his own procedures, he had stayed connected and now recognised his cue to speak.

'Provider is Vodafone, Eastings are 603228, Northings 170385, confidence approximately 80 per cent, operator to clear the line.' The man's voice was nasal, he allowed a moment's delay for Lynn to come back in with any questions. There was nothing more to ask and a click confirmed he was gone. She typed in the coordinates given; they related to the nearest phone mast to the caller rather than the caller themselves and gave a rough area. It came up with the entire Isle of Sheppey.

Thirty-six square miles.

'This is being treated as an emergency assistance call. We have officers in your area, are you able to confirm your location?' The headset was pushed so tight against her ear it hurt.

'Mum!' The voice was still distant, the word rushed, spoken like the caller had turned back into a room, away from the phone. There was another thud, then the same voice but louder, another layer of fear. 'Mum, is that you?'

CHAPTER 2

Saturday

Four days later

Her husband had gone down hard. Their hallway flooring was wooden and the vibrations spread out enough even to shake the part of the floor beneath where she was on her hands and knees. It was a connection, a reminder that she wasn't just an observer to the horror, despite the separation provided by the slatted door of her hiding place. She was there, she was part of it.

She could hear him too. He was in pain, choking and sobbing into his gag while turned on his side towards her. As she watched, his foot lifted then fell back down for the heel to thump. She felt that too; she'd splayed her fingertips against the floor, seeking more of that connection, trying to make it last. She wanted to feel him, his movements at least, even if it was flailing in pain. She could almost convince herself that the connection was two-way, that she could send something back to remind him that he wasn't alone.

But she had to stay quiet and she had to stay hidden. Those were his hurried instructions, instructions that had started even before the knock on the door, and his intensity had been such that she had followed dumbly. *You have to stay quiet! You have to stay hidden! You have to stay safe!* he had begged her, his palms raised out towards her to exert an invisible force that pushed her to the back of this cupboard and halted her questions.

She'd never seen him like that before.

She'd never seen him like this before, either: injured and wailing, his wide eyes towards her, searching the slats of the understairs cupboard, unable to see in, though she could see out. She found herself edging forward, still fighting her instinct to kick out at the door and rush to his aid.

Her nose brushed the cupboard door.

The sensation caught her out in the darkness, making her jerk back, her left elbow catching the underside of the cupboard in a glancing blow that made a scuffing noise. It was as good as silent, but to her it sounded like the loudest noise she had ever heard.

She froze.

She could see the legs of the stranger who had entered their home and now stood over her husband. She could see white trousers tainted with vivid stripes of red where the weapon had been wiped — one side, then the other, in a rhythmic movement. The weapon was gripped in a bloodied blue glove, the blade twisted and stubby. The stranger was unmoving, their stillness contrasting with her squirming husband who writhed like a snapped slow-worm. The stranger only moved to lash out, then was instantly back to still, back to silent; no pacing, no gesticulating, no shouting threats or demands. Just still, silent and cold.

And now turned to face the cupboard.

She couldn't see the face, the angled slats blotted out the top half entirely. For all she knew the stranger was staring down at the same gaps in the cupboard door as her husband was, searching for the same eye contact. Her internal dialogue told her to stay calm, that there was no way she could be seen, no way anyone but her husband even knew she was home.

The cupboard was an odd shape, made bespoke to make the most of the space under the stairs in their hallway. It rose in a sharp angle upwards, left to right, to chase the incline. But the first third, where the stairs were at their lowest point, was a bench with a padded top. It was a place where she had sat a million times to kick off her boots after a walk on a carefree Sunday, the whole family returning to be swamped by smells of dinner in the oven. Never could she imagine she would be cowering under it, pushed into it as far as she could muster, head first, with coats pulled from the hangers above as a way of adding an extra layer of concealment.

Maybe she should have run out of the back. She could have run the mile or so it took to get phone reception and called for help. Then at least she would be doing *something*, then at least she wouldn't be lying a metre away watching another flash of violence and feeling her husband's reaction through her fingertips.

* * *

Police Constable Vince Arnold upped his pace as the old railway bridge came into sight. The target address was just a couple of hundred metres the other side and knowing that gave him a boost. His legs were burning, he was built for sprints more than distance, but he'd run some distance to get here.

His chest burned as he made the bridge, the sound of his footsteps bouncing back like someone was running across the arched roof above him, keeping perfect pace for them both to burst out of the other side at the same time. The road had a gentle curve left, which meant he couldn't yet see the address, or the front door, but he was close.

One final push.

* * *

You will answer my question. The truth. That is all you will say.

The stranger had a voice. It was strong, determined and unflinching. There was no feeling to it, no weakness either. No single word spoken in such a way as to give any hope.

Her husband rushed a nod. He was still side-on, still facing where she was pressed up against the slats, her knees aching, merged into the darkness. His hands were pulled tight behind his back, his legs still fidgeting to make patterns in his own blood on the floor. He was sweating from his pain, crying in panic, his eyes blotched red and sopping as they followed the twisted blade that now moved slowly across his view. It came to a rest between his cheek and the material tied tight against his face to make up the gag. Another violent jerk and the material was yanked down around his neck. Her husband was like a listing ship, he spat and coughed towards the floor. His face jerked back up as the stranger moved directly towards the cupboard that concealed her, momentarily blocking her view.

The seat creaked and flexed above her. Dust fell onto her cheek and into her eyes that were turned upwards to the noise. Two legs in white now parted to frame her view out, the material so close she could have touched it. Her husband stared over, her new front door was directly behind him, it had a frosted glass surround, the low sun giving it a halo effect that now encircled him. She remembered the pride she'd felt when they had fitted it as part of the renovations they had always wanted, but had taken fifteen years to start. The birth of their son that had prompted the move to a larger place had then removed the finances required to improve it. The door had been last, the finishing touch and she'd never been prouder of their home, of what they had achieved together. It was everything she'd ever wanted: a forever home for her family somewhere quiet, isolated and peaceful.

That same cold, determined voice came back to fill the hall. This time it was a question that finally revealed the entire reason for this invasion of her home. The words meant nothing to the hiding woman, they might as well have been in a foreign language, but her husband's reaction was despair scrunched tight enough that a tear had to struggle its way out. And, in that moment, she knew that he had been a fool, that her dream of the perfect home with a perfect family was gone.

* * *

The house was now visible to Vince. The car on the drive and the tall tree in the front garden acted as an effective landmark. It was quiet out here, isolated and peaceful. He had barely passed anyone since breaking into a run.

His chest was close to bursting. His thighs were tightening up and he could feel the acid building in his calves as he pushed himself forward. His footfalls were heavier, the soles of his shoes slapping harder as he was getting tired and his technique was falling away.

But he couldn't slow down, he couldn't let up. He could only pray that he wasn't out of time already.

There was a garden path just the other side of that tree that cut through the front lawn. It was made up of polished stones mixed up in concrete and it led to a solid door with a glass surround. His soles squeaked at the sudden change of direction, his footsteps still heavy.

He only needed a few more.

* * *

The silence hit her the hardest. Every strike or slash of the blade had been met with noise: cries of pain, begging, scuffs against the polished floor where her husband had recoiled, or the clamour of him going down to the ground in the first instance.

But not this time.

This time there was no further to fall, this time his ability to push out his heels and scrabble away from the blade was gone. This time his voice was silenced. His face changed, too. He had been panicked and terrified, his eyes shifting from tightly shut to open wide, unblinking and chasing around the room. Now they were still, one eyelid lower than the other like a half-pulled blind.

The fingertips that had been splayed out against the wooden floor were now pressed hard into her cheek to stop any sounds leaking out as she struggled to look away from her dead husband. She was back to holding her breath then letting it out in controlled bursts, her mouth as wide as it would go behind her hand so it wouldn't make any noise.

There was movement from the stranger, back towards her, then a spin and a sit. The wooden bench squeaked and flexed once more, more dust shaken free to be sucked in through her fingers as she struggled to control her panic. She gripped her nose where it tickled like she might sneeze.

The weapon hung down in front of the slats, now held lightly between finger and thumb, and she could imagine her husband's killer slouched forward, taking a rest perhaps, looking out over a job done. This time the twisted blade hadn't been wiped clean and clumps of black and red mixed with the sunlight still bundling through the frosted glass opposite to give off an unreal, orange glow. She dared moved forward. Slowly, gently, her neck aching as she arched her head up, desperate to see those legs move away and leave her house.

Her eye was drawn to movement. It was a shadow that flickered across the glass of the front door in a blink-and-you'll-miss-it moment. But she hadn't missed it and the light was still changing: *someone was coming to her front door!*

The stranger must have seen it too, there was sudden movement, more creaking as the weight was removed. But then something unexpected, the legs turned again, away from the door, away from the movement and the voice returned. Three words that sliced through the silence like a scalpel to make her jump, three words spoken slow and deliberate like there was a need to be clear:

'*Sandy. Louise. Blackman.*'

Just three words.

Her full name.

ALSO BY CHARLIE GALLAGHER

DS MADDIE IVES SERIES
Book 1: HE IS WATCHING YOU
Book 2: HE WILL KILL YOU
Book 3: HE WILL FIND YOU
Book 4: HE KNOWS YOUR SECRETS
Book 5: HE WILL GET YOU
Book 6: THE DEADLY HOUSES
Book 7: LAST ONE ALIVE

LANGTHORNE POLICE SERIES
Book 1: BODILY HARM
Book 2: PANIC BUTTON
Book 3: BLOOD MONEY
Book 4: END GAME
Book 5: MISSING
Book 6: THEN SHE RAN
Book 7: HER LAST BREATH

STANDALONES
RUTHLESS

Thank you for reading this book.

If you enjoyed it please leave feedback on Amazon or Goodreads, and if there is anything we missed or you have a question about, then please get in touch. We appreciate you choosing our book.

Founded in 2014 in Shoreditch, London, we at Joffe Books pride ourselves on our history of innovative publishing. We were thrilled to be shortlisted for Independent Publisher of the Year at the British Book Awards.

www.joffebooks.com

We're very grateful to eagle-eyed readers who take the time to contact us. Please send any errors you find to corrections@joffebooks.com. We'll get them fixed ASAP.